Sherlock Holmes

and the

GIANT RAT

OF SUM

ALAN VA

An Otto

CARROLL & G

NEW

SHERLOCK HOLMES AND THE GIANT RAT OF SUMATRA

An Otto Penzler Book
Carroll & Graf Publishers
An Imprint of Avalon Publishing Group Inc.
161 William Street, 16th Floor
New York, NY 10038

Copyright © 2002 by Alan Vanneman

First Carroll & Graf cloth edition 2002
First Carroll & Graf trade paperback edition 2003

Library of Congress Cataloging-in-Publication Data is available.

ISBN: 978-0-7867-1125-3

Printed in the United States of America
Distributed by Publishers Group West

PREFACE

SEVERAL TIMES OVER THE past decade I have taken my pen in hand to describe the most remarkable of my friend's adventures. I have always been dissuaded, even with the assurance that the account would be withheld from publication until some years after both our deaths. "I should advise against it, Watson," Holmes would say with a shake of his head, refusing to add a word of explanation. Now that I have finally resolved to tell the tale and see it through to the end, I find myself all but overwhelmed by the task. I must remark at the outset that what I have to say will stretch any intelligent reader's credulity to the breaking point. I can only say in my defence that these things did happen. I saw them with my own eyes.

PART I

The Singapore Post

CHAPTER I

The Singapore Post

URDER, WATSON?"

"No, suicide," I responded, without thinking.

"Are you quite sure? The two so often blend together. The gradations are infinite. When does the lady arrive?"

The expression in my eyes must have revealed some measure of the exasperation I felt at his remarks. I dropped the letter I had been reading and sat back in my chair without speaking.

"My apologies, Watson. Forgive me for treating such personal news as a mere puzzle. Sad news coming from your poor wife's cousin in Singapore must be painful for you. It is her husband who is dead, is it not?"

For a moment I was silent. I poured myself a cup of coffee with an unsteady hand and wiped a suspicion of a tear from my eye.

"How do you know all this?"

In answer he picked up the torn envelope that lay on the table before me.

"The black border proclaims its message. The weave of the paper is distinctly non-European—rice paper, I should imagine—which points me towards the Orient. The amount of postage indicates a source beyond India, yet not so far as China. The handwriting is of an Englishwoman, and there are few Englishwomen in Asia beyond Singapore. I would also note that this stationery is in the best of taste. Bond Street would not offer better. Where in Asia beyond India but Singapore has our race so established itself that such refinements are available? Notice, too, that this is not official stationery. Of course, now that I examine it closely, the stamp of the Singapore post is plainly visible.

"The hand, as I say, is that of a woman. An acquaintance or relative of yours? Not likely. You could be fairly described as a closemouthed man, Watson, but I feel confident that if you had such a relationship, I would know about it. Furthermore, there is a striking resemblance between this woman's hand and that of your late wife's. I know, since she told me herself when she came to me as a client, that she was an only child. Yet the hand is that of a woman in early middle age. Surely her cousin, then, rather than an aunt.

"I cannot recall your ever speaking of this woman or receiving correspondence from her in the years since you have rejoined me here at Baker Street. Given such a tenuous relationship, it seemed unlikely that she would write to inform you of any death except that of her husband's. The expression on your face as you read the letter informed me that this death was not the result of age, illness, or accident. There was a particular mixture of horror and sadness, the pain that only an unjust death could inspire. As for choosing between suicide and murder, well . . ."

"Yes?"

"That part of the mystery can await its unravelling in due time. But is the lady coming?"

"Yes, though I'm not sure why. I only met her once in my life, and that seven years ago."

"Indeed. When may we expect her?"

"She wrote this the twelfth of November, with the intention of departing Singapore on the fourth of December."

"And today is the twenty-fourth of January. No mention of the ship itself, I imagine."

"No. Why all this interest?"

I may as well have addressed this remark to the toast rack for all the response I received. Holmes continued to subject the envelope to the closest scrutiny, going so far as to smooth out the flap where I had torn it open, as if he wished to see how the envelope looked while it was still whole.

"Then it will be perhaps a month before Mrs. Trent arrives. She seems intelligent, which would be a stroke of good fortune."

"There's a quality you rarely admit in a woman. I must ask the source of this gallantry?"

"May I see the letter?"

"Yes," I said, handing it over, "but why do you say that Elizabeth is intelligent?"

He ignored my question yet a third time, reading through the letter in absolute silence.

"Guarded," he muttered at last. "Very. Well, that's all to the best. What can you tell me of this poor woman?"

"I can tell you what I know," I remarked, with some irritation. "But first I would like you to explain why you concluded that Elizabeth was intelligent merely on the basis of the manner in which she wrote an address."

Holmes lit a cigarette and drew in the smoke gratefully.

"Child's play. She has received one of the most brutal shocks life can offer a young wife, yet she displays discipline and care in the most mundane of tasks—the addressing of an envelope. Notice how simple and elegant her hand is, how straight and well-spaced the lines are, the precision with which the return address is displayed. This is more than a matter of rote learning. The unaffected manner with which she describes the tragedy in her letter confirms my conclusion."

"You speak as a connoisseur of script," I said, still a little testy over the wait I had endured for this explanation.

"A mere student of human nature," he responded, pushing the cigarette box towards me. "Now, I have told you what I know of Elizabeth Trent. I must beg you to tell me what you know."

"There is little to tell, unfortunately. Elizabeth is the daughter of the sister of Mary's father. The poor woman died only three years after Elizabeth was born. For a number of years, Mary and Elizabeth grew up as sisters rather than cousins, living under the same roof in Bombay. Mary often spoke of it. However, the family paths separated. Elizabeth was sent back to England. They corresponded over the years, but never saw each other until Mary herself returned."

"Why was Elizabeth sent back to England, and who sent her?"

"Really, Holmes, I don't know! They grew up poor as church mice, I know that. Then she found this young fellow, Raleigh Trent, a clerk with a trading firm, Enderby & Cross, I believe it was."

"Yes, yes, Enderby & Cross. I know that firm. And what sort of a fellow was this Mr. Raleigh Trent?"

"Tall, quite blond, and blue-eyed. He looked far more like a well-bred yeoman than a London clerk. Well-dressed, without any flash, and good manners. Mary doted on him. I remember she was up half the night talking about how wonderfully things had turned out."

Here it was my turn to pause. Although a widower for five years, my Mary seemed to stand before me, young and full of life. I sought to compose myself by lighting a cigarette, and when I raised my eyes, I found myself confronting Holmes' hard, dry gaze. After a moment his eyes softened and he turned away.

"Sorry, Watson, sorry," he said, with a wave of his hand. "I have had nothing for some time to occupy my thoughts, and in searching to escape from boredom, I have intruded unpardonably upon most delicate matters."

"Not at all," I said. "There is pain in remembrance, but also joy. At any rate, I am close to the end of the story, so far as I am able to tell it. The two continued their correspondence, until, well, until Mary's own death. My understanding was that Mr. Trent had met with success in Singapore, that he and Elizabeth were happy. Of course, this was all a number of years ago."

"Hmm. Of course. And had you corresponded with either of them since that time?"

"Not a word until this minute. I can only hope that Mr. Trent left Elizabeth well provided for."

"She departed Singapore on the fourth," Holmes said, far more to himself than to me. He rose rapidly from the table and scanned the dusty, bowed shelves behind him, on which he kept his massive files. He pulled down a broad atlas and turned its pages rapidly with his long, nervous fingers. "Yes, yes," he murmured, picking up the letter once more and sorting through it. "Several weeks at a minimum."

"I should think so. Why all this concern?"

"You must be patient with me, old friend. In the current state of affairs, my mind is like a machine with nothing to feed on, in danger of tearing itself to pieces. You will alert me of Mrs. Trent's arrival, won't you? In case I am out?"

"Holmes, you are rarely out!"

"True, Watson, true. But the contingency could arise. Now, be a good fellow, and I'll trouble you no more on this matter."

But to my surprise, Holmes was not quite as good as his word. As the days passed, each post, each telegram provoked his eager interest. More than once he asked me point-blank if I had heard from Elizabeth. I replied in the negative, and when I attempted to question him on the source of his obvious concern, he withdrew into a rigid silence, consoling himself with tobacco and chemical experiments that often ran late into the night and occasionally well into the morning. I put down his interest in poor Elizabeth's story, which struck me as frankly ghoulish, to his own lack of employment, combined with his recent renunciation of cocaine. Since I had no wish to provoke him into resuming that disastrous habit, I determined to ignore his bizarre and intrusive behaviour to the very limit of my abilities.

At last the day arrived that Holmes had been anticipating with such unaccountable curiosity. The bell rang as Holmes and I were sitting down to breakfast, and presently Billy the page boy appeared with a message, which I opened and read while Holmes buttered a slice of toast with ostentatious unconcern. One word I could never apply to Sherlock Holmes was "transparent," but in this instance the expression would have been appropriate.

"Mrs. Trent will be calling on me this afternoon at two," I said. "Let me extend a formal invitation for your presence."

"Of course, Watson, if you wish it," Holmes replied blandly. "I shall be going out shortly to pursue a small piece of research, but I expect that I shall bring matters to a conclusion in advance of the hour you mention."

This elaborate pretence left me more in the dark as to my friend's motives than ever, for his blatant obfuscation removed any desire I might have had to seek an explanation. Holmes, for his part, ate his breakfast as rapidly as I have ever seen him and then left immediately, taking his *Times* with him. I was supremely unsurprised when he returned at precisely a quarter to two, his sharp eyes glowing. He disappeared into his bedroom without uttering a word and remained there until the bell rang once more. Billy opened the door and announced to me, "Mrs. Trent to see you, sir."

CHAPTER II

Visit From a Lady

s I told Holmes, I had not seen Elizabeth Trent for perhaps seven years. The memory I once had of her, as a sweet girl on the verge of womanhood, was so affected by my own loss, the painful missive I had received from her, and Holmes' mystifying behaviour in response to that missive, that I doubt very much if I could honestly say that I recognized the woman who entered our flat on that day. No longer in the first blush of youth, she had still a youthful dignity, a grace, and a sorrow that infinitely touched my heart. Her widow's weeds, so modest and simple, proclaimed a tragedy whose full extent only a few understood. As I took her hand, she drew me towards her with a gentle but persistent strength.

"Dr. Watson," she said, "I can scarcely say that I know you, yet I feel we are linked by the sad losses we have endured."

Her brief words summoned my Mary once more before me, and of a sudden I discovered that my cheeks were wet with tears. I, who had not wept once in the intervening five years, found myself weeping freely, without shame. I put my arms on Elizabeth's shoulder, whether to console her or myself I hardly know. As I wept, I heard her speaking in her low, musical voice.

"She was my dearest, dearest friend, and an angel placed here on earth, and yet now I have lost someone dearer."

Somehow we seated ourselves on the worn sofa in the sitting room Holmes and I used to entertain clients. We sat unspeaking for long minutes, when to my amazement Holmes entered with a shining silver tea service, which I had never seen before at Baker Street and never was to see again.

"Tea, Watson?" Holmes said, placing the gleaming tray before us. "You must be Mrs. Trent. I am Sherlock Holmes."

Elizabeth rose and extended her hand, which Holmes took and held briefly.

"Watson told me of your tragedy, Mrs. Trent," said Holmes. "I am sorry for you beyond words. I can only hope that returning at last to England can give you some opportunity to begin your life anew."

"Thank you, Mr. Holmes. It is such an honour to meet you. I have read much of what the good doctor has written of your exploits."

Holmes darted a sideways glance at me.

"Indeed!" he said after some pause. "I hope you were able to glean at least some small indication of my methods and objectives. Watson's compositions, I fear, are hardly the adequate vehicle for articulating the principles of scientific criminal investigation."

I opened my mouth to protest this unwarranted slur upon my authorial capabilities, but was forestalled by the lady herself.

"Oh, I found Dr. Watson's articles fascinating! Without them, I fear I should have given up hope entirely!"

I must confess I was not a little stunned by this encomium. I had the author's instinctive pride in his works, but even I could hardly imagine them to be as valuable as Elizabeth suggested. Still, my heart glowed within my breast to think they had been of service to such a charming and unfortunate woman.

"*De gustibus non disputandem,*" Holmes murmured. "But if the works in question made my poor name known to you, it is folly to complain. Perhaps I should offer you some tea before it grows cold?"

"I should love some," said Elizabeth, taking the elegant cup and saucer Holmes offered.

"And a biscuit? You seem to be in need of nourishment. Never fear, Watson. I shall provide for the two of us as well."

Elizabeth took a large drink of tea and sighed gratefully.

"It is so pleasant," she said, "to be enjoying a real English tea, here, with friends. I have felt so long that I have been living entirely with strangers."

"It is our pleasure to welcome you home, to do whatever we can. Let me offer you a sandwich. I can't vouch for them myself, but I'm sure Watson can."

I had little to say at this. Whatever little Holmes knew of the sandwiches, it was far more than I. I couldn't imagine where he had gotten them. There was nothing more removed from my friend's irregular mode of life than a proper English tea.

"Tell us, Mrs. Trent," Sherlock Holmes said, after Elizabeth had finished her sandwich and a second cup of tea, "of your journey. I understand that you travelled on the *Southern Star*. It must have been a tiring trip with so many weeks at sea. No doubt you had companions from Singapore to help you pass the time."

"Why, no," said Elizabeth, a little disconcerted by his questioning. "There were only a few passengers who departed with me from Singapore, and I believe they all disembarked at Bombay."

"Really? But perhaps you met an old face among those who boarded at other ports?"

"No, Mr. Holmes. I made a few acquaintances, but these were people I met on the voyage."

"Really? There was no one onboard the *Star* when she made port two days ago who was known to you? I mean, no one that you had seen before the voyage?"

"No. Should I have seen someone?"

"Oh, no, no. As an armchair traveller, no doubt my ideas about long ocean voyages are quite ill-founded. But, please, tell us your plans now that you have returned to England."

"My plans!" said Elizabeth, with a despairing laugh. "My

plans, Mr. Holmes, depend almost entirely on you!"

"Indeed, Mrs. Trent," Holmes said, reclining in his chair and arranging his fingers in the pyramidal fashion I knew so well. "Please continue."

I was instantly aware of the steel beneath the velvet glove. The intense interest that Holmes had taken in Elizabeth's story, which he had concealed beneath this show of hospitality, now rose to the surface once more.

"You know the tragedy of my husband's death," Elizabeth began. "However, you do not know of my conviction that he was driven to it by forces, powers, that I do not understand, but which I believe to be capable of any enormity, forces that now threaten me!"

With that statement, the remarkable composure that Elizabeth had exhibited before arriving at our rooms vanished entirely. She crumpled wordlessly against my arm, her body wracked by painful sobs. Only minutes ago she had been consoling me. Now I seemed powerless to offer any comfort. Holmes fidgeted in his chair, as helpless as myself and far more impatient with feminine distress. Fortunately, he busied himself by removing the biscuits and sandwiches and fetching a fresh pot of tea. When he returned, Elizabeth had calmed herself, though she had become dreadfully pale. At the sight of her, Holmes disappeared once more, returning with the brandy and a glass. Elizabeth moistened her lips, and a touch of colour returned to her cheeks.

"Thank you, Mr. Holmes. These are matters of which it is painful to think, much less to speak."

"I pray you, Mrs. Trent, to begin at the beginning and give us all the facts, no matter how trivial, in order that we may assist you."

"Perhaps it is best that I begin with this," she said, opening her bag and taking out a large envelope, which she handed to me. I opened it and found within a variety of newspaper clippings and handwritten documents.

"It would be perhaps best if you would read them aloud, Watson," said Holmes. "Mrs. Trent can add her comments when appropriate."

"I would appreciate that," Elizabeth said. She took the bundle from me and sorted through them. When she had finished, she handed them back to me. "I believe they are in order now," she said in a soft voice. She poured herself a cup of tea and sat back on the ottoman, a look of forced composure on her face. I took the first clipping and read aloud the following account:

TRAGIC DEATH OF RALEIGH TRENT

Our community has been shaken by the news of the tragic death of Raleigh Trent, chief assistant at Enderby & Cross for the China trade. Mr. Trent was found dead in his office on the morning of January 7 with a bullet through his brain. A small nickel-and-brass revolver of American manufacture lay at his side.

Inspector Howard Maul pronounced Trent's death a suicide. Trent left a note stating that he was suffering the effects of a progressive illness and could no longer endure the prospect of continuously declining health. Maul stated that the letter was indisputably genuine and that all the facts of the case corroborated the theory of suicide. Several witnesses have said that Trent had appeared to be in failing health for the past several months, though he had never complained of any illness. Dr. Thomas Matthews acknowledged that Trent had sought his assistance and that Trent's health had not been good.

Raleigh Trent and his wife Elizabeth first came to Singapore seven years ago. He had been in the employ of Enderby & Cross for the entire seven years, winning a reputation for probity and enterprise that will be sorely missed in our community. The editors of the *Straits Times* extend their deepest sympathy to the widow.

I passed the clipping to Holmes for his inspection.

"Unusual consistency," he said, fingering the paper. "No doubt the wood pulp of the Malay Peninsula differs considerably from the products of our northern forests. A pretty problem for another time. Type is good ten-point Caslon, well set. The colony seems prosperous to attract such competent printers. Mrs. Trent, were you aware that your husband possessed the revolver described in the article?"

"Yes, Mr. Holmes. In fact, I have the revolver with me." So saying, she drew out a small weapon that matched exactly the description in the article I had just read.

"May I see it?"

She handed the revolver over to Holmes, who undid the cylinder catch and held the gun upright. Five small cartridges fell into his hand. Aiming the empty pistol at the nearest wall, he pulled the trigger several times. Then he reloaded the weapon and handed it back to Elizabeth.

"A stiff pull, at least, which is some guarantee against accidental discharge. Still, a rare item for a lady's handbag. Why do you carry a loaded revolver, Mrs. Trent?"

"For protection, Mr. Holmes."

"Surely the danger of physical violence is minimal?"

"I cannot say that it is."

"Very well. Perhaps I should hear your tale to the end before reaching any conclusions. What's next, Watson?"

I unfolded a piece of stiff business stationery that bore the legend "ENDERBY & CROSS, Merchants Worldwide."

"To whom it may concern," I began, acutely aware of how difficult this must be for Elizabeth to hear, "I, Raleigh Trent, of sound mind but shattered body, write to explain the deed I am about to commit. For the past several years I have been suffering from a decline in the vital forces of my body. I have consulted every remedy known to man, to no avail. For the past few months my sufferings have increased daily. Regardless of the pain my decision may cause others, I make it knowing I am sparing them, as well as myself, from far greater. I have placed my affairs in order with my solicitor, although he knows nothing of my intentions."

"May I ask you, Mrs. Trent, said Holmes, "what you think of this note?"

"I can only say that it sounds utterly unlike my husband," she responded. "I knew for some time that he was under a terrible strain, though he always refused to discuss it with me. But I believe that it was this emotional stress that was the cause of his physical symptoms, rather than the other way round. I was never aware of a physical illness of any kind until a few months before his death."

"Then you are not inclined to believe this letter?"

"No, Mr. Holmes, I am not."

"Do you think it possible that someone forced your husband to compose this letter, or even forged it, and then murdered him?"

"I do not know what to believe. I only know that that letter is a deliberate falsification."

"May I examine it, Watson? Yes, good paper once again. Enderby & Cross is thriving, as well as Singapore. A steady hand, though obviously in the throes of a powerful emotion. Mrs. Trent, do you have another example of your husband's handwriting, say from six months or a year ago prior to this one, or even earlier?"

"Yes. This is a letter he wrote me two years ago while in Canton."

"Excellent." Holmes took out his lens and compared the two documents. "Definitely the same hand," he said at last. "But there is a terrible compression of the letters in the second, and the spacing of the words is erratic. On the other hand, what man could contemplate his own demise without emotion? Mrs. Trent, had your husband made any changes in his financial arrangements in the final few months prior to his death?"

"Yes. He used his savings to purchase annuities for myself."

"From which company were these annuities purchased?"

"From Enderby & Cross. Sir Henry explained them to me himself."

"Sir Henry?"

"Sir Henry Givens is the chief representative of Enderby & Cross in Singapore."

"And what sort of man is Sir Henry?"

"Very tall and very pale, with very thick black hair, though I believe he is approaching fifty. He is a very intimidating man and had said little to me in all the seven years I spent in Singapore. I was surprised indeed when he called on me after my husband's death. His words were considerate, though I found his manner exceedingly formal. He assured me that I would be provided for and suggested several times that I should return to England."

"And what was your reply?"

"I did not make one at the time. But I was determined not to leave Singapore until I had done my best to find out the true reasons for my husband's death."

"And what did you do to pursue these matters?"

"I began by speaking with Dr. Matthews. As I have already indicated, his statement, as reported in the *Times,* struck me as false. But when I questioned him, Dr. Matthews was very stubborn with me. He insisted that he saw no reason to doubt my husband's note and claimed that his statement, as reported in the paper, was entirely consistent with the facts."

"What do you think of that, Watson?" said Holmes, turning to me.

"Certainly it is difficult to agree with his diagnosis at this distance."

"Cautious as always, Watson! But it's hardly a fault under most circumstances. So the doctor would not assist you, Mrs. Trent. What was your next course of action?"

"Dr. Matthews' reaction left me bewildered for a time. For lack of anything better, I decided to undertake a thorough search of my husband's papers in the hopes of finding something that would tell in my favour. My husband's chief clerk, young Stafford, had always looked up to him and was willing to assist me, at least in the beginning. But his superiors must have learned of this."

"Why do you say that?"

"Because shortly after he gave me what papers he had, the company suddenly transferred him to Hong Kong. And Sir Henry made a second visit to my house. This time his words were not considerate. He accused me of slandering the company's name by my actions, and warned me that I should lose my annuity if I persisted."

"Dear, dear. One wonders if that would be legal. But in such a close-knit community as this colony must be, no doubt a powerful company such as Enderby & Cross has a large say in what is legal and what is not."

"Yes, Mr. Holmes, but I did find a solicitor, Mr. Arthur Craven, who was willing to take my case. He had been badly treated by Enderby & Cross and, I suspect, was quite willing to take any case whatsoever that they should find offensive. Mr. Craven was often erratic in his behaviour, but he was quite persistent. For the first time since my husband's death, I thought I might learn what had actually happened. However, less than a fortnight after Mr. Craven accepted my case, this appeared in the *Times*."

She handed me another clipping, which I read aloud.

STARTLING DEVELOPMENTS IN THE DEATH OF RALEIGH TRENT

The suicide of Mr. Raleigh Trent, reported previously in these pages, appears to have been a more sinister case than first appeared. According to sources connected with the firm of Enderby & Cross, Mr. Trent was not in failing health, as his suicide note stated. Instead, it appears that accounts managed for the firm by Mr. Trent are seriously confused. It now seems likely that Trent's death was actually a means of escaping exposure of a long series of criminal embezzlements on his part.

Sir Henry Givens, managing agent for Enderby & Cross in Singapore, refused to give a statement on the Trent case to our reporter, but also refused to deny allegations of possible malfeasance on the part of Mr. Trent. Mr. Harold Anthony, Sir Henry's assistant, said that the police had not been called in, as it would be impossible to charge a dead man with a crime. But Mr. Anthony did remark that some of Trent's expenditures seemed to be far in excess of his salary."

"And what do you think of that, Mrs. Trent?"

"I don't know, Mr. Holmes," said Elizabeth, dropping her eyes. "I remember Raleigh telling me after our first two years in Singapore that we were going to be rich."

"What year was that?" asked Holmes.

"Why, I believe it was in '92. Yes, I am sure, in January or February, for I had let Li Wu have the night off before."

"You're sure of that?"

"Yes. It was the Chinese New Year—the Year of the Dragon, I believe."

"And your fortunes did improve?"

"Yes. I do not believe we were lavish, but we accumulated many fine things. I sometimes feared that people in the company might complain, that we were getting above ourselves."

"And did they?"

"No. That helped reassure me. Sir Henry was extremely complimentary of Raleigh. I had no reason to suspect that anything was wrong."

"It would hardly appear that anything was wrong. And this continued for some time?"

"Yes, but in the last year I had the sense of a hectic excitement on Raleigh's part. When I questioned him about it, he would tell me that all would be well soon enough and we should never have to want or worry again. How wrong that was!"

Here poor Elizabeth burst into tears once more. A more poignant scene would be hard to imagine, nor one more calculated to try the patience of Sherlock Holmes. I soothed her as best I could, while Holmes chewed on the stem of his briar. At length she managed to calm herself and began her story over again.

"Once Enderby & Cross began to propagate these shameless innuendoes against my husband, Mr. Holmes, I determined to appeal to the authorities. I first took the precaution of having Mr. Craven review the annuities Raleigh had purchased. He informed me that Raleigh had been quite careful to obtain annuities that would withstand any legal test. Fortified with that knowledge, I wrote a letter to Lord Barington, who you must know is the governor of Singapore."

"Yes, I am familiar with his lordship's name," Holmes said. "May I offer you another cup of tea?"

"Thank you. After some delay, I received a notice requiring me to appear at Government House."

"Really?" said Holmes, in a languid voice. "His lordship was very considerate to favour you with a personal interview."

"I did not have the opportunity to speak with Lord Barington in person," said Elizabeth. "I—the interview was most difficult. I spoke with Sir Warren Clayborne, the lieutenant governor. He was cold and unfeeling. He attempted to smooth over what I knew to be lies. I insisted that my husband's death be investigated, and he refused. When I persisted, he simply terminated the interview and had a pair of footmen show me out."

"What did you do then?"

"I wrote a letter to Lord Barington protesting Sir Warren's behaviour. When that was ignored, I wrote another, and then a third. Finally I announced plans to send an appeal to London. That, I fear, was my mistake, Mr. Holmes. I thought I was dealing with honest men who were somehow miraculously obtuse. It cost me months to learn of my error. I have no doubt that my letter was intercepted. Shortly after posting it, I was summoned to Sir Warren's office. He said that he had been informed of my complaints by the Colonial Office in London. He gave me a very official-looking document, signed by the minister for colonial affairs, stating that if I wished to pursue my complaint, I would have to come to London in person rather than relying on correspondence."

"You amaze me, Mrs. Trent," said Holmes.

"He said the regulations on appeals were very strict. Naturally I protested. He said he would take my statement to Lord Barington. For a week I heard nothing. Then a man, whom I had never laid eyes upon, who had not even the decency to give me his name, appeared at my house and made the most dreadful threats."

"Indeed," said Holmes, "what was the date? Do you recall?"

"Why, I can't see that it matters."

"Perhaps not. Please go on with your story."

"At this point, Mr. Holmes, I was not sure what I should do. I had commenced several legal proceedings that would have been forfeit if I had not appeared personally in court. Then I learned that despite all Mr. Craven's assurances, Enderby & Cross had stopped payment on the annuities. They had transferred responsibility for payment to their London office, which meant that I had no legal redress in Singapore. I felt that there was no way to escape the web of intrigue that had been spun

around me but by coming here. To maintain the legal proceedings I had initiated and to pay for my ticket, I was forced
to sell our house in Singapore. This was rash of me, I know,
but there was no other avenue. And so I am here and only
hope that you good gentlemen can help me to clear my husband's name and regain what is rightfully mine!"

For my own part, my blood was aboil at this tale of official
incompetence and blundering, if not outright corruption.
Whatever the truth was that lay behind Elizabeth's sad story,
I was determined to get to the bottom of it. I was on the verge
of registering these sentiments in the most vigorous terms,
when Holmes spoke.

"I fear, Mrs. Trent, that it would be wisest for you to abandon this effort. Surely you would agree that it is impossible
for you to resume your life in Singapore. Instead, I would
advise you to inform Lord Barington of your plans to begin a
new life here in England and forget the past. I have no doubt
that if you make this appeal, your problems with Enderby &
Cross will resolve themselves as well. I can recommend an
excellent solicitor to you who will expedite matters."

"You make it sound so easy, Mr. Holmes. Do you really
advise me to simply give up after coming so far? To allow my
husband's good name to be permanently sullied in such an
atrocious manner?"

"Mrs. Trent, I can advise you that the trail, wherever it may
have once led, has grown cold. To adequately pursue your case,
I should have to journey to Singapore. You have described to
us how uncertain are your finances. I very much doubt that you
could assume the burden of such a lengthy investigation. For
my own part, I have numerous responsibilities here, which I am
very loath to surrender."

"Perhaps I could undertake the journey," I burst out, unable
to contain myself. "I should consider it a trust of the highest
order."

"No, Watson," said Holmes, with surprising quickness. "In
the first place, I need you here. Secondly, as I have already
indicated, what Mrs. Trent has presented us with is a nest of
theories spun around a dearth of facts. The facts needed,

either to confirm or deny the suspicions regarding her husband's death, are lacking. If they ever existed, they no longer do so. Research to ascertain facts is one thing; research to invent them is another."

"Then you feel there is no hope?" Mrs. Trent exclaimed in agitation. "I had expected better of you, Mr. Holmes."

"I am sorry you have found me lacking," Holmes said, with a note of sharpness that seemed to fade into the air. "I realize your case is an extremely painful one. But time and distance can be decisive barriers to investigation on occasion. You cannot neglect your own financial security."

"But what assurance is there that Lord Barington will even consent to this arrangement?"

"This was the course of action first urged upon you by Sir Henry Givens. From your account, the offer has never been withdrawn, nor could it be, from all that you have told us. Regardless of the rumours regarding your husband's conduct, the annuities he purchased are still valid and should remain so. No man can be convicted of a crime once he is in his grave. At this distance, it is impossible to unravel the confused events you have described."

I could sense the desperate struggle of emotions taking place in Elizabeth's breast. She saw the sacred memory of her beloved husband left with a permanent stain. For a long moment she waited, and then finally spoke.

"You believe I have acted as a child?" she asked.

"On the contrary. You have acted with intelligence and decision in a matter of the utmost difficulty. No man or woman could have done more. I simply ask you to think over the advice I have given you, and suggest that we meet in a few days to discuss this matter once more."

"You present me with very bitter choices, Mr. Holmes."

"You have been very patient, Mrs. Trent. I pray you to be patient a little while longer."

"Very well," she said at last. "Will Thursday be convenient for you?"

"Of course," said Holmes. "Are you staying with friends?"

"Other than Dr. Watson, I have no friends in England," she

said. "I have a sister, now living in Surrey, whom I have not seen for fifteen years. But I am staying in a rooming house kept by a cousin of my late husband, a Mrs. Keeps. I am as comfortable there as I can be anywhere. I will give every thought to your suggestion, Mr. Holmes, though I cannot conceal from you the fact that I am disappointed. I will return on Thursday."

"Once again, I offer my regrets that I cannot be of more assistance," said Holmes. There was a rigidity in his manner that I could not fathom. "I feel the course of action I have outlined to you is best."

"Thank you," said Elizabeth, rising from her seat. "John," she said, turning to me. "Will you be here on Thursday?"

"You may depend on it with your life!" I said, bursting forth once more. "I am eager to be of any assistance whatsoever. Please ask."

"Of course," she said, with a smile that sent my heart bounding. "You have always been very dear to me, and never more so than today."

"Yes, very good, then," said Holmes. "Good day, Mrs. Trent. Watson will show you out."

Ignoring the man's peremptory tone, I accompanied Elizabeth to the street and helped her to a cab. When I returned, I found Holmes already wrapped in a long travelling coat, with a scarf thrown around his neck and his deerstalker on his head. He watched Elizabeth's cab intently as it pulled away. I was about to address him when he turned abruptly.

"I shall be out, Watson," he announced.

Under the circumstances, I had no appetite for solitude, so I departed for my club, where Hoskins, one of the members, engaged me in a discussion of the latest cabinet crisis, which we pursued over dinner with several companions, though I found it impossible to forget entirely poor Elizabeth's situation. We continued our debate over port, with the result that I returned to Baker Street quite late. Holmes, however, was still up, sorting through the contents of one of the many dispatch boxes he used to save records of his old cases. After the events of the day, I hardly expected that he would be in the mood for conversation, but he sang out to me as soon as I set foot in the flat.

"That you, Watson?"

"Of course. Who else should it be at this hour?"

"True. I hope you are not too out of sorts with me over the way I handled Mrs. Trent. The poor lady's position is most unfortunate, but I am quite confident the remedy I suggest is the appropriate one."

"Are you sure?"

"Quite sure. One can stretch the law only so far. It is time for it to rebound in Mrs. Trent's favour."

"I hope that is true."

"Yes, Watson. The lady has suffered unconscionably. But I believe we can achieve some small measure of restitution."

Holmes faced away from me as he spoke, but there was a curious thrill in his voice as he spoke that left me even further at a loss as to his attitude towards Elizabeth. Seven hours before, he had treated her with coldness. Now he spoke as her champion. I was about to question him when he cut me off.

"It is extremely late," he said, rising. "I must bid you good-night."

As Holmes took his leave, I seated myself before the fire and meditated for a minute or two on Elizabeth's sad story, but found myself so fatigued that I could not concentrate. And I crawled under the sheets that night with no hope other than that the morrow might be a better day.

CHAPTER III

Murder in the Night

 WAS IN THE THROES of a most profound slumber when I was awakened by a confused succession of sounds and voices. I struggled to my feet, scarcely aware of where or even who I was, and pulled on my robe, more as an act of habit than thought. A flaring gas jet in the hallway, a sign that Holmes was already awake, provided the only illumination as I found my way to the front room. I entered to see Holmes opening the door. A police sergeant stood outside.

"Are you gentlemen Sherlock Holmes and Dr. Watson?" the man asked.

"Of course we are," snapped Holmes. "What can you tell us of Elizabeth Trent?"

"Well, sir, I have some hard news about that lady, though how you knew it was she I was to speak of I cannot say. Mrs. Elizabeth Trent is dead, sir."

"Is it possible?" I cried. "Elizabeth Trent was here in this room not twelve hours ago."

"I fear it is true, Watson," Holmes said.

"Good God, how could this happen?"

"I strongly suspect it was murder," said Holmes. "What do you say, sergeant?"

"No, sir, unless you say she murdered herself. The poor lady is a suicide."

"You're sure of that?"

"Oh, quite sure. Mr. Lestrade is investigating the matter. He sent me on ahead to inform you gentlemen that he would be calling on you at about nine this morning."

"Then why did you arrive at this hour?" I almost shouted. "It's a quarter to six."

I pointed angrily to the clock over the mantelpiece, at which the policeman could only stare dumbly.

"I apologize to you gentlemen," he said at last. "It seems there has been an error."

"No matter, sergeant," Holmes said. "It is impossible to begin an investigation too early. Watson, prepare yourself for a journey. I'm sure Sergeant Hall will be glad to accompany us in his four-wheeler to the scene of the crime."

"I cannot see how you know my name," the man began, "and I cannot allow you to ride in a police vehicle. And furthermore, sir, there has been no crime."

"I shall be the judge of that," shot Holmes. "I assure you, sergeant, that Lestrade will have no objection to our visit. Consider us as material witnesses, whom you are conveying for interrogation."

"I suppose I can do that," the man said, cautiously. "But just how is it that you know my name?"

"From the note protruding from your jacket pocket," Holmes said. "It is addressed to one Sergeant Hall in the inimitable hand of Inspector Lestrade, with the injunction, which you failed to obey, that we were not to be disturbed until eight. But as I say, your haste has been all to the good and will save your inspector an unnecessary journey. We will be with you shortly."

The sergeant seemed reluctant to follow the course of action urged upon him, but Holmes' decisive manner, plus the man's own error in arriving at our door some two hours ahead of time, prevented him from mounting an effective protest. Thus it was that Holmes and I found ourselves bouncing through the darkened streets of London that morning in the sergeant's company. The heavy press of commercial traffic was already gathering, but once we passed from the centre of London, we had the streets almost to ourselves. Few people indeed had any reason to be abroad that cold, sunless morning, and surely none had a sadder one than ours.

I was left alone with my thoughts. Sergeant Hall devoted all his attention to the horse, while Holmes was sunk in absolute silence and sat almost motionless, an empty pipe gripped between his teeth. I turned the terrible news over in my mind, attempting to make some sense out of it, without success. The more my clouded brain aroused itself, the more poor Elizabeth's tragedy pierced me. Two charming lives, begun with such promise, snuffed out, each dying by his own hand! And through the whole tale, there was no place where I could say "Here lies the blame! Here is the culprit!" Nothing but insinuations, rumours, guesses, suspicions, evasions, and half-truths! I struggled, as we rattled through the streets, to find some pattern in these terrible events and failed utterly. At last a painful sigh of frustration and sadness escaped me, and I shook my head in despair. At that moment I felt the grip of Holmes' thin, strong fingers on my wrist. Though his face remained an expressionless mask, he gave a powerful squeeze of reassurance. I felt he was absolutely committed to resolving these tangled affairs, wherever the path might lead.

At length we arrived at a capacious, four-story dwelling, whose faded magnificence signalled a long-term decline in the surrounding neighbourhood. The house stood out like a great steamer moored amid a host of coastal vessels. As we lighted from the four-wheeler, the first gleams of the rising sun could be seen over the chimney tops of the blocks of flats stretching back towards the heart of London. Inside the hallway a flickering gas jet revealed to us Inspector Lestrade, deep in conversation with an elderly woman whom I took to be the landlady.

"Eh? What's this? Mr. Holmes, what are you doing here? I had intended to call on you later this morning."

"I know you did, Inspector. But I decided to match your admirable devotion to duty as best I could and spare you the visit."

"Well, there's nothing to see here. It's a tragedy, all right, such a fine young lady doing herself in like this, but there's nothing for you to detect."

"I'd prefer to judge for myself. No doubt you are aware that the lady had called on me yesterday."

"Yes, Mr. Holmes, I did know that, which is why I wished to speak with you. But the evidence here of suicide is conclusive."

"As I say, Lestrade, I would like to judge for myself."

"You seem quite determined on this matter. I'd like to remind you, Mr. Holmes, that these are not matters for a private citizen to tamper with willy-nilly."

"Indeed, Lestrade. Perhaps I should remind you that in the past you have occasionally derived some benefit through my assistance."

"You have had your lucky guesses from time to time, I'd be the last man to deny that. But I do have my orders."

"Orders? What sort of orders?"

"Now, I can hardly discuss official police matters with the likes of you, can I?"

"Lestrade, don't you think you've taken up enough of this poor woman's time? I'm sure she has responsibilities she must attend to, regardless of these terrible events."

"I'm sure I do," the woman broke out, in an agitated manner. "I'm all broken up over the poor thing, doing herself in that way, though why she had to choose my house for it I'm sure I don't know. I've always kept a most respectable house, Mr. Holmes, really I have."

"Why, I knew that the moment I stepped in the door, Mrs. Keeps. I'm sure the inspector will let you go now, while we continue our conversation."

My analysis of Lestrade's mood was scarcely as sanguine as Holmes'. The inspector seemed to be a man on the point of overflowing with indignation. But with a rather surprising display of self-command, he managed to quell the rising flush in his cheeks and speak in a half-normal manner.

"It is never the intention of the police to inconvenience law-abiding citizens, Mrs. Keeps," he said at last. "Of course

you may go about your duties, though I may have a word
with you later."

"You see, Mrs. Keeps?" said Holmes. "The good inspector
can be quite reasonable when he wishes. Now, Lestrade, to
further assist Mrs. Keeps in calming her guests, I suggest that
you station Sergeant Hall out in the street with his four-
wheeler, while we retreat to the unfortunate lady's room."

"Oh, I would appreciate that very much!" burst out Mrs.
Keeps. "It is so upsetting for my guests to meet policemen in
the hallway. Why, they can talk for hours!"

Lestrade's temper was hardly improved by my friend's latest suggestion, but once more he mastered himself. As Mrs.
Keeps fluttered off, the three of us ascended the broad staircase that led to the second floor.

"Now, Lestrade," Holmes began. "What's all this about
orders?"

"As an inspector I have my orders," said Lestrade primly.
"Now I may ask you, Mr. Holmes, why you are being so
inquisitive as to this case, which as I have told you involves
no crime."

"This case concerns me particularly because Mrs. Trent
sought my assistance. I declined, in large part because I
believed her to be in no danger. I now see that I radically
underestimated the situation."

"The great Sherlock Holmes made a mistake! Well, that's
worth hearing!"

"Yes, and the result of it is that a fine young woman lies
dead! Now, if you have an ounce of gratitude in you, you will
take me to Mrs. Trent's room and leave your orders outside."

"Well, as to that, that may be as may be, Mr. Holmes. We
removed the young lady's body, but you may have yourself a
little look around if you make sure to tell no one about it."

As was the case with most large homes of the earlier part
of our century, the fourth floor of this house had originally
been given over to storage space. As a result, the flight of
stairs leading to it were narrow and wound themselves about
a stout chimney. As we ascended, they groaned with every
step.

"Not a stairway a man would want to walk down if he wished to keep himself a secret," said Lestrade.

"No," replied Holmes, "but then murderers may not always choose the settings of their crimes."

"No doubt, Mr. Holmes. But if I were so hard of heart as to wish to do a lady in, I'm sure I would not use a revolver if I had to run down three flights of stairs after I pulled the trigger."

"This revolver, was it nickel-plated and brass?"

"Yes, indeed, Mr. Holmes, so it was. Not very big, but sadly enough it proved fatal in the lady's case."

"Then it was not the murderer's weapon, for the lady showed it to me yesterday afternoon. No doubt the murderer had a more silent method, which the lady forestalled."

"Now, Mr. Holmes, who said anything about a murderer but you yourself? When you set to making difficulties where there are none, you'll soon be tripping over your own feet."

"Well, here's the room itself. You'll excuse me, Lestrade, if I concentrate on the facts of the case."

The shabby room where poor Elizabeth took her last breath had a grim and desolate look in the early morning light. The atmosphere was extremely close, and I made to open the one window in the room, but Holmes waved me off.

"Not just yet, Watson, if you please. I prefer to have things exactly as they were until I have completed my investigation."

So saying, Holmes began a most meticulous examination of the room. The furnishings were minimal—a small bed, neatly made, and a small table with a single chair. On the table was a half-burnt candle set in a brass holder, of the kind with a broad, flat saucer to catch the wax. In the saucer was a black wisp of ash. On the table beside the candle was a ghastly stain that I knew to be the blood of Elizabeth Trent.

"The lady was seated at the table?" asked Holmes.

"Yes."

"And she fell forward onto the table after she was shot."

"After she shot herself."

"The revolver was lying on the table?"

"No, on the floor."

"Ah. On which side?"

"On the right side, Mr. Holmes. On the same side as the bullet entered her temple. No doubt you observed that the lady was right-handed."

"Yes. At what angle did the bullet enter the body?"

"At a low angle."

"Then you conjecture that the lady held the revolver like this?"

Holmes held his right hand level with his jaw and directed his forefinger towards his temple.

"Yes. Approximately."

"Is that how you would hold a revolver if you wished to commit suicide?"

"I cannot say how I would commit suicide, Mr. Holmes. You seem to be searching for difficulties."

"Very well. Where is the pen?"

"Which pen?"

"The pen with which Mrs. Trent wrote the note."

"What makes you think there was a note?"

Holmes pointed at the table.

"See where the stain makes an edge. You are playing games with me, Lestrade. I have never known you to withhold evidence like this before."

"Very well, then, there is a pen, and a note," said Lestrade, with a malicious chuckle. "You are quite welcome to them, for they will destroy your case entirely. Here is the pen, and here is the note."

So saying, the detective took from his breast pocket a small, thin pen and a long envelope.

"The note was not in the envelope."

"No, it was not, Mr. Holmes. I put it there for safekeeping."

"Very well. This pen is most interesting."

Holmes held the pen lightly in his hand. It was exceedingly small and slender, made of dark wood, unpainted, with a point made of dull, silvery metal. He took out his glass and examined the pen exhaustively, the point in particular, turning the pen this way and that, so as to view the nibs from every angle.

"Yes," he said at last. "Murder, without a doubt. I had this case so wrong I did not know what to think, but now I am on firm ground."

"Really, Mr. Holmes? You know all that from the nibs of a lady's pen?"

"This is not a lady's pen. It did not belong to Mrs. Trent. Even the most delicate hand would find it inconvenient. There are issues here. . . . This pen is most unusual, Lestrade. May I have it?"

"I think not. If this is murder, as you claim, I cannot allow a mere private citizen to carry away evidence."

"Then you agree that this pen is evidence of a murder."

"I agree to no such thing."

"Well, I tell you that it is evidence. If you had examined this pen, Lestrade, you would have found that it belonged to a left-handed individual. And as you have noticed, Mrs. Trent was right-handed."

"Surely the lady could have obtained the pen from someone else. Perhaps it belonged to her husband."

Holmes held the pen before Lestrade's eyes.

"Do you believe any man or woman would write with such a delicate object?"

Lestrade shrugged.

"The lady came from Singapore, where there are many strange things. Perhaps she obtained it from someone else, a left-handed Chinese woman, perhaps."

"A left-handed Chinese woman!"

"That is only a conjecture, Mr. Holmes," said Lestrade, with some irritation. "No doubt there are other possibilities."

"I'm not faulting you, Lestrade. You have more imagination than you give yourself credit for. A left-handed Chinese woman is not a bad guess at all. Since I cannot supply a better, let it stand for the time being. Perhaps I could have a look at the note."

Lestrade handed Holmes the envelope and took back the pen. Holmes opened the letter and began to read, in his quiet, precise voice.

"I write this letter in clear awareness of what I am about to do. I am alone in this world, without hope or resources. I know now that I have been pursuing a phantom, something not of this world. Sherlock Holmes told me that I am behaving like a child. Now I see that that is true. I cannot bear to prolong the folly that is my life anymore. Let those who read this note take from it what they will.

"Mrs. Raleigh Trent"

When he had finished, Holmes fell silent. As he did so, the sordidness of the surroundings and the physical exhaustion of the early morning hour combined with the unutterable sadness of this last note to provoke in me a spirit of desolation that I have rarely endured. With every step, the mystery surrounding Elizabeth's affairs seemed to increase. Then Holmes spoke.

"You see it, Watson," he said, in a low, excited voice.

"See what?"

"That this is not a suicide note. This is Elizabeth Trent's last indictment of her foul murderers."

"Indictment?" cried Lestrade, snatching the paper from my friend's hand. "Where do you see that?"

"You are in no position to grasp the lady's clew," Holmes said. "This is the passage: 'Sherlock Holmes told me that I am behaving like a child.' Is that what I told her, Watson?"

"No, it isn't, by Jove! She said that, and you contradicted her."

"Precisely. In her last hour, Mrs. Trent had the wit and courage to contrive this message, in the hope that it would reach me. It has reached me, and, by heaven, those who are responsible for this lady's death will have ample cause to regret their deeds!"

After uttering these passionate words, Holmes glanced about the room in a kind of triumph. Finally, he returned his attention to Lestrade.

"Have I convinced you, Inspector?"

"I will take this under advisement, Mr. Holmes."

"Do so. Now that I have enlightened you, tell us what you have learned of the matter."

By his manner, Lestrade made it clear how little he enjoyed

being enlightened. He brusquely consulted his notebook and began reading, in the officious manner of a policeman speaking for the record.

"Mrs. Elizabeth Trent arrived in London two days ago as a passenger aboard the *Southern Star,* a steamer from the ports of Singapore, Columbo, Bombay, Diu, Alexandria, and Gibraltar. She had written ahead to Mrs. Keeps to secure lodgings. On her first day she remained within her room the entire time, so far as anyone knows, except for meals, which she took with the other guests. Yesterday afternoon she took a cab, to the address of 221B Baker Street, returning here from that address at close to seven o'clock."

"Ah, seven, you say?" interjected Holmes.

"Yes, Mr. Holmes. Seven was the hour of the lady's return."

"Very well, then. Continue."

"She did not appear for dinner, and there is no evidence that she left the house at any time after returning at seven. She had no guests. The lodger in the room next to hers, a Miss Mary O'Hara, insists that she saw Mrs. Trent coming up the stairs yesterday evening 'looking as though she had seen the devil himself,' to use her own words. Miss O'Hara is a shopgirl, of an extremely excitable nature, but it appears that under the circumstances her suspicions were justified. She states that at about two thirty in the morning she was wakened from a sound sleep by a terrible scream from Mrs. Trent's room. Because she had been so distressed by Mrs. Trent's appearance the evening before, Miss O'Hara made bold to enquire at Mrs. Trent's door, insisting in fact that the lady open the door and offer reassurances."

"That was shrewd of her," said Holmes. "What did she see?"

"Nothing," said Lestrade. "No sign of a forced entry, no sign of another human being whatsoever."

"She volunteered all this?"

"Now what is that supposed to mean?"

"I'm merely asking if this shopgirl thought to look at the time for signs of forced entry."

"It so happens she did."

"And on what account did she do that?"

"On account of the fact that she had been in the habit of filling her spare time with a book."

"A book, Lestrade?"

"Yes, Mr. Holmes. A book with the title of *Varney the Vampire, or The Goblet of Gore.*"

"I cannot say that I have read it. She feared that Mrs. Trent had been accosted by a vampire?"

"Yes."

"And after ascertaining that she had not, she retired?"

"Yes, but she did not fall asleep right away. She said that she heard voices from Mrs. Trent's room."

"Remarkable. Sometimes the most suggestible witnesses are the most valuable. What did the voices say?"

"That she could not determine. At this point, she apparently decided that Mrs. Trent had an assignation rather than an assailant, so that she dared not intervene."

"An assignation rather than an assailant! Really, Lestrade, you surpass yourself."

"Thank you, but the phrase is Miss O'Hara's rather than mine."

"Ah. The young lady appears to be a singularly industrious reader. How long did the voices continue?"

"For about twenty minutes. Miss O'Hara says that at some points she could hear Mrs. Trent crying. She theorized that the unknown gentleman was attempting to encourage Mrs. Trent to depart with him, and she was torn as to her duty. Then there was a period of silence for about ten minutes. Finally, she heard the shot. According to Miss O'Hara, the locks in these rooms are easily forced, and she entered almost immediately. She saw no one, heard no footsteps or other noises."

"Remarkable. I may say that my investigation bears out the young lady's story. If a man was in this room, he appears to have been in the habit of walking on air. But tell us, Lestrade, given this evidence, how can you possibly conclude that Mrs. Trent's death was a suicide?"

"For a number of reasons, Mr. Holmes. In the first place, Miss O'Hara is not what I would call a reliable witness. She is young, Irish, and excitable. You say your investigation corroborates the young lady's story, but if there is no evidence to suggest that a man was in this room, does that not rather suggest that there was no man in this room? The young lady's testimony may be anything from a dream to a deliberate falsification. Her people are not always helpful to the police, Mr. Holmes. Perhaps she would find it amusing to send the force on a wild-goose chase, looking for this winged assailant."

"Well, if the young lady's character is as black as you surmise, perhaps we had better have a look at her. Is she available?"

CHAPTER IV

Miss Mary O'Hara

VEN AS HOLMES SPOKE, the young lady presented herself. Mary O'Hara was Irish indeed, with the thick black hair and glowing complexion that are the pride of her race. It was immediately evident that she possessed the celebrated loquacity of the Celt as well, for as soon as she entered the room she presented her hand to me with astonishing impertinence.

"Oh, Dr. Watson," she began, "I am so honoured to meet such a great author as yourself."

I stared at her amazed, and then, foolishly, I admit, essayed an awkward kiss on her youthful hand.

"Well done, Watson!" cried Holmes, with a laugh. "It is so touching to see true merit finally receive its just reward."

"Oh, Mr. Holmes, I didn't mean to slight you," said the girl, with a graceful curtsey.

"Yes, Mary," said Holmes, flushing slightly. "Perhaps we ought to get on with the matter at hand."

"Oh, yes, Mr. Holmes. Such a tragedy for the poor lady. When I saw her coming up the stairs just a few hours ago, I knew in my heart that destiny had laid its hand on her."

"Indeed. And what makes you say that?"

"Why, the look on her face. As though she had seen the very devil himself."

"Yes, so you told Inspector Lestrade. Could you be more specific? Was she angry? Frightened? Exhausted?"

"She was terrified, Mr. Holmes. I wanted to speak to her, but she would not stay for me. The day before, she had been so polite, so kind, a perfect lady. But last night she would not speak to me, and I did not know her well enough to inquire."

"I see. And then last night you heard her scream?"

"Yes, Mr. Holmes. A terrible scream. And so I knocked on her door. At first she said nothing, but I persisted. Then she answered through the door, and I asked her to open it."

"Did you?"

"Yes, Mr. Holmes. She sounded so frightened I felt I had to. But when she did, I could see nothing."

"Did she open the door completely, or only part way?"

"Completely, Mr. Holmes, like she was showing me she had nothing to hide. You can see for yourself there is no place here for a man to hide."

"Just so. But he might have been standing directly behind her."

"Oh, I don't think so. I looked pretty sharp."

"Did you. And what did you see?"

"I saw the lady had burned a piece of paper in the candle, there on the table. You can see it now, that little piece of ash."

"So you can. Anything else?"

"Well, Mr. Holmes, the window was wide open."

"Really? What about it, Lestrade? Did anyone shut this window."

"Of course not. Not a thing has been touched."

"One wonders why the window was opened, and why it was closed."

"A woman bent on suicide will do strange things, Mr. Holmes. I see no great mystery in her first opening the window and then closing it."

"But the scream. How do you explain that?"

"Oh, any number of things. The sheer buildup of tension."

"Well, well, that may be. What do you think, Mary?"

"I believe the lady had a visitor, Mr. Holmes. A supernatural visitor!"

"And how do you come to this remarkable conclusion?"

"Why, by applying your methods."

"Indeed! I must ask you to elucidate. And I must ask you, Watson, to take special note. It was only a matter of time before my methods were adopted by a hand finer than mine. Please begin, Mary."

"Well, Mr. Holmes, consider first the extreme fright of the lady, which I observed on the staircase. And then her scream. Begging the inspector's pardon, a lady does not scream in such a manner because of tension. The lady screamed because she saw something that terrified her, something so dreadful that she lied to me rather than expose herself to its wrath. But most of all, Mr. Holmes, I would draw your attention to the creature's invisibility."

"Come now, Mary. Surely it would be possible somehow for a man, or a woman, to hide in this room?"

"I looked very closely, Mr. Holmes. Very closely, indeed. And after she closed the door and I returned to my room, I heard voices, I did. And the fellow who was talking had a high-pitched voice, not like a regular man at all."

"Then perhaps it wasn't a man. Perhaps it was a child."

"There was no child here, Mr. Holmes. I looked very closely."

"No doubt. Still, Mary, I should be cautious in resorting to the supernatural. When Mrs. Trent and this other person were speaking, did you hear anything they said?"

"No, it was just voices. They kept very low."

"No doubt. And then ultimately you heard a shot."

"Yes."

"What did you hear leading up to the shot?"

"Nothing, except a bit of a scratching sound."

"Like a pen upon paper?"

"Yes."

"Anything else? Anything at all?"

"No, just the scratching. Then there was silence for some time, and then I heard the shot. I pulled on my clothes and forced open the door."

"How long did that take?"

"About a minute. Perhaps two."

"There is some difference between one minute and two. You feel it was impossible for the intruder to have escaped through the door."

"Yes. I looked down the stair. I would have seen him, or heard him."

Holmes walked out into the hallway and looked down the narrow, winding stair. He paused to light his pipe and after a few draughts, seemed oblivious to us all.

"Yes, I believe we may dismiss the stairs as an escape route," he said, turning back to us again after a long pause. "It would take a cool nerve to creep down those steps after firing a shot. After the shot, and before you entered the room, did you hear any noise at all?"

"No."

"And what did you see when you opened the door?"

"What you see now, except that the poor lady was stretched out on the floor, in a pool of blood. Oh, I am glad you've cleaned it up, sir. It was very hard to look upon."

"I have no doubt, Mary," said Holmes. "You've been a great help to us. I think we better let you get some rest. You've had a long night."

"That I have, Mr. Holmes, and a sad one."

"Then here's a shilling or two for your troubles."

Holmes handed the coins to her, but she passed them right back.

"Oh no, Mr. Holmes, I couldn't. It wouldn't be right to prosper from another's sorrow. Keep your coins to say a Mass for the poor lady, and take a few of mine as well."

She suited her actions to her words, opening a small purse and taking out three shillings.

"That's a bit out of my line," said Holmes, offering her the coins once more. "Perhaps it would be better if you took care of it."

"If you wish, sir," she said, taking the money, "there's a very nice church not too far from here. I'll stop by on my way to work. It was a great honour to meet you fine gentlemen, and may God help you bring to earth the vicious miscreant who performed this awful deed."

And then, with another graceful curtsey and a saucy bob of her head, Mary took her leave.

"What an astonishing creature," I said, when she was safely out of earshot.

"Do you think so, Watson? Well, she has a sharp eye and a kind heart, and that's a combination that's all too rare. But I'm afraid we must take another look at this room. Miss O'Hara's testimony has raised a few additional points."

We entered the sad chamber once more, which Holmes surveyed with the utmost care. Taking out his glass, he examined the black ash on the candlestick holder for some minutes.

"May I take a sample of this residue, Lestrade?" he asked at last.

"You may, for all the good it will do you," said the inspector, somewhat testily.

"If we could read the words that were written here, we should solve this mystery."

"Oh, could we?"

"Yes. This scrap of paper undoubtedly gave the location of Mrs. Trent's last appointment, the one that so horrified her."

"Another appointment after visiting you?"

"Yes. Mrs. Trent left Baker Street shortly after three. She was distressed. She did not arrive here until seven o'clock. Obviously, she stopped elsewhere before returning. Despite Miss O'Hara's regrettable taste for melodrama, we may assume that her description of Mrs. Trent's mood was substantially accurate. Mrs. Trent had had an encounter that terrified her, with a person or persons who somehow pursued her to this room, shot and killed her, leaving hardly a trace of their presence behind."

"Not much to go on."

"No, I don't suppose it is. No doubt you will be pleased to permit me to make further examination of the premises."

I could see that Lestrade was becoming increasingly impatient with my friend, but once more he acquiesced.

"I fear I am not about to quit this room for at least an hour," Holmes said in response. "If you find my obsession with minutiae exasperating, perhaps you could summon a constable to act as chaperone for Watson and myself."

As Lestrade made no reply, Holmes set to work. With immense care, he examined first the floor, and then the window, collecting samples of dust and placing them in a series of small envelopes that he carried with him. The inspector soon quitted the room entirely, admitting by his actions if not his words the grudging respect he felt for my friend's powers.

Throughout this time, Holmes said not a word to me, as was his wont, other than an occasional request to stand aside as he pursued his investigations. He devoted particular attention to the window, examining its frame for fifteen minutes. When he was satisfied at last, he motioned for me to join him.

"Have a look, Watson," he said, pointing out the window with the stem of his pipe.

I gazed down at a sheer drop of forty or fifty feet. The building was made entirely of brick, except for some ornamental stonework. At each floor, a thin line of white stone had been set between the brick, running the length of the floor and level with the windowsills. The stone projected an inch or two beyond the brick.

"Do you see any footholds or handholds?"

"None."

"Now look up."

It was a good fifteen feet to the sloping roof, which had an overhang of perhaps two feet.

"Not an inviting prospect, would you agree?" he asked when I withdrew my head.

"Not in the slightest."

"Yet somehow our man entered through this window, murdered poor Mrs. Trent, and made good his escape. We have been here before, have we not?"

"You mean the murder of John Sholto?"

"Yes. The two cases are vexingly similar. But here the intruder has covered his tracks with much greater care. Look again at the white stonework. Could a man climb out one of the other windows on this floor, work his way along the ledge, and enter here?"

"Impossible."

"That was my reaction. It would require not merely nerves of steel, but fingers and toes as well. Unless he employed some sort of special climbing equipment, and I see no evidence of that."

"Perhaps he dropped a rope from the roof."

"Yes, I fear I shall have to explore that option. Will you join me?"

Several minutes later, Holmes and I clambered out onto the roof, whose numerous gables looked for all the world like vast, slate-covered waves. The morning frost still clung to the slates, rendering them slippery and treacherous.

"Be careful not to disturb anything," Holmes said sharply. "These slates give us our best chance for clews."

Many of the slates were indeed loose. It seemed unlikely that a man could walk across that roof without leaving an obvious trail. I attempted to follow Holmes in his search, but my every movement seemed to draw a cry of warning from him, and at length I gave it up. I rubbed the frost off a few slates and, bracing myself against a chimney pot, lit my pipe and relaxed as best I could in the cold, damp air.

Holmes did not reappear for the good part of an hour, and when he did he was much the worse for wear. His clothes were wet with perspiration and melted frost and smeared with soot.

"Nothing," he said bitterly as he seated himself beside me. He took out a cigar and bit off the end. Yet hardly had he applied a match to the tip but he dashed it out on the slate.

"I must have one more look at Mrs. Trent's room," he said, springing to his feet.

We retraced our steps down the ladder that led into the attic, and then down the narrow stairs to the top floor of the old house. I knew that Holmes was doubly irritated, by the lack of progress in the case and his own disreputable condition. Yet he somehow had recovered his temper when we returned to the sad room. Holmes led me to the window and gestured.

"You see the drainpipe," he said. "It's sound and runs the entire height of the building."

"Not an easy climb," I replied, shaking my head.

"Yes, and getting from the pipe to the window would be an even better trick. We have hold of the wrong end of the case here, Watson. There's no point in looking for clews where they don't exist. I fear I must undertake the very sad task of examining the body of Mrs. Trent. I don't ask you to accompany me."

As we descended the stairs, the landlady stopped us. She gave Holmes a look of silent rebuke and then addressed me.

"Now, are you Dr. Watson?"

"I am."

"Then I expect you'll be wanting your box."

"My box?"

"Yes, Doctor. The box Mrs. Trent brought for you. She had two men bring it down last night, and told me special who it was for."

"I must apologize for my friend, Mrs. Keeps," said Holmes, in a condescending voice. "Mrs. Trent told him about the box yesterday afternoon, and he has forgotten about it already."

"Indeed," said Mrs. Keeps, in a manner suggesting that she had not entirely forgiven Holmes for his appearance. "Well, if he wants it, he better fetch it today. I feel very sorry for the poor lady, but I have a house to run."

"Of course," said Holmes. "Why not have your boy find us a cab while we have a look at this."

Mrs. Keeps led us down into the cellar, where a stout wooden box, marked with all manner of foreign script, confronted us.

"This shouldn't be much of a task," said Holmes, rubbing his hands. "Now, Mrs. Keeps, why not leave us to it and get back to your guests."

"Thank you, Mr. Holmes," she said, eyeing us cautiously. "But why don't you just get it up the stairs first. I wouldn't want you breaking anything."

"Very good, Mrs. Keeps. Just one more thing. What about the poor lady's dog?"

"Dog, sir?"

"Yes. Mrs. Trent's dog."

"The lady had no dog, sir."

"Really? What about a cat?"

"No pets of any kind, sir. Not in this house."

"Are you sure, Mrs. Keeps? No animals at all? Not even a rat?"

"I am sure there are no rats under my roof, Mr. Holmes, and I'll thank you to be moving that box before I set the police on you! I don't allow no talk of rats in this house!"

After that admonition, we set to work without a word. The box, as it proved, was stout indeed and well filled, so that bringing it up the stairs was a task I scarcely relished. But we made it up, under Mrs. Keeps' watchful eye, and brought it out the front door, where a hansom waited.

"Sorry to cost you the exertion, Watson," said Holmes as we heaved the weighty object into the driver's boot, "but I hardly cared for Lestrade to get his hands on this. He seems peculiarly disinclined to pursue the case. I'll ride in with you and then find my own way to the police station. Once you've had a bath and breakfast, I suggest you start calling round at the steamship companies."

"Steamship companies? Why, whatever for?"

"Why, to book our passage for Singapore. What else?"

CHAPTER V

Lord Barington

HEN I RETURNED TO Baker Street that morning, I was famished and filthy from my exertions, but once I entered our rooms, my personal cares suddenly left me and I was struck all at once by a terrible sadness. Less than twenty-four hours ago Elizabeth Trent sat here on this sofa beside me, worn by care, yet charming and infinitely alive. How ready I had been to enlist in her cause! I threw back the curtains to admit the pale winter light. Outside, the eternal stream of London poured past, restless and self-absorbed. Inside, I was alone.

Given my mood, I had no choice but to immerse myself in the mundane tasks of daily life. I bade Mrs. Hudson prepare my breakfast and then bathed and shaved. As I ate I felt a growing reluctance to hurry forth in compliance with Holmes' request that I book our passage for Singapore. Lingering over a second cup of coffee, I was attempting to distract myself with a report in the *Times* of a crisis involving Her Majesty's yacht when I heard footsteps on the stairs. I thought at first it might be Holmes, but instead Billy the page boy entered with a large package, an unruly bundle wrapped in brown paper and bound with twine.

"What's that, Billy?"

"It's a package, Dr. Watson."

"I can see that. What's inside?"

"I don't know, sir, but it's for you. It's terribly heavy, sir. May I put it down? There's a note."

He set the package down on the table before me, endangering several plates. I sent him off and opened the note, which read as follows:

> Dear Dr. Watson:
> It was such an honour meeting you this morning! I am a great admirer of your work, which I have ever considered unexceptionable in the highest degree, sans flaw! And, you must know, I am also an author! I am enclosing for your perusal my first novel, which I dare to hope shall merit your distinguished approbation.
> I know that a man of your eminence has more demands on his time than are hours in the day, yet I know that a few kind words on your part to your publisher would be to me an act of infinite largesse. I only ask that you preserve the manuscript, as it is my only copy, and forgive the multitudinous imperfections of my unpolished discourse, as I write in haste under the unforgiving eye of a brutish employer! I hope indeed that we will have opportunity to discourse in person at a later date on the merits of my first poor attempt, when you have had leisure to peruse its pages. I am omnivorous for your concern!
> With deepest regards,
> Mary O'Hara

My first desire on reading this extraordinary missive was to take the entire package and hurl it downstairs in protest against the absurd presumption of this conniving creature. But it soon occurred to me that my choler was inappropriate. However gauche the young lady's appeal, her industry was commendable, and as Holmes had remarked, she possessed both a sharp eye and a kind heart. Fortifying myself with yet a third cup of coffee, I resolved to ascertain how these qualities might manifest themselves in literary form.

In bulk, at least, *Mary de Guize, or The Prince of the Iroquois* was a fair match for Gibbons. I took the first hundred pages in my lap in the easy chair by the fire and lit a cigar. The manuscript, I soon concluded, was surely the most absurd romance ever penned, yet it possessed an almost hypnotic power to seduce the reader. I found it the perfect antidote to the melancholy that assailed me on that dreary morning.

Mary de Guize, the fabulous heroine of Miss O'Hara's tale, was the product of an importunate marriage between Henri de Guize, heir to the throne of France, and Fionna O'Boyle, princess of Ireland. The two wed secretly, on the battlements of a high castle, after what the author describes as "a grand night of innocent passion, such as any high-born gentleman and lady might give in to when they were in love." Immediately after these hurried nuptials, an immense storm rouses itself, the first of many such atmospheric disturbances, which rumble through Miss O'Hara's narrative with the impact, and indeed the regularity, of express trains. An enormous lightning bolt, "such as no man ever saw," smashes the battlements, plunging the groom and the entire wedding party to their certain death, with the exception of the bride and her old nurse.

Fionna, "her lovely dress ruined and her shoes all squishy with wet," returns to the interior of the castle. Her half-brother, Count Modred, whose unprincipled character Miss O'Hara paints in the blackest of hues, emerges from her father's chamber, his drawn sword "with gore imbrued up to the hilt." Remarkably, indeed, almost miraculously, Fionna and the nurse evade the onslaught of Modred and his minions, which number in the hundreds. They flee to the forest, where they are befriended by woodcutters. It soon transpires that Fionna's one night of prematrimonial congress has impregnated her. When her pregnancy is well advanced, she goes out into the forest alone to pick wild flowers. At the edge of a clearing, she suddenly espies her husband, who miraculously escaped death during the thunderstorm that cut short their wedding. As the two race rapturously towards each other, an enormous boar bursts from the foliage and buries his tusks in the prince's thighs, somehow stripping him naked in the process. Fionna, gazing on her lover's "fair white skin, all sickled o'er with gruesome gore," collapses in a dead faint and proceeds to give birth. A simple charcoal burner, whose daughter had recently given birth to a stillborn child, comes upon the bizarre scene and carries off the babe, wrapping it in oak leaves, the mother and father both having conveniently expired.

When I came to the end of this passage I sat back in my chair, not a little dazed by the narrative's thunderous pace. I had read it in a sort of fever—similar, no doubt, to the one in which it had been composed. The absurd coincidences, melodramatic plot, and strange language, which lurched alternately from high-flown archaisms to contemporary slang, left me not a little stunned. Yet there was no denying its power to captivate. I was in the process of gathering up the second hundred pages of the manuscript when Holmes arrived.

"Sit down, dear fellow!" I cried. "You look all in."

"Not a bit of it," he replied, "though I confess my appearance has drawn stares from every respectable citizen from here to Bow Street. This suit, I fear, is fit only for the ragman. You must excuse me while I repair myself."

"Shall I have Mrs. Hudson prepare your breakfast?"

"Coffee only, Watson, and perhaps a bit of bread. I cannot think on a full stomach."

In something more than half an hour he returned, much restored. I detected, however, a certain nervousness in his behaviour, as though the special tension that always underlay his character had been given another turn.

"Have you been to the steamship companies, then?" he began.

"I'm afraid it rather slipped my mind," I replied, abashed by my carelessness. "Do you really think such an extreme step is necessary?"

"Quite necessary," he snapped, shooting me a hot glance of anger. He rose to his feet, and for a moment I thought he would walk out in his rage. Instead, he turned round about, as if in a momentary fit of irresolution, and then faced me.

"Sorry, Watson. I am directing the anger at others that I should reserve for myself. I have made a complete hash of things. But what's done is done. It only remains for us to play out our parts to the end."

He sat down and poured himself a cup of coffee from the fresh pot Mrs. Hudson had made. I placed a basket of rolls before him, but he motioned them away.

"You have perhaps wondered at the curious interest I have taken in Mrs. Trent's affairs since her letter first arrived," he said, leaning back in his chair and lighting a cigarette.

"Indeed I have. You have been most mysterious."

"Well, I have had my reasons. Tell me, Watson, what do you know of Lord Barington?"

"Not a great deal. He was born into one of the most distinguished families in the land. He held two or three cabinet positions, and as recently as five years ago was regarded as a possible prime minister. But his health failed him, and he had to retire from active life. Heart trouble, I think it was. Anyway, he resigned and ultimately accepted the governorship at Singapore. I believe there was some rumour in the Radical press about his finances not being all they should be."

"Indeed they weren't. And there was no heart trouble. Let me show you something."

Holmes rose and took down one of the enormous scrapbooks that he filled with clippings from the daily press. He sat down with the volume spread on his knees, flipping through the pages.

"Ah, McCardey. He cost me a sleepless night. Poisoned the needle of his wife's sewing machine. I fancy a murderer who keeps up with the times. And now Cates. Stuffed the seat of his brother's carriage with gun cotton. What crimes we'll have to look forward to in the twentieth century, Watson! But here's our man. What do you think of this?"

He passed the bulky volume over to me, his long finger pointing to a clipping with a leader that read "Splendid entertainment at Eddington Castle." I rapidly skimmed the article, clearly written some years ago, which gave an obsequious account of a formal ball given by Lord Barington, followed by a list of several hundred names. I glanced up in confusion, to Holmes' unmistakable pleasure.

"Remarkable, don't you think?" he chuckled.

"I can see no relevance to the case at hand."

"Who is on the guest list?"

"Half the nobility of England, I should say."

"Quite so. But go on down towards the bottom, where the noble lords give way to the honourables. Whom do you find modestly concealed in the third to last position?"

"Professor Moriarty!"

"Yes, indeed. The dear departed. You see, Watson, when Lord Barington was Home Secretary, he did a favour or two for the good professor. In fact, it was he who informed Moriarty of my researches and allowed him to escape apprehension, thus leading to our fatal encounter at the Reichenbach Gorge."

"But this is outrageous! How long have you been aware of this?"

"From the beginning."

"And you did nothing?"

"It was impossible to move against him, Watson. You say he is from a distinguished family. In fact, he is related by birth to two ducal lines, and by marriage to a third. Few men had closer social ties with the royal family. The mere attempt to bring an indictment against such a man would split half the governments of this century, while an unsuccessful prosecution would be enough to destroy a party. Show me the prosecutor who would want the case even if he won! If you were a civil servant asking for a departmental increase, would you care to explain to the Duke of Leicester why his favourite nephew had suddenly been compelled to take up residence in Dartmoor?"

"So even after Moriarty's death there was nothing you could do."

"Not with Colonel Moran on my trail. You recall my hasty departure from Europe to northern India and Tibet."

"A departure of which I knew nothing," I said, rather sharply, for the recollection of the deception Holmes had imposed upon me at the time still held a sting.

"Yes, Watson. But your account of my death, however erroneous, helped both to preserve my life and weaken Lord Barington's reputation. Despite his glitter, there was always something about his lordship that put people off, even in his best days. There was a certain flavour of corruption, a lack of restraint that seemed to grow rather than diminish with the years. It was Barington's ruinous appetite for gambling that put him in Moriarty's clutches, but I suspect that once he was there he rather fancied the man's company. After his master's departure, there was a dropping away from his lordship, due in large part to your account of the proceedings at the Reichenbach Gorge. The court invitations ceased. His day had passed and he knew it. He needed money and he needed to get away from London. It was a measure of his plight that he had to settle for so poor a plum as Singapore."

Holmes paused, charged his pipe, and lit it carefully.

"So, you see, when I saw a black-edged envelope arriving from that port, my attention was immediately aroused. I confess that I did not suspect his lordship of being capable of violence. His nature always struck me as pusillanimous rather than vicious. But I fear he has fallen in with some very bad companions now that he has gone east. I dangerously underestimated the man, Watson, and Mrs. Elizabeth Trent has paid for my folly with her life."

Holmes paused again and poured himself a second cup of coffee. He spoke in a low voice, full of suppressed emotion.

"I did not wish to alarm Mrs. Trent by informing her of the true nature of the evil confronting her. I assumed that Barington and his gang simply wanted her out of Singapore, with an end to her questions. The best thing, it seemed to me, was to convince her to drop the matter and settle here in England."

"So you had no intention of pursuing the case?"

"Not until she was no longer a part of it. I hoped to take up the case in a manner that would not direct suspicion towards her. But somehow either Barington or one of his associates learned of her plans to consult me. Or perhaps she was followed. In any event, they panicked and decided their only recourse was to silence her permanently. A devilishly clean job they made of it, too. Now I must make an end of this matter."

"Then you intend to go to Singapore?"

"I intend to go wherever this case takes me, Watson. And I shall not return until I have brought Lord Barington to earth."

"May I offer my services?"

"Indeed you may. I suspect your presence will prove invaluable."

"I hardly know if my practice could support such a venture."

"I could say as much for mine. I could undergo either the cost of a conventional passage or the loss of half a year's income, but the two combined would sink me. I suspect our mode of travel will be less than orthodox. But we will find a way, won't we, Watson? This morning's exertions have left a very bad taste in my mouth, and I intend to cleanse it."

"You can count on me. Do you have any clews at all?"

"Nothing to go on. There was an animal of some sort in that room last night, but the man who did the deed left not a trace. I shall consult the box that Mrs. Trent left you. I suspect that it contains her husband's papers. She was able to preserve that for us, and we must take advantage of it. And then there is the matter of the pen."

"And I shall attempt to book us passage to Singapore."

"Very good. I should remind you, Watson, that we are sailing into harm's way. Whatever ruse we employ to justify our presence in Singapore, Lord Barington will not be fooled. Our lives will be in danger, not once or twice, but for an extended period of time. Of course, he would like to avoid the outright murder of two respectable Englishmen such as ourselves, but as governor he will be in a unique position to stifle or misdirect any police investigation. And there are any number of other perils for the unwary traveller—fevers, typhoons, poisonous snakes, and insects, even the celebrated tigers of the interior of Singapore Island, though I doubt whether his lordship has command of those remarkable creatures."

"I shall carry my service revolver with me at all times."

"Excellent. I shall arm myself as well. And perhaps you could contrive to carry a knife in your boot and a derringer in your hat. But we will discuss these matters at greater length when you return."

CHAPTER VI

An Old Comrade

 COULD MANUFACTURE NO adequate response to these extraordinary suggestions other than to arm myself with my revolver, as I promised I would. So fortified, I left Holmes to the ledgers of Enderby & Cross and descended the stairs in search of a hansom.

The weather had changed sharply for the worse since our morning excursion. A bitter wind blew from the west, bearing occasional gusts of hail that stung like shot. Once I secured a cab, I wrapped myself glumly in my greatcoat as the driver jolted us over the cobbles. The cold had set the old wound in my left shoulder to aching, and I was beginning to grow drowsy. At length we arrived at Harcourt Street, where the steamship lines ply their trade. I tipped the cabman a half crown and made a cautious descent to the icy pavement.

As both Holmes and I had surmised, the price of a round-trip on a steamer was utterly beyond us. I was, in fact, a little stunned. There seemed to be nothing consistent with our finances other than the few all-sail vessels that still made the long journey, and they would take months. Despite the unwelcome news, I persevered, going from one shipping line to the next. I came at last to Archer & Company, whose window held a splendid model of an old clipper ship, dating from the great days of sail. But the model was fly-blown and covered with dust. As I peered through the window, it was more the weather that drove me inside than the hope that I might at last find affordable passage.

The interior of Archer & Company's office was as dusty and dreary as its window. A flickering gas jet supplied a minimum of illumination, while a small coal fire furnished a similar amount of heat. The solitary occupant was a white-haired old man seated behind a desk, with an enormous ledger spread out across its surface. He looked up and adjusted his spectacles as I entered.

"Excuse me," I said. "I am looking to book passage to Singapore for myself and a friend."

"Are you?" he said shortly. "You've come to the wrong place. We book no passengers."

"My friend and I have no need of luxurious accommodations. Any ship with a spare cabin will do."

"On the run, are you? And what might your name be?"

"I am Dr. Watson."

The man looked up at my words.

"Watson?" he said. "Tell me, Dr. Watson, have you ever been to India?"

"Yes, I have," I said, "but I hardly see that it matters."

"Oh, it matters, Doctor, it matters a great deal. For it was a Dr. Watson of the Fifth Northumberland Fusiliers who took two bullets out of old Sergeant Smith at Candahar. You don't remember me, then?"

"Why, I believe I do. You were my first battlefield case," I said, gripping his hand. "You had one in the thigh and one in the chest, as I recall."

"Now, Doctor, you've got a good memory. It was the one in the chest that worried me. When I saw that bloody foam I thought I was a goner. But you put me under and pulled me through. It was a long trip home, but I've never forgotten it. By God, those were hard times for an old campaigner. Sit yourself down, Doctor, and I'll make us a pot of tea."

It was a strange conversation we had in that old, darkened

office. I had, in fact, very little recollection of Sergeant Smith himself, but his wounds I remembered vividly, for as I had told him, they were the first bullet wounds I had ever treated. Naturally enough, the details of a man's wounds are withheld from him while he is convalescing, but at a remove of a good fifteen years I did not hesitate to portray Sergeant Smith's long-ago plight to him in the most vivid terms. Perhaps I exaggerated the gravity of his punctured lung and the delicacy with which I removed every bone fragment to forestall infection, but it was in a good cause. The old man, like all patients, delighted in the extremity of his condition once it was past, and I was compelled to recount the operation for him three times in its entirety while he savoured each horrific detail.

"Doctor," he proclaimed, when I had come at last to the conclusion of the second reiteration, "it was a good wind that blew you here to brighten an old man's day. Now let me see if there isn't anything I can do to get your friend and you to Singapore."

With that, he went back behind his desk and pulled out an ancient, leather-bound ledger, placing it on top of the first.

"Finding a ship that will carry you and your friend all the way to Singapore for steerage will take some doing," he said, turning the ledger's pages. "But perhaps we can patch a few things together."

I waited a few long minutes while the old man shuffled back and forth between the ledger and a stack of loose papers on a table behind the desk.

"Well," he said at last, "we have some thin pickings, to be sure. I don't know if I should offer this to a gentleman like yourself or not."

"Sergeant," I said, "it is imperative that my friend and I get to Singapore with the absolute minimum of delay. Price and speed, as I have told you, are our only concerns. I would get to Singapore if I had to fire the furnaces myself."

"Well, Doctor, it may not be so bad as that, but you can be the judge. Would you care to be a ship's doctor? It's a slow trip and low wages, but you won't be out when you get there."

I stared at the man.

"Why, what could possibly be better if there's room for my friend? She's not a sailing ship, is she?"

"Well, she's a bit of both, to tell you the truth, but the steamers only have a month or so to beat her. And on a boat like the *Prophet* there's always space for one with the brass to pay for it. But the captain, well, Captain MacDougall is a strange man."

"Is he competent?"

"Oh, no harm will come to you with the captain, I assure you. We've never lost a stick of cargo or spent a penny in late charges for one of his ships."

"What, then?"

"Well, Doctor, not to put too fine a point on it, the captain's a black man."

"A black man named MacDougall?"

"Yes, indeed, though of course that ain't the first name he's had. The captain is a purebred African, and he's a hard man to find on a moonless night."

"Does he speak English?"

"Oh, tolerably well, sir, tolerably well, with a bit of a Scots accent. You see, he was apprenticed to a Scots engineer as a boy, and that's how he came to take up the trade."

"But how could such a man become a captain?"

"Well, sir, there's many a strange thing in the South China Seas. It ain't so proper as London, don't you know. If a man can handle a ship, they don't inquire too closely as to his ancestry."

"Is he in London now?"

"Oh, no, sir. Captain MacDougall don't care too much for the metropolis, if you catch my drift. You'll find the captain and his ship in Tangier. You see, the captain's a Mussulman and don't like to travel in northern latitudes when he can help it."

"So we must travel to Tangier to find him?"

"Oh, yes, but you'll have several weeks. The *Prophet* don't sail for a fortnight. I know you and your friend are in a hurry, Doctor, but if you want to reach Singapore quicker, I'm afraid you'll pay for the privilege."

I told Sergeant Smith I would take his offer under advisement and hurried back to Baker Street to inform Holmes of the

meagre choices available to us. I found him dusty and preoccupied, taking notes in his fine, small hand from a great bundle of papers spread out on the table. At my appearance he
rang for dinner and began clearing off two areas large enough
to hold our plates. It was a simple meal of curried mutton, but
the events of the day had left me famished, so that it was not
until an hour later, as we sat over a glass of brandy, the remains
of one of Mrs. Hudson's noble blancmanges before us, that I
told him of what I had learned on Harcourt Street.

"The *Prophet* certainly sounds unusual," he said with a
smile when I described the ship and her captain.

"Unusual? I would have said unique."

"Quite possibly. But it is your sensibility that needs to be
consulted here rather than mine. How do you feel about serv-
ing under an African Mussulman?"

"It would be, well, irregular," I said, "but I'm not sure I
haven't had a heathen for a commanding officer once or twice
before. If there is no alternative, I shall at least be ready for
an interview with the captain."

"Well played," cried Holmes, laughing. "Let us turn over a
few stones more then before we essay the good captain's hospitality. Perhaps you may find a better ship, yet I can't help
but feel that the *Prophet* is the very one for us."

Exhausted by the events of the day, I retired shortly after
dinner. Yet I found myself unable to sleep and resorted in my
distress once more to Miss O'Hara's voluptuous romance.
Beguiled by her account of her heroine's childhood, I felt
myself surrendering insensibly to the demands of the flesh,
and fell asleep with the pages of the manuscript scattered
about me. The next morning I awoke much refreshed.
Immediately after regaining consciousness, however, my spirit was invaded by melancholy once more as I recalled the tragic events of the previous day. For a minute I lay almost paral-
ysed beneath the heavy coverlet, but then threw it off with a
single gesture as I recalled Holmes' fierce determination "to
play out his part to the end." Elizabeth was taken from us. But
her murderers must be brought to justice.

CHAPTER VII

The Southern Star

ULL OF RESOLVE I performed my ablutions and dressed for the day, though the hour was scarcely later than seven. A scribbled note from Holmes informed me that he was already gone, to the police station. I breakfasted rapidly and set off again to Harcourt Street in search of a fleet, cheap ship bound for Singapore. The pale, white glow of the false dawn was barely illuminating the eastern sky as I rode down toward the great London docks. When I rode back the sun was well past the midpoint and arcing down toward the horizon.

Holmes' prediction regarding the *Prophet* had rung true. The fare of the few ships that would be in Singapore before her was a good six months' earnings for myself. I never exchanged the lightest word with Holmes regarding finances, but I knew from long experience that his attitude toward money was supremely casual. When he had money, he spent it. When he had not, he went without. Despite his fame, and his intense pride in his abilities, he neglected every opportunity to increase or even stabilize his income. Somehow I had the feeling that what little I had to tell about Captain MacDougall appealed to his love of the *outré*. The only mark against the *Prophet* was her lack of speed, and that would have to be endured for the sake of economy.

As the cab halted before 221B, a tall man who could only
be Holmes sprang from the kerb, opened the door and vaulted in beside me.

"Farnsworth Docks, pier seven, the *Southern Star*," he
called to the driver, stowing a gladstone at my feet. "Excellent
good fortune to run into you like this, Watson," he said, turning to me. "I am on an errand that calls for a comrade."

"Is the *Southern Star* bound for Singapore?" I asked, embarrassed that I could recall no such ship.

"On the contrary, she arrived from there only three days
ago. Mrs. Trent was one of her passengers. I have spent the
day running down everyone else who made the journey with
her—a wearisome task, but not a difficult one."

"What did you learn?"

"A great deal or nothing, depending on one's interests. You
may recall that I questioned Mrs. Trent about her passage
rather closely. She never saw a familiar face the entire voyage. Yet undoubtedly she was followed. It is more likely than
not that Lord Barington has agents, or at least accomplices,
elsewhere than Singapore itself, yet the *Southern Star* remains
the one tangible connection we have with our quarry. The
passengers themselves we can dismiss. Mrs. Trent was the
only passenger to make the entire trip from Singapore to
London. I have seen the few who arrived with her on Monday
and am convinced they can have no connection with the matter. That leaves the crew.

"After I finished with the police yesterday, I went round to
the offices of Levant Shipping, which owns the *Southern Star*.
The clerk at Levant was quite helpful in giving me information about the *Southern Star*'s passengers, but about the ship
itself he was resolutely closemouthed. He refused to allow me
permission to come on board."

"So that has aroused your curiosity."

"Yes, and I spoke to Lestrade this morning. There was
much hemming and hawing on his part. I think the man is
coming under conflicting pressures. Some of his superiors
want to see this case pursued, while others do not, and a man
like Lestrade is left in the middle. This morning the better

angels of the force seemed to have the field, and I was able to obtain this."

Holmes handed me an official-looking document written on stiff paper, signed with a flourish by Chief Inspector Sam Hall.

"It looks proper enough," I said, perusing it.

"Yes, but it isn't a search warrant, which as a private citizen I would be unable to enforce in any event. Whether it is enough to bluff a suspicious sea captain remains to be seen."

Holmes paused as the hansom slowed to a stop and deposited us on the wharf. The *Southern Star,* a large, handsome ship, painted jet black, loomed before us. Holmes tossed the cabman half a crown and bid him to wait for us, but the minute our backs were turned we heard the scraping of the hansom's wheels as the man turned his cab about and left us.

"Deuce take the fellow," said Holmes. "The cold was too much for him. We'll have to make our own way back. It's well enough we have our revolvers."

It was a lonely walk up the gangplank of the *Southern Star,* with a cold wind blowing over the dark, sullen waves. A few electric lamps shone brilliantly on the ship, which was otherwise cloaked in the rapidly growing darkness. There seemed to be no one on board at all, but as soon as we set foot on deck we were met by a hard-faced sailor who barred our path.

"Good evening, gentlemen," he said. "Who gives you permission to come on board?"

"We are making an inquiry regarding one of your passengers," said Holmes, in his politest voice.

"There's no passengers on this ship, and no visiting. Seeing as you have no right to be here, I suggest you be gone."

"Perhaps we should discuss this matter with a superior officer," said Holmes.

"Oh, a superior officer? Very well then. I should have known you gentlemen were too grand for the likes of me." The ruffian glared at us and with an abrupt gesture rang the ship's bell. Scarcely had the bell ceased pealing when a half-dozen men sprang from the darkness and formed a semicircle around us. Though they made no move to advance, it was obvious that we would have to beat an ignominious retreat. Holmes glared at the men and seemed about to turn on his heel, when yet another figure stepped forward.

"What do we have here, Starkey? Who are these men?"

"They didn't give no names, Captain. Said they wanted to investigate."

"On my ship? Who might you gentlemen be?"

"I am Sherlock Holmes," my friend said. "This is Dr. Watson."

"Oh, Sherlock Holmes, the famous detective, is it? And what would you have with my ship?"

"We wish to investigate a crime, the murder of one of your passengers, Mrs. Elizabeth Trent."

"She was alive when she left this ship," the man said impassively.

"I am aware of that," said Holmes. "Still, the chief inspector at Scotland Yard has asked me to examine your ship for clews that might help identify her assailant." With these words he handed the paper inscribed by the chief inspector to the captain, who glanced at it with surprising shrewdness.

"Pretty," he said, "but it's no warrant. You have no legal right to be on my ship, do you, Mr. Holmes?"

"You have the right to deny me entry if you wish."

"Aye, that I do, Mr. Holmes, that I do. For I am the master of this ship. But far be from Captain Manning, who is only a poor sea dog, to interfere with the great Sherlock Holmes when he has detecting on his mind. You must excuse my sailor boys, Mr. Holmes, if they seem a little rough to you, for they have not had your advantages. Please, gentlemen, make way for Mr. Holmes and his friend."

The men parted to allow us movement but then regrouped, and we found ourselves accompanied across the deck by a circle of hard, grinning faces.

"You can hardly expect me to do any work under these circumstances," Holmes said, coming to a stop.

"You are particular, aren't you, Mr. Holmes? Now, boys,"

the captain said, turning to his men, "you must quit Mr. Holmes. A fine gentleman like himself has no time for the likes of you. Be off with you now! Be off!"

The men dispersed, with an air of smirking contempt that I found almost unendurable. We were left alone with Captain Manning, who continued to address us in his smooth, calculating manner.

"That's better now, isn't it, Mr. Holmes? But of course I have my duties as well, and so I'll leave you. I'll give you an hour, Mr. Holmes. Detect all you like, but port or starboard I'll have you off my ship in one hour."

As he uttered the last sentence, all the suppressed rage in his soul leapt into his face. But in a moment he mastered himself, and grinning once more he turned away and slipped into the darkness.

"What a scoundrel!" I said as soon as we were alone.

"Yes, it was a pretty drama," said Holmes. "They must have been watching us from the first."

"What can you hope to learn in one hour?"

"Nothing, I would imagine, given the captain's attitude. The whole crew has been primed against us, Watson. Poor Trent! He must have been in deep with a bad gang to have set all this in motion! Let us have one look in the ship's hold and then be off. I'm sure our host would be only too glad to feed us to the fish if we give him half a chance."

Holmes opened a door that took us into a narrow corridor, dimly lit by a few electric lamps. We had advanced only a few paces when the door slammed shut behind us and the lamps went out, plunging us into utter darkness.

"Bluff and counterbluff," Holmes chuckled. "Fortunately, I do have an alternative."

I heard him opening his gladstone, and a few moments later the round circle of light from a bull's-eye appeared on the wall opposite.

"That's better. Now I would like to see what's in her."

Moving slowly along the corridor, we found a spiral staircase and descended several levels into the ship's bowels. As we descended, the air grew warmer and charged with coal dust. We could feel as well as hear the dull throb of the ship's engines. When we reached the bottom of the stairwell, Holmes found the handle of a door and twisted it.

"At least they didn't think to shut us off at both ends," he said. "Ah, here come the lamps again. I didn't think they could do without them."

As he spoke, the lamps winked back on, and we found ourselves able to move about the ship's enormous hold without groping. Holmes stopped occasionally to gather dust from the floor.

"Just checking, Watson. Though Mrs. Trent's assailant left no footprints, there were traces of coconut matting, oak and mahogany splinters, gutta percha, rubber, pepper, nutmeg, and a curious substance known as gambier."

"An odd collection."

"Odd, indeed. And what more likely place for such a collection than the hold of a Pacific freighter?"

"Do you suspect a member of the crew?"

"Oh, any one of that lot would be glad to slit a throat for a hundred pounds. But we are looking for a man of extreme physical agility, and I doubt that . . . what's that noise?"

Holmes turned sharply about and drew his revolver. I followed suit. He motioned to me to move apart from him, and we advanced slowly toward the hull of the ship. There was a sort of raised metal fender or shield that ran along the hull, apparently to protect it from shifting cargo, barely two feet high. Holmes reached the fender and after pausing a moment, plunged his hand over it. Scarcely had he done so than he gave voice to a startled oath and pulled his hand back, streaming with blood. I heard a rustling sound and tried to get a look behind the screen, but found I could see little, due to the narrow angle of vision and the poorness of the light. I returned my attention to Holmes, who was calmly inspecting his wound.

"A mere scratch, Watson," he informed me.

"Let me look at it." I held the bull's-eye and examined his hand. As I suspected, he was understating the matter. In fact, there was a deep puncture in the ball of the thumb that would take several stitches to close, and the flesh was torn in a semi-circular pattern.

"I say, Holmes!" I exclaimed. "You've been bitten!"

"Yes. Remarkable dentition, isn't it? I can't think of an animal in Britain that could produce such a wound. By the way, did you see anything?"

"Nothing. We must get this cleaned immediately, along with an inoculation."

"No hurry," he said, binding his hand tightly with a handkerchief. "Pasteur assures us that the incubation period for rabies is at least twenty-four hours."

"I wish I had my bag. I could stitch you up right now."

"I think I'll forego any stitches. A natural scar should preserve the pattern of the bite far more effectively. I think we may as well depart. I don't think it would do to try the captain's hospitality."

We ascended the spiral staircase without difficulty and discovered that the captain was waiting for us at the top.

"Did you enjoy your tour, gentlemen? I apologize for the little trouble we had with the lights. This newfangled electricity is hard to work with."

"Our visit was most informative," said Holmes, giving the man a cold look.

"Found a clew, did you, Mr. Holmes? Ah, and what did you do to your hand?"

"I appear to have been bitten. Tell me, Captain, are there any apes or monkeys on board your ship?"

"Oh no, sir, unless you're referring to my crew, and I hope you wouldn't be, because my fellows don't care for such humour as that. No doubt it was a rat that nipped you, sir. They can be pesky fellows."

"This was no rat."

"Ah, well, you're the expert, and to tell the truth, I don't like thinking that I've got rats in my hold. But those rats, sir, they will give you a nip at times if you don't treat them right."

"Thank you, Captain. And now I think we will be leaving you."

"Must you, Mr. Holmes? I must say, my crew and I have enjoyed your visit. But we have a saying at sea, 'Once is enough.' Don't be coming back, Mr. Holmes, not without a warrant."

"I assure you, Captain, the next time you see me, I will have a warrant."

"Will you, then? Those are brave words. Mind the gangplank. I've seen more than one fellow slip through, just when he thought he was safe and sound."

And so we were ushered off, in a most vile and offensive manner, with the prospect of a long, cold walk through some of the most unsavoury areas of London.

"A poor night I've given you, Watson," said Holmes, lighting a cigar.

"Surely Captain Manning knows more than he is telling."

"It would be hard to imagine a less attractive character," said Holmes. "If ever a captain deserved to be hanged from his own yardarm, he is the man. No doubt our paths will cross again, if not in this case then another."

"You think he is guilty of the murder?"

"No, but I would bet a thousand pounds that he knows who is. I suspect our man is no longer in England, or at least well out of London."

"I am sorry you were unable to obtain more information."

"So am I. But at least I do have my wound. I must remember to keep it elevated. It would be a pity to preserve the clew and forfeit the detective."

CHAPTER VIII

The Persistence
of Miss O'Hara

 E DID NOT RETURN to Baker Street until after
midnight, chilled through and exhausted.
There I was able to properly tend to Holmes'
wound and, despite his remonstrances,
stitched it closed. The following day we returned to our separate tasks. I pursued an exhaustive search for an alternative
to the *Prophet,* consulting every major port in Western Europe
to no avail. Holmes divided his time between the most minute
review of the records Elizabeth had preserved and visits to
various government offices where he was known in the
hopes of creating a plausible fiction with which to disguise
our presence in Singapore. Ultimately, he obtained letters
from the Foreign Office that authorized him to investigate a
very real and disturbing crime, the theft of one thousand army
rifles, of the very latest type, taken from the transport
Columbine when she lay to in Singapore.

"His lordship won't care to see these," he said chuckling,
when he presented me with the documents, portentously
sealed with red wax and red ribbons. "They give us every
right to make a nuisance of ourselves. We can only pray the
rifles don't turn up before we do."

To while away the hours before our passage to Tangier, I

continued with my study of Miss O'Hara's manuscript. I had broken off shortly after the heroine had learned to walk. The author, though dilating on the "infinite, simple joys of child-hood," disposes of her heroine's first fourteen years in a few pages. However, when she reaches that age "when Nature upon her first began to shower the gifts of womanhood," the pace of the narrative slows appreciably. Young Mary takes to wandering in the woods, where she develops an astonishing proclivity for coming upon young gentlemen in a state of undress, a tendency she retains for the rest of her life. After one such misadventure, she finds herself being pursued by two young gallants "over fen and dell, by dappling springs and rumbling cataphracts [presumably, "cataracts"] that fair shook the earth in their thunder." During the course of her flight, twigs and branches repeatedly catch at her clasps and sashes, until she is "bare and proud as the day God made her." In this condition, she continues several miles through dense forest, until she encounters "Milord Henri de Coeur," a French noble-man of the highest blood and, even more fortunately, the high-est character as well. He generously surrenders his "elegant cloak, in just the very highest fashion and generously cut" to Mary, who springs lightly onto his saddle. The two gallop off to his castle, she "cuddling gently in the shelter of his strength."

At this point, I fear, my concentration began to waver. But the dreary weather without, and the tedium of our long wait before our departure for Tangier, left me without other occu-pation. I recharged my pipe with shag, prepared a mild brandy and soda, and took yet another hundred pages of manuscript into my lap, and then another, and another. I read on and on, though it became impossible to retain the details of the narrative in my mind. What passed between Mary and Milord Henri I cannot say. I suspect that like so many of the fine gentlemen who befriended Mary during the course of Miss O'Hara's opus, he endured a bloody and tragic death, quite possibly in *dishabille*.

Ultimately, Miss O'Hara launches her heroine across the Atlantic to French Canada, where the prospects of coming across nude men while wandering the woods are, of course, practically limitless. There she is abducted by Chi-anganagahouk, the Iroquois prince of the title, who quite naturally succumbs to her charms. But their romance is interrupted by an invasion of English troops, led by the sneering Lord Ramsbottom. When Chianganagahouk is wounded in battle, Mary rallies the Iroquois and leads them to victory, effectively reversing the battle of Quebec and rewriting history. In gratitude, the entire tribe converts to Catholicism, making Mary their queen, once she and Chianganagahouk marry. Together, the two preside over an Irish/French/Iroquois confederacy that stretches from the Atlantic to the Pacific, providing a refuge for all "whose hearts do beat with a strong and innocent passion."

I sat stunned in the twilight as the last page of Miss O'Hara's manuscript fell from my fingers. Never, I believe, had I encountered a narrative less bound by the laws of taste, propriety, and common sense. Slowly I gathered together the leaves of its enormous bulk and pondered what to do with it. No doubt a brief note expressing my disbelief in the work's ability to obtain a favourable reception in the marketplace would be best. Yet I doubted whether Miss O'Hara would accept such a politely worded rejection. On the contrary, it appeared only too likely that an evasive answer would only stimulate the tenacity that formed so great a part of her character. I came reluctantly to the conclusion that only personal interview, conducted at some length, would grant me the opportunity to satisfy her exceptional, though profoundly misguided, spirit. I was just considering how best to make my advance when I heard the bell and, almost immediately thereafter, a pair of light feet on the stairs. In another instant, the woman herself had entered our chambers, looking surprisingly elegant in a showy ensemble of dove-coloured silk. The costume, though far above her station, could hardly be faulted. The shimmering fabric accentuated her every charm, and I could not but admire in the warmest manner the superb elasticity of her carriage.

"Ah, Dr. Watson!" she cried, in a voice that reminded me irresistibly of her heroine. "I felt I should not come. Yet, I could not stay away!"

"Miss O'Hara!" I said, rising to my feet. "I must ask you to forgive this disorder. Why, I was just considering your manuscript."

"Were you, Doctor? You are too kind. Oh, I am exhausted! May I have a seat?"

"Of course. Would you like some tea?"

"That would be lovely."

I rang for Mrs. Hudson, who took my order rather grudgingly, I thought, and did not return with it for many minutes. However, subjected to the full force of Miss O'Hara's personality, I scarcely noticed.

"Dr. Watson," she began, "have you—have you any news of the terrible crime that took away poor Mrs. Trent?"

"There have been a few developments," I said, a little stiffly. "You know, Holmes—that is, Holmes and I are reluctant to discuss a case until it is complete."

"Of course! I'm sure that you know best in such matters. It must be dreadfully exciting!"

"Not really. So much of detective work is mere drudgery."

"Why, I am sure you are making that up because you are so modest."

In such a manner I found myself beguiled into delivering an extensive account of our adventures with Captain Manning on board the *Southern Star,* though with dubious accuracy. In fact, to my shame, I must now confess that I found Miss O'Hara's capacity for rewriting history so contagious that I concluded my narration by asserting that I had treated that oleaginous mariner to a sound thrashing! The young lady was quite captivated by this last and insisted on inspecting my hands for signs of the encounter. Unfortunately, I had none to show, but happily she discovered a slight injury I had done to my face while shaving the day before, which she immediately attributed to the imaginary scuffle. She kissed it repeatedly and then burst into tears.

"Oh, Doctor," she cried, "you are so heroic, so noble to avenge the poor lady's tragedy in such a manner."

After that outburst she suddenly fell faint, swooning in my arms. To revive her, I loosened the garment about her throat as best I could and uncorked the brandy I had earlier resorted to while reading her manuscript. As I moistened her mouth with it, her lovely eyes opened and looked directly into mine.

"Oh, Johnnie," she said, licking her lips, "do give us a glassful. Don't be stingy with the good stuff."

I was so startled by the impertinence of her language that I complied without thinking and had a glass for myself as well. By this time our tête-à-tête had already forsaken all compliance with decorum's rule. Whether the young lady was an angel or devil, I leave it to the reader to conjecture. All I can say is that I was powerless to resist the charms of this Irish Cleopatra. The stolid years of loneliness I had endured as a widower, the agonizing days occasioned by Elizabeth's foul murder—all these vanished in the steady, purifying flame of an afternoon's passion. I lay on the couch beside her in a state of blissful exhaustion, penetrated to my core. When at last the time came to stir, the sight of Mary, her flowing black hair all askew over her lily-white shoulders, her superb figure displaying every charm she had heaped upon her eponymous heroine, summoned me once more to the labours of Cupid, endowed with all the might of Hercules, until at last I could do no more. And so we lay when Holmes arrived.

"You surprise me, Watson," he said as he surveyed the devastation our passion had wrought on his bachelor abode. "I had not expected this for another week."

PART II

The Mediterranean

CHAPTER IX

Prelude

T WAS DIFFICULT, indeed, to accept a departure from Mary under those circumstances, but Holmes quite politely retreated while we repaired ourselves and I saw Mary safely off in a cab. He returned half an hour later with shining eyes and sealed lips, though in the following week he made occasional queries as to my progress in my "researches" and "experiments," to which I could make little reply. Thus it was that when the date for our departure for Tangier arrived, I took the precaution of securing a set of well-appointed and discreetly located rooms, so that Mary and I might take our leave unencumbered by extraneous concerns. I was able to deliver to the dear girl the news for which she so ardently wished, with all her heart and soul, that my publishers had agreed to give her novel the most careful consideration. Her gratitude, under the circumstances, was quite overpowering, so that when Holmes and I made our departure for that exotic port, I enjoyed a repose of flesh and spirit well beyond any that I had ever known.

Our voyage to Tangier, though brief, was a constant stimulus to my spirit, despite all odds. Each hour bore me further away from Mary, and considering her youth and passionate nature, the likelihood that I might return to find her affections still unencumbered was marginal at best; yet a curious appetite for adventure, such as I had not felt since I was a very young man, seemed to throb in my veins. I had travelled to the East then, to serve in Afghanistan, and now I was travelling East once more.

The dreary soot and grime of London departed. On the first day, we encountered nothing but fog and damp and chill as we made our way through the channel. But on the second, as we swung out into the open Atlantic, far from all land, the sun rose brilliantly, and though the hoar frost still glinted on the decks, the ineffable scent of the tropics wafted in the crisp, clean air. As we rode on the infinite blue bosom of the ocean, I felt that, somehow, nothing in my life would be quite the same.

Holmes, of course, remained unchanged. Though he joined me for a regular constitutional round the decks, before both breakfast and dinner, for the remainder of the day he kept himself immured in our cabin, working his way through the heavy mass of ledgers and other company records that Elizabeth had secured in the hope of clearing her husband's name.

While Holmes busied himself with his researches, I made a nuisance of myself on the bow of the ship, determined to be the first to cross every degree of latitude as we pursued our southern course. The crew, no doubt familiar with the middle-aged exuberance a sea voyage can inspire, treated my presence with amused contempt. My spirits, however, were proof against any ridicule. The months-long voyage stretched before me like a grand vista. The prospect of service under the mysterious black captain seemed as glorious to me as though I were enlisting under the colours of Nelson himself. And at the end of it all lay Singapore, the Lion's Port, the last great outpost of Empire, presided over by the murderous Lord Barington. Looking back on it all, it was well indeed that I commenced such an adventure fresh from Mary's exquisite embrace. Otherwise, I wonder that I would have had the stamina to endure all that befell us.

CHAPTER X

The Gates of Hercules

UR SHIP SOON BROUGHT us in sight of Gibraltar, the mighty rock that, perhaps more than any other spot of land, stirs the heart of the true Britisher. Holmes, to my surprise, insisted on riding in on the packet boat. The dock at Gibraltar seemed but a tawdry menagerie of shopworn curiosities designed to catch the eye, and even more the purse, of the unwary traveller. Only the sight of a red-coated military guard, tramping up the steep cliffs, reminded the onlooker that he stood at a very pivot point of the Empire. But Holmes was enthralled. He hurried me from place to place, stopping at last before an amiable ruffian who held on a chain one of the Barbary apes that infest the island. Behind the man a stack of cages held additional specimens, along with several other smaller monkeys.

"I say," cried Holmes, "that's a fine animal."

"Oh, indeed he is, sir," returned the man. "Smart as a whip. A man couldn't ask for a better pet."

"I fancy not. Does he bite?"

"Bite? Why no, sir. Never bit a gentleman in your life, did you, Jocko? He's tame as a kitten, sir. You can be sure of that."

"Pity. Do you mind if I have a look at his teeth?"

"Why, I don't know why you should be wanting to look at his teeth, sir. These apes is very polite."

"I'll tell you what. You hold him still, and there's a half crown in it for you."

"Well, sir, I ain't a man to turn down half a crown, especially from a fine gentleman such as yourself. But as I say, these apes is polite, and I don't know that you should be messing about with his teeth. Under the circumstances, he might take a nip at you."

"That will be my worry, my good man. You just hold your animal still while I examine him."

"Well, sir, I won't say no, but first I'd like to see my money."

Holmes dug a coin from his pocket and tossed it to the fellow, who caught it up with undisguised eagerness.

"Now there's a fine gentleman to be sure," he said, stuffing the coin in his purse and picking up the noisome creature. "Now, Jocko, you just hold still while the gentleman has a look at you."

Once the man had the ape wrapped in his arms, Holmes advanced a step, which produced a most astonishing reaction in the beast. Writhing in its keeper's grip, the little animal bared its teeth and shrieked as though in fear of its very life. Almost immediately, its caged brethren responded in kind. Mere words cannot describe the volume of their cries.

"What do you think, Watson?" said Holmes, oblivious to the creature's hysteria. He held up his left hand, whose wound had scarcely healed, and placed it next to the ape's face. "Different species entirely, wouldn't you say?"

"Yes, indeed!" I shouted, struggling to make myself heard over the appalling din. "Have you seen enough?"

"Not entirely," said Holmes, fixing his gaze on the contorted features of the frenzied beast with all the rapt attention of a connoisseur encountering an hitherto unknown Van Dyke. "The differences I find as instructive as the similarities. I confess to have neglected the study of comparative dentition, for I cannot recall a single case that ever turned on it. However, for the matter at hand, the issue appears to be a crucial one.

For example, consider the marked difference in the canines. Extraordinary."

"That's quite enough for half a crown, sir," snapped the keeper, turning away and struggling to secure the ape in a large wooden cage. When at last his task was done, he turned back to us with a look on his face that was far from friendly.

"I'm afraid I must ask you gentlemen to leave," he said, while the ape shrieked in protest of its confinement. "You have badly frightened poor Jocko."

"Here's another half crown for your troubles," said Holmes, good-naturedly. "Your animal was most instructive."

"Good day to you, sir, and thank you kindly for your generosity. But if you would be leaving, poor Jocko might calm himself. Once these fellows gets stirred up, there isn't much a man can do with them."

"So I should imagine," remarked Holmes dryly. "Well, Watson, let us be on our way."

From Gibraltar we had only a short distance to Tangier itself, a port as exotic as Gibraltar was commonplace. Few spots on the map, I fancy, offer such a mingling of peoples, races, tongues, religions, and cultures. Here the white-faced Englishman is an anomaly, surrounded by shades ranging from the lightest coffee to the deepest black. Here the Romans and Carthaginians trod, here the Vandals swept south and the Arabs east, here the Greeks gazed on the Pillars of Hercules. Though much of the population is sunk in appalling indolence and poverty, there is a strange charm to Tangier, an intoxication that the chill northerner is powerless to resist. So at least it appeared to me.

And it was at Tangier that we encountered at last Captain MacDougall. We had of necessity engaged a guide, a beggarly street Arab, who led us to the dock where the *Prophet* lay at anchor, along with several porters, who carried our baggage. The fellow assured us that he knew both the captain and the *Prophet* well, but when we reached the docks he suddenly grew silent.

"This is poor luck," I said angrily, gazing out into the forest of masts that confronted us. "The *Prophet* could be any of a dozen ships."

"It's not as bad as all that," said Holmes. "I believe this is our ship right here."

"How can you tell?" I asked, for he pointed to the high stern of a freighter that showed no identification.

"The captain, by the name of his ship, commemorates the founder of his religion, Mohammed. Observe the pennant trailing from the mainmast, covered with Arabic script. It is the custom of the Mussulman to adorn his vessel at its highest point with verses from the Koran."

Indeed, as we made our way round we discovered the ship's name, emblazoned in both English and Arabic. The *Prophet* was a remarkable ship, perhaps two hundred and fifty feet in length, made entirely of wood, with three masts, which, to my unnautical eye, appeared capable of carrying a full head of sail. Yet a large, black smokestack projected from the rear deck of the vessel, which had clearly been subjected to a substantial modification. The gangplank for the ship was a distinctly makeshift affair, little more than a rope bridge, and exceedingly difficult to use, owing to the steep angle of ascent.

As we made our way to the deck, we were suddenly halted, in a manner unpleasantly reminiscent of our encounter with Captain Manning aboard the *Southern Star*. A muscular, yellow-skinned fellow, clad in nothing but a pair of tattered black breeches, thrust himself in our way, gesticulating fiercely and sending forth a stream of gibberish that left us both speechless. We turned as one to our guide and discovered him, along with the porters, in full flight from their position, leaving our baggage abandoned on the dock. We ourselves took several steps back along the makeshift gangplank, which seemed to calm the man a bit.

"Apparently we face the enemy alone, Watson," Holmes said to me. "What do you suggest?"

"I cannot imagine what would appease the fellow," I said.

"Obviously he has no idea who we are. Captain MacDougall seems to have been remiss in informing his crew."

But at my words a man appeared who could only be the captain himself. He was well over six feet, a good two inches taller than Holmes, with a splendid physique and a skin that shone like polished ebony. He was dressed in tropical navy whites and carried himself with the assurance and grace of a natural athlete. At his approach, the sailor instantly withdrew and the captain took his place before us.

"Request permission to come aboard, sir," I cried, matching my words with a salute. My actions drew a startled look from Holmes, and I was not a little surprised myself at this sudden reversion to half-remembered military formalities.

"Not a bad salute for a soldier," the captain laughed. He spoke in dark, liquid tones, with a soft Scots burr that was as unmistakable as it was unexpected. "Welcome aboard, gentlemen. I informed the crew of your arrival, but Wu Si here hasn't much patience with a white face."

"I am Sherlock Holmes," said Holmes, advancing up the gangplank. "I congratulate you, Captain, on your remarkable ship."

"Welcome, Mr. Holmes, but right now I am more concerned to meet my ship's doctor. You are Dr. Watson, are you not?"

"I am indeed, Captain," I said, introducing myself. "Is there an emergency?"

"None, Doctor, other than that I am in haste to get under way and would like you to examine our stores before we do so. I will have a few of the men tend to your baggage."

I had hardly expected to be set to work in such a manner immediately upon arrival, but the captain was obviously a man who brooked no delay. I accompanied him belowdecks to a large section of the hold that was filled to the bursting with every manner of foodstuff. I stood outside, while a pair of sailors, one black and one yellow, brought forth bread, cheeses, salted sides of beef, and even fragrant crates of cantaloupes that the captain found questionable.

"We will have many stops along the way," he explained, "but

the prices at Tangier are favourable. Besides, I work my men hard and find I have to fill their bellies well as a consequence."

As we went abovedecks, I discovered just how true these words were. No sooner had we seen the sunlight than the captain began barking orders to the crew, who scurried about in preparation for casting off.

"Remarkable, wouldn't you say?" said Holmes, suddenly appearing at my elbow.

"Exceedingly!" I exclaimed. "But to what, precisely, are you referring?"

"Yes, that is the question," he replied, laughing. "I refer to the entire affair—the captain, the ship, the crew, and the voyage. We are a long way from London, Watson."

"We are indeed."

As we spoke we heard the powerful blast of a steam whistle, and a mighty plume of smoke arose from the stack at the rear of the ship. We felt the decks tremble with each piston thrust as the engines below began to build power.

"I fear we are in the way here," said Holmes, watching a cargo hook swing past us. "Perhaps we should retire to the cabin."

Our cabin, located belowdecks and forward on the ship, consisted of two rooms, which were comfortable but hardly commodious. The front room, where we were to spend most of our time, was equipped with a few stiff, formal chairs of an earlier era, somewhat miniaturized for life aboard ship. The sleeping room was so small that our baggage, which had been placed there for us, filled it almost entirely.

"One hopes for fair weather," Holmes remarked, as we set about unpacking. I was pleased to see that he had no intention of reproducing the bohemian clutter of Baker Street. The sailor's apothegm—"a place for everything, and everything in its place"—guided us, until at length everything was stowed away, with the exception of the sad trunk that contained the records left to us by Elizabeth. There was no room for it except in the exact centre of the front room. When we had positioned it there, Holmes drew from his gladstone a silver cigarette box, which he placed on the trunk with a ceremonious gesture.

"We have the comforts of home, if not the spaciousness," he said, taking a cigarette and offering me one. "This trunk shall serve us as table and desk, and constant reminder of our task."

"I suppose there is little we can do but wait until we arrive," I said.

"True. So far I have learned little from all this"—here he thumped the trunk by way of explanation—"that would be of interest to anyone except an historian of Enderby & Cross. Certainly I have a fair knowledge of the commercial ebb and flow in the Malay Straits for the past half-dozen years, but why this should drive one man to suicide, and others to murder, remains hidden. Fortunately, this voyage will give me the leisure to master this material in its entirety."

"Indeed. But I am curious to discover what my duties will consist of. I don't believe I counted thirty men on deck."

"Oh, no doubt you will save a life or two before we reach Singapore. There are all sorts of ways a man can break a leg, or his neck, on a ship like this."

As he spoke these words, we heard repeated, shrill blasts from the ship's whistle. The pant of the engines grew louder and faster, and through the tiny porthole that gave us our only view of the exterior world, we could see the dock begin to slowly slip past our eyes.

"Under way at last," cried Holmes, springing to his feet. "We must be on deck for this, Watson."

The sails of the *Prophet* were still furled as she swung slowly about in the harbour, which was dotted about with all manner of small, exotic craft. We found ourselves a section of the deck near the bow that seemed not to require the attentions of the crew and took our positions along the rail.

"There is no turning back now," said Holmes, producing his pipe. "The die is cast."

I looked out to the cool, blue, rippling waters of the Mediterranean stretching before us.

"We have many seas to travel before our destination," I remarked.

"True. Lord Barington will have months to prepare himself for our arrival. Never have I given an adversary such advance warning."

"What about the ostensible purpose of our visit, the missing rifles? Have you heard anything?"

"Only that they are still missing. As governor, it is Lord Barington's responsibility to find them. I understand that at first he bitterly protested my appointment as special investigator. The rifles themselves are an interesting issue. If his lordship was instrumental in their theft, it suggests that once more he is only an underling."

"How so?"

"Unless his lordship is planning an insurrection, I imagine he would rather return the rifles than endure an extended investigation into his affairs. And I can think of no one less likely to embrace the rigors of a rebel camp than Lord Barington."

"Perhaps the rifles have been sold."

"There is that possibility. But the theft of military rifles is a daring undertaking. Only organized men, entirely outside the law, would pay the price for them. If it were India one could understand. But rifles taken in the Malay Straits would have to travel a thousand miles to find a buyer. It's a pretty tangle we're walking into, Watson. I must repeat my remark to be on your guard at all times. By the way, have you paid much attention to our crew?"

"Not really. Not a white face among them, I should say."

"Perhaps that's all to the good. I shouldn't want to be reacquainted with any of our friends from the *Southern Star*."

"I say, do you think that's possible?"

"At this point, no. During our stay in Tangier, I employed several men to observe us to see if we were being followed, and they reported in the negative."

"But why didn't you discuss this with me?"

"My dear Watson, in the first place, I did not wish to spoil your holiday, which you have obviously been enjoying to the fullest. In the second place, if I had alerted you to the possibility, you would have been on your guard, which would only have served to put an observer on his guard. Nothing makes the hunter more careless than an unwary prey."

"I should think you might trust me more."

"I do trust you, Watson, entirely, to be yourself. And you have been far more useful in that role than any other. Our crew, as you say, seems entirely exotic. Since we know nothing else about them, I suggest that we be on our guard throughout this trip."

"In what manner?"

"I think it best if we avoid appearing alone on deck at night, or even to frequent a solitary spot during the day. While we may have eluded Lord Barington's agents for the present, I wonder if it is possible for two English gentlemen to make their way from Tangier to Singapore without being noticed by someone."

"You take a very dark view of this matter."

"I do. Elizabeth Trent was murdered because of what she might do, or cause others to do. We are committed to the destruction of Lord Barington and all his confederates, whoever they may be. I do not think they will look lightly on our progress."

I must confess that Holmes' words cast a chill over my heart. I had felt invincible on our voyage down to Tangier. Now it seemed that somewhere beneath the Mediterranean's serene charm there lurked an obscure but murderous evil, like some hideous monster of the deep. I brushed my hand against my jacket pocket to encounter the reassuring weight of my revolver. If our journey was to be as fraught with peril as that of Ulysses some three thousand years before, at least we would be prepared.

CHAPTER XI

Captain MacDougall

ESPITE HOLMES' FEARS, which were indisputably well-founded, our first night aboard the
Prophet proved remarkably pleasant, providing
us with our first real acquaintance with Captain
MacDougall. Throughout the day he had busied himself with
supervising our departure, but in the evening we received an
invitation to join him for a late supper, which we were very glad
to have, for we had been without food the entire day. We were
in the process of discovering that the captain expected his
guests to live and eat according to his schedule, which was not
that of other men. He rose before the first light for his breakfast,
and lunched promptly at noon. After lunch he slept for several
hours and did not dine until ten, or even later, depending on
the press of business. So it was that we joined him that first
night on the foredeck at a quarter to eleven.

Fortunately, the meal was worth the wait, for the captain
was a remarkable combination of parts, a black man who
spoke English with a Scots accent, cursed his crew in Malay
and Arabic, and dined like a Spanish grandee, though his religion bade him to forego the wines that grace an hidalgo's
table. We dined chiefly on fish, bread, and melon, prepared
in a manner more associated with a gentleman's yacht than a

South Seas freighter. The plate, china, and glasses were of the humblest manufacture, but the food was remarkable.

The meal was rendered all the more pleasant by the weather. A breeze had sprung up, stiff but by no means uncomfortable, sufficient to propel our ship without use of the engines. As a result, we sat beneath an immense canopy of sail that towered a full one hundred feet above our heads and carried us effortlessly along the wine-dark seas. The sensation of travelling on a sailing ship on a fair night with a clean breeze is intoxicating indeed. So it was that I found myself remarkably at ease on that occasion, despite the unusual nature of our company.

"May I ask the purpose of your journey, gentlemen?" the captain asked, once we had been served.

"We are on a mission of Her Majesty's Government," returned Holmes.

"Indeed? I find it rare that English officials travel in such a manner as yourselves."

"Ah, but we are unofficials," said Holmes. "We must bear the cost of our journey, and so cannot ignore the advantages of thrift."

"I understand. Have you been to Singapore previously?"

"Never."

"I thought not. You do not have the look of travelling men. I imagine you have not spent much time in Asia."

"I am entirely a novice," said Holmes. "However, my friend served as an army doctor in India and was wounded in the Afghanistan War."

This information appeared to amuse the captain.

"Really?" he said, chuckling. "Which one? Your government seems addicted to wars in that obscure and ill-defined nation."

"That is one of the responsibilities of the Empire," I interjected, rather stiffly.

"No doubt, Doctor, no doubt. I meant no disrespect to your sufferings, and I rate a man highly who dedicates his life to medicine, at least until he proves himself unworthy of his calling. But you see by the colour of my skin that I am likely to

have a different perspective of your Empire than you yourselves. Tell me, Doctor, did your troops refer to the people of
India as 'niggers'?"

"On occasion," I conceded, not liking the conversation but
finding it difficult to avoid the force of the captain's remarks.

"Yes, and no doubt they resented the term bitterly, for they
did not wish to be compared to people of my race, though
there were black kings in India in times past."

"And how did those black kings rule, Captain?" said Holmes,
fixing the man with a sharp gaze.

"Oh, some well and some poorly, I should imagine, like all
monarchs, though surely none had the grace and grandeur of
your Victoria Regina," said the captain, smiling again. "But tell
me, how is your turbot? My cook is Chinese, and his sauces
are not always welcome to the Northern palate."

"Why, this is the finest meal I've ever had on board ship,"
I burst out. "An army man never got a meal such as this from
the British navy."

The captain seemed delighted by my response.

"Now here's an honest man," he cried, slapping his broad
hand hard upon the table for emphasis. "A man with a taste
for Chinese cooking has some good in him. I shall inform my
cook that there is a gentleman at the table. Now I must excuse
myself. I have my duties to attend to, but you gentlemen may
feel free to enjoy a cigar. I allow no liquor on my ship, but
permit my guests a limited use of tobacco, provided they are
sensible to the risks of fire."

"You are most indulgent, Captain," returned Holmes, rising
as the captain did so. "We will make ourselves worthy of your
trust."

"Singular fellow," said Holmes, as the captain headed
belowdecks.

"You chose not to inform him of your adventures in the
Himalayas," I remarked, referring to my friend's travels in
northern India and Tibet after the death of Professor Moriarty.

"Yes. It is almost always advisable to present oneself as an
innocent. The captain is a guarded man, but he may perhaps
be less guarded if confident of my ignorance."

"What do you make of him?" I said, not a little anxious to know what my friend could deduce of the man's background and character.

"What can a 'Northerner' know of the Dark Continent?" said Holmes, with a smile. "Clearly, our captain is a well-travelled man. He has been a captive, a slave on at least two continents, and a professional boxer of remarkable skill. As a boy he was an enthusiastic Presbyterian. Later, he rejected the teachings of the West in favour of some sort of revolutionary doctrine, which he later discarded in its turn in favour of the Islamic faith. Of his later career as a sailor and engineer we already know something."

"Whatever makes you say he was a Presbyterian? I never met a man further from that faith in my life. Besides, Sergeant Smith said he learned English from a Scots engineer."

"He may have learned about engines from a 'Scottie,' but he learned to speak from a man of the Book," said Holmes, lighting a cigar. "How fortunate that the captain has granted us an indulgence. Otherwise this voyage would be unendurable."

"Yes, indeed," I replied, lighting one of my own. "But explain to me your theory that he studied religion under a Scots missionary."

"Well, the captain's English may be curiously accented, but he speaks with precision and care. He is not merely comfortable with English, but literate in it as well. Furthermore, he is educated in our culture. His use of the phrase 'Victoria Regina' was most instructive. Imagine a man such as our captain, living entirely outside European civilization but speaking English. He hears of our faraway country, a nation ruled by a woman, which he no doubt finds amusing. He understands that this ruler's name is Victoria Regina. An uneducated man would naturally assume that 'Regina' is Her Majesty's last name, as mine is Holmes and yours is Watson. But the captain pronounced the name precisely as you or I would pronounce it. He knew that 'Regina' is a word foreign to our tongue, knew furthermore just how an educated man in England regards Latin, understood its prestige among us as a mark of learning and social position. This is a man who learned about the English tongue and the English people from a man at his ease among the classics. And how could an African boy meet an educated Scot except in the form of a missionary?"

"You mean Livingston himself?"

"As likely as not. How many Scots missionaries have seen the interior of Africa? Besides, you see how the captain values your medical training. One questions whether a man of his background would appreciate the significance of modern science had he not been exposed to it at an early age."

"But this is remarkable."

"Indeed. But the captain is a remarkable man."

"But what about the rest?"

"Oh, that is less mysterious than it appears. You notice that the captain is so unfortunate as to have a notch in his ear."

"Yes. A cutlass wound, perhaps."

"Ah, Watson. I have often told you how your penchant for romance leads you astray. The reality is more prosaic, and more tragic. That notch is the mark of an Arab slave trader. Undoubtedly, the captain was abducted as a youth and sold in the slave markets of Arabia. From thence he must have made his way to India—indeed, Bengal, since he cites the history of that land so confidently."

"As a boxer?"

"As the property of a sportsman."

"But how do you deduce that?"

"From the man's hands. One would expect a sailor to have a powerful grip, but the captain's knuckles are singularly enlarged and marked with numerous scars. Only bare-knuckled boxing, and a great deal of it, could induce such injuries. It is, after all, an exceedingly unnatural, and unwise, occupation."

"Why do you say he was competent?"

"Because his hands were bruised and his face unmarked. And it is obvious that he suffered no mental deterioration from his career, which is unusual. One imagines he contrived to make his escape while still a young man. Perhaps this marked the initiation of his revolutionary activities, for which he endured penance in the custody of the Raj."

"Are you sure of that?"

"Look at the marks on his wrists. I know the effects of English bracelets—Pennington-Martins, from the looks of it—but then I am not familiar with the constabulary equipment of the Bengali police. No doubt an expert from the area could tell us of the political intrigues that led to the captain's imprisonment."

"What makes you so sure he was a revolutionary? Why not a common criminal?"

"His criticism of our empire shows more than mere pique. There is an intellectual edge to his words that only comes from the study of abstract thought. But I am entirely at a loss to determine which sect engaged his allegiance. I should have thought to have equipped myself with more extensive files. At any rate, our captain obviously obtained his freedom in one manner or another and made his way to the sea. Since then, it appears, he has travelled all over Asia and now ranges from Tangier to Hong Kong on a vessel of his own design."

"It sounds like a tale from the 'Arabian Nights',"

"Indeed."

We paused for a moment from the intensity of our conversation. Amongst the taut canvas above us the constellations blazed in the cloudless sky with a brilliance and a profusion inconceivable to the Londoner, hemmed in by fog and smoke and blinded by his own gas lamps. We were a thousand miles from the din of Baker Street. The only sounds were the soft rush of the waves and the slow creak of the ship.

"A remarkable case, Watson," said Holmes at last, extinguishing his cigar. "The fox is far distant and snug in his burrow. But our mount is a good one, and the scent will not fail us."

CHAPTER XII

The Injured Sailor

HE FOLLOWING DAY, we learned more of the habits of our captain. As a devout Mussulman, he made his bows to Mecca five times a day, using a special compass to orient himself in the proper direction. He was joined in his worship by every member of the crew who was not held to his post by the press of duty. At dinner that night I made bold to compliment him on the religious quality of his men.

"They are not all of the true faith," he said with a certain formality, "but I accept all who wish to honour Allah, even if they have not come to recognize His truth."

"Your ship is ecumenical, then?" Holmes asked.

"Sailors are cautious men, Mr. Holmes," the captain replied. "Several seasons ago, I had one holdout among all the crew. I applied no pressure, but one morning he had the misfortune to fall overboard. Just as we were pulling him out, a large shark appeared and bit him quite in two. Since then participation has been unanimous."

"Really?" said my friend. "In that case, perhaps Dr. Watson and I should join you."

"Oh, I think not," said the captain. "It is well known among the crew that you are English and as such, unworthy of trust.

No one would accept your obeisances as genuine. Your participation, I fear, would be more likely to affright the men than calm them."

The absurdity of the captain's logic was so palpable, so absolute, that no rational man would attempt to refute him, and so this preposterous slur on our race, doubtless among the most ludicrous ever perpetrated, passed without comment. I well remember the smile on Holmes' face when I discussed the matter with him after dinner. "Most preposterous indeed, Watson," he said, his eyes shining.

Subsequent conversations with Captain MacDougall demonstrated to us the uncompromising rigidity of his view of the world. Men, nations, events, indeed all natural phenomena, were viewed through the blinkered lens of the Koran. Holmes and I quickly found that virtually any statement made in the captain's presence might meet with the instant rebuff of being "contrary to the will of Allah," and we tempered our observations accordingly.

Once we accustomed ourselves to the captain's peculiarities, the voyage passed uneventfully. For my part, I found the duties of ship's doctor less than onerous. In the interests of economy, the captain kept his crew small. In the interests of efficiency, he chose men of exceptional physical agility and strength. Injuries were rare and slight, despite the remarkable effort required to keep a three-master at full speed twenty-four hours a day. As a result, I devoted my time to the study of medicine rather than its practice. However, on the sixth day out, I was summoned from a dead sleep at three in the morning. The seaman who wakened me, like most of the crew, spoke no English at all, though it was clear enough that an emergency was at hand. I dressed myself as best I could in the dark, swaying ship and grabbed my medical bag.

Once on deck a dramatic scene confronted me. The night sky was without a cloud, and a full moon poured its white light on the deck below. But a high sea was running, and an unceasing wind pushed the vessel forward like a powerful hand. As the ship rose and plunged, I advanced toward a knot of men, several bearing lanterns. In the centre lay a man,

writing and hysterical with pain. His left leg was covered
with blood, and as I moved closer I could see through the tattered rags of his trousers the terrible whiteness of bone protruding from his lower leg. I could not tell from the situation
what had caused the fellow's injury, but now in his delirium
he was refusing all assistance, frantically waving a knife at any
man who might approach him. I stopped at a safe distance
and held up my medical bag in the hope that it might reassure him.

"Please calm yourself," I told him, though I was sure he
spoke no English. "I am a doctor. I am here to help you."

Unsurprisingly, my speech had no effect.

"Keep talking, Doctor," said a voice behind me, which could
only belong to Captain MacDougall.

"The fellow can't understand a word I'm saying," I replied
over my shoulder.

"I am aware of that. I just ask you to engage his attention."

I did as I was bid, held up my bag and opened it, and took
out my stethoscope as the badge of my profession, to no
avail. But as I spoke the captain slipped behind the men surrounding their fallen comrade. Crouching low, he crept up,
and with a sudden spring grasped the man. As they rolled on
the deck in a brief struggle, the captain threw his powerful
arms about the arms of the sailor, pinioning them to his body,
the knife falling harmlessly to the deck. At the same time, the
captain wrapped his right leg about the sailor's uninjured leg.
Thus bound, the man was as helpless as a kitten.

"You may proceed, Doctor," said the captain, in an unruffled voice.

I approached my patient with some trepidation. Although
the captain held him as tightly as could be, the rising and
falling ship made a poor platform for surgery. In addition, it
was clear that I would have an audience, for the members of
the crew on deck made no move to quit the scene. Indeed, I
required the presence of a few men simply to bear the light. I
positioned those holding lanterns so that I would have constant illumination and set to work. I removed the poor fellow's
trousers and examined the wound. As is so often the case, it

was a mixture of good and bad. Despite the shattered bone, there had been no damage to a major artery. The bleeding, though significant, was not severe. There was no need to apply a tourniquet, no danger of losing the man even as I worked on him. Instead, I had a good chance of saving his leg.

With the captain's assistance as translator, I had a man bring soap and hot water, and set about cleansing the wound. The danger of infection under such circumstances is ever present, and I had to remove every fragment of dirt, filth, and bone before setting the leg. At first, the poor fellow shouted with every touch of my probe, but as I worked he gradually came to endure my ministrations without struggling, so far as he was capable.

The task I had set upon was no easy one. The deck of a tramp freighter like the *Prophet* is rarely free from some debris, and the man had been rolling about in it for some time. But despite the hour, I felt no sense of fatigue, doubt, or confusion as I knelt there on the deck, under the warm light of the lanterns. I seemed to find myself back on the battlefields of India, in a hot, canvas tent, the smell of blood in my nostrils and the groans of the dying in my ear. I shut out all that surrounded me and concentrated on my work. When the wound was perfectly clean, I prepared to give the fellow some brandy to relax him, when I felt the captain's firm hand on my shoulder.

"Enough of that," he said, sternly. The look in his eye brooked no argument. I replaced the flask in my breast pocket. "Please hold him steady, Captain," I said. "I fear I must enlarge the wound with my scalpel if I am to restore the bone to its proper position. You might explain to him that this is necessary if I am to save his leg. And later we will need your ship's carpenter to make this fellow a splint."

As I took out my scalpel, both my patient and the onlooking sailors flinched. But the captain simply locked his arms even more tightly around the sailor and spoke a few brief sentences into his ear. The man trembled and shook, but relaxed at last. I gave him a bullet to bite on and set to work. As I cut gently through the poor, bruised flesh, I felt a curious satisfaction. My career as a physician had been unremarkable in the extreme. I had never scaled the heights of modern surgery. I had been a follower, not a leader, in the scientific revolution that has reshaped the medical art in our era. Yet there have been times—in Afghanistan, in a humble London flat, and on board the *Prophet* that night—when I have felt worthy of the title of "healer." I could see through the tortured, bloodstained flesh and the shattered bone to the restored, healthy leg that somehow lay beneath it. As I laboured to ease the broken tibia back in place so that it would knit properly, I was already deciding how I would construct the cast to hold the leg immobile, and wondering about the feasibility of a special hammock I had seen in a book on nautical surgery. An hour passed, or even two, before I was ready to finally extend that poor limb, ease the broken bone back so that the two ends properly abutted one another, massage the muscles in position over the bone, and begin to stitch up the wound, but I hardly noticed. The degree of my effort seemed trivial, so long as I might somehow contrive to allow this poor, black-skinned fellow to stump along the path to his grave on two good legs instead of one.

When I snipped the thread on the last stitch, the knot of sailors around me gave an involuntary gasp of relief, which caused me to look up in surprise. I had completely forgotten their presence.

"You are finished, Doctor?" the captain inquired.

"Halfway, at least," I replied. "Now we must prepare the splint. Has the carpenter been summoned?"

The carpenter, who, of course, also spoke no English, presented himself. With the captain as interpreter, we assembled a proper selection of boards and poles, wrapped them in cloth, and bound them together against the man's leg to provide a rigid cage for the entire leg. At this point the captain could at last relax his grip. I was a little startled to realize just how long he had been holding the fellow. With the major part of the task completed, I explained to the captain how we could sling a hammock in a central spot belowdecks with a set of guy ropes that would minimize the shocks of the rolling ship. He agreed to the idea and we went below, several members of the crew following to fetch the hammock and the ropes. Once the hammock was hung properly, I climbed into it and flung myself about to see if it would in fact protect a man. Satisfied of its capabilities, I climbed out and informed the captain that we were ready for the patient. As the sailors left to bring the fellow down, I gave the ropes a few final jerks and adjusted their tension slightly. Then I took a worn blanket and spread it out over the stiff canvas. When I was done, I turned about and found myself looking into Captain MacDougall's eyes.

"Yes, Captain?" I said, a little unnerved by his intense gaze.

"You show a great concern for the comfort of a common seaman."

"A physician's duty is to his patient," I said crisply.

"Indeed," he said, inspecting the hammock. "Do you know, Doctor, I have been on ships where a man with an injury like that, especially a black man, could expect to be cast overboard."

"Not on an English ship, surely!"

My reply appeared to catch him by surprise. He stared for a moment and then burst into laughter, as a broad, unfeigned grin of delight, such as I had never seen on his features before, spread across his face.

"No, no, Doctor!" he cried, between spasms of merriment. "Not on an English ship! Never!"

For some obscure reason he found my remark entertaining to the extreme. Not only did it serve to heal the breach that had existed between us, but for the remainder of our acquaintance he would refer to it, in a wide variety of circumstances, always with a hearty burst of jocularity, though its significance, if any, was apparent to himself alone. On this occasion, he put his arm around my shoulder in a remarkable display of comradeship.

"Now, Doctor," he said, "once you have completed your duty toward your patient, you must join me on the foredeck for breakfast, for you have had a good night's work. Are fresh duck eggs and duck sausage to your liking?"

"Very much so!" I replied. The mention of food suddenly awakened the appetite that had been building during my labours.

"Excellent. Then I will see you shortly."

With that he turned on his heel and disappeared out the door. A half hour later I joined him on deck, the breeze still high but not uncomfortably so, thanks to the shelter of some immense boxes that were stacked near the very prow of the ship. The morning sun, not yet hot, bathed us in light. We began with hot green tea and a cool slab of white, juicy melon, followed by the duck eggs and duck sausage to which the captain had alluded, complemented by slices of dry wheat bread, which were rendered quite agreeable when dipped in duck fat. His cook, stationed nearby with a small, portable charcoal fire, prepared the eggs to our order in an ancient iron pan that rested directly on the coals. With such service placed at our instant command, I could not refrain from consuming four of the large eggs and an equal number of sausages.

While we ate, the captain inquired more specifically of my experiences in Afghanistan as a surgeon. He told me frankly that he had not expected me to save the injured sailor's life, much less his leg. His lack of squeamishness allowed me to give full vent to the enthusiasm I felt for the operation I had just completed. As we ate, I explained to him in some detail exactly why I had been able to save the man's leg. The captain had a very rude and practical knowledge of human anatomy, such as a man living in a brutal physical environment might be expected to know, and was intrigued when I explained to him such matters as the circulation of the blood and the difference in significance of an injury to a vein and an artery. As a result of his curiosity, our conversation transformed itself into a sort of lecture on the rudiments of modern science and medicine. I invited the captain to come to our cabin later in the day to take advantage of the powerful microscope Holmes had brought with him, which would provide visual proof of much of what I had said.

I returned to the cabin with a pleasurable sense of fulfilment and was rather surprised to discover that Holmes was up and about, heating a pot of water for tea. Notwithstanding the supposed charm of "sea air," my friend often preferred to delay his hour of rising until the sun had climbed well toward the meridian. Finding him awake, I greeted him and gave a full account of my night's adventures.

"Splendid, Watson," he remarked when I came to the conclusion of my narrative. "Since the captain will be our intimate companion for the next several months, it is of infinite value to have him as an ally rather than adversary."

"Do you think we can be certain of his nature?" I asked. "I cannot deny that the events of the last ten hours have given me a new perspective on the man, but how much do we really know of him? You said yourself that Barington's agents could be anywhere. And what of the crew? I should say that several of the fellows on board could have made the climb into Elizabeth Trent's room, if any man could."

"The point has not escaped my attention, Watson. But I doubt that even these fellows could have done the deed. I am convinced that only a very small man could have made his way along that ledge or across that roof without leaving any traces. Indeed, I am still unsure how it could be done. I only know that it was done. Five years ago I would have suspected the Mendoza brothers, but now they are dispersed."

"The Mendoza brothers?"

"Surely you have heard of them. Three brothers from Andalusia, none over five feet high, and Diego, the most gifted, only four feet ten. The three were superb acrobats, who travelled with their parents as circus performers throughout northeastern Spain. They amused themselves by robbing the great houses of the towns they visited. Success came so easily that they soon migrated to Paris, where the rewards for their enterprise were, of course, far greater. They were the despair of the Paris police, until they overreached themselves while pilfering the casino at Monte Carlo. A remarkable case, in which I played a secondary role. Fortunately, I was able to resolve the matter without quitting London."

"I have no recollection of the crime."

"Oh, it was kept out of the papers. Naturally, the casino was loathe to admit that its celebrated security had been penetrated and its customers' valuables exposed to theft. The Mendozas had discovered that the great skylight of the casino would bear their weight if they made the trip across it in well-spaced intervals. However, they neglected to consider that a man adds significantly to his weight when he fills his knapsack with gold coin. As a result of this miscalculation, both Hernando and Luis came crashing down upon the roulette tables, to the consternation of those beneath.

"The casino claimed the two were workmen, which was the account accepted by the press. Diego, more cunning as always, used the confusion to make good his escape to South America, his pockets full of jewels and carrying a satchel stuffed with five-pound notes fresh from the Bank of England. I was called in to locate him, which was not difficult, and return him to justice, which unfortunately proved to be impossible. Today the celebrated Diego takes his ease on the finest verandas in Buenos Aires, surrounded by tall, lovely women, beloved by all."

At the end of this peroration, Holmes finished his tea and began carefully charging the stained calabash pipe that he turned to when contemplating the most abstruse issues.

"Are you certain he's still there?" I asked.

"Yes. Before leaving London I telegraphed the police commissioner in Buenos Aires, who informed me that Diego remained in that city throughout the time period in question."

"Then we know no more now than we did that sad day when we learned of Elizabeth's death."

"I did not say that," he returned. "Indeed, the method of Mrs. Trent's murder has proved extremely resistant to analysis. But the affairs of her husband, and those of Enderby & Cross, are beginning to make sense."

"You have found a clew?"

"I have found dozens, and if I had more records I could find dozens more. Enderby & Cross is a vast shell, Watson. It's an old firm, and I don't know its full history, whether it was corrupt from the first or only recently. I suspect the latter. But certainly long before Raleigh Trent ever hung his hat in their offices, the company had been infected."

"What, precisely, are they doing?"

"That's the devil of it. They don't make money the way other firms do, but they enjoy a fabulous rate of return. A good deal goes into the pockets of the partners, of course. You remember Mrs. Trent telling us how her husband expected to become rich. But the greater amount simply disappears off the books entirely. Why do the partners allow it? Why have thousands when you could have millions? Enderby & Cross is a leading purveyor of virtually every product that moves through the tropics, yet their sources of supply are invisible. They do not buy on the open market. Tin, rubber, hardwoods, spices, coconut oil, gutta percha, gambier, and the rest simply appear at their door. Remarkable, is it not?"

"It is indeed. What do you think is behind it all?"

"Slavery, Watson, pure and simple. A crime as old as the pharaohs."

"In this day and age? And by a company based in London?"

"Yes, I found it difficult to countenance myself at first. But the more I read of these documents, the more I am convinced. Before I left London, I was able to obtain a compendium of financial dispatches concerning the Far East from the *Times*. Every company in the eastern trade of any size has been complaining incessantly to Parliament of the predations of the new German companies. Enderby & Cross alone has been silent. While profits stagnate or decline for others, Enderby & Cross records a steady increase. This last I was able to obtain only from Trent's records. Enderby & Cross is the most secretive of firms. Compared to it, the Rothschilds themselves are an open book."

"But how can such an outrage be countenanced?"

"Oh, success, particularly in the remote corners of the globe, can answer all questions."

"And you think Lord Barington is behind it all."

"No. The plan was far advanced before his lordship ever set foot in Singapore. It appears to be an indigenous matter. The wire-puller, whoever he is, and whatever his game, is entirely unknown. Trent, I am sure, never set eyes on him. The closer he approached to the secret of the place, the more terrified he became, and rightly so, because it cost him his life. It's a sad business, Watson, but it's drawing us to the unmasking of an immense criminal enterprise, one whose final purpose is only beginning to be made clear."

"Whatever do you mean by that?"

"I mean insurrection, or revolution, or something of the sort. Investigating the theft of those thousand rifles will not be a cover for our true investigation, but a part of it. But where this insurrection is to take place, and for what purpose, and for whose benefit, I am entirely at a loss."

"At least you have the time to review the evidence entirely."

"Yes, indeed. We are only two days off the pace of the fastest boat to Alexandria, but the time is already starting to weigh heavily. And our voyage cannot be said to properly begin until we pass through the canal. You have certainly prepared yourself. I was remarking on your library just prior to your return."

I was indeed prepared. Any reader familiar with my works must have realized how extensively I had neglected my medical practice in order to serve as Holmes' chronicler and assistant. I had, in fact, for the past several years confined my medical efforts entirely to the care of several elderly families whom I had served for decades and who displayed that resistance to change that is inseparable from advanced age. However, my professional vanity forbade me from acknowledging that I was little better than retired, and I maintained subscriptions to every manner of medical publication, as if I were new to the profession and determined to be familiar with every modern discovery. As a result, the successive issues accumulated insensibly in my study. I had gathered them together for our trip, thus supplying myself with enough reading for several circumnavigations of the globe. I had read little enough while we made our way to Tangier, but since then I had become almost as much a scholar as Holmes himself. As a result, I was brimming with more medical theory than at any time since I was a student. I explained as much to Holmes.

"That's well enough," he said. "I hope you took the precaution of augmenting your collection with several volumes on diseases of the tropics."

"Do you really fear some plague engineered by Lord Barington?"

"You put the matter too lightly, Watson. I do not fear Lord Barington so much as I fear the unexpected. Besides, as ship's doctor, you should be prepared for the treatment of such diseases as beriberi and scurvy."

"I am well aware of my duties as ship's doctor," I retorted, stung by Holmes' magisterial tone. "Certainly, the captain has had no cause for complaint."

"Yes, but surely a fracture of the tibia, however spectacular to the layman, is simple stuff compared to the complex maladies of the tropics."

"Then let me put your mind at rest. I completed a study of Cobalt's *Maritime Physician* and Putnam's *Compendium of Naval Surgery* prior to our departure, as well as Emerson's *Diseases of the Tropics*. Furthermore, I have numerous bound volumes, containing the past decade of the *Malay Lancet,* so that I think I am tolerably well supplied."

"And well primed," said Holmes, laughing. "I must apologize, Watson. I see I must quicken my pace if I am to equal your level of preparation. I would like to consult the *Malay Lancet* myself. Any recent information emanating from the colony could prove useful."

"In that case, I shall begin my studies with the oldest volumes."

"Excellent. But for now, I must prepare for the little demonstration you have promised the captain."

CHAPTER XIII

A Strange Turn

HE PRESS OF BUSINESS kept the captain away until the middle of the afternoon. When he arrived, there was a certain diffidence in his demeanour, as though the enthusiasm engendered by our long night of surgery had dissipated during the day. However, the impact of Holmes' microscope, together with the slides we had prepared for his viewing, soon aroused him to a remarkable pitch of interest. In my mind's eye I can still see him, the full vigour of his immense frame poised over the microscope's slim brass tube, fiercely gazing into the universe contained in a drop of seawater, muttering to himself in Arabic. On occasion I would attempt a brief explanation of the phenomenon he was observing, but words seemed to be lost on him. When he was done, he rose swiftly from his chair and gave us each a brief bow.

"New miracles from the infidels," he said in a light, mocking tone. "I have not seen one of these since I was a boy. You have made numerous improvements since then. Now I must bid you good day. We will continue our conversations at dinner."

As might be expected, our relations with Captain MacDougall rapidly improved following these events. His taciturn, ironic manner at meals vanished, and he became voluble

to the extreme. I was astonished to discover through our conversations that he was an avid reader of the *Times,* contriving
to lay his hands on virtually every issue of that faraway journal,
though often weeks, and sometimes months, out-of-date. He
seemed to take a profound intellectual pleasure in piecing
together an idiosyncratic view of world events, which combined in an uneasy meld the mouthings of Tory club land with
the gossip and rumour of a hundred ports.

Unsurprisingly, he was an aggressive partisan of the
Ottoman Empire, whose continued decline filled him with dismay. Like monarchists of all climes and ages, he attributed all
fault to the ruler's advisors and none to the chosen one himself. He had no love for the British Empire, though he made his
living entirely within its ambit and was of course employed by
a British firm. The rise of Germany he regarded with great satisfaction, though I noticed he had very sharp words for the few
German officials he had met in his career. He had great admiration for at least one Englishman, the late Lord Beaconsfield,
and he frequently insisted that England owed her "decline" to
her neglect of his heritage. What the "heritage" of that dazzling
yet duplicitous statesman was, I could never determine.

The change in the atmosphere at our mess was not altogether to my liking. As the captain felt freer to state his opin-
ions, I grew all the more constrained in the expression of
mine. I was, after all, in the awkward position of both inferi-
or officer and guest, and could hardly respond comfortably to
the captain's occasional gibes regarding British policy.
Captain MacDougall was entirely lacking in that officious
punctilio that is all too often the hallmark of the Royal Navy,
but there was never any question as to who was master of the
Prophet. He ruled that eight-hundred odd tons of wood, iron,
rope, and canvas as surely as any sultan, sheik, shah, or czar.

Holmes, of course, was in a different position. His own
sardonic nature had many points of similarity with the captain's. Moreover, his own lack of interest in political affairs
allowed him to tolerate the captain's more outrageous con-
ceits with more grace than I could manage. Holmes could
also, on occasion, guide the captain's review of contemporary

events into discussions of a more historical nature—on the movements of peoples and cultures in India and Southeast Asia, for example, which were, by their nature, bound to be less controversial. And Holmes himself displayed a familiarity with these topics that I found surprising.

"There is no particular mystery, Watson," he said one evening when I taxed him on the matter. "The unfortunate Mr. Trent was an enthusiastic amateur anthropologist, and corresponded extensively with a number of like-minded individuals. Perhaps it diverted him from the uneasiness he felt in conjunction with his employment. I had previously some knowledge of peoples, language, and religion throughout the East, most particularly northern India, Afghanistan, Tibet, and Mongolia, from my travels there, but thanks to Mr. Trent I am becoming somewhat familiar with the peoples of southern India as well, along with the cultures of the Malay Peninsula and the islands of Java and Sumatra."

"All that?"

"Yes. What I have read would fill several stout volumes. Mr. Trent copied all his own letters and kept those of his correspondents. He knew several retired civil servants in India whose knowledge of the East was extraordinary. Trent himself was eager to exploit his location by collecting a mass of folklore about the ancient inhabitants of the Straits. There are layers and layers of peoples, religions, commerce, and conquest, and Trent chronicled them all. The original inhabitants of Singapore Island, one gathers, were a race of cannibals, rather less than three feet high, equipped with sharp teeth and long, naked tails."

"Preposterous!"

"Mr. Trent's informants assured him that the creatures originated on the island of Sumatra, where they still hold forth in the interior."

"How absurd!"

"And a few of them may still be found in the back alleys of Singapore itself."

"The man must have been unhinged even to record such rubbish."

"Oh, he was quite struck with the theories of Darwin, which he was anxious to apply to the development of the human race."

"I can only think how unfortunate it was that Elizabeth became linked with such a man."

"So it proved. But I think Trent was weak rather than wicked. He got in over his head and paid the price."

The fact that Holmes was pursuing such nonsense suggested to me that he had lost his bearings on the case, but of course I was too discreet to breach the subject directly. From the first, he had felt the responsibility for the terrible tragedy of Elizabeth's death all too keenly. Now it was clear that the loss of his Baker Street routine had seriously disrupted his delicately balanced mental apparatus. He read endlessly from the great mass of material Elizabeth had assembled, and questioned the captain repeatedly on events shrouded in the mist of centuries. I even made the effort, on occasion, to guide him back to more substantive issues, but the only reward for my pains was either a stinging rebuff or, more often, complete silence. For my part, I occupied myself with my medical texts and my duties as ship's doctor, stitching wounds, salving burns, and setting a few broken bones, none of which were as spectacular as that of my first patient, whose convalescence was progressing nicely.

So matters stood between us until the day before we were scheduled to arrive in Alexandria. That morning, the captain appeared at our door. Holmes, still in his robe, sat motionless in his chair, lost in thought, his breakfast sitting untouched before him.

"Good morning, gentlemen," said the captain. "You seem to lack an appetite, Mr. Holmes," he remarked, observing the basket of rolls and bowl of sliced fruit that sat before my friend.

"It is my mind, not my body, that is in need of nourishment," said Holmes.

"Then perhaps I may be of assistance. You gentlemen have had things for me to look at, and now I have something to show you."

With that, he handed Holmes a small, rough sheet of paper. On the sheet was a tiny sketch of a man's head, scarcely two inches high.

"Do you recognize this man?" the captain asked.

"I think so," Holmes replied. "What do you say, Watson?"

He held out the page to me. I stared in amazement. Though strangely drawn, there was no doubt that it was a portrait of Holmes himself.

"Good heavens!"

"It does have a certain charm, does it not," said Holmes. "Where did you get this, Captain?"

"From a member of the crew. A shifty fellow. I have him below in irons."

"An excellent precaution. I suggest that you send him on his way when we reach Alexandria."

"I had already reached that conclusion, Mr. Holmes," the captain replied. "Would you care to question the man?"

Holmes took out the powerful lens he always carried and held it up to his eye.

"Later, perhaps. I doubt if he has anything to tell us. Ah, rice paper. We have seen this before."

For several minutes he said nothing, examining the sketch with relentless care, both with lens and the naked eye. Repeatedly, he held the paper at arm's length and slowly drew it toward him, until it was touching the very bridge of his nose.

"Remarkable," he said at last. "I had doubted, but this seems conclusive. Poor Elizabeth! What a damnable fate! But it all hangs together now. What do you think, Watson?"

"It's remarkably crude," I said, glancing at the drawing. "And what possible purpose could it serve?"

"Why, to mark me for murder, what else?"

"Do you really think so?"

"I do indeed. Was that not your conclusion, Captain?"

"Yes, it was. Before you ever set foot on this ship, I had heard reports that there might be a price on your head. And where there is one of these sketches, Mr. Holmes, there will be others. You must know that you are going forward into danger."

"Yes, Captain," said Holmes, with a smile. "But tell me, isn't a marked man a dangerous passenger? I think perhaps the *Prophet* would float more lightly if Watson and myself were not aboard."

"Oh, I am used to such matters," returned the captain.

"No doubt, no doubt. But I am losing my thread. Watson, tell me more of your impression of the drawing itself. You called it crude. But look at the rendering of the hair, and the ears. This is not the work of an untrained hand. And what about the treatment of the jaw, particularly the upper jaw?"

As he spoke, Holmes handed me the drawing. I struggled to find some correspondence between his remarks and the miserable sketch I was holding, but gave it up at last.

"I scarcely see what you mean," I replied. "There is some art in the depiction of the hair, I grant you, but the fellow makes you look like a malignant rodent."

"A malignant rodent! Well put, Watson. Yes, that may be the very thing. Tell me, Captain," said Holmes, his eyes flashing, "what do you know of the monkey boys?"

"The monkey boys?" said the captain, with a short laugh. For a moment he seemed to hesitate, as though caught off guard, but then collected himself.

"I'll tell you this, Mr. Holmes. Before you go to meddle with the monkey boys, be sure you have a stout ship and a full load of coals." And with that he turned and left us.

"What on earth did he mean by that?" I asked, when the captain was out of earshot.

"Oh, the captain is an infidel in these matters, while I am a believer," said Holmes, obviously pleased. "It is this sketch that has made me a convert. If I could document its history, there isn't a university in Europe that wouldn't pay a hundred thousand pounds for its possession."

"What on earth for?"

"Because, my dear Watson," said Holmes, throwing me a sharp glance, "this was not drawn by a human being."

CHAPTER XIV

A Questionable Clew

 STARED AT HIM. There was no doubt that he was in complete earnest.

"How can you possibly say that?" I managed at last.

"Recall our endless difficulties with the manner of entry by Elizabeth's assailant."

"You suggested an acrobat."

"I was grasping at straws. Could any human being be capable both of making that ascent and then traversing that ledge? The stone projected only an inch and a quarter from the brickwork. I measured it myself."

"But what other explanation is there?"

"Precisely. That is where I foundered. But this illustration has made everything clear. Look at the size in the first place. Would Scotland Yard ever distribute anything so minute? And what artist would choose to work in such a limited frame? Then consider the perspective. It is not adjusted to human eyes. The foreground and background have a tendency to shift when one tilts the picture. No doubt a skilled artist could create such an effect deliberately, but this was done for utilitarian purposes. I am confident that proper analysis would demonstrate that the artist who created this drawing had eyes set no more than one inch apart. Tell me, did your medical training involve any special study of the mechanics of sight?"

"No, it did not."

"Pity. The final point, of course, is the rodentlike features, which you described so admirably."

I shook my head, still overwhelmed by the line of thought my friend was pursuing.

"You question an artist's—his, his species—because he makes you look like a rat?"

"Really, Watson, you outdo yourself," said Holmes, obviously amused. "A man could not ask for a more searching, a more pungent critic. Yes, an adversary might well say that my conclusions rest on vanity, motivated by spite toward an artist whose genius enabled him to capture my true nature. But in reality my deductions have a more objective basis."

He stopped to charge his pipe, his fingers showing that quick, nervous eagerness that marked his motions in moments of extreme excitement.

"You see, Watson," he said, once his pipe was fairly lit, "every artist, no matter what his subject, ultimately depicts himself. The fellow who did this could no more escape depicting me as an exceptionally large rat than a human artist could avoid depicting him as an exceptionally small man. To change the line of analysis, consider the pen work, the almost infinite delicacy of the strokes that depict the hair. The strictest drawing masters in France would put forth such effort only in their finest work. Yet here it is thrown away on an ephemeral sketch. Why? Because the fellow worked naturally in this scale. Recall that singular pen found in Elizabeth's room. Even the most affected dandy would hardly write with such a miniature. Merely reduce the size of the hand that would hold it, and the problem disappears."

As I listened to these ramblings, I felt increasing confusion and dismay over the decline of my friend's powers. He seemed to have fallen away entirely from the precise scientific accuracy that had hitherto characterized his work.

"I cannot say that I am convinced by your analysis," I said at last, hoping to avoid giving a direct contradiction of his reasoning.

"My analysis is hardly dependent on this drawing alone," he said shortly, "though in my opinion it is conclusive. The data collected by Trent, though entirely anecdotal, are entirely consistent with the hypothesis that ours is not the only rational species to have emerged on this planet. Fifty years ago men would have thought Darwin's theory of human origins sheer insanity. No civilized man had ever laid eyes on either the gorilla or the chimpanzee. But if one beholds these creatures, the theory suggests itself. The Malay archipelago is the most extensive on the planet. The opportunities for evolutionary change observed by Darwin in the Galapagos are multiplied a thousandfold."

"Surely you cannot rely on the reports of credulous natives?"

"Natives, like all humans, report what they see. It is in their interpretations that they go awry. Besides, I do not rely on their testimony alone. The recent discoveries of the Belgian Dubois on Java, of which you may have read, are extremely suggestive."

"Dubois said the skullcap and femur he discovered were of a primitive man, not a colossal rat."

"True, but it does suggest that the archipelago served as a birthing place for intelligence. And what Nature does once she can do twice. Finally, I do have some evidence of my own, which you must agree is 'firsthand', even though faint."

Smiling, he held up the hand that had been bitten that night on the *Southern Star.*

"As I feared, the scar proved to be temporary. But I did have the foresight to have the wound photographed before leaving London. No doubt the dental studies of the rodents of the archipelago would be most illuminating. Perhaps you have found some discussion of the topic in the *Malay Lancet.*"

"I have not. The authors confine themselves entirely to humanity."

"Well, that is understandable, though unfortunate. There are times, Watson, when common sense is the worst of guides. I urge you to maintain an open mind in these matters."

"Open, but unconvinced."

"Very well. But you must excuse me. I must review Trent's correspondence in light of this glorious find. I suspect the man knew more than he was willing to say to others. This is the thread, Watson," he said, holding his newfound portrait before him and tapping it with the stem of his pipe, "the thread that will unite every fragment of this monstrous case."

CHAPTER XV

The Captain's Evidence

AVING UTTERED THAT remarkable but dubious statement, he withdrew into that contemplative silence that he so often preferred. Shortly thereafter I left to tend to my patient, whose wounds, though progressing, could still not be trusted to untrained hands. I changed the dressings and inspected for any sign of infection. Fortunately there was none. I washed the wounds carefully, applied disinfectant, and bound them with fresh linen. The captain had instructed his cabin boy, a lad of no more than twelve, to assist me in these matters. Though his name was indecipherable to my ear, he spoke some English, and I had trained him to wash and boil the bandages. Having set him to that task, I was confronted by a dislocated shoulder and a broken wrist, which occupied my time for several hours. When I returned to our cabin, Holmes had not moved an inch from his previous position. As he took no notice of my arrival, I took up a volume of the *Lancet* and continued my own studies. I learned, for example, that "a physician treating a patient suffering from lacerations owing to the jaws of the Bengal tiger will frequently be perplexed by the tendency of disinfectant to drain from the injured area, owing to puncture wounds occasioned by the creature's canines. These puncture wounds must be identified and sealed if infection is to be avoided."

I continued to read from the *Lancet* into the evening, lighting the lamps as darkness fell. Holmes' concentration on Trent's correspondence was such that I thought him utterly lost to the outside world, but when the faint chime of the ship's bells signalled eight o'clock, he suddenly sprang to his feet and murmured, "I must dress for dinner."

He withdrew to the small bedchamber that served the both of us, reappearing an hour later, looking perfectly refreshed.

"Why, look at you, Watson," he said with a smile. "You must hurry, or the captain will be displeased."

I obeyed without protest. Frequent though they were, I could never accustom myself to my friend's sudden changes in mood. At dinner he amazed me by embarking, without the slightest prologue, on a long and florid account of the marvels that awaited us in Alexandria, the quaint shops, the fantastic architecture, and the ancient culture. The captain listened without comment for close to half an hour, but then interrupted with an abrupt remark.

"What you say of Alexandria is all very well, Mr. Holmes, but I should guess that your real object of concern in that city is Sir Roger Ainsby-Gore."

"Sir Roger," said Holmes, blinking. "You mean Lord Cromer's first lieutenant?"

"Lord Cromer is in London, attempting once more to undo the effects of Mr. Gladstone's folly. In his absence, Sir Roger acts in his place."

"I believe the scope of Sir Roger's authority is more limited than you suggest."

"You have secret information, then?"

"You exaggerate, Captain. As I told you, Dr. Watson and I function in an essentially private capacity."

"Now, now, Mr. Holmes." The captain broke off a piece of bread from the loaf on the table and buttered it thoughtfully. "A man that draws the attention of the monkey boys won't live long without help. I've seen three of those pictures in my time, and I've seen three fellows turn up drowned two days later, with their throats torn out."

"Indeed," said Holmes, taking a piece of bread as well. "I was not aware of that."

"Yes," said the captain. "I've always kept my distance from the monkey boys, and to go against them for the sake of a passenger who says less than he knows is bad business. Perhaps you'd better tell me a little more about Sir Roger and Lord Barington, and Mr. and Mrs. Trent."

Holmes hesitated, then gave in.

"What you say is persuasive, Captain," said Holmes. "I am dependent on your hospitality if I am ever to reach my destination, and as you say, my activities hardly make me a welcome passenger. You appear to know half my story already, so you may as well hear the rest of it from my own lips. When I say that Dr. Watson and I are acting in a private capacity, that is at least a half-truth, because we go against an English official. Our quarry is too exalted to allow us the full backing of the government."

"You mean Barington himself?"

"Yes."

The captain leaned back in his chair, shook his head, and smiled.

"You seek no small game, Mr. Holmes. East of India and west of China, there is no man who can stand against Lord Barington. What is your quarrel with the man?"

"Elizabeth Trent was my client, and his lordship had her murdered right under my nose."

"I read some account of that in the papers. The police were baffled, as I recall."

"For once I found myself in the same position. However, thanks to the drawing you gave me this morning, the matter is as clear as crystal."

"You believe Barington and the monkey boys are confederates?"

"I do."

"A remarkable theory, and not altogether unbelievable. But I find it hard to conceive that the monkey boys would make league with such a creature as Barington. From what I know of them, they prefer to be left alone."

"And what do you know of them?"

"As much as any man, and that's little enough. They inhabit chiefly the island of Sumatra. For the most part, they do not meddle in the affairs of others. Yet they will undertake journeys of a thousand miles and more to conclude a vendetta. On occasion, their activities betray an extreme intelligence and purpose. What that purpose is, no man can say. But I have heard that they have a leader of gigantic stature."

"Really? My deductions had led me in the opposite direction."

"I can only tell you what I have heard. I can also tell you, Mr. Holmes, that you are an object of particular interest to the monkey boys, for I have never seen one of their drawings west of Suez."

"That is gratifying. We seem to have struck a nerve, Watson," said Holmes, turning to me. I nodded without speaking. Their conversation seemed too fantastic for me to venture a comment of even the most equivocal sort.

"But tell me, Mr. Holmes," said the captain, picking up the thread. "What do you hope to learn from Sir Roger?"

"That is hard to say. You know, of course, that he is closely linked with Barington?"

"Yes."

"And that his position in Alexandria is tenuous at best?"

"I did not know that."

"Yes. Lord Cromer despises him. I had some hand in Lord Barington's forced retirement to Singapore, Captain. I understand that his lordship has tired of the climate and is seeking to engineer his return to England. The appointment of Sir Roger, Barington's cousin, as Lord Cromer's second in command is a first step in effecting that return."

"Then Lord Cromer is linked with Barington."

"Not a bit of it. The two men are deadly enemies. Without Lord Cromer's intervention, Watson and I would not be here on this ship. Lord Barington was forced to swallow us, and as a consequence Lord Cromer was forced to swallow Sir Roger."

"The English tit for tat. Well, gentlemen, thank you for this conversation. I can tell you that I have already had my ship searched for stowaways, with negative results. We should arrive in Alexandria by morning. I suggest that while in that port you avoid dark streets, secluded vistas, and everything unknown. On land nothing is simple."

After the captain left, Holmes took out a cigar. He trimmed it with the small penknife he always carried for that purpose, lit it carefully, and then sat back in his chair. Shutting his eyes, he smoked wordlessly until the cigar was a butt no more than an inch long.

"I wonder," he said at last.

"Wonder what?"

"What particular animus the captain bears toward Lord Barington."

"Why do you think that he bears an animus?"

"Because otherwise he would not have endured our presence on board his ship."

"What convinces you of that?"

"It is clear from the captain's words that we have strolled half-knowing into a monstrous world of intrigue and corruption. Lord Barington, whether he deserves the credit or not, seems to have taken a remarkable step. He owns the distinction of being the first man to join a criminal league with a separate species."

"Ridiculous!"

"Still a sceptic, Watson? There is no doubt that these creatures exist. The captain does not doubt. He has seen many things, Watson—the top and the bottom, the black and the white. He has been both slave and master. He knows these creatures and knows the peril they represent. Yet he keeps us on board. He preserves us. He sees us as a weapon to be used against Lord Barington, who must be his mortal foe." Holmes emptied the last of the teapot into his cup. "We must lay in a proper store of English tea and coffee when we arrive in Alexandria," he said, after tasting the cup. "It is remarkable how the trivia of daily life affect the workings of the intellect.

The mind should be indifferent to its surroundings, but manifestly it is not."

"I should say not, if you convince yourself of such nonsense."

"There is that possibility to consider. Well, Watson, you shall be my governor. A slow ship and a burst boiler are equally to be deplored."

"Seriously, Holmes, do you really think the captain sees us as a tool to be used against Barington?"

"You heard his words. I suspect he knows much about his lordship that we do not. And whether or not we believe in these creatures known as the monkey boys, it is manifest that the captain does. And yet, as I say, he keeps us on his ship."

"If he is telling the truth."

"Yes. But tell me, Watson," said Holmes, with half-closed eyes, "how would you describe the captain? I feel you know him better than I."

The question was well posed. I sought to respond, but found myself speechless. After long thought, I finally uttered one word.

"Formidable."

"Excellent, Watson, excellent," murmured Holmes. "'Formidable' is the very word. And why would this formidable man guide us and confide in us unless he were convinced of our worth and our use? Undoubtedly, it was your noble work of surgery that gained his confidence."

I could not suppress the glow of pride I felt at these words, though I said nothing. We sat listening to the quiet rush of the sea past the ship, when the silence was suddenly broken by the deep cough of the engines. A plume of sparks from the smokestack illuminated the rear of the deck, and the whole vessel seemed to plunge forward as the propellers took hold. Holmes glanced at the display and then turned back to me.

"We shall be in Alexandria by morning," he said with a smile. "This is not a slow ship."

CHAPTER XVI

Alexandria

 KNOCK ON OUR CABIN door at a quarter to six announced our arrival at the Egyptian port named for the greatest of all conquerors and forever associated with the greatest of all sailors. As Holmes and I arrived on deck, we found the *Prophet* surrounded by a variety of small craft, their crews earnestly offering their services as seafaring hansoms. We had gathered together sufficient baggage to maintain us for a week-long stopover, and soon we were pitching across the waves in a long, narrow, shallow boat that rose barely a foot above the water.

"We have done the first leg, Watson," said Holmes, surveying the ancient port from our precarious perch as it rose up before us.

"Yes, but what can you expect to learn from Sir Roger?"

"In all probability, nothing," said Holmes, lighting his pipe with some difficulty. "But we may discover what it is that he and Lord Barington want to know, and what they particularly do not want us to know. We may consider ourselves at this point only a reconnaissance party, selected to determine an invasion route. The main assault will come later. On an outside chance, we may learn enough about Sir Roger to enable Lord Cromer to dispense with his services."

As we spoke, our swarthy crew brought us alongside a primitive wooden dock that stood well above our heads. We clambered up the ladder affixed to it as best we could, and then watched as the crew passed up our luggage. When they were finished, I tossed them a coin in payment, which was greeted with howls of disbelief at my penuriousness. I repeated the process several times, until, to my unpractised ear, at least, it appeared that the howls had begun to ring hollow. In the meantime, Holmes had collected bearers and a guide. So equipped, we set off in search of the British Consulate, which proved to be a dry, dusty journey indeed.

The consulate is an edifice of surpassing elegance, though the passerby will see nothing but a massive, blank wall, some ten feet high, covered with masonry and broken by a single pair of heavy iron gates. This preoccupation with security well symbolizes the painful, and often tragic, history of our nation's presence in this most ancient of all lands. Alexandria, at least the "official" portion of it to which our visit was confined, had for me little of the strange mystery and charm of Tangier. On its streets we saw Englishmen and Egyptians. The marvellous variety of Tangier, the interplay of race and culture, was largely absent.

As we stood before the gates, Holmes gave me one final word of instruction.

"While we are within these walls," he said, "always speak as though in the presence of others. We cannot afford to give our adversaries the slightest advantage."

As he spoke, the gates swung open, exposing a verdant expanse of smoothly mown lawn. Directly before the entrance of the consulate stood a magnificent circular fountain of light-brown marble, cut in the intricate Moorish fashion that so delights the traveller in Spain. From its broad rim the water descended in stately, unbroken sheets, which gleamed like fine lead crystal in the afternoon sun. But whether its beauty welcomed us into paradise or a prison remained to be known.

CHAPTER XVII

Coming to Grips

LTHOUGH THE VOYAGE FROM Tangier to Alexandria was comparatively brief, the confines of the *Prophet* had already begun to chafe, so that it was difficult not to welcome the commodious suites that Sir Roger placed at our disposal. However, the rooms assigned to Holmes and myself could hardly have been more distant. "Divide and conquer" was evidently Sir Roger's maxim. The knowledge that one's host is also one's foe is most unlikely to put a man at his ease, so that even as I enjoyed the supreme luxury of an English bath with hot water, I found myself far from composed.

After recovering from the effects of my journey, I set about inspecting my surroundings. My suite was large and airy, well suited to the near-tropical environment of upper Egypt, and equipped with sound English furniture of traditional design. I was pleased to discover that I had an excellent view of the gardens at the rear of the consulate, through a pair of arched windows. These were large affairs, taller than a man, consisting of many panes and set in heavy frames made of bronze. A small but powerful crank, set at the base of the frame, allowed one to open and close them with relative ease. They were hung with great curtains that obscured the midday heat, but could be drawn back at night.

However, these luxuries did nothing to compensate for the isolation to which I was subjected. I could see, and hear, no one. So greatly did the situation prey upon my nerves that when Holmes rejoined me several hours later, I could scarcely refrain from exclaiming my relief at the sight of him. However, we had not the slightest opportunity for a private discussion, because we were immediately joined by Mr. Archibald Beamish, Sir Roger's private secretary, a remarkably smooth and oily young man, whom it was impossible not to dislike. Mr. Beamish clung to us throughout the afternoon, and saw us off to our rooms when it was time to dress for dinner. He proved to be an equally tenacious after-dinner companion as well. At no time were Holmes and I allowed a moment to ourselves.

The next two days proved to be mere copies of the first. Holmes sought unsuccessfully to obtain an interview with Sir Roger, while we jointly and severally fended off the constant inquiries and assistance of Mr. Beamish. Most trying of all were the personal "servants" assigned to each of us, Morris and Simpson, two silent, hulking fellows who were nothing less than spies, and who dogged our steps from morning to night.

Under such supervision, there was little to do but accept our status as unwelcome guests and make the best of it. I found myself cultivating the company of a Mrs. Saunderson, who graciously offered to show me the "sights," allowing me to escape the overzealous attentions of Simpson. Emily was the wife of an army officer stationed with the legation, the kind of woman who is often unkindly referred to as being "past her prime." It is true that Emily did not take well to exile from London, and that as a consequence she frequently succumbed to the temptations of the table, yet one can hardly say that the pleasures of the world should be reserved exclusively for the young and slender. Emily had a generous nature that chafed at confinement and refused to let itself be dominated by convention and chance, an attitude to which I was

now more responsive than in the past, for I must confess to
the reader that my brief acquaintance with Mary had opened
my eyes to possibilities of companionship between a man and
a woman that my earlier, perhaps adolescent notions of
chivalry had denied me. In any event, an extended afternoon's journey in Emily's carriage afforded us an opportunity
to escape, if only for a short time, the oppressive weight of
propriety, an occasion that culminated, for good or ill, in an
amorous interchange that may not have been the most graceful the sun ever shone upon, but was surely among the most
heartfelt. And as we returned to the consulate that evening, a
strange, twilight sense of well-being stole over me, a vague
reassurance that Holmes and I, despite the twin burdens of
constant separation and supervision, would see this matter
through and would ultimately subdue Sir Roger in this mad-
deningly slow chess game he waged against us.

It was well indeed that I had gained in Emily such a willing and restorative ally, for in fact another full week passed
by before we were able to make a move against Sir Roger.
During that time I paid a visit to Captain MacDougall, accompanied, I might add, by both Simpson and the indefatigable
Beamish, to determine our sailing date. I discovered the ship
piled high with merchandise, to the point that she fairly wal-
lowed in the water, and was more than a little surprised to
learn that the captain was almost indifferent as to his time of
departure. "We are in no special hurry, Doctor," he told me.
"We will keep you informed." I returned with this message to
Holmes, whom I found encumbered with Morris.

We were forced to endure another three days of boredom
before an opportunity presented itself. I returned to my rooms
from lunch to discover that the usually omnipresent Simpson
had disappeared. I settled down with a cigar, wondering if it
might not be possible to seek out Emily's company, when I
heard a knock on the door. Opening it, I discovered Beamish,
looking rather less self-satisfied than usual, though I could not
fathom the reason why.

"Sir Roger extends his invitation to dinner this evening," he
said abruptly, without the slightest preamble.

I attempted to stammer a reply, but he strode away without listening. Stunned both by the invitation and the manner of its delivery, I had no other recourse than to return to my chair, where I recovered my cigar and picked up a volume of the *Malay Lancet*. I spent the next several hours immersed in an account of the horrors of beriberi, until the lengthened shadows on the floor informed me that it was time to begin preparing for dinner. I had almost completed my dress when I heard a sharp knocking, not on the door but from the window. As a precaution, I took my revolver from the bureau drawer where I had secreted it and advanced on the heavy curtains. As I did so the thought crossed my mind that my visitor could only be Holmes himself, for an assailant would hardly announce himself, and no one else would hazard so eccentric an entry.

My surmise proved to be correct. I found Holmes standing on a window ledge somewhat less than a foot in width, dressed in the worn dinner jacket he favoured on formal occasions.

"I hope my appearance has not startled you, Watson," he said, with a look that rather suggested the opposite. "I determined on our first night here that the window ledge offers a most satisfactory footpath. It was only last night that I discovered it was possible to descend from floor to floor as well. You see, I am on the third, while you are on the second."

"Will you come in?"

"Only for a moment. I do not wish my absence to be discovered."

"What do you make of the invitation from Sir Roger?"

"Clearly, something is up, though I have no idea what. Neither Simpson or Morris are present, and Beamish shows evident signs of distress. When you return from dinner, do not retire, but change instead into more comfortable clothes. There may be opportunities for espionage later tonight."

As Holmes turned to go, a deep, distant rumble of thunder announced the looming presence of a storm.

"Nature seems inclined to furnish a suitable backdrop for the night's activities," he remarked. "One imagines that conversation at dinner will be somewhat strained."

CHAPTER XVIII

Sir Roger's Soiree

O IT PROVED. Our host, whom I had never laid eyes on before, was tall and imperious, but intensely preoccupied and made no attempt to disguise his lack of interest in his guests. Due to my friend's celebrity, the dinner had been made something of an occasion in the Anglo-Egyptian community, with the result that we had the company of several ambassadors, lords, sheiks, millionaires, and ministers extraordinary—altogether the cream of Alexandrian society. I searched through the crowd for Emily's charming face and figure, and when she arrived we were able to exchange a warm hand squeeze. Our greetings, however, were cut short by an icy stare from Captain Saunderson, her husband, who had unfortunately returned from the Sudan. The captain, a bluff and rude fellow, all but trod on my toes and made it clear that I would be well-advised to maintain a proper distance from his wife. His suspicious manner, though eminently justified, I found hard to bear under the circumstances, for I feared that these might be the last hours that Emily and I should spend together.

With Emily's company denied me, I should have been lost entirely if I had not made the acquaintance of Dr. Bouvier, a French physician who spoke flawless English and was an immense expert on tropical disease, having spent some years in French settlements on the Ivory Coast, as well as French Cochin China. Fortunately, my shipboard reading, and my prior experience in India and Afghanistan, allowed me to hold my own in the conversation, though my simple tales of gunshot surgery could hardly have provided much illumination for him.

The dinner itself proved to be tedious in the extreme. The evident discomfort of Sir Roger could not help communicating itself to his guests. Several times I observed him conferring with Beamish in a distinctly agitated manner. My own position at the table proved unfortunate. I was seated far distant from Dr. Bouvier and flanked by a pair of painfully bored young English wives, who soon discovered I knew nothing of London—at least, nothing of the London about which they cared. The gentleman seated across from me was a junior partner from the banking firm of Baring & Brothers, who bored us all with his incessant complaints about exchange rates and the unreliability of the "natives."

At length the ladies departed, and the servants passed around the brandy and the cigars, the last being surpassingly fine, "the one thing Sir Roger did right," Holmes remarked to me much later. After the cigars were lit and the brandy sampled, there was a long stretch of desultory conversation, followed by a lull. Then, to my surprise, all of the suppressed tension of the evening burst forth, in a manner deliberately contrived by Holmes himself. One of the junior members of the legation gave my friend his cue, asking if there was anything he might tell them about his mission.

"I am not at liberty to say much," said Holmes, in a loud voice, "but I will say this. This case cuts very deep. It appears that a number of consulates are involved."

"Oh, come, Mr. Holmes," responded Mr. Beamish, in a sharp tone. "Surely you overplay your hand."

"I do not think so," said Holmes.

"But I say you do," said the private secretary. "There had been some bungling in the previous administration, and you have been hired to put a good face on it. These stolen rifles that you pretend to miss so dearly were undoubtedly sold to buy a few baubles for some liberal lord's lady."

This sally was greeted by a round of appreciative laughter, which Beamish clearly enjoyed. Smirking at his own wit, he struck an oratorical pose and continued.

"Yes, I believe that fits the facts of the case," he said, striding about as though he imagined himself on the floor of Parliament. "Then when the Tories got in, some of the bolder spirits wanted to take a look at these things. The opposition, dreading a parliamentary enquiry, proposed this 'special investigation' instead. The cabinet unfortunately lacked the stomach to undertake the task of rolling over Mr. Gladstone's rocks and acquiesced. As a result, instead of suffering the rigours of another English winter, you and your friend are sitting here in this delightful city, enjoying Sir Roger's most excellent cigars."

As he concluded, the young man flourished his own cigar and took a long puff. I regret to say that this display of delicately malicious cynicism brought forth a round of applause, with not a few cries of "hear, hear." Even Sir Roger relaxed, to a degree, and grinned at his protégé's audacity. Holmes, however, was not intimidated.

"I only wish the case were as trivial as you suppose," he retorted. "But these were a thousand military rifles of the very latest design. Does that strike you as cause for levity, Major Thomas?"

Holmes turned to the major, who was chief of security at the consulate. The major, though every inch the stalwart officer, proved a poor ally. Despite his gilt decorations, he was a simple soldier at heart, who requires orders before he can act, and here he had no orders. Sir Roger quickly intervened to remind the fellow of his place.

"Yes, Major," the vice consul said, in a cold, clear voice. "Tell Mr. Holmes what he wants to know."

"Any theft of Her Majesty's property is a cause for concern," he said, twisting uncomfortably in his chair. "Here, of course, I have no official knowledge of the case and thus cannot comment."

"You see, Mr. Holmes?" said Beamish. "Perhaps if you had a case we would be interested. But you have no case, no evidence, no facts."

"I have a great deal of evidence," returned my friend.

"Really? Then why, after almost two weeks of dining here at the British taxpayer's expense, have you not made one allegation, not one arrest? As a detective, Mr. Holmes, you really should arrest someone, if only to keep up appearances. May I suggest myself? I should not resent it at all, I assure you."

"I have no power to arrest anyone," said Holmes quietly.

"No? How unfortunate," returned the secretary. "I fear, Mr. Holmes, that well-meaning people have led you into waters over your head. You have been made a pawn, and now you stand naked and alone on the chessboard, a poor piece indeed. Your place is in London. Dr. Watson has written so agreeably of your adventures there, defending the honour of governesses and shopgirls, protecting the goods of High Street merchants. You must miss the middle-class hustle and bustle of your dear metropolis, Mr. Holmes. Return to it! Leave the great world of diplomacy and affairs of state. This is a stage upon which, unfortunately, you have no role to play."

As the secretary finished his peroration, his brash and insulting words seemed to hang in the air. The assembled gentlemen smiled awkwardly and silently among themselves. All eyes were on Holmes as he made his reply.

"There is much in what you say," he began. "After all, I have made no study of political life. But there is one thing I do know, Mr. Beamish, and that is crime, crime in all its aspects and manifestations. And having made crime my study, Mr. Beamish, there is one thing I find. A man may take a wrong step for many reasons—he may be ignorant, lazy, reckless, careless—it scarcely matters why. For having taken that first step he will likely take a second, and a third, and a fourth. And then he will inevitably come to that point where he has to consider whether to go forward and turn back. And almost as inevitably, having reached that point, he will decide that he has already come 'too far.' But, do you know, Mr. Beamish, no man has ever gone 'too far.' The way back is

always shorter than the way forward, for the way back leads
to forgiveness, while the way forward leads to perdition."

Holmes paused and sipped his brandy. For a moment he
seemed utterly lost in thought and oblivious to us all, but then
he resumed his speech.

"You must excuse me, gentlemen," he said, turning his
attention from Beamish to Sir Roger, "but I was thinking about
something I recently had read. Something about a rat."

"A rat, Mr. Holmes?" responded Sir Roger, in a trembling
voice.

"Yes. Curious creatures. All very well in their place, but no
good all over the shop."

"What have rats to do with us?" exclaimed Beamish, almost
shouting.

"Why, nothing, I should hope. I would, in fact, advise you
to steer clear of them at all costs."

"I find I tire of your humour, Mr. Holmes," said Sir Roger,
testily. "The weight of affairs is very pressing. I must ask Mr.
Beamish to assume my role as host." And with that Sir Roger
bustled off.

"Dear, dear," said Holmes to the assembled company. "I
have most foolishly offended my host. I am sure I could convince Sir Roger that he and I see eye to eye on this matter.
But we should follow his example, don't you agree, Watson?
We have an early day tomorrow."

"Yes, of course," I returned, "and today's events have been
most fatiguing."

"So soon, Mr. Holmes?" said Mr. Beamish, rising quickly to
his feet and stepping between us and the door. "While I cannot agree with your provocation of my chief, there is much in
what you say about the consular service. I'm sure the other
members of the legation would have you remain a while
longer."

"Ah, that is impossible. As Watson has said, our day has
been tiring."

"Surely not! Why, Mr. Holmes, you are the most wideawake man here."

"Appearances are deceiving," returned Holmes. "I must bid

you adieu, gentlemen," he said, turning to the guests. "Will you join me, Watson?"

"At least let me join you," said Beamish, linking his arm with Holmes'. "I would be remiss if I did not accompany you."

And so it was with this unwanted companion that we left the gathering and strolled upstairs to our rooms, Mr. Beamish making sure all the time that Holmes and I were unable to exchange a single word. When I entered my room, I had not the slightest idea if Holmes still intended to pursue the midnight excursion he had earlier described to me, but I felt it best to prepare for that eventuality. Outside my window, the storm that had been brewing all evening now announced its arrival with tempestuous violence, as sheets of rain lashed against the glass. The thought of essaying a narrow marble ledge under such conditions was hardly an agreeable one, but there was nothing I could do other than to select a pair of rubber-soled tennis shoes instead of the leather boots I had originally chosen. Once the substitution was made and my revolver loaded and placed in a holster that fastened conveniently to my belt, I settled into an easy chair and lit a cigar, which proved a poor companion. The lonely room, and the brutal storm without, filled me with the greatest trepidation. At length I heard a sharp rapping on my window. I threw back the sash to discover Holmes perched precariously outside, the storm howling about him.

"Holmes," I cried, straining to make myself heard. "Do you really intend to make the attempt?"

"No time for questions, Watson. It is now or never. The ledge is quite commodious."

This I discovered to be a gross exaggeration. The sill was perhaps eight inches wide and, thanks to the rain, slick as glass. We inched our way along, pressed against the exterior wall, for perhaps fifty yards before reaching one of the massive columns that stretched the full height of the building. Holmes paused and turned to me.

"This is a bit more difficult," he said, gesturing at the column. "We must go up a story."

"Difficult" was not the word I would have chosen for the task before us. The deeply incised stone gave our hands and feet some manner of purchase, but the climb, more than thirty feet up, the wind and the rain tearing at us, tested my strength and determination to the limit. More than once, the sudden shock of a lightning flash almost caused me to lose my grip. When we gained the upper ledge at last, we were able to take refuge in a carved and fretted niche that surmounted the column we had lately ascended.

"You see the light in the last window?" Holmes asked, pointing down the long line of portals that stretched before us into the gloom.

"I see nothing."

"It is Sir Roger's study. Half an hour ago I observed a large coach pull up to the front of the palace. A shrouded figure entered, accompanied by two men, I believe Morris and Simpson. As soon as I saw them enter, I left my perch and came here. As I did so that light came on. It is here that Sir Roger is entertaining his mysterious guest."

"If your calculations are correct."

Holmes raised his head sharply at my words.

"Perhaps you would care to verify them!" he responded, indicating with a gesture that I should precede him.

Recognizing that no good could come from pursuing a dispute at this juncture, I stepped ahead and made my way along the marble ledge as rapidly as prudence would allow. However, I had not reckoned that the marble itself would be unsound. I had not advanced twenty feet when a large piece gave way beneath my weight, and I found myself plunging downward. Fortunately, I was able to catch hold of the groove where the sill had torn itself out and halt my fall, but the jagged edges of the shattered marble made it impossible for me to maintain myself in that position for long. My feet struggled to obtain a purchase on sheer wall itself, to no avail.

"Hold on, Watson!" Holmes' powerful voice rang out above me over the roar of the storm. "For God's sake, hold on! Hold on for thirty seconds and I shall have you out of there."

It seemed I endured that hideous uncertainty for closer to

thirty minutes than thirty seconds, the pitiless marble cutting into my flesh, but at length I felt Holmes' steel-like grip around my wrist. I looked up, and as I did so, an enormous lightning bolt crashed directly over my head. I saw Holmes silhouetted against the darkness, the rain streaming down from above. His legs were spread-eagled on either side of the broken marble with his back braced against the wall. Somehow he managed to maintain his balance while pulling me slowly upward by both wrists.

"Put your right arm around my waist," he said, his voice trembling with effort.

I struggled to comply, fearing both that I might fall and that my exertions to avoid that fate might destroy us both. As I struggled to inch myself upward, using Holmes as a support, I found that my dangling feet might at last find some purchase in the niche that my fingers had found so torturing. After such a trial the temptation to relax was almost overpowering, but to do so would almost certainly have been fatal. I transferred my grip from Holmes' waist to the wall, and as he withdrew his leg, I clambered onto the unbroken portion of the ledge that lay before us. Trembling and uncertain, I forced myself to move several anxious feet forward, allowing Holmes to join me.

"Can you continue?" he asked, once he had crossed over.

"There seems to be little alternative."

"True. But I suggest that we tread our pathway with increased care. Would you prefer that I lead the way?"

"No. If you fell, it would be impossible for me to pull you back."

"Very well. We cannot allow Sir Roger to escape us."

With my friend's last words urging me on, I hastened rather than retarded my pace, despite the circumstances. Fortunately, the ledge proved sound for the remainder of its length, and we arrived at the hooded and masked window that Holmes had marked as our quarry without further mishap. Thick, black curtains concealed the interior, but a few small chinks of light escaping into the darkness gave evidence of habitation. With a gesture to me that commanded silence,

Holmes positioned himself in front of the window and took from his coat what I recognized to be a sort of suction cup made of india rubber and a glass cutter.

"Glazier's tools," he whispered to me. "I thought it best to be prepared for any eventuality."

With a few expert motions he freed a small pane of glass from the window. As he did so, I was rather surprised to hear a loud, angry murmur of voices. For the first time since we had begun this journey, Holmes betrayed a smile of satisfaction.

"Can you make out what they're saying?" I whispered.

"No. We had better listen and hope a thunderclap doesn't betray us."

We remained in that situation for perhaps twenty minutes. Fortunately, we were shielded from the rain, which fell steadily but without the thunder and lightning that Holmes feared. At length the voices grew louder, though still indistinct. All at once our nerves were shattered by a bloodcurdling scream.

"Give me a hand here, Watson," shouted Holmes as he struggled with the window. "We're going in."

The window at Sir Roger's study was even more massive than the one for my own room. Operating the mechanism from the outside in that downpour was no easy task. We had forced it open a crack, when the air was rent by a second scream, more horrifying than the first, which ended with a dreadful gurgle. We redoubled our efforts until at last, with a supreme effort, Holmes wrenched open the groaning frame, and we plunged through the curtain.

CHAPTER XIX

Sir Roger's Fate

E FOUND OURSELVES in a large, high-ceilinged room, appointed with all the opulence appropriate to a great lord, only to be greeted by a sight of nightmarish horror. The figure of Sir Roger was seated at a massive mahogany desk. His head hung down at a ghastly angle, for his neck had been broken and his throat torn out, as though he had been mauled by some great beast of prey. An enormous pool of his life's blood spilled out across the desk and down onto the carpeting.

"The door, Watson!" Holmes commanded.

We both flew to it, but found it locked from the outside. Holmes flung himself against it in a fury of frustration, but the heavy oak was proof against the stoutest shoulder.

"Is there another exit?" he cried, glancing around eagerly, but in vain, for there was none.

"I'll ring for the servants," I said, reaching for the bell cord.

"Excellent. With any luck we'll have our man within the hour."

"It is no use," said a thin, despairing voice.

Holmes and I stared at each other. Beamish, who had evidently been crouching behind the desk, rose uncertainly to his feet. The silky, assured courtier had vanished. We saw before us a sickly, trembling figure, his evening clothes daubed with blood, with a pasty complexion and a hectic eye.

"Do you have a key?" Holmes shouted. "We can still catch him if you have a key."

"It is no use," Beamish repeated, staggering forward.

"See if he has a key, Watson," Holmes instructed me. I turned the man's pockets out but found nothing. In the meantime, Holmes picked up a letter opener from the desk and set about prying the lock, which defied our best efforts. Precious minutes slipped by until we heard voices outside. There was a rattling of the key in the lock and the door swung open, revealing Stebbins, the aging butler who had greeted us upon our arrival at the consulate.

"Bless me," he said, "what are you gentlemen doing here?"

"Never mind that," cried Holmes. "Have you seen anyone?"

"Why, there's no one to see. Is anything amiss with Sir Roger?"

"Yes," said Holmes, pushing past the man. "Something is very much amiss with Sir Roger."

Holmes and I raced down the broad, darkened hallway towards the stairs. After the endless vexations of the last several hours, culminating in the gruesome murder of Sir Roger, the mere ability to move about freely was an inestimable tonic to the spirit. We flung ourselves down the long, processional staircase, which led to the entrance hall. At the great glass doors we found ourselves barred once more. With an oath, Holmes grabbed a ceremonial lance that hung from the wall and smashed the butt through the ornamental glass, which seemed to explode at his touch. We stepped through the naked frames, our shoes crunching on the gleaming splinters that littered the step.

Once outside, the unrelenting rain lashed our faces. If anything, the darkness had deepened, and more thunder muttered in the far-off distance.

"Do you see anything, Watson?"

"Nothing."

We paused for a moment at the top of steps.

"Do you think he could still be on the grounds?" I said, almost shouting to make myself heard over the rising wind.

"It's possible," replied Holmes. "Damn this weather! The fiend could be a dozen paces away and we would never know it. I should have persisted with Sir Roger. I could have . . ."

But Holmes' words froze on his lips as an enormous lightning bolt crashed above us. The driving rain gleamed white as the gigantic electrical charge coursed through the atmosphere. Far in the distance, almost precisely at the marble gates that opened onto the grounds of the consulate, we could see the distinct outline of a coach speeding away from us. Holmes flung himself down the steps to the drive, which was nothing but a sea of mud. He fell once, collected himself, and fell again. Descending the steps more cautiously, I soon joined him.

"It is impossible, Holmes!"

But he ignored my words and began striding through the thick mud. There was nothing for me to do but follow. We had gone perhaps fifty yards when he stopped.

"You are quite right," he said, as though no time had lapsed between my remark and his response. "We must question Beamish. We should communicate with the captain in the morning as well. His information has proved to be more reliable than mine."

Once we had returned to the consulate, Holmes and I learned that our discovery of Sir Roger's mutilated body had far from exhausted the night's horrors. In an obscure, darkened corner of the entrance hall, we found the bodies of Morris and Simpson. Sir Roger's murderer had evidently killed them by dashing their heads together, a scarcely credible feat.

"This fellow must be a man of enormous strength," I said.

"I doubt very much that he is a man of any sort," Holmes responded. "Recall the captain's remark that the leader of these creatures was of gigantic stature. He was here, Watson. He was here, and we let him slip through our fingers."

It was impossible for me to answer such a remark directly. Instead, I suggested that we seek out Beamish.

"He is our only remaining resource," agreed Holmes. He shook his head in the direction of the bodies of the unfortunate men. "Poor fools. No doubt they believed they had found the perfect employer."

When we made the weary journey back to the tragic study, to which we had obtained entry with such difficulty, we discovered that Major Thomas had taken the matter in hand.

"Mr. Holmes!" he exclaimed as we appeared. "You are the man I have been looking for. I want a full account of your activities for this evening."

"That will take some time, Major," my friend replied. "Might I trouble you for a cigar? Dr. Watson and I have had a full night of it, and with little to show for our time."

"Tell me at least what you make of these horrible events," the major said, producing a fine black cheroot and a match.

"I am reluctant even to venture a guess," answered Holmes, lighting the cheroot. "What has Mr. Beamish said? He is the one man who could tell us what occurred within these four walls."

"Mr. Beamish, sir? I have not seen Mr. Beamish at all this evening."

"He should not have been left alone," Holmes said sharply. "Come, Watson."

When we arrived at the secretary's room, we were too late once more. There, from the chandelier, the poor man's body swung in a slow spin. The major cut him down and laid him on a sofa, but there was nothing anyone could do to revive him. What he had just witnessed had destroyed his mind, and now the body had followed. He lay sprawled on the cushions like a ghastly puppet, arms and legs dangling. Holmes stood staring down at him for a long moment, drawing thoughtfully on the cheroot. Then, with a sudden inspiration, he unbuttoned the secretary's waistcoat and pulled it back.

"There, Watson, there! What do you think of that?"

Amazement and horror swept through me as I stared at the incredible evidence Holmes had uncovered. There on the white cloth was the print of a huge hand, in blood, but with three rather than four fingers, and the fingers were furred and equipped with long, curving claws!

PART III

East of Suez

CHAPTER XX

The Departure of Holmes

HE SENSATION CREATED BY the horrible murders within the consulate can scarcely be exaggerated, but the impact of these tragedies upon our investigation was the opposite of what Holmes could have wished. With all my confidence in my friend's remarkable abilities, I had refused even to consider his analysis of the case. Even now, in the face of incontestable evidence, I could only say that I saw no way to refute his conclusion that we were joined in the pursuit of an adversary that was less, or perhaps more, than human. But no evidence could convince a simple soldier like Major Thomas that heaven and earth contained more than was dreamt of in his philosophy. The three of us spent the remainder of the night, and the whole of the next morning, reviewing the case. No matter how Holmes tried, nothing could budge the major from the conclusion he had formed when entering Sir Roger's study, that all this was the doing of "El-Kavil and those damned meddling Turks."

"I see no hope for the major," said Holmes, as we shared a late, miserable lunch in his rooms. "Apparently he has been wanting to hang this El-Kavil for some time, and now he sees his chance."

"Do you think it possible that the major himself was part of Sir Roger's conspiracy?"

"That is highly unlikely. If he had been, surely he would have participated in the conference as well. Yet he shows no sign whatsoever of fearing exposure, and I never met a man less capable of dissimulation."

"What do we do next?"

"I must obtain permission to cable London and save the neck of this El-Kavil, whoever he may be."

"Then what?"

"That is more difficult. I doubt whether it is possible to present my conclusions in this case to anyone. Still, my hand has been strengthened immeasurably. Lord Barington's supporters can hardly claim now that this case is a matter of all smoke and no fire."

But again events did not go entirely as Holmes predicted. Major Thomas arrested El-Kavil, who proved to be a stoop-shouldered, astigmatic scholar who could have been no threat to anyone other than his own students. In the meantime, cables sped to and fro between Egypt and England. On the third day following the murders, Holmes strode into my rooms and flung himself into an available armchair.

"I have received disagreeable news from London," he said bitterly. "Lord Cromer tells me that he cannot maintain his position before the cabinet without my personal testimony."

"Then you must return?"

"Yes. The German ambassador has presented an official statement to the government saying that the recent events here cast doubt on the right and ability of England to manage the affairs of Egypt. They are proposing an international commission consisting of Germany, France, Austria-Hungary, and the United States to assume control."

"How abominable!"

"Indeed. This must be headed off at all costs. Otherwise, there will be no end to delays. There could be a crisis, a new government, anything. Meanwhile, Barington would be free to hatch new plans at his leisure. As a result, I depart tomorrow, courtesy of the Royal Navy."

"Then I must go with you."

"On the contrary. You must go onward to Singapore. We cannot allow Barington any respite. Besides, it would be a pity to leave the *Prophet* without a doctor."

The next morning Holmes and I rode out from the consulate in an open carriage. The sun was already hot and the atmosphere moist and cloying, but the sheer relief we both felt at being outside those grim and dismal gates was palpable.

"A ghastly business, Watson," said Holmes, as he lit a cigar and watched the consulate recede slowly in the distance. "I don't know when I have enjoyed a place less. I deeply regret having to leave you in the major's company."

"Think nothing of it," I returned. "The *Prophet* is set to sail in less than a week. The major is busying himself with El-Kavil. The excitement is subsiding, and I shall enjoy the quiet."

"Yes, of course. And I understand that Captain Saunderson has been ordered to return to the Sudan."

To this outrageous jibe I made no response, and we made the rest of the journey to the quay in complete silence.

It is a measure of the government's concern over the developments in Alexandria that the light cruiser *Intrepid* had been assigned the duty of bearing Holmes back to London. The sight of the great, sleek warship riding at anchor in the harbour reminded me forcibly of the enormity of the events that had been set in motion by Elizabeth's letter to me only a few months before. As if in response to our presence, the stacks of the mighty ship gave vent to a great blast of coal smoke, and the scream of a steam whistle pierced the torpid Egyptian air. On the dock itself a young lieutenant, accompanied by a brace of sailors, saluted us as we arrived.

"Mr. Sherlock Holmes, sir?"

"Yes, I am."

"Captain Jones extends his welcome, sir, and requests that you come aboard immediately."

"I share the captain's concern for promptness," said Holmes, taking a final puff on his cigar. "Your men will find my luggage in the boot. Tell me, what are the size of the *Intrepid*'s largest guns?"

"Six-inchers, sir. And she can show her heels to any ship on the Mediterranean."

"Excellent! That allays a few of my fears. Please allow me a few words in private with my friend here, Lieutenant, and I will be with you in a minute."

"Very good, sir."

The lieutenant saluted, turned on his heel, and barked an order to the men, who had burdened themselves with Holmes' luggage. The three of them marched off toward a staircase that descended to water level.

"I shall be safe enough, at least," said Holmes, turning to me. "If all goes well, I should arrive in Singapore only a few weeks behind you. I am not sure if we will be able to communicate. It is best to assume not. In the meantime, learn what you can from the captain. And remember, Watson, that you are engaging the enemy on his home ground. Singapore is the centre of danger. Once you leave the *Prophet,* you must be constantly on guard."

"I shall do my utmost," I responded, gripping his hand.

"Good, Watson, good."

With that, he sprang from the carriage and strode off to join the small party from the *Intrepid.* As I watched that tall, spare figure that I knew so well disappear down the stairs, I could not help but feel a momentary sense of panic. I was all alone, on a journey spanning thousands of miles of trackless ocean, engaged against an enemy so monstrous I could not well conceive his nature. But then I recalled my promise to Holmes, and the tragic fate of poor Elizabeth. Having come so far, it was impossible to weaken now. My spirit stiffened inside me, and I bade the driver return to the consulate.

When I arrived, I learned that Lord Cromer had at last dispatched word to Major Thomas to release El-Kavil. Although the evidence exculpating that bemused scholar was irrefutable, the loss of his intended victim left Major Thomas in a malignant rage, in part because he had already set about the construction of a special gallows for the man's execution.

The major's ire was such that I deemed it best to remain in my rooms to the extent possible, with the result that I was almost as much a prisoner after Sir Roger's death as I had been before. However, since Emily's rooms were located on the same floor as mine, I was able to put the window ledge, which I had cursed so heartily on the dreadful night of Sir Roger's death, to a more gentle and more elevating purpose. As Emily remarked, "The architect of this building must have been a most understanding man."

It pained me greatly to exchange the tender abandon of Emily's company for my Spartan quarters aboard the *Prophet*, but the call of duty could not be denied. Absurd as it may sound, I felt myself rather like one of the great sultans, relinquishing the pleasures of the harem for an arduous and uncertain campaign against the infidels. And it was in such an inflated and inflamed spirit that I finally bid Emily a passionate adieu.

The warmth of our ardour clung to me as I boarded the *Prophet* on the following day. Given the captain's concern for punctuality, I thought it best to go on board the night before our departure. I was awakened considerably before six by the thud of cargo, shouts from the crew, and the hiss of the *Prophet*'s steam winch. After dressing, I went on deck and located the captain, who was perched halfway up into the rigging, dressed as usual in an immaculate white uniform.

"Dr. Watson," he shouted, "good to have you on board! You must give me an account of your adventures once we are properly under way!"

I shouted my assurances in return and found a comfortable spot from which to view the morning's activities. The *Prophet*'s extended layover in Alexandria had brought it a rich harvest of cargo. Indeed, the deck was so covered with crates, barrels, and boxes, not to mention the multitude of red earthenware jugs and urns, that it was difficult to make one's way across it. Many of the boxes stood as high as a man, or even higher, and had to be specially lashed to the deck. As the hour of departure approached, Captain MacDougall swarmed down from his lofty vantage point and leapt from one box to the next in the performance of his final inspection. When he had satisfied himself that every last jug was secure, he gave the signal to cast off. One by one the heavy cables fell to the dock; the engines snorted, and the long prow of the *Prophet* swung slowly around. The second leg of the voyage had begun.

CHAPTER XXI

East of Suez

 UR PROGRESS AROUND THE northeast corner of Egypt was slow, stopping at Port Said before entering the canal and at Suez itself as we completed the passage between Africa and Asia. Consequently, it was not until we were in the Red Sea that the captain was free to discuss with me in detail the atrocious events at the consulate. He questioned me with particular closeness regarding Sir Roger's wounds, a distasteful but significant issue.

"You are sure they were caused by an animal?"

"I state it only as the most likely conjecture. I cannot imagine the implement that would cause such wounds."

"Teeth, then."

"Probably. But not fangs. There were no circular punctures, such as the canines produce. Of course, I am no expert in the area of animal bites. But I have seen sheep with their throats torn by dogs, and the wounds were dissimilar."

"Have you seen anything that resembles these injuries?"

"I once had a patient who had been severely bitten by a horse."

"Really, Doctor? Do you think Sir Roger was attacked by his mount and later brought to the study?"

"Not at all," I retorted. "The quantity of blood on his desk, the freshness of the wounds, the screams Holmes and I heard, all confirm that he was killed only minutes before we entered the room. I only suggest that the marks on Sir Roger's throat resembled more closely the spadelike teeth of a plant eater than the fangs of a carnivore."

"Of course," said the captain. "I have heard," he continued, in a slow voice, "that the leader of the monkey boys is nothing less than a gigantic rat, the size of a man."

"Impossible!"

"Doctor, you speak as a man of the West. You are so pleased with your own miracles that you neglect those of others."

"You call this supposed monster a miracle?"

"Not a miracle, precisely, but rather something outside the normal course of events. It is a vanity to insist that your learning has exhausted the resources of the world."

"Then what do you know of this creature?"

"I know nothing of him. I know what a few men will say, with great reluctance. Most men of the East will not speak of him at all, though all know of him."

"Then what do they say?"

"That he resembles a monstrous rat, that he has lived for centuries, that he rules over the monkey men, and that he has an implacable heart. I am amazed to hear that he has journeyed as far west as Alexandria, but the evidence you and Mr. Holmes have compiled appears conclusive."

"Does this creature have a name?"

"He is called Harat, which simply means 'leader,' 'the great one.'"

I shook my head in frustration.

"What distresses you, Doctor?"

"This case distresses me," I said a little sharply, because I believed I caught a trace of irony in the captain's tone. "When I think of poor Elizabeth dying such a pitiful death, and now, months later, there is nothing to show for all our effort but a handful of rumours that would have us committed to Bedlam if we dared to make them public."

"A man who would serve Allah must be patient. This case, as you call it, involves far more than the death of one woman, however tragic that may be. The evil of Harat has endured for centuries. Do you think that you and Mr. Holmes could wash it away in a fortnight? This is not a case of simple London thuggery that you describe so charmingly in your little stories. You have had a sample of Harat's work at the consulate. He can do much more. Do you see this?"

Here he pointed to the notch in his ear.

"Yes," I responded, in a reluctant voice.

"And do you know what it means?"

"Holmes said it was the mark of an Arab slave trader."

"Mr. Holmes seldom disappoints. Does it surprise you to know, Dr. Watson, that the number of Africans sold and stolen into slavery by Arab traders has increased significantly each year over the past ten years, under the very noses of the so-called civilized nations?"

"I knew the slave trade has not been eliminated."

"It has not been eliminated. It has increased." The captain paused and glanced away at the slow, calm swells, black in the darkness. Without returning his gaze to me, he resumed speaking.

"I have travelled this sea many times, but first as a boy, chained belowdecks, with this ear still raw and bleeding. Your papers tell us of progress, yet thousands more still follow my path. Why, Doctor?"

"Holmes said he believed the firm of Enderby & Cross was using human slaves to work its plantations and mines in the Malay Peninsula and archipelago."

"Then once more I must applaud that gentleman's acumen. Do you know, Dr. Watson, I have read your *London Times* for years and have followed the fortunes of Enderby & Cross with the closest attention. I have seen dozens of articles praising that company's shrewdness, industry, and opulence. In all that time, I have never found a single article willing to look beyond that company's profits to discover their source. Do you not find that remarkable?"

"Success, particularly in remote corners of the globe, can answer all questions."

The captain appeared amused by my remark, which I confess was not designed to displease him.

"Excellent, Doctor. You are beginning to think like a believer. Let me tell you something. There is a temple in southeast India, in Mahabalipuram, where you can learn more about Harat and the monkey men. It is an infidel temple, most impious, but the priests there will help you. But you must be patient."

The captain did not speak lightly. The passage to Diu, our first stop in India, took over a week, sailing around the Arabian boot and stopping over at both Aden and Muscat. At this point, we were still more than a thousand miles from Mahabalipuram. Diu, a dusty port founded by Portugal in the sixteenth century, is located in the Gujarat, in extreme northwestern India. I felt a special thrill as we rode into the harbour, for it was at Diu that I first set foot in India, preparatory to making the long march north to Afghanistan.

Now as then, Diu has little to offer the European traveller. Yet as I sat in the cafe of the one decent hotel in the city, sipping a glass of Madeira, the memories of my hasty, confused youth jostled in my brain. In the company of a few smooth-faced, whispering traders, I recalled the endless tramp of marching feet, the heat and the dust, the cries and curses of the mule skinners, the creaking oxcarts, and the long whips that cracked like rifle shots. I recalled India and its people, that great, endless, eternal, alien presence, through which we crawled like a trickle of ants. Now I had come to India again.

I sat lost in my thoughts until my reverie was interrupted by the voices, and perhaps even more by the uniforms, of a group of young British army officers, hot and dusty from the trail, loudly and in good humour demanding refreshment from the bar. One of them, recognizing me as a fellow countryman, engaged me in conversation, and after I informed them of my history they naturally made me one of their party. They bore my old war stories well enough, for they were too young to have seen action, and insisted on treating me to drinks.

As the evening wore on, their lively companionship provided such a diversion from the serious business at hand that I found myself insensibly becoming not merely an accomplice but a chief in their merriment. Emptying our pockets, we commanded that an impromptu banquet be prepared on our behalf. While that was being done, one of the officers concocted a heady punch of brandy and champagne, which served to banish all restraint.

Thus fortified, we strode into the hotel's small banquet room and dined capitally on curried chicken and mutton, suet pudding, and trifle, all washed down with liberal draughts of champagne. We toasted Queen and Country and sang innumerable choruses of regimental songs, hailing our own and damning all others. It is safe to say that I had not spent such an evening in twenty years.

After we had consumed all the champagne the hotel had to offer, we departed for another establishment, which to my shame I must confess was little more than a house of assignation, of the most disreputable sort. Young ladies of every hue, and the most casual modes of dress, presented themselves to us immediately upon our arrival. As a young surgeon, I had always refrained from visiting such establishments, and in fact knew little more than that they existed. My experiences on this night did not cause me to regret my previous innocence. My recent involvements with Mary and Emily, however inconsistent with the dictates of conventional morality, had a charm, and even a nobility, that I would never have cause to regret. But the mingling of commerce and passion seems to me entirely repugnant, despite the evident enthusiasm that I saw displayed that night on the part of both my countrymen and their dusky courtesans.

Such excesses are, of course, far more excusable in the young than the old. While I would not condemn my comrades, neither would I join them. An older woman, quite obviously the mistress of the house, as hardened and shrewd as her charges were young and impressionable, sought to interest me in a variety of diversions, ranging from the vulgar to the unspeakable. However, I declined them all and finally convinced her that all I desired was a quiet bed for myself, which was indeed not far from the truth, for the innumerable bumpers of champagne and brandy punch I had consumed were now taking their toll. Spurning all assistance, I made my way up a steep and ill-lit stairway, thinking vaguely that a room on the top floor would distance me from the raucous hurly-burly enacted below. With each step, I felt more sharply the burden of my earlier dissipation. My head ached and my body trembled. I was reduced to crawling on my hands and knees to avoid toppling over entirely. At last I reached a hallway and crawled my way painfully into a large, bare, empty room, devoid of furniture of any kind. Scarcely had I passed through the doorway than I fell thankfully into a debauched and dreamless slumber.

How long I slept, and why I awoke, I do not know. The room was black as pitch, but the darkness was broken by the flickering light of a small candle. As the light seemed to move toward me, I struggled desperately but helplessly to rouse myself, my brain stricken with a vague but overpowering sense of danger. In my pathetic condition, I could do no more than raise my head and stare at the apparition that approached.

It was a giant rat, perhaps three feet high, moving easily on its hind legs, its long, naked tail trailing off into the darkness. In one hand it bore a candle, while the other carried a small but cruel knife, whose gleaming blade looked as sharp as a razor. A thick leather belt worn over the creature's left shoulder and around its waist was hung with several small pouches and other accoutrements, whose nature I could not distinguish. The creature's head was enlarged but still clearly rat-like, covered with short, brown fur. Its close-set eyes, black as buttons, regarded me with calm intensity, while his enormous, curved teeth shone whitely in the flickering light of the candle's flame.

All this I saw with the lunatic clarity of a nightmare. But the rest was confusion. I had forgotten where I was and how I came to be there. All I knew was that I was lying alone on the floor of some strange room, staring into the eyes of a creature whose existence would have been dismissed by the wisest heads of Europe as the merest moonshine.

We remained regarding each other for a long time. How long, I cannot say. I dared not move. Indeed, I could not. If the creature had attacked me, I do not know if I could have defended myself. But it did not attack. At times I could swear that a look of understanding, almost of amusement, passed over its hirsute and rodentlike features. At times I thought it was on the verge of speech. But only silence prevailed between us.

The minutes passed by endlessly. At last I thought I must rouse myself. I drew my legs awkwardly beneath me. Instantly, the creature jerked its head in an attitude of suspicion and impatience. The hand that held the knife thrust the keen blade warningly toward my throat. I raised my hand, half to defend myself and half to beg for mercy. I sought to speak, but my tongue seemed swollen and frozen in my mouth. I gagged on my own words and fell once more into a dark and dreamless swoon. In such a state I must have lain for hours, until I felt a hand upon my shoulder. I struggled wildly at the touch, for I thought the creature must have returned, but when I regained my senses at last, I found myself confronting the grim visage of Captain MacDougall.

"Ah, Doctor, I was told I might find you here. Have you seen enough of Diu?"

Only the captain's eyes betrayed his amusement at my plight. Taking his hand, I rose unsteadily to my feet, my every movement betraying my debilitated condition.

"I had the most hideous dream," I said. "You will not believe this, but I dreamt I saw one of the creatures, the rat-men."

"That was no dream, Doctor," replied the captain, in a sharply altered tone. "Look!"

He pointed to the floor. There in the dust, we could see clearly the footprints of a small animal. A long, slithering line in the dust gave evidence of the creature's tail.

I stared, amazed, bitterly regretting the injudicious behaviour that now left me scarcely capable of absorbing the astounding evidence before me.

"It had a knife," I said at last. "Why did it not destroy me?"

"That is impossible to say," said the captain. "What can you recall of the encounter?"

"Only that we stared at one another for a long time without speaking. I sought to rise, but could not. I must have lost consciousness. From that moment to this, I remember nothing."

"You have had a rare encounter, Doctor. I would advise you not to speak of this to anyone. The monkey men place a great value on their privacy."

Whenever the captain spoke of the monkey men, he adopted a light, ironic tone, but I could see from the expression in his eyes that he was in deadly earnest. For my part, I could only nod miserably and hope that when I had recovered from the night's dissipation, I could give this most bizarre and momentous encounter the consideration it deserved.

Wishing to avoid temptation, I spent the remainder of our stay in Diu on board the *Prophet*. The captain instituted a quiet but extremely thorough search of the ship, and informed me that he found no evidence that any of the creatures had been living within its confines, "but it is impossible to know." I contented myself with that faint reassurance and continued my perusal of the *Malay Lancet*.

CHAPTER XXII

The Naval Interest

HAT DRY BUT ESTIMABLE publication proved to be my main companion as the *Prophet* made its long voyage down the Malabar Coast of the Indian subcontinent. Oppressed by the tropical weather, I found myself sleeping twelve hours out of every twenty-four. I awakened early, enjoyed a brief breakfast with the captain, and took a morning constitutional around the ship. Then I retired to a shady spot on deck and continued working my way through the *Lancet*. After a light lunch, I read for an hour more and then returned to my cabin for a nap, which invariably lasted for the remainder of the afternoon. I would take a second constitutional in the fading light of evening, bathe, and read in my cabin until the captain was available for dinner. After dinner I would immediately retire, and thus begin the cycle all over again.

This monotony continued for several weeks, broken only by the occasional medical emergency and our stops at Bombay and Goa. To avoid temptation, I remained on board for the entirety of our stays at both ports, much to the captain's amusement. When I had apologized to him for my behaviour at Diu, he replied, "You should not apologize, Doctor. It is the way of your race." Naturally, this only encouraged me to demonstrate that not all Europeans were hopeless inebriates, and the only way I could do so was to remain both continually present and sober.

Throughout our voyage from Alexandria, we had made no contact with British officialdom. However, as we were approaching India's southern tip, the captain summoned me to the quarterdeck and handed me a pair of powerful binoculars.

"What do you make of that?" he said, pointing into the distance.

With the naked eye, I could barely discern a spot on the horizon with a smudge of smoke rising above it, but the glass revealed a powerfully built warship, smoke rolling from its stacks.

"It appears to be a warship of some size."

"She is the *Black Prince,* one of your newest heavy cruisers, bearing down on us at top speed. She has several destroyers in her wake as well."

"What can this possibly mean?"

"I expect we shall find out soon. The *Prince* is good for twenty knots."

An hour later the great ship was no more than a mile distant. A string of collared flags fluttered from the ship's mast.

"They invite us to lunch," the captain said, with the binoculars at his eyes. "I have never been on a British warship before—at least, not as a captain. The experience should prove informative."

The thought of mingling socially with the senior officers of such a prestigious vessel filled me with dismay. Nonetheless, I retired to my cabin to obtain those garments I had with me that would be least inappropriate for the occasion. I returned to the foredeck to find the captain resplendent in a white uniform that shone with gold braid. A motor launch from the *Black Prince* was already splashing its way toward us. As I stood by the captain's side, I was suddenly struck by the fear that the *Black Prince's* captain might be another of Barington's confederates, and that the captain and I would find ourselves imprisoned on some trumped-up charge. I suggested as much to the captain in a whispered voice, but he dismissed the idea with a shake of his head.

"Sir Harry Speers is her captain. Though cunning, he is entirely devoid of initiative. He would not harm us unless he had orders. If he has orders, the entire fleet has orders. And there is no escape from the entire fleet."

I could not but admire this bluff fatalism.

"What, then, do you think he wants with us?" I asked.

"Information, of course," replied the captain. The impending collision between Lord Barington and your friend has aroused the interest of the entire East. I heard much talk in Bombay and Goa. Men worry over everything from the price of tin to the price of a captaincy."

The appearance of an impeccably dressed British ensign cut short our conversation. Ten minutes later we were aboard the launch, riding over the slow, heavy swells toward the enormous ship, which rose up above us like a great cliff. When we reached the ship, we transferred to a sort of landing platform and then ascended a long flight of stairs to the main deck, where a phalanx of officers greeted us beneath the *Prince*'s eight-inch guns. The captain squared himself, saluted confidently, and cried, "Request permission to come aboard, sir!" in a powerful voice. He may as well have been the first sea lord, come to inspect his fleet.

As we stepped past the assembled officers to meet Sir Harry, I was struck forcibly by how carefully the captain must have studied the means by which one man may gain mastery over the mind and thoughts of others. On the decks of the *Prophet* he strode as a unique figure, unlike any other. On the decks of the *Black Prince* he did the same. The great black boots he wore, despite the summer heat, added at least two inches to his already immense height, so that he towered over every man on deck. His uniform, which he must have reserved especially for rare occasions such as this, proclaimed that a black man could be just as regardful of his appearance as a white. Above all it was his easy, yet dignified confidence, in a situation that must have been entirely new to him, that commanded the respect of those around him.

At the luncheon itself, Sir Harry applied all of his consider-
able charm to learning how much I knew about what he
termed "your investigation," as though I were in charge
of affairs. My responses, of course, were quite guarded. I
expressed my deepest regrets over the tragic events in
Alexandria without making the least reference to the monstrous nature of the culprit involved. I was glad that our investigation had assumed an official nature, for this allowed me to
announce pompously that "the matter is too delicate to discuss" whenever the questioning took an undesirable path.

In any event, there was little that I could tell Sir Harry, for
his main concerns revolved around the arcana of imperial
politics, of which I was entirely ignorant. He was vitally concerned to know who would have Sir Roger's place, and who
would have the place to be vacated by the person to have Sir
Roger's, what would happen to Major Thomas, and, most of
all, how much credence to attach to "those disturbing
rumours concerning Lord Barington." My frequent pleas of
ignorance never distressed him; instead, he simply offered me
another glass of the superb claret that graced his table, which
I was always careful to decline, in part because of the captain's amused yet censorious eye.

The captain was, in fact, an extremely close observer of the
exchanges between Sir Harry and myself. He was quick to
insert a technical question regarding the operation of the
Black Prince whenever the opportunity was presented, rather
to Sir Harry's irritation, I should judge. That the captain was
present at the table at all suggested how urgently Sir Harry
wished for news. I strongly suspect that never before had a
black man sat at the captain's table of a major British warship,
and I doubt that Sir Harry cared for the honour. To have a
black man present was bad enough; to be on the receiving
end of his repeated questions, regardless of their harmless
subject matter, was close to insupportable.

Conversation ultimately languished, and it appeared that
complete silence should fall over the table, until the captain
engaged one of the more junior officers in a discussion of the
newly developed steam turbines that propelled the ship. The

man, it appeared, needed little prompting to wax eloquent on the subject. He let forth a stream of abstruse detail that evidently pleased the captain as much as it angered Sir Harry. After a few minutes, the latter brusquely rose to his feet, which was of course a signal for all the others to rise as well. As we stood there, Sir Harry bade us farewell with what struck me as a rather strained smile. The same ensign who had fetched us from the *Prophet* was deputized to return there, a duty that I believe he would have preferred to avoid. The captain made the return trip without speaking a word. When we arrived at the *Prophet,* he saluted the ensign graciously and we clambered aboard.

"This will not be the last time we enjoy a lunch at your navy's expense," said the captain, as we stood on deck and watched the launch make its way back to the warship. "If Sir Harry will suffer to have a black man at his table, the rest will follow."

The captain's assessment proved to be sound. As we made our way up the Coromandel coast, we were repeatedly hailed by British vessels. The smaller ships seemed to have orders simply to verify our position, but we dined twice with captains of frigates on our way to Mahabalipuram.

When we arrived at that ancient city, the captain spent the first two days disposing of the *Prophet*'s cargo and purchasing new stores, but on the third day we departed the ship prior to the first light. At the captain's suggestion, I wore my stoutest pair of boots and wore my revolver and holster on my belt. When I met the captain on deck, he handed me a rifle, which I put over one shoulder, and a swollen leather water bottle, which I slung over the other. He was similarly equipped. We trod the darkened, mysterious streets in silence for almost an hour before reaching the outskirts of the city. There we came to a ramshackle corral of sorts, in which a handful of horses and mules grazed, their powerful teeth gnawing audibly on the sparse, wiry stubble. A small outbuilding, worn and washed by the monsoon rains and seemingly in imminent danger of collapsing, stood by the gate. A nodding Hindu sat cross-legged with his back against this structure, a coil of rope sprawling across his knees.

"Aziz!" the captain's voice shook the man awake in an instant. "Where are our mounts?"

"A thousand pardons, honoured captain," the man cried. "My duties are most heavy."

"Where are our mounts?"

"They will be ready immediately, most honoured captain. My boy, a most vile and corrupt fellow, has deserted me. You shall have my finest mules."

"The supplies. Have you stolen those as well?"

"I have stolen nothing, your excellency. I have kept them safe."

"Fetch the mules. Dr. Watson and I will do your work for you."

While Aziz began his slow pursuit of our mounts, the captain and I retrieved saddles, bridles, and provisions from the gatehouse. As Aziz brought forward each sleepy, recalcitrant beast, the captain would sling a saddle over its back and cinch it tight. I assisted in the burdening of the creatures as best I could, but more than an hour had passed before the captain and I were bestride our animals. The slight coolness of the night had vanished, and the dull heat of the late Indian summer was already upon us.

"Where do you journey, great captain?" cried Aziz, as we began our departure.

"Not far. We should be back in a day. Two perhaps."

"Mysterious journeys are most dangerous," the man called, trotting beside us. "You must tell me your destination, so that I can come to your aid if you do not return."

"You will have your mules, Aziz. That is all you need to know."

"Of course, Captain, of course. The great captain is always most wise. But caution is also great wisdom. There can be much danger for two men travelling alone."

"Take care, Aziz, that you do not run into danger. You will have your mules. Return to your corral, and have fresh water for us when we return."

"Of course, Captain," said the man, slowing his pace at last. "May the gods smile on your journey."

"May they indeed," said the captain. "Remember, Aziz. Fresh water."

With that last stricture the captain turned his back on the Hindu. Orienting our course by the sun, I marked our direction as vaguely northwest, but beyond that I knew nothing. We rode in silence through an endless series of rising hills, green from the summer monsoon but baked by the heat. Sweat soaked every inch of my clothes. Taking my example from the captain, I drank deeply from my water bottle whenever he refreshed himself, though I found some difficulty even in that act when performed on the bony, rolling back of a mule. As the glistening sun rose ever higher in the sky, the captain at last halted and pointed to a distant hill.

"Beyond that hill is a ruined temple and a spring. We can refresh our mounts and wait for dark."

Mercifully, enough of the temple was standing to provide shade for both us and the mules, while the spring, swollen with the monsoon rains, assuaged the thirst of our mounts. The captain filled his water bags, selected towelling and a change of clothes from his baggage, and disappeared outside. In his absence I washed and changed. He returned in twenty minutes, looking refreshed, but already sweating.

"We have missed the great heat, but a man should not be travelling by late morning," he said, joining me on a fallen timber that provided the only seating in the ruins. "That fool Aziz did us no favour with his delays. We should eat and rest, Doctor, and pray that no Hindu arrive. Though this temple is abandoned, they would not care for our presence, nor that of our mules."

He took out a loaf of bread and cut off a slice with the great knife he kept thrust in his belt. He handed it to me and cut himself another. When we had consumed the loaf, washed down with draughts of cold spring water, we swept most of the debris from the floor and spread our bedrolls. I must not have realized the extent of my exhaustion, for no sooner had my head touched my pillow than I fell into the most profound slumber. I awakened hours later to feel the captain's hand on my shoulder. Working in wordless haste, we saddled our mules and returned to the trail, riding from about eight in the evening until two in the morning, when we made a rude camp under the stars. On this occasion, it was all I could do to complete the routine tasks of preparing the mules to pass the night unattended before falling once more into a deep and dreamless sleep. The relentless heat and monotony of the trail were such that I could hardly keep the hours of waking and sleeping separate in my mind. They all seemed to form one dreamy and exhausted whole, as though I were never truly asleep and never truly awake, but always in the act of passing from one stage to the other.

Fortunately, on the morrow my mind retrieved its normal clarity. As we shared another loaf for our breakfast, the broad, whitening sky revealed to us at last the object of our quest, a squat, brown, crumbling temple, situated no more than a mile distant on a high hill. We finished the bread quickly, saddled our mules, and were on our way.

Seen through the half light of dawn, the temple seemed scarcely more than an outcropping of rock from the hill itself. As we approached more closely, the structure's dimensions became more apparent, for it was no inconsiderable piece of work, but its outlines remained vague and indistinct. It was not until we gained the hill itself that the nature of the temple revealed itself to our eyes.

Though surrounded by a broad, stone wall and a number of smaller buildings, the temple seemed to rise directly out of the rock it rested upon, being built from the same brownish stone as the hill itself. The front of the temple was massive but low, while the rear soared upward several hundred feet in the air in a series of ungainly, bulbous protrusions. As we rode around the low wall to the central gate I was able to inspect the character of the architecture more closely.

The precision of the Classical school and the soaring grace of the Gothic are equally alien to the Hindu genius. It can surely be said of that religion that it inclines to emphasize the multitude of creation rather than the unity. No one who has not seen a Hindu temple firsthand can imagine the tropic profusion of form characteristic of this religion. It is the custom to adorn such structures with literally hundreds, nay, thousands, of sculpted images, which mingle the sacred and profane, human and animal, celestial and bestial in a manner that defies all comprehension. The artists who had decorated this temple appeared to have had a particular obsession with the female figure, which they presented with a voluptuousness and directness that would reduce the Venus di Milo herself to a shrinking schoolgirl in comparison.

I was amused to note that the captain gazed steadfastly at his saddle horn as we approached these wanton images, looking neither to the right nor the left. For my own part, the superhuman dimensions of these stone enchantresses possessed all the powers of Circe, and I shifted uneasily on my mount, plagued by thoughts of Mary's youthful embrace, longings that I cannot but acknowledge were entirely inappropriate for a man of my age.

"We may as well tether the mules here," said the captain abruptly, as we arrived at the temple gates. He vaulted to earth and busily gathered the mules' reins together, still keeping his eyes fixed to the ground.

"Yes, of course," I replied, dismounting as well. It was remarkable to see the captain, so masterful in all other circumstances, rendered so ill at ease. No wonder, then, that he had described this temple as "most impious"!

As we tied the mules, we heard the vicious barking of dogs, which reached a cacophony as we approached the temple gate itself. Through a gap in the gates I could see a furious pack of ill-coloured mongrels, all about the size of terriers, with fearsome teeth, fairly leaping in the air at the prospect of assaulting our persons.

"Monkey dogs," said the captain, with a quiet smile, as if this reception suited him. "The priests here do well."

The dogs continued their hysterical reaction to our presence for another ten minutes, finally falling silent at the approach of a small, brown-skinned, bright-eyed, barefoot girl. From my vantage point I watched as she grasped a thick rope and, exerting a strength of which I scarcely felt her capable, pulled the gates open. As she did so, the dogs clustered round us, silent but watchful, and baring their fangs at our least movement.

"You are visitor?" the girl asked, in the unmistakable lilt of Babu English.

"Captain MacDougall and Dr. Watson," I responded, feeling that under the circumstances I ought to take the lead.

"You come," the girl said, turning and trotting off at a brisk rate. The captain and I strode after her. The dogs followed at a cautious distance and, as we continued our journey, ultimately dispersed.

It was only once we were inside the temple gates that I could truly appreciate the size and complexity of the edifice that was the object of our quest. We found ourselves in a large courtyard, surrounded by small temples that reproduced features of the large one in miniature. Rather than true buildings, they appeared to be carved bodily out of immense blocks of stone, a sort of three-dimensional *trompe-l'oeil* to which the Hindu are much addicted. Before us lay an enormous tank, with row upon row of steps leading down to it, used by worshippers for ritual ablutions. While we stood there, a wizened man of painful thinness appeared, with no more clothing on his body than a rag tied about his waist. He greeted us with a low bow and a few words of Hindu. To my surprise, the captain returned the bow, and I thought it best to do likewise. However, our bows appeared to alarm the man, who fell to his knees and literally grovelled before us. At this behaviour the old fire returned to the captain's eye.

"You see these people's folly," he growled. "He will be another ten minutes cleansing himself of the taint he has acquired receiving our bows."

"One must be patient to serve Allah," I responded.

A momentary look of amusement shone in the captain's eyes.

"He is of the lowest caste allowed within the temple itself. Orders to care for our mules must pass through him to the lower orders outside the gates. We must find a member of a higher caste to inform the priests of our presence."

We stood in silence until the man finally returned to his feet. The captain spoke a few halting words in what I took to be Hindu, which seemed to distress the man almost as much as our bows. He burst into tears and gesticulated helplessly with his aged limbs. The captain repeated his words, which summoned forth another torrent of tears. The captain repeated himself a third time, and at last the old man shuffled off.

"Was that Hindu?" I asked, as we watched the poor fellow make his painful way toward the temple gates.

"My dear doctor," said the captain with a laugh, "did the British army not teach you that India has as many languages as gods? I spoke southern dialect, though not well. I had occasion to learn it while enjoying the hospitality of your government."

I was about to make some response when a young man approached, dressed in a simple robe of fine white cloth, with an air of self-possession that immediately marked him off as a member of the priesthood. He nodded, and spoke a single word. The captain replied in kind, and the youth motioned for us to follow. Instead of walking directly to the temple, we turned to the left, walking past a series of fantastically carved pillars.

"In a Hindu temple you must always walk to the left," said the captain in a low voice. "Otherwise you profane their gods. These pillars commemorate the manifestations of their god Shiva. We must pause and pay our respects to each. It is the last manifestation that we seek."

"Who is Shiva?" I asked.

"A very great demon, much beloved in these parts."

The system of the Hindu mythology, if indeed it has one, must surely remain a closed book to the Western mind. The reasons why a god might have two arms on some occasions and four on another, might sometimes be a shrivelled ascetic and on others a brutal and corrupt libertine, and finally, why he might prefer on occasions to substitute a jackal's head for his more normal human one, are never explained. Yet each of these transformations was compellingly depicted in the carvings we passed on our circumferential journey.

"You spoke of the final manifestation?" I said to the captain, as we approached the completion of our cycle.

"Yes. That uncarved stone up ahead. As these people believe in everything, so they believe in nothing. We must persuade them that, unclean as we are in their eyes, still we may approach Shiva in this last manifestation."

I could only marvel at the captain's confidence that he could somehow navigate the mysteries of this infinite, and infinitely confusing, system of belief. His own faith seemed to have the razor edge of a scimitar, ready to cut through anything, but how to cut through everything and nothing? We came at last to the uncarved post and stopped before it. The priest, who had previously walked well before us, came back and joined us at the square, blank stone pillar. A slight superior smile played at his lips. When he judged that we had genuflected enough, he motioned to us to follow and led us before the very entrance of the temple itself. There he picked up a small bucket of water and, using a gourd for a ladle, scattered a few drops on our foreheads, the same slight superior smile playing at his lips, as though amused, if not amazed, at his own kindness to the unwashed.

"Very well, Doctor," said the captain, who in his own way was as amused by the proceedings as the priest. "Let us see what Allah will grant us from the hand of the infidel."

With that we began climbing the broad steps leading into the temple. We passed through several antechambers, each worked and carved in such detail as to all but overwhelm the observer. Belgian lacemakers never plied their craft with more delicacy than these artisans of stone. The rising sun, shining through carved stone windows, bathed the walls in curious patterns of light and dark, throwing some details in bold relief, while casting others in impenetrable darkness.

We came at last to the central temple, immediately turning to the left down a long corridor, whose ponderous columns called to mind the tread of elephants. The priest led the way, pausing occasionally before the more impressive statues, which either smiled beneficently or grimaced in mysterious anger. The captain, who never appeared distressed or pleased by these delays, maintained a respectful silence, and I did the same.

After we had completed our journey around the exterior of the temple, the young priest suddenly led us through a narrow doorway into a corridor that was almost pitch black. Despite the gloom, our guide set a brisk pace down the long, twisting passageway, which soon bereft me of any sense of direction. I stumbled along blindly, desperate to keep up with the steady tread of the captain's boots. At last we came to an ancient spiral staircase, hewn of massive timbers. On either side of the entrance, brass oil lamps burned quietly, sending forth a welcome illumination.

"These stairs will take us to the inner sanctum of Shiva," said the captain. "The Hindu say that those who profane Shiva's temple are the food of demons. I will trust in Allah for this encounter, but you must make your own provisions."

Fortunately, the young priest seemed deaf to this sardonic account of his religion. Almost invisible in the darkness, he sprinkled us once more with what I presumed was the Hindu version of holy water, murmuring soft prayers all the while. Then he blew out the lamps and chanted in a singsong, high-pitched tone. At last he relit the lamps and hurried out the doorway. Once the sound of his footsteps had faded from our ears, the captain began the ascent of the stairs.

The task was not an easy one. From the outside, I had estimated the height of the temple as more than two hundred feet, and we must have climbed fully three quarters of that distance before reaching the top. Far more inconvenient than the height was the darkness. We quickly left the light of the oil lamps behind and found no others along the way. An occasional whisper of fresh air alerted us to the presence of a window of some sort, but these openings, wherever they were, provided no illumination whatsoever. As a result, we climbed upward in perfect darkness.

"The fellow could have at least provided us with a candle," I remarked, after a stumble by the captain had brought us into a brief collision.

"The Hindu build their temples for gods, not men," he

replied. "As those of no caste, we are privileged even to be here."

I could not but bow to the captain's superior knowledge of the East, and so continued the rest of the climb in silence. We arrived at last in a circular room, virtually identical to the one we had quitted below, whose lamps flickered gently at our approach.

"What do we do now?" I whispered.

"We wait, of course," returned the captain.

The room was lacking in furniture of any sort, so we remained standing for an interminable length of time, until at last a single spark of light emerged from the darkness. A boy holding a candle appeared and motioned us to follow. The prospect of yet another mysterious journey exhausted my patience.

"Where are we going now?" I demanded.

"To a large room directly beneath the central dome," the captain explained. "Speech is not forbidden within these walls, Doctor, but neither is it encouraged, particularly in English. If there is anything you need to know, I shall alert you of it."

Such an answer was hardly to my liking, but the matter was obviously out of my hands, and so I followed in silence. As we continued along our way, I was glad to notice a gradual increase in illumination. After several hours of almost complete darkness, it was a profound relief to be able to see one's hand before one's face. We could see the end of the corridor now, which seemed to be almost ablaze with light. This proved to be the large room the captain had spoken of. As we approached it, our guide politely stepped aside and ushered us in. He pointed to a pair of pillows on the floor, richly embroidered, that were obviously intended for our comfort. Once we were seated, the young man disappeared.

The room we found ourselves in was, in fact, more than large. It was enormous. It was lit with dozens of candles, each more than three feet high and as thick as a man's arm, dripping beeswax. The heat they generated in that already tropic climate can scarcely be imagined. The warmth and languor of the atmosphere was further enhanced by smouldering spirals of incense, which hung from the ceiling on immensely long cords.

The candles gave fitful illumination to the carved interior of the dome, which has seemed to me ever since a sort of apotheosis of the Hindu religion. The entirety of creation was depicted in that mute stone, in a manner that irresistibly recalled Michelangelo's sublime decorations of the Sistine Chapel, but also perhaps more reminiscent of Homeric myth than the chaste homilies of our own Book. At the apex of the dome, a god and goddess were locked in the most lascivious embrace imaginable, surrounded by lesser deities, all similarly occupied. As one descended from this most peculiar heaven, the entire phantasmagoria of the Hindu pantheon was displayed. In the flickering candlelight, women with six arms, men with the heads of elephants, seemed to issue forth from the stone and then return. At the sight of such metamorphoses, Ovid himself would have shattered his pen in despair.

Below these minor gods was the realm of our own hapless race, crushed beneath the great wheel of birth, life, and death. As the observer's eye made its way about the silent chamber, women endured the pangs of childbirth with the dumb suffering of medieval maids, boys and girls were dragged insensibly to adulthood, men and women flourished in the brief midday of their lives before displaying the pinched, wizened limbs and hunched backs of old age. As if this were not enough to chill the heart of the most carefree observer, there was yet another circle, that of the Underworld, where pitiless demons tore the flesh of the damned. The care the sculptor took to capture both the gluttonous delight of the demons, and the intimate details of their victims' anguish, sent an endless thrill of horror through my soul.

Confronted by this nightmarish tableau, the eye had no place to turn other than the great, freestanding statue that dominated the room, placed at the very centre of the chamber. In this apparition, the god, whom I took to be Shiva, had four arms and stood on one leg, the other thrust out across his body. The face of the god betrayed that curious, impassive beneficence that the Hindu find appropriate for scenes of unrelieved carnage.

Seated around the circumference of the room were dozens of silent motionless monks, clad in white robes, so lost in meditation that they hardly seemed alive. I ignored their presence entirely as my mind wandered back and forth across the great panorama that arched above me, returning again and again to the mysterious statue that appeared to reign as the special genius of the place.

How long my head swam in this reverie, held captive by this unholy intoxication of the soul, I am unable to say. But a touch on the arm from the captain awakened me with a jolt. He, of course, was staring steadfastly at the floor, trusting fiercely in Allah. But his touch was not intended to rescue me from the maelstrom of death and desire that writhed above my head; rather it was to alert me to the presence of a tiny, bustling man, almost naked, who suddenly appeared before us. He was accompanied by a short, plump, and yet stately man of early middle age, obviously a priest, dressed carefully in white robes, with a shrewd, bland face. His face had the patient cunning of an able bureaucrat rather than the vacant holiness of a monk. I wondered how he could endure the solitude of his calling.

Captain MacDougall rose at his approach and bowed, and I followed suit. The younger man nodded in the captain's direction and spoke.

"It is pleasant to encounter such promising acolytes," he said in remarkably unaccented English. "I trust your journey was not unduly arduous."

"Our journey is nothing. We seek the special learning of this place," replied the captain.

"Indeed? And for what end?"

"To put an end to suffering."

The priest smiled at the captain's words.

"The world never changes," he said.

"No," the captain replied. "That is why we have come to you."

"You are welcome to what we have. What, precisely, can we tell you?"

"We wish to know the lore of the Bada."

"To pursue such things is not wise."

"Then we will grow wise along the way."

"Sit, Captain. The old man will read for you."

We sat again on our pillows, while the old man arranged his shrunken limbs on the stone floor. When I saw this, I offered him my pillow, but he waved me away.

"The master disdains the needs of the flesh," the younger priest remarked serenely, yet with a hint of sarcasm that seemed grotesquely out of place in such a setting. After speaking he turned and clapped his hands twice. The young man who had accompanied us earlier reappeared, bearing an armful of tattered scrolls, which he deposited at the side of the ancient priest. Then he left but returned once more, bearing a small stool, upon which the younger priest immediately sat. The captain fixed his eyes on the old man and spoke.

"Who are the Bada?"

"The Bada are not of our race," said the old man, in a painfully thin, singsong voice. "They are not of the dark race. They are the seed of the blood of Shiva."

"When was the blood of Shiva shed?"

"In the Millennium of the Immortals, when the sun swallowed the earth. Shiva saved the earth, and the sun slew him. From his blood the Bada were born. With their blood they washed him, and he was reborn. The Bada are sacred to Shiva, and he forgives their evil."

"Who is their leader?"

"They have no lord but Shiva."

"Who is their leader?"

"I have told you. You must not ask again."

"Who is Harat?"

The old man dropped his eyes and began to fumble with the manuscripts. I thought he would read us something, but instead he simply untied and retied the worn black strings that bound the rolls of paper.

"Tell us about the Easterners," prompted the captain.

"They came. They did not seek gold. They sought wisdom."

"They came to this temple," said the captain, as both a question and a statement.

"They came," echoed the priest.

"What did they leave?"

The old man shook his head. "Impurities," he said, at last.

"Here? Within the temple?"

"You are tiring him," interjected the young priest. "Father, do you grow tired?"

"I grow tired," echoed the old man.

"The little father disdains the flesh," replied the captain, with a flash of anger. "Tell us of these impurities, little father."

"Shiva preserves his own. They could not be destroyed."

"These were relics of the Bada?"

"Shiva's hand was upon them. He sent his fire to those who opposed him."

"Then the relics are here."

"Father grows very tired!" the young priest shouted, leaping from his stool.

"I am not tired," the old man responded.

"You grow tired," the young priest insisted, bending over him.

"There is a time for all things," said the old priest, untying one of the scrolls and unrolling it. His movements were calm and unhurried, though the young priest seemed on the verge of ripping the document from his hands at any moment. A vague but insistent murmur arose among the assembled monks. For my part, I was appalled at the dissension that the captain had provoked with his questioning. We were but two, far from any possible assistance and surrounded by an angry and suspicious multitude. Yet the captain, though he may have been intimidated by stone goddesses, had no fear of men. He continued to question the old priest.

"Do these writings speak of the impurities?"

"There is a time for all things," the old man repeated, as though he had not heard the captain. "There is a time for all things, even the dance of Shiva."

"The impurities," said the captain once more. "Can you tell us of the impurities?"

"Yes," replied the old man, mournfully. The excited murmur around us grew louder.

"Read to us," said the captain. At his words, the young priest sputtered, and then clapped his hand to his mouth and shut his eyes, as though physically overwhelmed.

The old man spread out the scroll before him with elaborate care. The faded parchment was covered with a faint, spidery script that should have been indecipherable in that light. Yet the old man, bending far forward, commenced to read it in his quavering, singsong voice. He would read a passage, halt, and then wait while the assembled monks began a slow and lugubrious chant, devoid, to my ears at least, of any musical form whatsoever and, like so much of India, seemingly without end. When the chant came to an end at last, the old priest would read another passage and the cycle would begin again. As for the words, they were entirely unintelligible to me, and the captain's expression gave me no evidence that he found the recital more profitable than myself.

As the reader may well imagine, I had long since given up all hope of obtaining any information that might have even the slightest bearing on the case. Indeed, the only question before my mind at this point was whether the captain and I could contrive to escape with our lives. As the chanting droned on, the old man hunched before us appeared to sink into a stupor, his bowed body crumpling up like a discarded handkerchief. The younger priest, still seated on his little stool, chanted with the rest, but I could observe his shrewd, restless eyes darting maliciously about the room beneath half-closed lids. I glanced numerous times at the captain, hoping for some indication of his intent, but he remained impassive, his eyes staring into the stone floor beneath us.

At last the chanting faded, and silence reclaimed the room, like the morning light asserting itself against the darkness. When the silence was complete, the captain spoke.

"Where lies the Bada now?"

"Gone. All gone," replied the old priest.

"Yet they are sacred to Shiva."

"All gone."

"There is a grave within this temple."

"No."

"There is a grave sacred to Shiva, accurst to men."

"No."

"There is a grave you cannot purify, cannot cast out."

"It is forbidden! The children of light must obey Shiva."

"This is a temple of Shiva."

"The children of light must obey Shiva."

"Shiva is angry."

"Men must endure the anger of Shiva. It is their lot. The children of light must obey Shiva."

The captain held forth his arm.

"Am I of the children of light?"

The old man shook his head wordlessly.

"Am I one of the children of light?"

"This is forbidden."

"I have come to cleanse you, to bear away the grave of the Bada."

"You cannot know these things."

"I have come to bear away the grave of the Bada."

The old man did not reply. The captain thrust forth his arm again.

"Am I of the children of light?"

The priest shook his head fearfully.

"Am I of the children of light?"

"No," cried the old priest, "you are of the dark race. You are a son of the night."

"I am a son of the night. I have come to bear away the grave of the Bada."

The old priest fell silent for a long time.

"He is the one of whom you spoke," he said at last, staring into the ground.

"He is the one," said the young priest.

"I am the one," said the captain.

"You will bear this burden?" the old priest asked.

"I will bear it," said the captain.

"Your soul is very dark."

The captain smiled.

"There is a place for all things," he said. "Your house has borne this matter long enough. It is time for me to bear it away."

With these words the captain rose to his feet. That simple exercise of his commanding physical presence sent an electric thrill throughout the room. The assembled monks quavered and fell back. The young priest sprang from his stool and glanced uneasily from the captain to the old man, still cross-legged on the floor. At length the ancient priest warily raised his head, only to encounter the captain's penetrating gaze. He cringed and shrank back down onto the floor.

"Show him," he whispered at last. "It is the dance of Shiva." With that, he climbed painfully to his feet and seemed to scuttle away like a crab.

The captain turned his attention to the young priest.

"For your sake, I hope you know what you are doing," the priest said. His brisk, modern tone jerked me back to the present. The world of Shiva was suddenly far away.

"For my sake, and yours," returned the captain.

"You were foolish to come. You are meddling in affairs that are none of your concern."

"Perhaps. What news have you from Sumatra?"

The young priest glared at him in speechless horror. He clapped his hands twice and turned away from us. At his action the monks silently rose to their feet and filed out, bearing their candles. The chamber darkened rapidly as they departed, and we were in danger of being plunged once more into complete darkness, when a slender, cringing figure appeared, bearing a flaming torch.

"Undoubtedly, our guide," the captain said to me in an ironic tone. "It has been a long day, Doctor, and I apologize. But this should put an end to it."

We followed the man back down the winding tunnel that led to the stairs and made our descent. Then we passed through another tunnel and descended another set of stairs, these of stone and very ill-made. At length we found ourselves in a room whose dimensions I was utterly unable to comprehend.

Our guide's flickering torch revealed a floor of natural stone, strewn with ridges of earth and gravel, and a low, vaulted ceiling, but the walls themselves were not apparent. I heard distinctly the sound of rushing water and sensed its coolness. As we walked across the bare stone, I could hear scurrying feet and occasionally catch a glimpse of small, fierce eyes, reflecting back the light from the burning torch.

"Rats," said the captain by way of explanation. "You are not afraid of them, are you, Doctor?"

"If that's all they are."

"Ah, your imagination runs away with you. But do keep an eye out for cobras."

With that charming injunction in mind, we continued our exploration of the chamber. I was struck by the coolheadedness of our guide, who led us without the slightest hesitation, though for any Hindu the place must have been swarming with supernatural danger. At last we came to a simple box of stone, set on a massive plinth of dark granite. The proportions of the box were unmistakably those of a sarcophagus and provided mute testimony of its contents. The stone itself was well-worked and unmarked, except for a faint inscription on the cover. The captain held his torch over the cover and blew the dust from the inscription.

"'Sacred to Shiva'," he muttered. "'Let none approach who cannot endure his dance.' Well, Doctor, let us see what Allah has reserved for us."

So saying, he passed his torch to me and grasped the lid of the box, a large, heavy slab of stone, at one end and jerked it upwards. As he raised the one end of the slab, the other began to slide downward, slowly at first, but then gathering momentum, until it fell to the floor with a crash that echoed ominously throughout the cavern.

Here our guide's courage deserted him, and one could hardly blame him. Murmuring prayers and apologies, he quickly made his retreat.

"Try to mark his path," said the captain, as we watched the flame recede into the darkness. "I don't fancy getting lost in this place."

When the last trace of light faded from our vision, we turned to the open vault. The sight that greeted us was not what I expected. There was no ghastly, shrunken corpse, wrapped in decayed finery. Instead there was a wooden chest, perhaps three feet long, obviously of extreme age, bound with dark metal. Otherwise, the resting place was empty.

"Let us be off," said the captain, scooping up the box. Then he paused and handed it to me. He walked round to where the lid rested on the floor and, taking it up once more, carefully slid the massive slab back into place.

"A thief should honour the god he robs," he said by way of explanation. "I believe that I should carry the box. We may encounter some of the monks on the way out, and it would alarm them less to see it in my possession."

"Yes, of course, if you think it best," I responded. "What do you think can be in the box?"

"Not a great deal, to judge by the weight," he said. "But I prefer not to open it until we are on board ship. We have tried these people's patience to the limit already. There is a limit to the amount of sacrilege we can expect them to endure."

"May I ask how you were able to induce them to allow us to come this far?"

"That is a story for another time, Doctor, when we are safely on board the *Prophet*."

"But can you tell me, at least, what is the dance of Shiva?"

The flickering light of the torch allowed me to see a brief smile decorate the captain's normally austere visage.

"The Hindu believe many things. When Shiva dances, all things come to an end and are reborn. The great statue we saw above was of the dance of Shiva. Let us be off, Doctor. My torch is growing faint."

By great good fortune, we found our way through that dank, black cellar, up the staircase, and out through the last of those infernal, twisting tunnels without a single wrong turn. We found ourselves at last in the great outer hallway of the temple, lit from the west by soft shafts of evening light. We had spent an entire day in the temple. In the twilight we could hear the faint buzz and murmur of hidden voices.

"We are being watched," said the captain softly, without turning his head. "Let us be off."

As we strode out into the courtyard I observed our mules waiting for us, tied at the gatepost.

"These people want us gone," said the captain, "but it will be a dry ride home. The water bags are empty."

"Shouldn't we fill them?"

"Not here. And I doubt that the local water would suit your belly, Doctor. You must have had ample experience with such things. I shall buy you a glass of Madeira when we return to Mahabalipuram."

Despite my fatigue, I could not help but be amused by the captain's offer. By their history, the Mussulmans seemed to think it more holy to slaughter the infidel than to buy him a glass, but I hesitated to broach the subject. While I pondered the question, the captain wrapped the mysterious box in canvas, bound it with rope, and lashed it securely to one of the pack mules. Examining the saddlebags of his own mule, he drew forth his revolvers, holsters, belt, and knife.

"These people take nothing and leave nothing. Did you not find that to be the case, Doctor?"

"I prefer not to generalize."

"Ah. Most wise. I have bread for our dinner. A dry meal, but worth having. I suggest we eat in the saddle."

An account of our long, hot, dusty ride back to Mahabalipuram would, I fear, bore the reader as thoroughly as it did the captain and myself. On the outskirts of that city, we made our way to Aziz, the ragged and raffish gentleman from whom the captain had rented the mules.

"The distinguished captain," he cried, bobbing his head energetically, as we came into sight. "Your journey was most fortunate, I am sure."

"That remains to be seen," said the captain, descending from the saddle. "Perhaps you would allow us a drink in exchange for the safe return of your mules."

"Yes, you have given them such splendid care. Here is my Englishman's water for your convenience. Please drink heartily at my expense."

I confess that as I staggered down from the saddle I could scarcely resist drinking directly from the urn itself, so great was the dehydration I had suffered on the journey. But I managed to contain myself as the captain ladled out a brimming cup, which I instantly drank down. The temperature of that viscous liquid must have been well over one hundred degrees, but seldom have I had a more welcome draught. I returned the cup to the captain, who filled it and drank it down himself. While Aziz busied himself with the mules, we continued to reduce his precious supply until, as the captain proclaimed, there was nothing left but mud. Aziz, who no doubt had had one eye on us the entire time, instantly flew to our sides.

"One glass only, gentlemen, please! I am a poor man, proud to serve such gentlemen as yourself, but you must consider other gentlemen as well!"

"Only a parched man would drink your water, Aziz," returned the captain. "Besides, you will have no more customers today."

"I am sure the great captain is correct," cried Aziz, shifting his ground with that exuberance so characteristic of the Eastern trader. "Please tell me more of the great success of your journey."

"There is nothing more to tell," said the captain, lifting the box to his shoulder.

"The little monks were helpful? They have great wealth. Blessings be to Shiva."

"Praise be to Allah," returned the captain.

"To be sure, Captain, to be sure. But Shiva is a great god as well."

"There is no god but Allah."

"The captain is most wise. But those who wrong Shiva are the food of demons."

"Those who serve Allah can do no wrong," said the captain, shortly. "Come, Doctor. We have had enough of this fellow."

"Farewell, Captain!" shouted Aziz, as we made our way through the marketplace. "You will remember my splendid mules!"

"Why did he enquire of Shiva?" I asked when we were well clear of the mule trader's hovel.

"Word has spread more rapidly than I would have wished. You will have to forego your Madeira, Doctor. We depart from this foul port tonight."

CHAPTER XXIII

The Curiosity of the East

HEN WE RETURNED TO the *Prophet,* the captain instantly set about preparing to cast off. Evidently he had anticipated that an immediate departure might be required, for the entire crew was already on board. I retired to my cabin with the mysterious box, washed myself as best I could, dined on cold chicken sent down by the cook, and collapsed on my bunk, the mysterious box stowed safely beneath it, still bound in canvas. I fell instantly into a dreamless sleep, from which I was awakened by an insistent rapping on my door. To my befuddled wits the interlude seemed only a matter of moments, so great was my exhaustion, but in fact I had slept for hours, for my cabin was almost pitch black, the small port-hole revealing only a faint gleam of moonlight on the restless waves.

"You are awake, Doctor?" said the captain's soft voice.

"Barely," I replied.

"Good. Please join me in my cabin at your earliest convenience."

Minutes later, I made my way abovedecks, the box on my shoulder. I encountered only a few of the crew members, none of whom gave me a second glance. When I arrived at the captain's cabin, the door opened at my first knock and the captain silently ushered me in. I placed the box on a table that he had obviously cleared for that purpose. The curtains for his windows, I noticed, were drawn.

The captain pulled off the canvas and inspected the curious lock that bound the casket shut.

"I should hate to destroy Mr. Holmes' evidence," he said. "Perhaps it would be wiser to cut through the metal." So saying, he took a small metal saw from a tool kit resting on the floor, and carefully cut a small piece of metal from the hasp of the lock, which he then opened.

"That should do it," he said. "Now let us see what we have."

He pushed back the lid. Inside was a small, mummified skeleton, wrapped in bands of crumbling cloth. The bony fingers, resting on the chest, held a small, golden sphere. The blank eye sockets of a tiny skull stared up at us in silence. The slow passage of the centuries only seemed to enhance the solemnity of death that lingered about the minute figure.

"A child," I said.

"No," said the captain, "look at the teeth. This is one of the Bada, the monkey men."

I stared in amazement. There was no doubt that what he said was true. The tiny skull was distinctly nonhuman, and the mouth showed the enlarged incisors so typical of rodents. As I looked more closely, I marvelled at the skeleton, at once so similar to that of a human and yet different in numerous details. The head was large, yet perhaps not quite so large in proportion to the body as is the human head. The neck was short. I wondered if the creature would be able to turn its head as easily as a human. The arms were very long, halfway between a man's and a monkey's, with grasping hands and opposable thumbs. The pelvis would clearly permit an upright gait, though I doubted that the creature was capable of running for long distances.

"What is this?" I asked, touching the golden sphere.

"A bughola, a world ball, like one of your globes," said the captain. "The Hindu make them. You can see that it is engraved with coastal markings."

I brought my eye close to the globe and could indeed see the outline of the coast of Africa traced delicately in the shining metal. Intriguing though the object was, it held far less interest for me than the skeleton. Here at last was conclusive evidence that the mysterious encounter I had in Diu was more than an inebriate's fantasy, that Holmes' bizarre theory of Elizabeth's murder was in fact correct.

"Incredible," I said, more to myself than to the captain. "I must make a thorough examination."

"Of course," he replied, in a low tone, "but not at the present time. I must urge the utmost caution in the handling of this entire matter."

So saying, the captain shut the lid of the box and motioned me to a chair.

"There are matters we must discuss," he said, speaking to me in a more intimate tone than before. "Our visit to the temple of Shiva is already known. If there is anyone who knew of this casket, then they will know that we have it. One of the legends of the monkey men is that they keep their graves inviolate of humans. When the old priest warned us that we would be food for demons, he was not speaking figuratively. I would not have any member of the crew know of this, and there are few secrets aboard a ship."

"Then what do you suggest?"

"I suggest that I put this box in a secret place, where it shall remain until we arrive at Singapore."

"You don't feel your caution is excessive?"

"I do not. I almost wish that we had thought to bring the box aboard secretly, except that efforts to avoid attention so often attract it. Now, Doctor, I suggest you depart. Let us return precisely to our former schedule."

The slow pace of our journey, which had been only tedious, now became exasperating as well. Every morning I arose at dawn with the knowledge that the key to the entire mystery was in our possession, yet there was nothing I could do about it. When we reached Calcutta, I made immediate inquiries to learn if Holmes had dispatched a cable, but was unsurprised to learn that none had arrived. There was little news that could travel safely through a medium so exposed to interference.

The vagaries of trade required us to spend more than a week at the capital of India, but I was so belayed by fever that I could scarcely stir abovedecks and so was unable to inspect the city's fabled elegance. I could not but feel that my recent adventures with the captain had made me a possible target for assault, or even murder, and in my weakened condition I thought it unwise to expose myself unnecessarily to danger. My illness persisted after we left that port and entered on the ultimate leg of our journey, first swinging east to Rangoon across the Bay of Bengal before making the long descent down the Malay Peninsula to the Malacca Straits.

It appeared that our stay in Rangoon was particularly lucrative for the captain. He never spoke to me of such things, but it was impossible to ignore the sale of the ship's cargo, in its entirety, to an aged Chinese broker, and its subsequent replacement by an enormous and diverse lot of manufactured items, "parasols and bicycles," he liked to say, though that was hardly an adequate description of the goods that filled the *Prophet*'s hold and crowded her decks.

It was not until we quitted Burma that my health began to recover and I felt it once more safe to go above. The weather out of Rangoon was uncommonly pleasant and clear. We were travelling in the main shipping lane bound for the straits, and it was a rare moment when we were out of sight of either smoke or sail. On the third day out, I joined the captain at the rail at the stern of the ship. He was gazing intently out to sea through a pair of enormous binoculars. By straining my eyes to the utmost, I could barely observe a faint smudge of smoke on the horizon. If the day had been less than perfect, I am sure I could have seen nothing.

"We are being followed," the captain muttered, taking the glass from his eye and passing it to me. "She came closer yesterday, but now that she has marked us she's fallen back. What is she waiting for?"

The day provided no answer to the riddle. The three days following were overcast, but the fourth dawned with an almost incandescent clearness.

"She is still with us," the captain reported to me over breakfast, "so far back I can make nothing of her. We arrive in Penang in two days. When we leave Penang we are in the straits proper. If anything is to happen, I believe it will happen today, or perhaps tonight."

The day passed without incident. At dinner the captain informed me that he had doubled the watch, and I retired that evening with a distinct sense of unease. But I was not prepared to be awakened as I was, by a blinding flash of white light that blazed through my small porthole with all the intensity of the direct rays of the midday sun. After about thirty seconds the illumination ceased, leaving me groggy and stupefied. I stumbled into my clothes and ascertained the hour, which proved to be well past midnight. Then I went out abovedecks and sought out the captain.

As soon as I was abovedecks, much of the mystery resolved itself. An enormous warship, even larger than the *Black Prince,* loomed out of the darkness, scarcely a thousand yards off our port bow. The low rumble of its powerful engines filled the air. A beam of light, of amazing intensity, shone from the great ship on to ours. I found the captain conferring with a crew member, who was in the process of raising signal flags.

"Who is she?" I cried.

"The *Indomitable,*" he replied, "your newest and most powerful battleship. Equipped, as you see, with the latest in electrical illumination. I believe I could replace the *Prophet* with the price of such a lamp. I am informing the *Indomitable* that we mean her no harm."

"What does she want with us?"

"Why, I believe she is sending us a passenger."

"A passenger? Under these circumstances?"

"Yes," replied the captain, obviously amused by my incredulity. "I believe this is your navy's idea of a clandestine rendezvous."

Indeed, I could already see a small boat putting out from the *Indomitable*. Suddenly the great electrical beam flickered on again, first capturing the pilot boat in its glare but then travelling rapidly across the water until it shone directly into our eyes. A moment later it switched off. The abrupt shift from artificial brilliance to natural darkness left me virtually blind. I gripped the rail before me for reassurance. While I struggled to regain my vision, the few members of the crew on deck lowered a rope ladder over the side to welcome our mysterious guest. Minutes later I heard a voice that, all unconsciously, I was already expecting.

"Good evening, Watson. I apologize for disturbing your slumbers in such a manner, but Admiral Watkins insisted that we make the transfer at night. I understand that you have raided the crypt of the Bada."

CHAPTER XXIV

The Crypt of the Bada

ESPITE THE LATENESS OF the hour, Holmes insisted on inspecting the casket the captain and I had retrieved. When we laid it before him on the captain's table and opened the lid, he stared down at its contents with a degree of concentration such as I had rarely observed.

"Remarkable," he said at last. "You observe the dentition, Watson?"

"Of course."

"I wonder what became of the creature, the one that bit me aboard the *Southern Star*. I strongly suspect . . ."

"Yes?"

"That that creature was Elizabeth's murderer. A pretty problem for the English legal system. I doubt that such a beast could be brought to trial. Tell me, Captain, have you ever heard of the Bada travelling so far west as London itself?"

The captain shook his head.

"I would have said it was impossible. They are never seen outside of Malay. It was centuries ago when they came as far as India, and this is the only one that remained."

"Are you sure?"

"How can any man be sure?"

"True enough. What is it he holds in his hands?"

"A bughola—a world ball, a globe, as you would say."

"Does it contain anything?"

"Perhaps. We decided not to perform an examination."

"Then let us have a look now."

So saying, Holmes delicately plucked the shining gold sphere from the creature's bony grasp and surveyed it intently through his most powerful lens.

"Extraordinary workmanship," he said, laying it down on the table for our inspection. "When do you date it, Captain?"

The captain smiled.

"Why do you ask me?" he inquired.

Holmes threw him a sharp glance.

"The penal records of the India Office are exceptionally complete," he said. "Ten years ago, the Helena Barracks in Delhi played host to a remarkable congeries of offenders, including a Brahmin priest turned social revolutionary, several aged but apparently dangerous scholars, and a gentleman referred to only as 'a black revolutionary calling himself MacDougall.' Furthermore, Captain, I have the distinct impression that you have made a special study of the Bada's lore."

"Perhaps."

"Well enough. How old is the temple in which you found this?"

"Well over a thousand years. It was constructed during the time of Narasimhavarman, who founded the port of Mahabalipuram. But this casket came much later, after the revival of Krishna, perhaps around 1450."

Holmes stared at the golden ball, rubbing his forehead in vexation.

"The workmanship is indisputably Chinese," he said, as though he half expected the captain to contest the point. "But how can you be so confident of the date? The revival of Krishna worship itself began more than a thousand years ago."

"True. But the inscription on the block of stone Dr. Watson and I removed asks forgiveness of Shiva and begs revenge on the Cursed One, the bringer of great uncleanness, and that could only have been Muhammad bin Tugluq, who conquered the area at the beginning of the fourteenth century, by the will of Allah, though the Hindu will not tell you that."

"That still gives more than a century to account for," answered Holmes, turning the sphere gently in his hands. "What is more, Chinese travellers have been known in India almost since the birth of Christ. Why pick the date of 1450?"

"Have you never," said the captain, "heard of the great junks of Cheng-Ho?"

"Never."

"Cheng-Ho was an admiral of the Ming Dynasty and a remarkable man, Mr. Holmes. A representative of a seafaring nation such as yourself should know more about him. In his time, his voyages dwarfed those of the West. He visited the Malay archipelago and India several times, and ultimately came as far west as Aden and Jidda. He most assuredly would have gone farther had not his imperial masters decided to turn their backs on the outside world. There is a legend that Cheng-Ho defied his masters, that he sailed off on a final voyage and never returned. I believe that one of his junks bore the Bada to Mahabalipuram, that it was by his hand that this casket was sealed in the temple."

"By 1450 the Portuguese themselves were knocking on India's door. The occurrence of something so remarkable should have been recorded."

"There were records. They were destroyed, and the ashes strewn on a Chandala burial ground."

"I congratulate you on your erudition," said Holmes, "but you will have to explain one thing to me. If this device dates from 1450, why does it depict the western coasts of North and South America?"

Holmes handed the tiny sphere to the captain, who pondered it wordlessly.

"Notice as well," said Holmes, "the spacing of the continents, the width of the oceans. It tallies very well with a modern globe. I cannot imagine a western globe of 1550, or even 1600, showing a similar accuracy."

The captain turned the globe slowly over in his hand, rapt in thought.

"I cannot dispute you," he said at last, setting the sphere on the table before us. "But 1450 still seems the only possible date for the visit of the Bada. This deepens the mystery rather than detracts from it."

"Indeed," said Holmes, taking the globe up once again. "But if its surface confounds us, perhaps the contents may be more enlightening."

With that, he gently twisted the north and south hemispheres apart. Inside was a small cylindrical object, made of gold and inscribed with oriental markings. Holmes plucked out the cylinder and handed it to the captain, his eyes glittering.

"What do you think, Captain?"

"It is a miniature Chinese scroll box, from all appearances. The characters are definitely Chinese, though I can't read them."

"Yes, a scroll box. The captain proved an excellent guide, Watson. You gentlemen have done very well."

Holmes took a pair of tweezers from his vest and carefully opened the tiny box. Inside was a miniature scroll, perhaps two and a half inches long, also crafted of gold. Holmes picked up his lens again.

"It is the scroll," he murmured, half to himself. "Gold in its entirety. The workmanship beggars the imagination. Take a look, Watson."

I crouched over the table, staring down at the miniature through the glass. Remarkably, it appeared there was a real scroll bound round the spindle, held in place by a golden rope scarcely thicker than a thread. Yet this rope was itself woven of at least a dozen strands, and its ends were marked with tiny tassels.

"It would dazzle any collector," I said with a shake of my head.

"Indeed. But I suspect that the workmanship is the least of its value."

Taking another pair of tweezers from his vest, Holmes patiently set about untying the golden rope. Once that was done, he began to unroll the scroll itself, a shimmering strip somewhat more than an inch wide. Holmes held the strip up to the light and viewed it through his glass.

"What is it?" I ejaculated.

"Gold," Holmes replied, "pure gold, beaten to the very limit of its malleability. No thicker than one ten-thousandth of an inch, I should say. And covered with the most delicate characters."

Holmes perused the strip in silence for a few seconds.

"Remarkable," he said at last. "These characters are not Chinese. Have a look, Captain."

The captain studied the miniature scroll under the light.

"Not Chinese," he agreed at last. "And certainly not Arabic, Farsi, Hindu, Sanskrit, or any other writing I have seen. Perhaps the doctor's microscope could tell us more."

"Perhaps," said Holmes. "Watson, you must have a look too."

A glance through Holmes' glass enabled me to verify his statements, as well as the captain's, to the extent that my limited knowledge could apply. The entire surface of the scroll was covered with ideograms, engraved into the beaten metal. Even under powerful magnification, each character was perfectly distinct, though totally unrecognisable.

"The scroll itself must be fifty feet long," Holmes said, rewinding it carefully. "But now let us bring this conversation to the present day. When I learned that you had been to Mahabalipuram, I immediately guessed your objective. The story of the cursed temple of Shiva, and the Scroll of the Bada, though obscure, is widespread. I learned of it several years ago while in Tibet, though I never dreamed that I would be staking my life on the truth of such a legend. Yet certainly this Harat, if such a creature exists, must know far more of these matters than we."

"He exists, Mr. Holmes, as you of all men should know. And if you are telling me my life is not safe, I know that. Indeed, I knew it when I accepted you as a passenger in Tangier. I saw you then as a possible instrument against Sir Roger Ainsby-Gore, though in fact at first I could not tell if you were an ally of that gentleman or his adversary. If the former, I was determined to turn you over to the monkey men. If the latter, to assist you. Since then, I have found that to strike at the slave trade as I had wished, I must strike at the monkey men as well. But now that we have seen this, I have one more thing to show you."

With that he stood up from the table and went over to a cabinet, from which he took several maps. I removed the casket from the table, while Holmes replaced the scroll in its two carrying cases. The captain spread out the maps on the table, depicting the Indian Ocean.

"You see the Maldives," he said, indicating with a sweep of his finger the thousand-mile strand of islands that runs north and south below the subcontinent. "The lower islands are among the least visited in the world. They are of no importance in themselves and far from any shipping lanes. Yet for several years one of these islands attracted constant attention."

He spread out the second map, one he clearly had prepared himself, which showed perhaps two dozen small islands.

"Each year, one or two ships filled with African slaves travelled to this island." He pointed to a spot on the map, outlined in red. "It has no name. Few of them do. Other ships came from Singapore, and from India."

"Intriguing," said Holmes. "Trent was there."

"He was?"

"Yes, he makes a guarded reference in one of his letters."

"Did he say what he saw?"

"No. Only that he was there."

"Do you recall, Mr. Holmes, a year ago, reports of a spectacular volcanic eruption in these waters?"

"Yes. A fishing vessel reported it. Then a scientific expedition set out from Bombay to investigate."

"Which never returned."

"No," said Holmes, sitting down and staring at the map. "It never returned. You remember, Watson?" he asked, turning to me. "Sir Edward Havisham was the leader. The *Times* called him 'the modern Pliny.' But it seems the case cut deeper than that."

Holmes took out his pipe, which in unthinking deference to the captain he did not light but only placed between his teeth.

"Tell me, Captain," he said after a long pause, "have you seen this island?"

"I have, Mr. Holmes. Two years ago. Ten thousand people were on that island, almost all of them black as myself. But if you search for that island today, you will not find it. Nor the people who were on it."

"The volcano . . . "

"There was no volcano. And today there is no island. I found one man—an Indian trader—who could speak of it. He said it was the dance of Shiva."

"And what do you think it was?"

"An explosive device of undreamed of power, with a strength coming from the very earth itself and brought about by this creature Harat. I believe such a device existed before, hundreds of years ago, when this scroll was written. I believe the story of this device has been handed down in legend as the dance of Shiva and that Harat has anticipated its secret. But there is much more on this scroll that he does not yet possess. The priests at the temple knew of this. Otherwise they never would have allowed us to enter."

"Indeed. But this Indian you speak of, in the Maldives. He saw the explosion?"

"Yes. He said it burst from beneath the ocean like a great fire, thrusting the seawater high into the sky."

"And what became of him?"

"He died, Mr. Holmes, like many others, the hair falling from his head and the skin from his body, not from the explosion itself but merely from the watery mist that descended from the eruption."

Holmes received this information in silence.

"You're sure of this?" he said at last.

"I am."

"What else do you know?"

"Nothing."

"So be it. We are far, far behind, but we do have the scroll."

"What do you propose we should do with it?"

"For the present I am at a loss. I should like to put it in Admiral Watkins' safe aboard the *Indomitable,* but I am not sure that even there it would be secure. Tell me, what are your plans for your ship when we reach Singapore?"

"I expect a layover of at least a week, if not more. Then, if there is nothing to detain me, I leave for Macao and Hong Kong. Then I shall retrace my steps, returning to Singapore in three months or four."

"Then perhaps it would be best to take the casket and the scroll with us. The casket simply confirms that the Bada exist. The scroll is another matter."

"It is indeed," said the captain, with a grim smile. "I can assure you, Mr. Holmes, he who keeps the scroll will most assuredly encounter Harat."

"True enough. Once we are in Singapore, Dr. Watson and I will be more protected targets than yourself. It would be most inconvenient for Lord Barington, and Harat, if anything were to happen to us while we are in Singapore."

"Do you think Harat concerns himself with the concerns of Barington, or any other human?"

"Up until this point, Harat's greatest strength is that no European believes him to be real. He would not abandon this advantage until he feels he is their equal. While he undoubtedly cares nothing for Barington, he needs him as a tool, to do the things he cannot do for himself. Watson and I will simply take the chance that Barington's value to Harat does not expire whilst we are residents of Singapore."

So saying, Holmes took out a black leather jewellery case from his pocket, opened it, and set it on the table. He placed the golden bughola carefully on the crimson velvet that lined the case and then snapped it shut.

"Will you do the honours, Watson?" he said, handing the box to me. "As I understand it, this is mostly your doing."

CHAPTER XXV

The Gates of Singapore

HERLOCK HOLMES HAD A remarkable ability
to disengage his mind from a problem whenever he felt he lacked the evidence needed
for its resolution. During the remainder of our
voyage before arriving in Singapore, not once did he make
reference to the stupendous anthropological find the captain
and I had presented him with. He did not examine the casket, the contents, or the mysterious golden scroll, nor did he
say a word to me concerning Lord Barington. Instead, he
immersed himself in a translation of the *Mahabharata,* an
Indian epic poem of gigantic length, supplied to him by the
captain. "It sheds invaluable light on the Krishna cult, which
has long puzzled me," he stated in response to my inquiry as
to why he should occupy his days and nights with a poem
that filled ten stout volumes.

For my own part, I could do little more than pace the decks
by day and bore myself with dated copies of the *Times* at
night. Once, in Holmes' absence, I cleaned my revolver—a
reasonable precaution, considering the ill effects of salt air on
metal, but one that gave little comfort.

The morning of our arrival in Singapore found both
Holmes and myself on deck before sunup. As is so often the

case at sea, a thick mist shrouded the water, reducing visibility to no more than several hundred yards.

"We close at last," said Holmes, gripping the rail.

"What reception do you expect from Lord Barington?" I asked.

"I expect him to be the soul of cordiality. I have seen to it that his lordship can never return to London, except in irons, but here his word is still law. The European trading community thinks only of its profits, and has united behind him. The Chinese, the Indians, and the rest feel this is a mere dispute among white men, which cannot concern them. They deal with Barington, not with us, and while he stands they will not abandon him. Then, too, the shadowy presence of Harat and the Bada inhibit our cause no end. In London, of course, one cannot speak of such things."

He paused to light his pipe.

"But if we are hobbled, so is Barington. He is being watched, and he knows it. No overt harm can come to us, nothing that can be traced back to him. Of course, we must still be on our guard."

"Then what course of action do you propose?"

"We still have the matter of the rifles to attend to. That is a mere blind, and Barington knows it. But I have no doubt that Harat has control of those rifles. One path to this creature will do as well as another, and what we cannot accomplish directly we can accomplish indirectly. Barington will, I am sure, make a great show of cooperation. I shall be given barrels of evidence, all of it useless, and we shall dine royally, at the government's expense, as the unfortunate Mr. Beamish put it."

"It seems intolerable that after so many crimes we still cannot bring Lord Barington to justice."

"Patience, Watson, patience!" said Holmes. "This is not mere police work. We cannot simply lay our righteous hands on his lordship and summon the nearest constable. This is war, war by disguise and indirection, to be sure, but war nonetheless, and war with no quarter asked or given. As long as Lord Barington has control over the machinery of government in Singapore we must maintain the charade."

"Then you expect another interlude as frustrating as the one we endured in Alexandria?"

"I should not be surprised. But I am sure you will find a diversion with which to amuse yourself. For the present I suggest that we go below and enjoy a final ship's breakfast. We should not reach port for several hours."

We returned to our cabin for a breakfast consisting of bread, tea, and fresh papaya.

"A most ingenious fruit," said Holmes, slicing his papaya. "What a pity that it does not travel well. I shall miss the simple elegance of the captain's table. I doubt very much that our traditional northern cuisine is suited for these climates."

"Have you made arrangements to communicate with the captain once he begins his voyage to Macao?"

"The navy will be of assistance there, but of course we must first contact the navy. Barington's spies will be everywhere. I am afraid we will be largely on our own."

"And you have no strategy at all?"

"On the contrary, I have the perfect strategy."

"And what is that?"

"Why, to befriend the harbourmaster, of course."

"The harbourmaster? What can he tell you?"

"He can tell me about shipping, Watson, and shipping is the key to the puzzle. What is Singapore but a vast depot, an exchange point between East and West? Everything goes into Singapore by ship, and by ship everything comes out. The captain tells us that the one true thing known of Harat is that he inhabits the island of Sumatra. Undoubtedly, he does not advertise his location, nor do his goods travel by commercial packet. But wherever he is, he has spun a web that links himself with Barington and, no doubt, a dozen other ports across the East. It is a web whose threads are composed of junks, sloops, dugouts, and tramps, and I shall find it. And when I do, we shall trace those threads, one by one, until our spider is flushed from his lair. And we have, in addition, one more string to our bow."

"What is that?"

"Why, you, Watson, or rather the scroll that you bear. Unless I am very much mistaken, Harat would give half of what he owns, and risk all of it, to obtain possession of that rarely worked bit of gold. I would suggest that you oil your revolver if you have not seen to it already. The salt air can be most corrosive."

"I have tended to the matter," I replied, a little stiffly.

"Excellent. And the knife for your boot? You recall I mentioned such a device in London."

"Unfortunately, I neglected to acquire one."

"Then you must consult with the captain. No doubt he has something along those lines that you can obtain from him. Now, if you will excuse me, I think I will devote the remainder of the time before we dock at Singapore to a perusal of the *Mahabharata*. I find the verse of the Aryan has a remarkable ability to refresh the mind. I did not dare expose my Stradivarius to the sea air and until now despaired of finding a substitute."

So saying, he picked up one of the volumes, which he had reserved from his baggage, and opened its pages. With nothing else to occupy my time, I decided to go on deck once more.

A fresh breeze struck me in the face as I opened the door and stepped out onto the deck. In less than an hour, the sea had taken on an entirely new appearance. The somnambulant mist of early morning had blown away. The slow, sullen swells had been transformed into boisterous whitecaps. In the east the sun gathered its brilliance. And directly before us lay the port of Singapore.

I walked to the bow of the *Prophet,* my heart soaring in response to the change in the weather. The months-long journey seemed to vanish from my mind. It was as though we had left London only one day before, as if the tedium and horror of Alexandria, the long, slow journey along the coast of India, the nightmarish adventure the captain and I had shared in the cave temple at Mahabalipuram, had all been but a single night's dream. Now I had awakened, refreshed and ready to grapple with the murderer of Elizabeth.

Behind me I could hear the crew making ready for our arrival. Though Singapore itself was no more than the promise of land on the horizon, the sea was already dotted with all manner of craft—junks, prahus, sampans, lorchas, pukats, and tongkangs—names that were as foreign to me then as they are likely to be now to the reader—as well as the occasional European ship. I was struck by the paucity of modern steamships, until I realized that for the unhurried East speed was a dispensable luxury.

Occupied by such thoughts I stood at the rail for an hour or more, one of the last of poor Sir Roger's fine cheroots between my teeth. I was interrupted from my reverie by a hand on my shoulder.

"Good morning, Doctor," said the captain. "Mr. Holmes suggested that I give you this."

So saying, he handed me a long, flat knife, perhaps six inches in length, fitted snugly in a leather scabbard. I drew it out and examined its fearsome blade.

"There is no need to test its edge," the captain advised. "It is extremely sharp and made of the finest Sheffield steel. The clips at either end of the scabbard facilitate its attachment to a gentleman's boot. Mr. Holmes assured me that this feature would be of particular interest to you."

"My friend believes that, as the bearer of the golden scroll, I may be in some danger."

"Mr. Holmes is most certainly correct. Harat cannot allow that scroll to remain in the hands of a European, least of all you and Mr. Holmes. As long as Harat lives, Doctor, you must be always looking over your shoulder."

With that cheerful admonition, the captain departed. I sat on a box and after a little work managed to attach the scabbard firmly to the interior of my left boot. By adjusting my boot and the leg of my trousers, I achieved a perfectly natural appearance, though I could not help feeling that the arrangement was more appropriate for a Limehouse ruffian than a man of medicine.

In less than two hours time we entered the port itself. Boats, large and small, crowded on all sides. The *Prophet* slowed its pace to a crawl, and in the distance the white stone walls and red tile roofs of the city came into view. Holmes joined me on the foredeck.

"A trip worth taking, Watson?"

"So it has proved."

"Indeed. And yet, after these four months, here is the true beginning of our quest. Ah, I see his lordship has prepared a proper reception for us."

Holmes pointed with his pipe at the dock. I could observe a number of red coats arranged in formation and a glint of brass instruments. When the *Prophet* cut its engines preparatory to its final glide to the dock, the unmistakable strains of "Rule Britannia" emerged in the hot, humid air. As we drew closer, I could see several dozen soldiers, in full rank and display despite the heat, along with several distinguished gentlemen in diplomatic regalia. There was, in addition, a small crowd of well-dressed, European gentlefolk, which was constantly being enlarged by new arrivals in carriages. Beyond this was another, larger crowd, of Chinese, Malays, and Indian labourers, attracted both by the arrival of the *Prophet* and the reception that had been prepared for it.

"There is our man," said Holmes, pointing once more with his pipe. "The fellow in white."

It suddenly occurred to me that I had never laid eyes on Lord Barington in my life. From a distance I could only see a tall, spare figure, dressed in a white uniform. As the *Prophet* slowly advanced, I strained my eyes to catch a fair glimpse of the foe we had pursued for so long, but, because of the shifting crowd, I was unable to see him clearly.

As the *Prophet* floated slowly toward the dock, its steam whistle blew a shriek of greeting to the assembled crowd. The music continued to play as the crew struggled with the immense coils of rope that would bind the ship to her berth. The gangplank descended, and Holmes and I advanced to it. As we did so, the captain happened past. He paused for a moment, laying his hands on our shoulders and whispering in our ear: "Good fortune, gentlemen. Keep always the will of Allah foremost in your mind." And with that fierce injunction to guide us, Holmes and I set foot at last on the island of Singapore.

PART IV

The Giant Rat of Sumatra

CHAPTER XXVI

Lord Barington

ORD BARINGTON HAD EVIDENTLY decided to make the best of a bad occasion. He stood before us in the resplendent white uniform of his office. His gold buttons gleamed like the sun itself; a snowy ostrich plume draped his conical helmet; and a polished sword glittered at his side. He greeted us with a grace and ease that were worthy of his exalted rank. But all that elegance of manner was for display. At close range one could see the ravages that dissipation had wrought on his face. He looked out at the world with dark, suspicious eyes that darted from one object to another like birds of prey. His thin, cruel mouth, forced briefly into a smile, betrayed the temperament of a voluptuary. His cheeks were daubed with rouge, a curious affectation indeed for a gentleman of his position and rank. Beneath this polished exterior, one sensed, lived a man capable of insensate rage and unrestrained debauchery, a man who, even before arriving in the tropics, had cast off the ennobling bonds of civilization and honour.

"Ah, Mr. Holmes," he said, extending his hand. "We meet at last. You must forgive my little extravagance at your expense. But there is so little that happens here that is remarkable."

"From what I understand, your lordship, there is much in

this area of the world that is remarkable," returned Holmes. "But Dr. Watson and I are most grateful for your hospitality."

We strode between a double line of uniformed guards as though we were dignitaries of the first rank, and then stopped before a gleaming coach, obviously the property of his lordship. I marvelled at the brilliant equipage, which would not have been out of place at Buckingham Palace itself.

A uniformed lackey descended from the driver's seat and opened the door at our approach. Although I only laid eyes on him for an instant, his appearance gave me a start. He was a short, powerfully built man, with stocky legs but immensely long arms. His hands were enormous and covered with hair. Matted black hair bristled in every direction from under the military cap jammed upon his head, pulled down low over his small, round, wizened face. As we entered the carriage he stared at us with sullen eyes, then slammed the door shut as we were seated. Out of the corner of my eye I watched him return to the front of the carriage with a slow, shambling walk. Reaching out his long arm, he swung himself into his high driver's perch with stunning ease. Lord Barington gave the command for our departure and the procession began.

"I hope the men will be dismissed immediately after our departure," said Holmes, settling himself on the rich leather cushions. "This is hardly suitable weather for such uniforms."

"It is particularly important to keep up appearances," Barington returned. "The further one is from the centres of civilization, the greater the temptation to let standards decline."

"Yes, indeed," said Holmes. "The temptations the Orient offers to a man of position and power must at times be almost overwhelming."

"Almost, Mr. Holmes," returned his lordship, a little too quickly, for it was clear that this thrust, though lightly given, had gone home. He glanced away as we passed along the broad avenues and the proud structures of official Singapore.

"These buildings are most agreeable," said Holmes, as though nothing had happened. "Watson and I have had a great deal to look at on our journeys."

"I have had the honour of overseeing much of the most significant construction during my terms as governor," said Lord Barington in his most pompous manner. "Only the finest and most costly materials have been used."

"No doubt it is imperative for important men to have fine things to look upon," said Holmes. "Ah, that statue, that must be Raffles himself."

As he spoke, we passed the bronze visage of Sir Stamford Raffles, the visionary founder of Singapore, staring forever out into the harbour he had selected to anchor England's greatness in the Far East. I could not help thinking that his genius, so often thwarted by the incompetence and blundering of other men, would have thrilled to our quest to cleanse this latest and most heinous stain from his beloved Lion's Port.

"I have arranged for you to stay at a most charming villa, quite secluded," said Lord Barington, interrupting my thoughts. "My driver, Molo, will escort you. Molo knows Singapore well and will make an excellent factotum for your visit. But first I must invite you to join me and my staff for a brief reception."

"You are very kind," said Holmes. "However, Watson and I have made our own arrangements for our stay in Singapore. And I would not dream of depriving you of your driver. But I would be delighted to attend your reception. One cannot begin on a case too soon."

"This is hardly intended to be part of your investigation, Mr. Holmes," returned his lordship, with amused disdain. "This is a purely social gathering."

"But I have no doubt I shall find the event most informative. On such occasions, the shrewdest criminal finds it difficult to maintain his guard."

"You will find no criminals at Government House," Lord Barington replied sharply. "The finest gentlemen in Southeast Asia have not assembled themselves so that you may go prying about in search of clews."

"Of course," said Holmes, sweetly. "I only meant that such high-placed gentlemen will be able to provide me with all the information I require regarding the missing rifles."

"The missing rifles, about which you inquire so assiduous-
ly, were undoubtedly stolen by natives," said his lordship.
Though his manner was perfectly cool, there was a slight
flush in his cheek, which betrayed itself despite the cloying
rouge. He paused, and looked directly at my friend.

"Let me give you a bit of advice, Mr. Holmes. As you are
aware, I have told the Foreign Office repeatedly that I thought
your appointment to this position was a mistake. They have
overruled me, and I accept their decision. I do not fault a
man, particularly a man of your economic and social position,
for seeking to advance himself. But you will do very well to
confine your investigation to those rifles. Do not attempt to
meddle in affairs that are not your own. The East is not the
West, Mr. Holmes. The penalty for failure is extraordinarily
high."

"Certainly Sir Roger found it to be so," returned my friend
dryly. "But surely this magnificent structure must be
Government House. I thank you humbly for your advice, your
lordship. I shall keep your words constantly in my mind."

The carriage halted, and Lord Barington nodded dismis-
sively in our direction. An elegantly dressed subaltern
approached and opened the carriage door. Lord Barington
arose and descended from the carriage with the imper-
turbable mien of a great and noble lord, leaving us to bring
up the rear in a distinctly awkward fashion. We passed up a
great staircase into a great hall, where we were greeted by an
elegant assembly of military and foreign service officers,
brought together, it would seem, for the single purpose of
snubbing Holmes and myself. I was particularly offended by
the attitude of Sir Warren Clayborne, the lieutenant governor
of Singapore, who had bullied poor Elizabeth so unconscionably after the death of her husband, and could scarcely
restrain myself in his presence. After enduring close to two
hours of haughty condescension, we were ushered out the
door by an officious lackey, without so much as a word of
farewell from our erstwhile host.

"An instructive experience, Watson," said Holmes, as we
descended the steps of Government House. "It seems his

lordship wishes us to understand that we are not welcome in Singapore."

"I don't know when I have been more insulted," I said angrily, for I was unable to bear the contumacy of his lordship's entourage with Holmes' equanimity.

"Yes, it was the death of a thousands cuts with a vengeance," said Holmes. "But, on the whole, instructive nonetheless."

"In what way?" I asked.

"I would call your attention to the curious issue of his lordship's right cheek," he replied. "But we must now seek lodgings. I have been in touch with Arthur Craven, who was Elizabeth's barrister. He suggested that we might prefer a host other than his lordship, and I agreed. I have the address of his place of business, and we must hurry if we are to be sure of locating him today."

We engaged the services of two native taxi drivers, who quickly conveyed us in their rickshaws to what I subsequently learned to call "Chinatown," an area of Singapore greatly unlike the European. The drivers assured us in broken English that Arthur Craven was well known to them and deposited us before a large, decrepit building that I could only assume was the office or domicile of this legal person. We paid their fees without haggling—a great error, no doubt, but one we could scarcely avoid making—and they departed with much haste and merriment. Holmes shook his head.

"I fear, Watson."

"What?"

"That we should have ascertained whether Mr. Craven is in fact at this address before having paid their wages."

Holmes' scepticism was entirely justified. The front door was locked tightly, and no amount of knocking could summon assistance. We circled the building twice in search of entry, but could gain none. In any event, the edifice gave every impression of having been abandoned for several years.

"We shall have to make inquiries," said Holmes at last.

This, unfortunately, proved to be easier said than done. Our drivers had deposited us in an almost deserted area of the city. Our attempts to obtain information from the few passersby elicited nothing but mute shrugs. We began walking and soon found ourselves in a teeming slum that could have matched the worst that London has to offer. Gambling dens, brothels, taverns, and opium shops confronted us at every turn, while the narrow, crooked streets were filled with Asians of every breed and hue, but chiefly Chinese, all laughing, shouting, and cursing in their strange, high-pitched voices. I was a little startled to discover that the population of Singapore, in Chinatown at least, was almost entirely masculine. The few women who did appear were all invariably painted in a strange manner that cast the strongest possible doubt upon their virtue.

"I hardly think we will improve our situation if we take up residence here," I observed, stepping around a drunken Malay who had fallen at our feet.

"Perhaps not," said Holmes, "but this is undoubtedly the worst, rather than the best, that Chinese Singapore has to offer. We would not judge London by Cheapside. What we need to do is find Mr. Craven. Ah, we are being observed."

"What makes you say that?"

"That young boy in the alleyway. I saw him two blocks before. I think perhaps it would be best to have a word with him."

I half expected the boy to bolt at our approach, but he held his ground. He was a lad of twelve or thirteen, very slight, and dressed in the simple tunic and trousers worn by virtually every Chinese in Singapore. A neat pigtail hung down his back, tied with a bit of grey wool.

"Good afternoon, young man," said Holmes, as though he were encountering the son of a schoolmate on the Strand. "Are you in the employ of Mr. Arthur Craven?"

"Mr. Craven he be big bossman," said the boy. "You be bossman Mr. Sherlock Holmes?"

"Indeed I am," said Holmes. "This is my friend Dr. Watson. We are most anxious to make the acquaintance of Mr. Craven."

"You come. I take you to big boss man."

"How on earth did you know he worked for Arthur Craven?" I asked, as we followed the boy along the thoroughfare.

"His queue is tied with wool from a barrister's wig," said

Holmes. "I've spent enough time in Old Bailey to recognize that shade of grey anywhere."

We followed the boy for perhaps a dozen blocks. During our journey a distinct improvement in the quality and condition of the buildings was apparent, although we remained the sole Europeans on the street. When the boy led us down a long and distinctly unprepossessing alley, I began to fear an act of treachery. I slid my hand inside my jacket and rested it on the butt of my revolver.

"Always cautious, eh, Watson?" Holmes said. "Well, the suspense should be over soon. I believe this is our destination."

The boy stood with a slightly self-conscious air beside a doorway.

"You enter," he announced. "Big boss man Mr. Arthur Craven Esquire to receive you now. He is third floor."

"Thank you for your assistance," said Holmes.

I have rarely been in a building so unkempt as the one that housed the apartments of Mr. Arthur Craven. The narrow stairs that we trod to his abode were littered with rubbish and groaned at every step. We startled more than one rat as we ascended, and by the time we reached the third floor, perhaps half a dozen were scurrying before us. They disappeared into a hallway but soon returned, racing down the stairs and fleeing past us with blind haste.

"Deuce take the creatures," said Holmes, fending one off with his forearm. "What can have provoked them?"

We found the answer to Holmes' question at the top of the stair, in a foul-smelling corridor so dirty and ill-lit that one could hardly see. A large, blue-black snake lay in the dust, knotting its coils around a hapless rodent. I drew my revolver in case the scaly brute should prove to be poisonous, but the Chinese boy dissuaded me.

"Billy be very good snake," he said. "Catch many rats. He no hurt you."

With that, he led us past the foul creature, which was fully occupied in the revolting process of crushing the life from its verminous prey. We advanced halfway down the hall, and the boy stopped beside a doorway.

"You enter," he said.

We entered a large room that was filled with a strange collection of both Asian and Western bric-a-brac. Several high windows, hung with bamboo curtains, provided a hazy half-light that was a vast improvement over the almost Stygian gloom of the hallway. Our feet sank into a luxurious but painfully worn carpet, which seemed to bear the ill effects of more than a century of hard use. A fine lacquered cabinet, black and gold, was set against one wall, but the main object of furniture in the room was a large mahogany desk placed before the windows. Both the cabinet and the desk, and indeed much of the rug, were covered with dusty piles of yellowing paper. A few nondescript hunting prints decorated the unpainted plaster walls. But the most distinctive, and most unpleasant, feature of the room was an all but overwhelming stench of rotting fruit.

"Is it Mr. Holmes, then?" rang out a voice from behind the mass of paper on the desk. "Mr. Holmes, I'm glad to see you, I am."

Arthur Craven stepped from behind the desk and shook hands, first with Holmes and then with me. His personal appearance was in keeping with that of his office. He was a large, unsteady man, with a flushed face and a broad, theatrical manner. A thick, poorly trimmed moustache covered his upper lip. He wore a thin, white linen shirt without collar or cuffs, while an oversized kimono of worn green silk hung about his shoulders.

"Dr. Watson, I presume," he said with a laugh as he shook my hand. "Eh? Eh? Always wanted to say that. 'Dr. Watson, I presume.' I enjoy your work exceedingly, sir. You see, I keep you in my files."

Here he pointed to an immense stack of back issues of the *Strand* magazine, almost three feet high, set in a corner to keep them upright.

"Get them from the steamers. I'm only a few months behind. Four or five, at the most. Wu Shih, get these gentlemen chairs. And let me introduce you gentlemen to a doorian. Ever had one before? The nectar of the gods, gentlemen. Worth a trip to Singapore all in itself."

So saying, he went behind his desk and brought out the most bizarre fruit I have ever seen. It was almost the size of a man's head, the exterior covered with knobs and spines, split open to reveal the remains of a soft, custardy flesh that was the undoubted source of the foul odour that so permeated his rooms.

"Thank you, no," said Holmes. "We have just lately dined."

"You sure? Don't be put off by the smell, Mr. Holmes. A man can't be too finicky if he wants to enjoy the pleasures of the East."

"I think not," said Holmes rather sharply.

"Ah. Another time, perhaps. Can't leave Singapore without splitting open a doorian or two. Mark my words, gentlemen. You'll live to regret it."

"No doubt," said Holmes. "But for the present, perhaps we could tend to more pressing matters."

"Of course. But first, I've a question for you, Mr. Holmes, about the *Study in Scarlet,* that Mormon fellow with the bloody nose. How could you be so sure about the poison?"

"A scientific presentation of the evidence would have provided ample justification for my conclusions," said Holmes. "My friend's account of the case was not entirely coherent."

"You don't say," said Mr. Craven, who evidently had appointed himself as my champion. "I found it gripping. Yes, sir, that is the word. Gripping. I don't mind telling you, Dr. Watson, you've kept me up many a night with your tales. I ain't ashamed to say that I wept the time poor Mr. Holmes here went over them Riding Back Falls with Professor Moriarty. Thank God you escaped, Mr. Holmes. Thank God indeed."

"If I had known my feigned demise would be the source of so much distress, I would have chosen some other means to escape the attentions of Colonel Moran," said Holmes, with some irritation.

"Oh, now, you knew best I'm sure," continued Mr. Craven, unabashed. "A fine gentleman like yourself always knows what's best for himself, and it's a man's duty to look out for himself, whatever the circumstances. Here now, have a seat, and if you won't partake of some doorian, help yourself to a cigarette."

Wu Shih entered with a pair of curious folding chairs, one
under each arm, which when unfolded proved to be scarcely
more than footstools. Holmes and I perched carefully on them,
while Mr. Craven transferred several heaps of paper from his
desk to the floor, revealing a gleaming silver cigarette box.

"Thank you," said Holmes, opening the box. "What a fine
cigarette box. Do you know, I saw a box remarkably similar
to this not one month ago in the cabin of Admiral Watkins
aboard the *Indomitable.*"

"Did you now," said Mr. Craven. "That is a coincidence."

"It is indeed," said Holmes, taking out several cigarettes and
passing one to me. "What is perhaps even more remarkable
is that your cigarette box bears the admiral's flag."

"Indeed it does, Mr. Holmes, and if that distresses you, perhaps you should discuss the evils of gambling with the
Indomitable's executive officer."

Craven rose from his chair and went over to the lacquer cabinet. He opened it and took out a tray bearing a decanter and
several glasses. He placed the tray carefully on the piles of
paper that covered the cabinet and unstoppered the decanter.

"You see, Mr. Holmes," he said, pouring a glass, "I have
taken it upon myself to provide certain services for young
gentlemen visiting Singapore who have a mind to sample the
pleasures of Chinatown. Chinatown is a very fair flower, Mr.
Holmes, very fair. But she has exceedingly sharp spines. May
I offer you some brandy?"

"Thank you, no. What can you tell us about Elizabeth
Trent?"

At the mention of Elizabeth's name, the swagger and brag
suddenly disappeared from Craven's manner.

"A fine lady," he said soberly, "the finest lady that ever trod
the streets of Singapore." He sat down, clutching the glass of
brandy in his fist. He set the glass down before him and
passed a trembling hand over his face. "I felt I should have
done something more."

"She said you were the only man in Singapore who helped
her at all."

"It's a cruel crew we have here. You can take your choice

of Sir Henry or Lord Barington—cross either of them and you're dead."

"What brought you to Singapore, Mr. Craven?"

"Oh, I think you know well enough. The great Sherlock Holmes doesn't ask a question like that without knowing the answer. Credit a broken-down barrister with knowing a few tricks. I had my difficulties with the bar. I wasn't the right sort, and didn't know my place. I got myself all mixed up with foreigners and anarchists."

"The Masetto case. I remember it well. The man was innocent."

"He was indeed, though convincing twelve Englishmen of that took a bit of work."

"As I recall, no one else would handle the case."

"No, they wouldn't. Mr. Masetto was not what you would call a charmer, except with the ladies. A jury don't like to see a foreigner having his way with our English girls. That case did me, Mr. Holmes, I have to say. I walked out of that courtroom on top of the world, but poor Mr. Masetto didn't have a quid to his name. And then when he up and took off to Naples on me, well, I was left flat. I looked about me, and I said, 'Arthur, my boy, it's time for a change of venue.'

"So I thought I'd come out here, where life would be simpler. You see the results. But I like Singapore. I like the Chinkies. They'll treat you square. They're a hard people. They won't take you in, but they'll treat you square. So I'm the Chinkies' man. They don't like law courts, but when they're in a jam, it's me they come to. That's my place, and I like it. I'm a long way from Bow Bells, but London's not much of a place for a fellow like me, who didn't get his head screwed on quite right. Singapore's better."

At the conclusion of this remarkable speech, he toasted us with his glass.

"To your health, gentlemen. To your health, and to the memory of Elizabeth Trent."

With that, he drained the glass and set it down. After a moment's hesitation he reached for the glass again, but then drew his hand back.

"It's a fine vintage, Mr. Holmes, and I do love my brandy. But when I'm talking with the great Sherlock Holmes, I'd best have my wits about me. You sure I can't talk you into splitting open another doorian?"

"Thank you, no," said Holmes.

"Then what about you, Dr. Watson?"

I shook my head wordlessly at the thought of consuming such a grotesque repast.

"Ah, you still have your Western stomachs and Western noses. There's time enough to learn better. But for now, Mr. Holmes, I have found you, and I have also arranged for lodgings for you and Dr. Watson. What else is it you will be requirin' of me?"

With these words, Arthur Craven took a cigarette from the silver cigarette box that had lately been aboard the *Indomitable,* lit it with a flourish, and sat back in his chair with a sort of boyish smirk.

"I should like," said Holmes, in a manner that ignored all the eccentricities of our host, "to know of all contacts between Lord Barington and representatives of the firm of Enderby & Cross and the island of Sumatra."

"Ah, now that would take some doin', Mr. Holmes. Sumatra is a big island. You might be bitin' off more than you could chew. That's a bad habit for a man, especially in Singapore."

"You agreed to help us."

"So I did, Mr. Holmes, and so I have. But Singapore has its own set of rules. I'm not liked here, Mr. Holmes. You won't find a white man in the straits less welcome than I. But I am tolerated, because I do play by the rules. But I'm already stretched to the limit. I've given you a place, and you and his lordship can fight it out here, and may the better man win, and I'm sure hopin' it's you. Because if Lord Barington had his way he'd ruin me. It wouldn't spoil his breakfast to see me floatin' face down in Singapore Bay. It wouldn't at all. That fellow would dance a jig at my funeral, and to tell the truth, he may live to do it. But old Arthur Craven won't go down without a fight. That's why I'm so agreeable to you, Mr. Holmes. I do have a great respect for you, for all you've done, but Arthur Craven knows what side of his bread the butter's on, so if I invited you in, it's because you can help me. And if you go messin' about in Sumatra, you're no good to anyone, Mr. Holmes, least of all yourself. You see, Mr. Holmes, I fancy my throat. I fancy my throat the way it is. And I don't think it would improve appearances much to have it slit from ear to ear. And that's what happens to folks that go messin' about in Sumatra."

"You state your case very well," said Holmes with a smile, evidently amused rather than offended by this appalling display of petty self-interest. "But tell me, aren't you taking too much of a risk simply by taking me in. If I fail, won't Lord Barington be down on you in an instant?"

"That's true, Mr. Holmes, that's very true. But it's not as if his lordship and I were bosom buddies to begin with. You see, when I came here from London, I was to work for Enderby & Cross, but we had a fallin' out, so you might say, and I happened to bring a case against them on behalf of a Chinese gentleman. I say gentleman, Mr. Holmes, because I think a man can be a gentleman even though he wears a pigtail, especially if he pays his bills regular. In fact, Mr. Holmes, I've found that gentlemen that has pigtails is more likely to pay their bills than those that has not. And so that's how I've made my living, though the folks at Enderby & Cross haven't much cared for it. They've treated the Chinese right sharp, and now I've spoiled their little party. But I must confess I got myself into it with Mrs. Trent. I was so charmed by the lady that I went a little far, and then a little too far—too far to turn back, do you understand? So that his lordship hadn't much use for me anymore. And you see, Mr. Holmes, I haven't much choice in the matter. You're the only horse I've got. But to put your shirt on a horse is one thing. To put your life on a nag is another. He who fights and runs away lives to fight another day, if you catch my drift."

"I do exactly, Mr. Craven. If I could obtain from you all the material that you obtained from Mrs. Trent, perhaps it would be best if Dr. Watson and I should repair to our new lodgings."

"You know, Mr. Holmes, you took the words right out of my mouth. Because I have what you're lookin' for right here, everything I received from the dear lady."

Craven pulled open a drawer from his desk and took from it a large, worn leather satchel that bulged with papers. Holding the satchel carefully with both hands, he passed it across the desk to my friend.

"Excellent," said Holmes, glancing through the voluminous files.

"It's all in order, Mr. Holmes, you needn't worry yourself about that. The lady was very organized, and I kept everything just the way she had it."

"These are essential elements to the case," said Holmes, as much to himself as to Craven and me. "But tell me something, Mr. Craven, just to satisfy my curiosity. Did you arrange to work for Enderby & Cross before coming to Singapore?"

"Aye, Mr. Holmes, that I did."

"Do you have any idea why they chose you in particular?"

"They seemed to be looking for a fellow they could get on the cheap, that's what I thought. They're a tight-fisted crew, Mr. Holmes, though I can't see why. They have more money than they know what to do with."

"Ah, but perhaps it's money they can't call their own. Who did you report to here in Singapore?"

"Why, to Sir Henry. He was the headman when I came here."

"And what kind of a man was he to work for?"

"Nervous, Mr. Holmes, very nervous. Nothing was ever quite right for that man. He could be hard as nails, but underneath I thought he was always ready to crack."

"Curious, that success seemed to bring so little happiness."

"My sentiments exactly, Mr. Holmes. What is life if you can't have a little happiness? Life's not bad in Singapore, not bad at all, if a man don't push himself. If you push yourself, the heat will break you. I've seen it happen time after time. A man ought to take a leaf from the Chinkies and live like they do."

"I am sure your advice is excellent," said Holmes, rising to his feet. "However, I doubt that Watson and I will be able to abide by it. We will try to make our stay here as brief as possible."

"Good luck, Mr. Holmes," said our host, also rising. "Please call on me whenever you feel the need. Wu Shih will take you to your quarters."

We followed the Chinese lad's footsteps back down the stairs and out into the alley once more. He led us along a narrow, tortuous path from one alley to another. At length we arrived at the rear of a broad, tall building, whose exterior, though clean, appeared as nondescript as the one we had lately quitted. But when we entered the wide door that opened for us at Wu Shih's knock, the transformation was as great as any to be found in the "Arabian Nights." Instead of climbing a dingy stairway, we found ourselves in a large, airy, well-lit room, hung with Chinese tapestries of enchanting delicacy. A pair of enormous ceramic lions, brilliantly painted, stood guard in this sanctuary. The furniture was Chinese as well, massive pieces of oak carved with incredible depth and detail. We advanced slowly over rich, silken carpets, as though preparing ourselves for whatever the next wonder would be to confront our eyes. As we did so, a tall, elegant Chinese lady appeared, dressed entirely in black silk, her carefully arranged hair as black and gleaming as her gown, with a cheek of porcelain.

"Good day, gentlemen," she said, with a gesture of infinite dignity. "I am the Widow Han. You will be my guests."

CHAPTER XXVII

The Widow Han

UR HOSTESS LED US to a high-ceilinged room, a portion of which was open to the sky. Directly below the open portion was a large marble tank, filled with constantly flowing water. Large, golden fish swam within the tank, which was set about with exotic tropical flowering plants. Their delicate perfumes formed the greatest possible contrast with the loathsome stink of the ghastly fruit that Mr. Craven had been in the act of consuming when we had arrived at his premises. The elegant silk cushions on which we now reclined made a similar contrast with the strange folding chairs with which our previous host had provided us.

"You gentlemen are weary from your travels," said the Widow Han, surveying us with a sharp, amused eye once we were settled.

"Yes," said my friend, "though our destination has proved more than worthy of our effort. May I enquire if it would be possible to have servants sent to attend to our baggage? It would be convenient to have it brought here as quickly as possible."

"Of course," said our hostess.

"Excellent," said Holmes. "Our baggage is located on board the *Prophet,* the ship on which we arrived."

"I will have my servants obtain it at once," the Widow announced. "Please make yourselves at home. I hope it is to your liking."

"It is indeed," I exclaimed. "Your house is most charming. I cannot recall such a lovely home."

"For once Dr. Watson has conveyed my own sentiments correctly," said Holmes, with a quick, ironic tone. "You must tell us the history of some of your pieces."

"Yes!" I said eagerly. "Your fish tank, for instance. It is so finely carved."

"Later, gentlemen, when you have recovered from your journey," said the lady, with a polite laugh. "For now, I will attend to your luggage and my servants will show you to your rooms."

Our rooms were small but quaint, unlike any that I have ever seen. Though the Widow Han was obviously quite familiar with Western ways, the furnishings of her home were thoroughly Chinese, and it required no small amount of ingenuity to determine the purpose of the various items that confronted me. Fortunately, the Widow had assigned to me a maid, Soo Ling, a tiny, shy girl barely in her teens, who spoke no English yet always seemed to know what I wanted. She brought me what I needed most, hot water and towels, of which I made good use. I then took the opportunity to recline on the curious bed with which my apartment was equipped, only to fall into a sound sleep, from which I did not awaken until several hours later. I descended the stairs and followed the murmur of voices until I came upon Holmes and our hostess, enjoying a quiet dinner.

"Dr. Watson," cried the Widow Han, rising at my approach, "it is so good of you to come. Please to sit here."

She indicated a place to her right and clapped her hands vigorously. This action summoned a pair of servants, who quickly provided me with plates and saucers, along with Western tableware. The Widow Han, of course, ate with

chopsticks, which she employed with a finesse I had not realized could be possible. She had changed her dress and now
wore an elaborate gown of white silk painted with gold. Her
hair was arranged in a much more formal manner, and her
face was highly painted. I could not say that I preferred the
change, but the effect was undeniably striking.

The dinner gave me the opportunity to examine the person
and character of our hostess in more detail. Though Holmes
and I remained in her house for more than a month, the additional familiarity I gained with her over that period of time
only served to confirm my first impressions. She was above
medium height and appeared taller, for she always held herself with the greatest possible erectness. Like so many Asian
women, she was remarkably slender, with surpassingly delicate hands and features. Her manner was calm and dignified,
yet in her slightest word and gesture, there was as well the
inexpressible charm and spontaneity of youth, which could
not be denied. Her voice was gentle and low and remarkably
musical, so that her curiously accented English never failed to
delight the ear. She seemed always to know when she was
mispronouncing a word, for her dainty mouth invariably
assumed a droll expression when she stumbled. All in all, it
would be difficult for the dullest man alive to spend an hour
with her without falling hopelessly in love, and as the reader
may guess, I was soon her all-too-willing captive.

Even Holmes, notoriously impatient as he was with the fair
sex, appeared to show some submissiveness to her charms,
though throughout the meal he persisted in questioning her
about Lord Barington and the affairs of Enderby & Cross. In
her replies, the Widow Han seemed resolved to play a game
of cat-and-mouse with my friend. She declined to take refuge
in the traditional and rather tedious feminine pose of helpless
ignorance when confronted with anything having to do with
"business," but neither was she willing to discuss these matters in detail. Instead, she sought to turn the conversation to
the delights of Singapore itself, the sights we ought to see,
and the pleasures we ought to sample. The quick enthusiasm
of her gesture, the soft thrill of her voice, and the ineffable

sparkle of her jet-black eyes, all held me spellbound, but I could tell that my friend was growing restive.

The conclusion of the dinner arrived all too soon for me, but when it did Holmes rose almost immediately and asked me to join him outside for a walk and a cigar. Since exercise for its own sake had no appeal for Holmes, I deduced that he wished to discuss matters with me without the possibility of being overheard.

"A mysterious woman, Watson," Holmes said, almost with a note of anger, once we were well away from her house.

"What makes you say that?" I replied, a little stunned by the force of his remark.

"In the first place, why does she take us into her home? She must know that Lord Barington is keeping a close watch on our movements. Why antagonize the most powerful man in the colony?"

"Perhaps Mr. Craven has told her of your great reputation."

"This is hardly the time for levity, Watson. I tell you frankly that I do not trust our hostess. Fortunately, it is possible to lock the bedroom doors from the inside. I would prefer that you give me the bughola. If it is ever missing, I should prefer to have no one to blame but myself. And I suggest that you keep your revolver close by. I doubt we are safer now than in that miserable bungalow provided by his lordship."

This tirade by my friend left me not a little offended. That the Widow Han had offered her hospitality to two strangers, not of her race, against the known wishes of the authorities, meant nothing to him. I could only put it down to his rigidly logical nature, which revolted against any appeal to the emotions. His hard and exclusively masculine intellect could only rebel when confronted with the quintessentially feminine spirit of the Widow Han.

Naturally I did not share this analysis with Holmes. I concurred vaguely with the various suspicions he voiced against our hostess, and agreed to take all the precautions he suggested against the possibility of a nocturnal assault. We continued our walk some distance further, while Holmes outlined in general terms his plans for research now that we were in

Singapore, and then made our way back to the house. Upon returning to my bedroom I was delighted to discover that our luggage had arrived, including the casket. I found as well a fresh copy of the *Straits Times* laid out on my bed, which recalled to me poor Elizabeth's visit to our rooms on Baker Street, now six months past. I read the paper through, including a short article that discussed the arrival of Holmes and myself in guarded terms, until it was time to retire.

I was awakened early the next morning by a dull boom, like a single stroke of thunder, which left me well puzzled until I recalled that the Widow had told me that life in Singapore was regulated by cannon fire. The entire populace, she assured me, arose at five A.M. in response to a salute fired by a venerable sixty-eight pounder. They ventured forth at six for a morning walk, returning home at seven or so to prepare for breakfast. I confess that I had not actually believed my hostess at the time, and now that I found myself awake so early in the morning, I wondered how my friend might adapt, who was far more likely to retire at five o'clock in the morning than to awaken at such an hour. Yet the thought of beginning a new day with a walk through the streets of Singapore with my charming hostess on my arm aroused and elevated my spirits no little extent. I dressed quickly and descended the stairs, to find myself alone. I made my way through the darkened rooms to the large, central atrium, where a faint shower of rain fell through the air shaft, lightly sprinkling the surface of the water in the fish tank below. I sat in the chair nearest the tank and watched the fish swim silently, their golden colours muted by the overcast sky.

"Dr. Watson, you arise so early! You will be a true resident of Singapore!"

I turned and saw the Widow Han coming towards me, followed by a pair of servants bearing trays. She was dressed in a wrap of yellow silk, which contrasted charmingly with her beautiful black hair, brought up in a bun behind her head and thrust through with several long needles. She sat in the chair opposite me, while the servants placed the trays before us on a table. Needless to say, the trays bore a tea service of fine

Chinese porcelain. While the servants retreated, the Widow poured a dainty cup and handed it to me.

"It is the custom of Singapore to take a walk before breakfast, but we must wait until the rain ceases. Will Mr. Holmes be joining us?"

"I'm afraid my friend does not keep regular hours," I said, tasting the tea, which was unlike any I had ever encountered. "He is rarely awake before noon."

"You should confine your slanders of my person to matters less easy to refute, Watson. I assure you I was up before the cannon."

I turned round to discover my friend entering the room, clad in his old robe that he had worn for so many years at Baker Street.

"Oh, Mr. Holmes," cried the Widow Han, "we shall enjoy your company after all. You must please join us."

With Holmes as our third, we completed our tea. When the rain ceased, our hostess insisted that we accompany her on her morning walk, an act of some social significance, as I understood from her gentle suggestions that we make ourselves more respectable. I struggled to recall the dress of the European contingent that had crowded the dock on our arrival two days before, and was not a little worried that my extended sojourn on the *Prophet* had rendered my wardrobe incurably bohemian. Fortunately, I was able to recover enough respectable items of clothing to make myself presentable, though their condition, after months of storage at sea, left much to be desired, and I resolved to seek out a competent tailor as soon as the opportunity presented itself.

Our morning walk proved to be a tour of the finest neighbourhoods of the Chinese section of the city. As might be expected, the Widow Han knew everyone, though the greetings we received struck me as guarded in the extreme. Of course, no one could be more ignorant of the niceties of Chinese etiquette than I, but nonetheless I felt a distinct chill in the manner of those we encountered on our walk. It was not until the following day, in a conversation with Arthur Craven, that Holmes and I learned the true position of our hostess, and thus of ourselves, within the community of Singapore.

"The Widow Han, you see, she's a bit of a mystery," said Arthur Craven, biting off the end of a cheroot and then applying a flame to its tip. "Help yourself, gentlemen," he added, lifting the lid of an elegant silver cigar box. "Fresh off the boat, from the captain's table of H.M.S. *Ajax*. Nothing but the best for the bloody Royal Navy."

"Thank you," said Holmes, taking two cheroots from the box and passing one to me. "I must confess that I have felt the absence of adequate tobacco exceedingly for the past few months. But you were telling us about the Widow Han."

"Yes, Mr. Holmes." Arthur Craven leaned back in his chair with the contented air of a man with a good story to tell and in no hurry to tell it. "You see, the Widow Han is what you might call *sui generis*. She's the richest woman in Singapore, and Singapore is a man's city. She has no man to look out for her, excepting for yours truly on a few occasions, and she goes her own way. I ain't saying that she's popular, not with the Chinese or the English, but as long as you've got the dollars, you can do as you please, and the Widow has the dollars. There aren't many on the island who can touch her. She buys cheap and she sells dear, and I've never known her to lose a bargain."

"How did she come to this wealth?" asked Holmes.

"That's a good story, Mr. Holmes, which many people will be pleased to tell you, for she married well and she married early, if what people say is true. You see, Mr. Holmes, John Chinaman takes a dry view of things, very dry. If he wants a woman, he don't woo her, he buys her. And there's folks who'll say the Widow was raised for sale, that she was bought more than once, and when she was a mere slip of a girl."

"How do you know that the people who say such vile things are not simply speaking nonsense?" I burst out, unable to contain my disgust at the thoughtless repetition of such a dubious calumny, particularly when I considered the grace and dignity of its object.

Mr. Craven colored a little at my rebuke.

"I only repeat what others say," he said hastily, "to help you with your investigation. I mean no disrespect to the lady. I assure you, few have done as much for her as I have, and to be honest, none have done as much for me as she. But the lady does go her own way, and that will attract comment."

"Perhaps you have encountered similar reactions in your own life, Mr. Craven," said Holmes with a smile. "But do not let Watson's words discourage you. It is important to have all the facts, and all the rumours as well."

"I mean no disrespect," said Craven again, flushing and obviously uncomfortable. He drew out a rumpled handkerchief from one of the pockets of the kimono he wore and mopped his forehead.

"The ways of the Chinese ain't our ways, and you must take them as they are if you are to do anything with them at all. Now the Chinese do love their gossip, and the fact is, the Widow Han, rich as she is, ain't entirely respectable. You see, folks in England have the wrong idea about China. China ain't a country, like England or France. It's a continent, like Europe or India. A Chinaman from Canton can't talk to a Chinaman from Fukieng. They're all split up at home, and it's the same way in Singapore. But the Widow Han, for all anyone can say, was born in Hong Kong, with a father from one province and a mother from another, so she ain't rightly from anywhere, if you catch my drift. The Chinese, as I say, are a hard people, so for them that knows the East, it ain't surprising that the Widow may have come up the hard way."

"When did she arrive in Singapore?" asked Holmes, apparently determined to lead Craven's ramblings onto firmer ground.

"Before my time, Mr. Holmes. About fifteen years ago, as near as I can estimate. She was then the bride of Mr. Fu Yen Han, one of the richest men in Chinatown. He was a bachelor all his life, but he took this twelve-year-old girl as his bride. They lived together for eight years before he up and died, and when he did he left her the opium farm."

"The widow owns an opium farm?" I asked, not a little astonished at the news.

"Not a farm, Doctor, the farm," explained Mr. Craven. "You see, here in Singapore, opium's a monopoly, and the Widow had it. How she held onto it when her husband died I'm not so sure, though there are many tales about it, but she did. It was about that time that old Arthur Craven arrived here in Singapore, and I handled a few cases for her, but she always held me at arm's length, so you might say. I didn't get to know the particulars of her business. I wouldn't think any man has. The Widow knows where to place her foot, if you catch my drift."

"What connection has she with Barington?"

"Ah, now that's a good question, Mr. Holmes, because you'd be thinking, why should she take you in? Why cross his lordship? I can't tell you that exactly, for they got along well enough in the early years, but they had a falling out some time ago. That's when she lost the farm. Now, some folks will tell you some things about the Widow and his lordship, but people do love to talk about a pretty woman, don't they? But, as I say, the Widow always knows where to place her foot, and I don't see her getting in too deep with the likes of Lord Barington. But it did give me a turn when she asked to take you folks in. That's not done, Mr. Holmes. And for the most part the Widow's no gambler. But she's put a fair stack of chips on you."

"Indeed," said Holmes, rising to depart. "In that case, let us hope my talents prove worthy of the lady's wager."

CHAPTER XXVIII

The Charms of Singapore

N THE DAYS THAT followed, I had the intense pleasure of accompanying the Widow on a round of social visits undertaken in my honour. During the course of these visits I was forced to admit that an element of calculation was never entirely absent from her actions. We visited homes of many wealthy merchants, Chinese and European, as well as a number of Eurasian families. Despite the Widow's superabundance of charm and tact, I could not help noticing, when we would drive homeward in her coach after a successful visit, the slight flush of triumph that would decorate her lovely cheek. And I could not ignore her gentle but persistent prodding when I failed to dress entirely in accordance with her notion of the proper attire of an English gentleman. Surely no one was a more ardent foe of "going native" than the Widow, and despite the intense heat, I was forced to array myself with the formal broadcloth, stiff collars, and pinching shoes so preferred in London.

For this reason I felt it fortunate that Holmes always refused to accompany us. Months of travel in the tropics had bred in him a thorough eccentricity in dress that belonged to no one race or culture. His shirts came from Spain, his trousers from

Turkey, and his shoes from India. The only English item of his
dress at all was a pith helmet, which had just recently come
into use among the English residents of the East. The protection these hats offered to the unwholesome rays of the midday sun was bruited to be so potent that gentlemen wore
them even while swimming, preposterous as it may sound.

As the Widow's frequent companion, I had extensive opportunity to study her way of life, which was indeed well worthy
of contemplation. Her house was staffed inside entirely with
female servants, perhaps a dozen in number, though she had
several footmen who attended her when she travelled beyond
her walls, along with a number of simple, honest fellows who
lived over her stables. But the introduction of two gentlemen
guests required her to hire two servant boys to attend our
needs within the house itself. I soon found that the ubiquity
and plenitude of servants in the East, at least in an establishment such as the Widow Han's, verged on absurdity.

Soo Ling cared for my room and clothes. She brought me my
copy of the *Straits Times* every day, and indeed almost had to
be restrained from turning the pages for me as well. Despite her
shyness, she had an enormously winning manner, which quickly endeared her to me. Ming Pao, a boy of no more than ten,
assisted me in activities too trivial or too intimate to fall within
the purview of Soo Ling. I required his assistance chiefly in the
bath, for the customs of Singapore require a gentleman to bathe
by standing naked in the bathhouse while a servant dashes
water on him, the water being stored in an immense earthenware jug. After bathing I would have the pleasure of being
shaved by an itinerant barber, who arrived at a quarter to six
each morning for that purpose. The man was remarkably skil-
ful, and always insisted on anointing my face after each shave
with Poindexter's Bay Rum, reputedly the choice of the Prince
of Wales. I detected the Widow's hand here, for it was no doubt
her conviction that I ought to smell like an English gentleman
as well as dress like one. Dressing was a remarkably simple
task, for Soo Ling laid out my clothes each morning (not, I suspect, without prompting from the Widow), while Ming Pao
helped me put them on. Thus bathed, tonsured, scented, and

dressed, I would descend the stairs each morning to join the Widow in her atrium for tea prior to our morning walk.

The Widow's morning was less leisurely than most of Singapore's. Directly after returning from our walk we would have a light breakfast, after which she would plunge into her work. From eight until two each day she met with a steady stream of merchants in a large front room, which functioned as her office. An office boy with an abacus was constantly at her side, while an ancient, wrinkled clerk silently wrote down all the transactions in Chinese script. Hundreds of paper rolls arranged in a large rack contained the records of all her affairs. At two in the afternoon she would stop for the mid-day meal, called "tiffin" in Singapore, after the Indian usage.

For the Widow, tiffin was almost entirely a matter of fruit, unless special guests were present. The island offers an enormous variety, most of them unknown to Europe. We lunched pleasantly on pineapples, plantains, ducoos, mangoes, rambutans, pomeloes, and mangosteens, the latter especially delicious. The Widow always insisted on having English food for Holmes and me to eat, though such fare as mutton chops and beef and kidney pie have limited appeal when the thermometer is hovering at the ninety-degree mark. A fresh, savoury bowl of elegantly sliced and prepared fruit, on the other hand, is pleasing to both the palate and digestion, particularly when cooled with ice ingeniously supplied from North America by the American Tudor Company.

I may say that I never saw or smelled a doorian within the Widow's house, though I was frequently assured by a variety of wagging tongues that she ate little else. One particularly malicious lady, Madame Rainier, the wife of the French legate, even claimed that it was the Widow's invariable custom to dine in the nude, the better to enjoy the voluptuous succulence of that dubious fruit unhindered by concern for her wardrobe. This from a woman whose highest ambition was to sup from the table of Lord Barington! But such slander is ever the reward of those who exceed the common mark.

Afternoons the Widow reserved for visits to her other places of business, a pair of well-kept godowns on the

Singapore River, which housed the great variety of goods that
passed through her hands. These were pointed out to me by
Ming Pao, for the Widow did not care to bring her guests in
close contact with her commercial affairs. Evenings were
spent in a steady succession of social functions, often of
wearisome formality. Before retiring, each night the Widow
would kneel before a simple shrine located in a private corner of her house to meditate in the presence of her ancestors
and the compassionate Buddha.

Once a week the Widow would entertain a group of
women friends, all Chinese, whose appearance and manner
were curiously at variance with the standards the Widow so
carefully enforced at all other times. Gentlemen were, of
course, rigorously excluded from these gatherings, and the
endless succession of feminine shrieks and giggles that
attended them quickly convinced me to absent myself from
the house when they occurred. On such nights I would venture forth with Arthur Craven, who introduced me to a decidedly different side of Singapore.

Strangely enough, I found myself most at home when visiting among the rather pathetic colony of well-to-do Eurasians
that the Widow was acquainted with. Barred by active preju-
dice from full and easy participation in the social life of the
European elite, they nonetheless chose to follow the dictates
of England rather than Asia in matters of manners and dress.
I was quickly adopted by this group, who, I must confess, displayed a certain touching charm. My hostess, I could tell,
thought little of them, and they returned the favour, particularly the ladies, but the peculiar stratification of Singapore
society thrust them together. Besides, from what I could gather, the Widow was closely allied commercially with several of
the gentlemen of the group, which inevitably led to some
measure of social intercourse. In any event, I walked frequently in the mornings with Mr. and Mrs. Amspray, both
Indian/English, and Mr. and Miss Botts, a brother and sister
who were Chinese/English. We were joined on various occasions by Mr. and Mrs. Winifred-Owen, Chinese/English, and
Mr. and Mrs. Sampson, Chinese/English as well.

All of my acquaintances were painfully interested in anything I could tell them of London, which they all regarded as a metropolis of unimaginable wonders, a city where no one did anything except wear expensive clothes, appear at court, and ride in railway trains travelling at speeds in excess of one hundred miles an hour. Nothing that I could tell them of the real London could make a dent in these preconceptions. In fact, to avoid being rude, I found myself ultimately embroidering on their fairy tales rather than refuting them.

When the opportunity presented itself, I questioned the gentlemen regarding the firm of Enderby & Cross. The four of them were all merchants and uniformly regarded the firm with distaste, though if they had any knowledge of palpable wrongdoing, they withheld it from me. Despite the awkwardness of their position racially, they were, after all, members of the great freemasonry of commerce and sworn to keep its secrets safe from outsiders like myself. They were much more comfortable discussing tiger hunting, a very gentlemanly sport on the island. In the recent past, depredations by the great beasts claimed several hundred lives a year, but a bounty had been placed upon their slaughter by Lord Barington, with the presumably desirable effect that now more tigers died each year than men.

The gentlemen were all members of the Tiger Club, which they had founded in competition with an all-white society, though only Mr. Winifred-Owen had been on a hunt. He was a particularly small man, quite successful in business and older than the rest, which gave him more leisure to pursue his hobby. Several months before, he had bagged his first tiger and could talk of little else. He maintained a trophy room, whose floor was decorated with the skin of the beast, and he loved to reenact the hunt, clad in a dinner jacket and brandishing his tiger rifle, which was fully as long as he was tall. The boyish enthusiasm with which he performed this ritual never lost its charm for me, though I must have seen it a dozen times, for he could scarcely look at the rug without initiating it once more.

Holmes did not participate in any part of the Widow's social schedule. As I suspected, he did not care to be roused at five in the morning on a regular basis and rarely made an appearance until tiffin. He persisted in his manner of formal politeness to the Widow despite her constant efforts to comply with his every wish, so that I was hardly displeased when he began to take most of his meals in the special room she had appointed for his use as a study, a chamber that soon acquired the same clutter as our rooms on Baker Street. For reasons known only to himself, he had attempted, for some time, to translate the inscriptions on the golden scroll and had copied out a number of them in his own hand, which he left scattered about the room, along with a quantity of maps, bills of lading, and other records.

His plans to examine harbour records had been delayed on the specious grounds that preparation for an impending visit by the capitan general of the Philippines necessitated the closing of Government House to all visitors, while his efforts to pursue the case through the records of Enderby & Cross met a similar dead end. The senior partners all took the precaution of absenting themselves through trips to Hong Kong and Calcutta, leaving a few junior clerks in charge, who knew nothing and would give Holmes no access to company files.

The effectiveness of these dilatory strategies threw my friend into the blackest depression, until I feared that he might resort for relief to the opium that was so plentiful in the city. Instead he bought a violin, which he pronounced an "adequate" substitute for his beloved Stradivarius. He was wont to play only during the afternoon, sometimes for the Widow and myself, but more often for his own amusement, favouring those strange and melancholy airs that always recalled to me our early days together.

I was awakened one night at the extremely unreasonable hour of three thirty in the morning by the sound of Holmes' instrument emanating from his study. The piercing, lugubrious wail seemed well capable of arousing the entire house, and so I ventured in to make a protest. At the sight of me Holmes put down his violin.

"Sorry, Watson," he said, his bitter mood reflected in his voice, "but I am letting this case get the better of me. I have wound myself too tightly and cannot bear the inaction. I have done nothing but rattle the handles of locked doors since arriving in this wretched place."

"You should not speak so harshly of my island," said the Widow Han, entering suddenly. She wore a soft, white robe and her long, black hair, undone for once, fell over her fine shoulders with inexpressibly feminine grace. "But you are my guest. If you are unable to sleep, I shall find a way to calm you. Please wait for my return."

She returned perhaps fifteen minutes later, with her hair up and bearing a sort of Chinese lute. Seating herself comfortably, she began to play and sing in a plaintive manner that was at once strange and soothing. She sang, of course, in Chinese, with the unspoken confidence and pride of a trained professional, which suggested to me that Arthur Craven's blunt comments about her early years might in fact be well-founded. But lulled by her delicate, silvery voice I had no time for such unkind thoughts.

After half an hour Holmes rose to his feet.

"Thank you, gracious Widow," he said, with a smile. "You have indeed soothed your savage guest. I shall retire and approach this problem anew in the morning, and promise not to disturb the slumbers of your house again."

"I am pleased that my music pleases you," the Widow said, with a quick bow of her head. "I will leave you now."

Turning to go, her eyes brightened suddenly and she picked up a sheet of paper.

"You are trying to read the rock," she said, studying it.

"What?" said Holmes.

"The writing of the rock. Where did you obtain this?"

"You have seen this writing before?"

"Of course. From the rock."

"What rock?"

"The great rock that was once in Singapore Harbour. An Englishman blew it up because it was in his way. This was many years ago. I was given a piece for good luck."

With these words, she took from around her lovely neck a locket that was set with a scrap of stone, inscribed with characters that strongly resembled what Holmes had written on the paper. Holmes took the locket and studied it for a long while.

"Remarkable," he said at last. "Do you have any more fragments?"

"No. They are very few. That is why they are thought to be good luck."

"I see." Holmes handed the stone back to the Widow and threw me a glance with his weary eyes.

"Devilish tantalization of the gods, Watson," he said, shaking his head. And on that strange note our conversation ended.

CHAPTER XXIX

Curious Events

 THOUGHT THAT THIS CHARMING encounter with the Widow would have dissipated entirely my friend's scepticism regarding her motive and purpose, but I was mistaken. The next day at tiffin he seemed to regard her with particular reserve, as if the warmth he had displayed toward her the night before were a matter to be regretted, and he persisted in this attitude during the days that followed. Strangely enough, it was the visit from the capitan general of the Philippines that provided the occasion for his final decision in the lady's favour. I could not imagine why the prospect of such a deadly ritual as a state visit, particularly one conducted out of doors under the equatorial sun, would interest him, but he insisted on our attendance, despite the torrid heat. "I would attend were the event held in Hades itself," he told me when I warned him of the dangers of prolonged exposure.

When we arrived at the gathering, Holmes insisted on taking a position as close to the reviewing stand as possible, and even brought along a small pair of binoculars through which to view the proceedings. So it was that we endured several hours of gleaming swords and droning speeches, half of them in Spanish, before he suddenly announced that we had seen enough. Our departure was far from inconspicuous, but that did not concern him in the least. In fact, I was confident I could discern a thin smile of satisfaction on his lips, but strangely mixed as well with both anger and determination.

"You have seen something?" I asked when we were well clear of the crowd.

"Yes, Watson, I have. I have seen that I have wronged our hostess."

"How so?"

Holmes paused and lit a cigar.

"I do not apologize for questioning the Widow's motives, Watson," he began, "though by your tone you still hold it against me. Mr. Craven, whose chivalry is scarcely less florid than your own, raised the point very well. Craven himself is the sort of man who will always set himself up against authority if given half a chance, but the Widow is another matter. If she were truly on our side and against his lordship, there had to be a reason. I made guarded enquiries regarding their relationship, but came up with nothing. Half the colony says Barington intends to destroy the Widow, and half says she is his mistress. Whenever I mentioned his lordship in the lady's presence, there was a noticeable stiffening in her manner, but I could never divine if this were due to anger or fear of discovery. Her own comments regarding Barington have always been resolutely noncommittal. Have you ever heard her say anything either decidedly for or against him?"

"No," I admitted. "But what have you learned today to make you change your mind?"

"What do you say of Lord Barington's fondness for rouge?"

"Repulsive and bizarre," I said, though I could hardly tell what his lordship's rouge had to do with the Widow's honour.

"I quite agree. But what caught my attention upon our arrival was the lack of symmetry. You recall my remark regarding his right cheek?"

"Yes."

"His right cheek was significantly more marked with rouge than his left. The area covered was larger, and the material more thickly applied. In my few encounters with his lordship in London, I never knew him to use cosmetics of any kind, and the climate of Singapore is unlikely to cause a pallor of the skin. Why has he taken up the practice now, and why does he do the job so poorly?"

"I have no idea."

"For concealment. Because he has some mark on his right cheek that he wishes no one to see. But the sun has sweated the truth out of him."

"Well, what did you see?"

"I saw six puncture marks, Watson, arranged in pairs, each pair perhaps two inches from the other."

"And what could this possibly have to do with the Widow?"

"Let me raise two other questions before answering yours. What could cause such scars, and why should his lordship be so anxious to conceal them? The marks, though noticeable, are hardly disfiguring."

"I have no idea."

"I shall tell you, Watson," Holmes said, his eyes narrowing. "Have you ever noticed the pins with which the Widow secures her hair? They are long, strong, and sharp, made of unusually fine steel, with heads carved of ivory. Wielded by a determined hand, they would make a dangerous weapon. The thought occurred to me when we first met, and Mr. Craven's information suggested to me that a young woman, raised in a harsh environment, might well feel the need of a means of defence both unobtrusive and convenient."

"Do you really think the Widow wears her hairpins as weapons?"

"I am sure of it. Have you noticed that the Widow is left-handed?"

"Of course."

"And have you noticed that her hairpins are always inserted from the left to the right, which would facilitate their quick and easy removal?"

"Perhaps she simply inserts them that way herself," I said, a little dazed by my friend's seeming obsession with minutiae.

"Not a bit of it. Her maid, who by the way is right-handed, inserts them."

"How do you know that?"

"Come, Watson, come," said Holmes, with a note of asperity. "Surely a lady of the Widow's station would not fix her own hair. I might also draw your attention to the eight ladies who visit the Widow each Thursday. Six are right-handed and two are left. All eight wear hairpins, and the six wear them right to left, while the two wear them left to right.

"A left-handed woman defending herself would naturally wound her attacker on the right. From what I know of his lordship's character, I would be more surprised to learn that he had not made an attempt on her virtue than the reverse. But the lady acquitted herself more adroitly than he could have imagined. Barington could ill afford an open scandal, so he concealed his wounds and went no further than to confiscate her monopoly on opium. But he doubtless longs for a more complete revenge."

"How monstrous!" I exclaimed. "But can you be sure it is true?"

"It is true, Watson. The Widow has taken a great risk by placing her trust in us. We must prove ourselves worthy of that trust!"

Naturally, the atmosphere at the Widow's house changed enormously when we returned that afternoon. At first I was so charged with indignation over the ill treatment the Widow had received at Lord Barington's hands that I found it difficult not to allude to the outrage, but as the evening progressed I gradually came to master my emotions. After dinner that evening, Holmes courteously requested that the lady play and sing for us again. She acceded most graciously, with the proviso that Holmes play as well. He responded with several bravura pieces by Paganini, performed in a most impassioned manner, which I had never heard from him before. The Widow, I fear, was more amused than impressed by these fervid renditions, so unlike the delicate melodies of her own repertoire, though she applauded politely in the Western manner. Holmes, to my amazement, bowed earnestly after each piece, as though he were the great virtuoso himself.

In the evenings that followed, the Widow sang dozens of songs for us, in a series of simple concerts that have always held a special place in my heart. Her songs were wonderfully soothing to the ear, though I could never tell one from the other. Their meaning was equally obscure. When Holmes or I asked her what a song was about, she would never provide a translation, but only say that it was an old, old song, sung by a poor girl whose lover had betrayed her. This statement was invariably accompanied by a half-humorous, half-censorious glance of her beautiful eyes, as if to hold us each personally responsible for the unexpungeable perfidy of the male sex down through the ages.

These weeks were, as my friend put it, "amiable but unproductive." As Holmes had predicted, the government at Singapore provided him with endless records, with the hope of discovering the lair of the mysterious "Harat." For my part, I continued to accompany the Widow on her numerous social rounds, although an undefined malady, which seemed never to affect her physically, often confined her in the evenings.

On such nights, for lack of a better resource, I sought out the company of Arthur Craven and joined him in his nocturnal rambles. Craven took me to the gambling "hells" that are a singular feature of the island. The Chinese are immense gamblers, and previous governors of Singapore concluded that, in this case at least, an open vice is less of an evil than a secret one. Lord Barington, of course, was most tolerant in these matters, so that one could hardly find a block in Chinatown that did not echo with the joyous shouts of the winners and the piteous groans of those who had lost all.

Craven took great pleasure in visiting these and other dens of iniquity, though he appeared to have no real vices other than alcohol, tobacco, and his beloved doorians, which he pressed upon me on every occasion, and which I just as frequently declined. With his battered black wideawake tilted far back on his head, he would stride each night through the streets for hours, marvelling at the gamblers, drunkards, pickpockets, thieves, and prostitutes who streamed past our eyes.

When he tired of this sport, we would seek out one of the disreputable establishments he favoured. Here we would sit over glasses of iced brandy and coconut milk, brought by shy, giggling waitresses, while Craven excoriated Barington and all his works.

Surprisingly enough, we were usually not the only white faces in the bar. The demimonde of Singapore included a number of Europeans who had "gone native," a vulgar American named Brennan in particular, who claimed to make a living as a tiger hunter, though to me he seemed a man far more at home cadging drinks in a bar than sighting down one of the great cats that infested the island. Whenever we came across one of these debauched characters, he would quickly attach himself to us, for Craven, though hardly rich, was not a man to let another man go dry. Yet he kept himself within limits. Each night, somewhere between midnight and one in the morning, he would abruptly announce that he "had had enough," and together the two of us would walk back through the crowds of gamblers, undiminished despite the lateness of the hour.

On more than one of these occasions I noticed Lord Barington's driver, Molo, keeping me under observation. There was something in the man's bearing and appearance that filled me with an unaccountable loathing. On these rambles I took the sensible precaution of arming myself both with my revolver and the knife the captain had given me, and I consciously refrained from ever surrendering entirely to the lure of alcohol. I had the sense, indeed, that however slow the pace of Holmes' investigation, events in Singapore were beginning to draw to a climax. Molo's attentions, it seemed to me, were growing increasingly open and persistent, and I felt that my excursions had the welcome though inadvertent effect of diverting scrutiny from Holmes himself.

After one such night, I returned especially late and noticed the light still on in Holmes' study. The door was open, and I entered as quietly as I could. The room was strewn with maps and ledgers, and Holmes was down on his hands and knees, with his back to me, surveying the largest, an enormous chart that must have measured six feet in either direction.

"Ah, Watson," said Holmes, "you have arrived just in time."

"I did not alarm you?"

"Not in the slightest. A man would have to be careless indeed to be threatened by an assassin with such an uncertain tread. What do you think of my handiwork?"

He pointed to the map with the pencil he held in his hand. Singapore Island was located in the righthand corner of the map, with the peninsula of Malaysia stretching off to the north. The island of Sumatra was depicted in its entirety, as were many of the smaller islands that form a fraction of the entire Malay archipelago. I could see innumerable pencilled lines emanating from Singapore, threading their way through the straits or heading off to China, Java, Australia, or other parts of the Pacific. By each line was written, in Holmes' precise hand, the name of a ship, its owner, and the date of its departure from Singapore.

"What have you learned?" I asked.

"I have learned that our adversaries have gone to great lengths to cover their tracks. The captain, you remember, was most insistent that Sumatra is the true home of the creatures we seek."

"Yes."

"If that is so, and I am inclined to believe that it is, then there must be some regular line of communication between Lord Barington here in Singapore and his allies in Sumatra. But look at the movements of cargo. Ships from Singapore touch Sumatra here, and here, and here on a regular basis. But none of these ships are controlled by Enderby & Cross. Most are Dutch, while the rest are Chinese. I have made enquiries, and none of the owners involved bear the least goodwill toward Barington or Enderby & Cross."

"Then where is the link?"

"I do not know. I am inclined to think . . ." Here Holmes broke off, leaning forward to examine the map more closely.

"What is it?" I said.

"Here," he said, laying his finger on a point in the open sea.

"I see nothing but water."

"There is nothing but water to see. But notice how many

ships have passed by this point in the last year, in every manner of direction. Their paths form the rough outline of a circle. And these are outbound ships only, and only those whose first port of call led them beyond this point. Look where they are bound." Here he pointed rapidly to a dozen points on half as many islands. "Have you heard of any of them?"

"No."

"Nor have I. That in itself is hardly meaningful. But three of these islands are mere bits of land. And here. The *Crown Royal,* fifteen thousand tons, the first ship in the Pacific, bound for Renggano. There's something out there, Watson. I'm sure of it. A rendezvous point of some sort, perhaps."

Struck by the force of Holmes' observations, I had joined him on the floor. In doing so, my hand brushed against a small, soft, black object.

"What is this?" I asked, holding it carefully, for fear of damaging another clew.

"That? Why, it is nothing, nothing. I will dispose of it."

So saying, he literally tore the object from my hand, but not before I had recognized it for what it was—the silk slipper of a Chinese lady, such as I had often seen adorning the tiny, elegant feet of the Widow Han. For a second, Holmes' eyes and mine met. Then he quickly turned away. I rose to my feet, amazed. The great Sherlock Holmes was blushing!

CHAPTER XXX

Finding a Ship

 HERE WAS, OF COURSE, no further conversation between Holmes and myself that evening. I retired immediately, but then rose a few hours later for my morning walk, despite my lack of sleep. I cannot say that my conversation with the Widow that morning was unforced, but she smiled sweetly, as she always did, and appeared completely at her ease. On our walk we met the Winifred-Owens, who invited us to breakfast. The Widow insisted that I accept, though she herself declined, protesting a headache. When I returned, I was surprised to find Holmes in the atrium with Wu Shih, Arthur Craven's errand boy.

"Good morning, Watson," said Holmes, as though nothing had passed between us the night before. "I have spoken to Arthur Craven about my findings. Wu Shih and I are preparing to make a visit to the docks today. I would be most pleased if you would join us."

"In search of a ship?" I asked.

"In search of a ship and a captain," he responded. "Once Wu Shih has completed a few errands for his master, we shall be on our way."

Two hours later we were riding to the docks in the small carriage maintained by the Widow, pulled by a pair of diminutive horses, who rather laboured under the unaccustomed weight of two Englishmen. Wu Shih was our coachman, to his infinite delight, for he spent most of his waking hours running errands for Craven. Throughout the journey, he cracked the whip with boyish glee over the heads of the two ponies, who fortunately took no notice of this constant goad, proceeding at a modest pace until we reached our destination.

We drove right past the main harbour area, dominated by modern steamships from Europe, and stopped at one of the Chinese docks, where dozens of exotic junks rose and fell gently with each passing swell. The dock itself was made of wood, a good twenty feet wide, and stretched out into the harbour for two hundred yards. At right angles to the main structure were smaller walkways, a dozen feet wide at most, and several hundred feet long. It was to these walkways that the junks were tethered. Beyond this dock, one could see several similar structures in the distance.

"You must be our interpreter, Wu Shih," Holmes said, climbing down from the carriage. "We require a safe ship and a discreet captain, if such is to be found in these waters. Mr. Craven has suggested Captain Lin for the task. If he is not available, ask for Captain Tang or Captain Wu."

Holmes and I found a seat beneath a spreading "cannonball" tree, so called because of its solid, spherical fruit, while Wu Shih set off on foot to seek the three captains. After an absence of more than an hour, he returned to report that all three were at sea.

"We cannot afford to wait," said Holmes, grimacing at the unwelcome news. "Try Captains Liu, Shan, and Soong."

Wu Shih was off again, returning in another hour to inform us that Captains Liu, Shan, and Soong were all at sea as well. Holmes frowned.

"They can't all be at sea," he said. "I had not counted on such uniform resistance."

He appeared on the verge of an additional comment, but

instead nodded in the direction of a pair of British officers who were approaching us.

"A most striking confirmation of our deductions, Watson," he said in a whisper.

"Whatever do you mean?"

"We shall find out soon enough."

The officers saluted at our approach and stood their ground.

"Are you two gentlemen Sherlock Holmes and Dr. Watson?" one of them asked.

"We are," said Holmes. "What is your purpose, Lieutenant?"

"My purpose, Mr. Holmes, is to place you under arrest. Please come along quietly."

A few moments later, to my intense surprise, the officers bound our hands behind our backs and led us to a heavy coach with barred windows. In the driver's seat sat Molo, dressed in a grotesque, ill-fitting uniform and grinning with malicious pleasure at our discomfort. The officers locked us inside the coach, mounted their own horses, and led us off in a grim procession.

"Well, Watson," said Holmes, struggling to seat himself on the coach's unyielding cushions, "we make progress."

"In what sense?" I replied, amazed at his optimism.

"You recall that several weeks ago I said that we were in no real danger as long as we did not threaten Lord Barington directly. It appears that we have crossed that line."

I hoped that Holmes' sanguine view of the matter was justified. For my own part, being jolted through the streets of Singapore in a prison cart hardly constituted progress. We passed through the entire city and out into the countryside. At length it appeared that we had gone beyond all trace of civilization, other than the road upon which we travelled, for on both sides we could see nothing but the immense tangle of the primeval jungle. However, when we finally came to a halt after a journey of several hours, we found ourselves in a vast clearing of some sort, whose purpose I could not well imagine, covered with thick grass that rose almost to the height of the knee. The carriage door opened, and before we could move an inch, Molo had us both in his iron grip and fairly hurled us from the coach. The vigour of his assault left both Holmes and myself sprawling in the dirt.

"That's enough of that, fellow!" shouted one of the officers, his horse prancing at the commotion. "We are in charge of these men. Be off, and stand until you are called."

As was his wont, Molo snarled wordlessly at this check to his foul and bestial nature. He slammed the heavy door shut and swung himself back onto his perch with near-simian nonchalance. Once there he lashed the horses off in a fury, the coach's iron wheels passing within inches of my limbs. As I staggered to my feet, I could not but shudder at the limitless disparity between the man's physical grace and his moral grossness.

The two officers dismounted and passed their horses over to a pair of servants who had appeared on the scene.

"Could we trouble you to remove our chains?" asked Holmes. "Surely there is no question of our escape at this point."

"We have our orders, sir," said one of the officers, a little uncomfortably. He seemed to regret our ill-handling, but dared not do anything about it. "I must ask you to step this way."

The officers led us out into the clearing. In the distance I could see a thin line of sportsmen carrying shotguns, and presently the air was filled with the reports of those weapons. A formal hunt of some sort appeared to be in progress, with unseen beaters driving the game toward the aristocratic executioners. At length we spied the elegantly dressed figure of Lord Barington, who appeared utterly engrossed in his sport. We stood for some time behind him, waiting until the flow of birds ceased. Eventually one of the officers spoke.

"Lieutenant Dinwiddie reporting, sir, with the prisoners."

Lord Barington turned his attention to us with a studiedly casual air.

"Ah, Mr. Holmes and Dr. Watson. I hope your journey was a pleasant one."

"I suggest you call this farce to a halt immediately," said Holmes, glaring into his lordship's eyes.

"Oh, I think not, Mr. Holmes. The day is hardly begun. By the way, what do you think of my new Purdy? It just arrived last week. They do such fine work."

He held out his gleaming, double-barreled shotgun for our admiration, the muzzle pointed directly at us. It was indeed a superbly crafted, polished, and burnished weapon, but under the circumstances his action was nothing less than a direct threat to our lives.

"I have learned that you are attempting to leave the island, Mr. Holmes," continued his lordship. "That is not in your charter."

"My charter is to pursue my investigation wherever it leads me," said Holmes.

"I shall give the orders in Singapore!" said Lord Barington, his face flushing with sudden anger. "I have endured the insolence of your presence far too long already, Mr. Holmes. You speak of your charter. I will give you your charter. Conclude your investigation within the week!"

"That will hardly be possible, your lordship," said Holmes sternly. "I must remind your lordship that the memorandum from the cabinet addressed to you specifically forbade any interference of my investigation on your part."

"The cabinet!" said Barington, almost with a sneer. "What does the cabinet know of these things? Let me warn you, Mr. Holmes. The East is far different from the West. Christian notions of clemency have not penetrated these regions. The rewards of success are without limit. The penalty for failure is equally so. You had best accustom yourself to our ways, or you will be destroyed."

Holmes smiled briefly at this outburst. Despite the extreme heat, he seemed utterly cool and collected.

"I thank your lordship for the advice," he said. "But I fear my character is already fully formed and not susceptible to the influence of longitudinal change. Perhaps a common acquaintance of ours, the late Professor Moriarty, had occasion to remark to you of this defect in my nature."

"You are a fool, Mr. Holmes, a meddling fool. Do as I say, and you can depart Singapore a rich man. Violate my word, and you will depart this earth!"

For a long moment Lord Barington stood before us, the gleaming barrels of his shotgun poised at our breasts and his finger upon the triggers. The cries of the beaters, the occasional gunshots from the other hunters, the faint murmur of the wind, all seemed to fade into a perfect silence. Yet Holmes continued to stare directly into the eyes of his foe, while I stood by, not daring to move an inch. At last a strange look, a look of fear, almost of terror, seemed to spread over Lord Barington's face, superseding the rancour that had prevailed before.

"Lieutenant!" he cried.

"Yes, sir," responded the lieutenant, racing to his master's side, halting, coming to attention, and saluting, all in an instant.

"Remove their irons," Lord Barington muttered, in a low, strangled voice. He turned away from us and stared out into the broad field before him. Suddenly, he fired two rounds at a rising bird, which spun sideways in a slow arc and then fell to earth. Grinning slightly at his success, he opened a small brass compartment in the butt of his gun and removed four shells, loading two into the breech of his weapon and pocketing the others. When the lieutenant had removed the handcuffs that bound us and retreated some distance, his lordship turned his attention to us once more. He looked shockingly wearied, and stared out at us with the eyes of a cornered beast.

"You know so little of these matters, Mr. Holmes," he breathed. "So little. Now, for God's sake, go!"

CHAPTER XXXI

The Doorian and Its Power

 N INSTRUCTIVE SESSION, was it not?" said Holmes, rubbing his hands with pleasure as we walked away from the distraught nobleman, who had used so ill his illustrious family name.

"We might have been killed, Holmes!"

"There was that possibility. His lordship would have given much to pull those triggers. However, he didn't. What did you think of his mental state?"

"He appears to be under enormous stress."

"Yes. Clearly, we are on the right track. Fortunately for us, his lordship is still under orders to leave us unharmed. The trick now is to find a ship, and a captain, who will take us where we wish to go before those orders are changed. I would much prefer not to involve the Widow more deeply in this, but she may prove to be our only resource."

At the mention of the Widow's name, we suddenly heard the shrill voice of Wu Shih calling to us. We turned and saw him riding up to us in the Widow's carriage. In the back rode the Widow herself, slim and erect, a fringed parasol raised above her head. From the corner of my eye, I saw my friend straighten slightly and his face flush with pleasure. Naturally, I said nothing.

"Dr. Watson, Mr. Holmes," she called. "English gentlemen search for ships in such strange places. But I am pleased that you are both well."

"Well indeed and grateful indeed for your hospitality," returned Holmes. "I fear Lord Barington neglected to allow for our return to Singapore."

"Then you shall be pleased to accept my assistance," she said, opening the door.

The three of us weighed her carriage considerably, but neither the Widow nor Holmes seemed to mind the deliberate pace of our homeward journey. Undoubtedly, news of our arrest had filled the Widow with the utmost trepidation, though she disdained to show it. Now that Holmes had been returned to her, she was more than content to sit next to him in a slowly swaying carriage for hours, and his emotions were similar. For me, the circumstances were less ideal. I was clearly unnecessary, if not actually unwanted, and out of respect for the Widow's wishes, I was denied even the solace of tobacco. It was difficult even to enjoy the charm of the countryside when in the company of two who so clearly would rather have been alone.

When we arrived at the Widow's house, I immediately announced a fictitious dinner engagement with Arthur Craven—a transparent ruse, for it was well past the normal dining hour for Singapore, but one that was eagerly accepted by my friend and the woman who had laid a claim to his heart such as no woman had ever essayed before. To bar with my presence the full expression of that tender and profound regard that had arisen between these two remarkable persons was clearly insupportable. Thus it was that I found myself out on the street at eight o'clock in the evening with an empty stomach, a fine cigar between my teeth, and hopes of joining Arthur Craven in one of his late-night revels.

But I was to be disappointed in my expectation. After climbing those rat-infested stairs and renewing my acquaintance with Billy, I discovered Arthur Craven to be in the throes of preparing a legal brief for a court case he was trying on the morrow. Whether other lawyers prepare their briefs in the manner of Arthur Craven I cannot say, but I am inclined to think not. His method involved a great deal of running about, of shouting for Wu Shih, and of angrily rummaging through dusty heaps of yellowing papers, along with the consumption of significant quantities of coconut milk and brandy. I joined him in the last, and after my third cup set off alone in hopes of discovering Brennan or some other of his cronies.

I felt a sense of both elation and fatigue as I walked the crowded streets of Chinatown that night. My nerves, strung to the highest pitch by our near-fatal encounter with Lord Barington, demanded release. I took some measure of vicarious pleasure at the joy of my friend and his beloved, but at the same time could not help but feel frustration at my own lack of companionship. My steps led me insensibly to an establishment I had frequented with Craven and Brennan in the past, which Craven liked to call "the best gin shop and casino in the East," though in fact there was little to distinguish it from a hundred others. The proprietor alone was distinctive, being Indian rather than Chinese, by the name of Ramajan Mukerjee. He was assisted in his duties by an unusual young woman who seemed to be neither his daughter nor his sister nor his wife, a woman whose physical charms seemed the earthly validation of the sublime sculptures the captain and I had viewed on our memorable journey to the temples at Mahabalipuram.

I entered the establishment and inquired of Mukerjee, who spoke tolerable English, if Brennan were present. He replied in the negative but assured me that the tiger hunter was expected soon, a statement whose veracity I doubted, but since it was accompanied by a large glass of beer, which refreshed my thirst exceedingly, I decided to remain. The young lady, who went by the improbable name of Deirdre, joined me at the table and, after a certain amount of conversation, invited me to dinner in a private room. This invitation, accompanied as it was by a slight pressure of her foot against mine, prompted a firm and energetic response from an area of my anatomy that had not hitherto played a role in our relationship. I assented eagerly and set off with her at once.

The room to which Deirdre led me was small and indifferently furnished, but reasonably clean and quiet. I relaxed in a worn easy chair with my pipe while Deirdre served the meal. Mukerjee proved a more than competent cook, providing us an excellent chicken and vegetable curry. In an act of importunate bravado, stimulated by Deirdre's charming presence and attentiveness, I ordered a bottle of champagne as an accompaniment. Deirdre joined me in the consumption of the bottle, which was followed by a second. When the second bottle was approaching its extinction, she said something to me that I could not well follow, but in the spirit of intense goodfellowship that had settled over me, I assented eagerly once more. I must confess that at this point in our acquaintance, it is doubtful that I would have rejected any suggestion whatsoever, provided it came from her lips. Deirdre disappeared, returning several minutes later, dressed somewhat more casually and bearing the largest doorian I ever saw. She placed it on the table before me and handed me a stout cleaver.

With one blow I split the swollen fruit asunder. At once our nostrils were assailed by that rank, pungent, and unmistakable odour that had so offended me in the past. Tonight, however, was no ordinary night. Tonight the scent of the doorian was an incitement to my appetite rather than a deterrent, as if my reticence itself were a challenge to be overcome, a wall to be breached, a citadel to be conquered. Disdaining cutlery, I plunged my hands into the soft, shimmering, custardy flesh and hungrily transferred the warm, succulent gobbets to my mouth. Their savour, at once delicate and earthy, provoked me to heartfelt groans of pleasure. Deirdre clapped her hands with delight and joined me in the feast. Again and again our hands dug into the soft, intoxicating flesh, as though we had not eaten for days. We sucked the seeds and licked the rind to capture every last voluptuous morsel, like debauched schoolchildren at a forbidden feast. A second melon was summoned, and fairly torn asunder. Then a third, which Deirdre splashed liberally with fine brandy, a glorious concoction that enraptured my senses beyond recall.

I must draw a veil over what later befell me that night. Suffice to say that no Arcadian youth stumbling upon a nymph's enchanted bower, no shipwrecked sailor bewitched by the mermaid's song, nor Solomon in his tent beholding the charms of Sheba, enjoyed such a night of wanton abandon. The swelling treasures of India enfolded, enveloped, and conquered me. Again and again I rose, only to fall, drifting at last into a slumber of profound satiety.

Never was sound so unwelcome to my ears as the dull boom of the fort's sixty-eight-pounder that next morning. As the reader may well imagine, the night's revels had left a decided impression on both my person and my apparel. I was fairly bathed in the fatal liquor of the doorian. Indeed, such was its potency that I dared not give Deirdre even a parting glance for fear of falling victim once more to her immense and quivering charms. In a shameful state of *dishabille,* I whispered my farewells while exiting out the door, one boot in my hand. I set out in the faint light of early morning, desperate to arrive at the Widow's house before the most Spartan residents of Singapore began their morning constitutional. By great good luck I made my way unobserved to her grounds, entered, and found the bathhouse, where I disrobed and washed and rinsed myself thoroughly. In this manner I judged that I had at least freed my person from that most unchaste scent, but my clothes were another matter. Having dared so much I went further, depositing the reeking garments in the refuse bin in the alley behind the Widow's house and assuming for a few minutes the costume of Adam. It was in such attire that I ventured silently into the house itself, up the stairs and into my room, where I shaved and dressed as rapidly as possible, rubbing my scalp with a heavily scented hair oil as a final precaution against discovery. Satisfied that my appearance, though far from fresh, suggested no more than a late evening, I descended the stairs and entered the atrium to discover the Widow at her morning tea.

"My dear doctor!" she exclaimed, wrinkling her tiny nose in malicious delight, "the odour about you is most obscure! If I did not know you better, I would think you had been corrupted by a doorian! I fear Soo Ling can no longer be your maid. Her virtue would not last an instant!"

I attempted an explanation of my condition, but this effort only prompted a silvery burst of laughter, which I would have found enchanting had I not been its cause.

"Please, Doctor, please!" she said, rising from her seat and waving her hands delicately in the air, "I think it is best you should rest rather than exert yourself further. My servants will accompany me this morning. I will inform our friends that you are indisposed."

And with that she walked from the room, her graceful shoulders trembling with amusement. I had nothing more to do than retire to my room, to which I repaired with the utmost pleasure.

CHAPTER XXXII

An Unexpected Blow

OR THE NEXT SEVERAL days, I saw rather less of both Holmes and the Widow than had been my habit. To my dismay, Soo Ling was duly replaced by a young boy, courteous and competent, but of course entirely lacking Soo Ling's ineffable charm. I spent my evenings with Arthur Craven, who was glad enough to find a sympathetic ear, for his brief had apparently been well received, despite the unlikely circumstances of its genesis. I kept resolutely away from Mukerjee's establishment, returning home each night at a reasonable hour and taking care to make my arrival known in the household.

On the third morning, I felt comfortable enough to walk with the Widow, who managed to keep her composure even when we were so unfortunate as to pass a doorian tree. Later that morning we were joined by Holmes for breakfast. My friend, despite the Widow's soothing presence, could not conceal his irritation with his lack of progress in finding a captain and a ship.

"We are up against it, Watson," he told me. "Our adversary has closed the ports of the East against us. If I could find a way to contact Admiral Watkins, perhaps the British navy would be willing to supply us with a craft, but with Lord

Barington in control of the port itself and all lines of communication, I am not sure how even that can be done."

"Perhaps we should announce our return to England. Once
out of Singapore we would have less difficulty in making contact with the navy."

"That is a possibility. But we would lose time. I fear we
have wasted far too much already."

I was about to respond when a servant entered. She spoke
in Chinese to her mistress, whose face expressed some alarm.

"An officer," she said to Holmes. "With a message from
Lord Barington."

Holmes and I immediately rose and went to the door. A
young officer stood stiffly at attention as we approached.

"Do I have the honour of addressing Mr. Sherlock Holmes?"
he asked.

"Yes, Lieutenant," said Holmes. "What can I do for you?"

"I am instructed to convey this message to you from his
lordship, sir."

With that the man handed Holmes a large, official-looking
envelope. My friend tore it open, hardly concealing his impatience. He unfolded a single sheet of paper and read its contents in silence. Then he handed the sheet to me without a
word.

> My dear Mr. Holmes,
> You will be infinitely pleased to know that the miss-
> ing rifles, which you have been at such pains to locate,
> have been found. Army officers operating under my
> direction discovered them in the port of Malacca. A ring
> of thieving Chinese merchants have admitted their guilt,
> and so the matter is at an end. You are to be congratu-
> lated on the diligence of your investigation, though it
> proved, in the end, to be entirely unsuccessful. I have
> already dispatched the full details of the matter to the
> cabinet. Your commission, of course, is now revoked. If
> you and Dr. Watson lack funds to finance your return to
> England, Her Majesty's Government will be pleased to
> arrange gratis third-class passage on the vessel
> *Cormorant,* in recognition of your efforts on behalf of
> the Crown and the Crown Colony of Singapore. The *Cor-*
> *morant* departs from Singapore in three days.

I raised my eyes from the paper.

"What effrontery," I muttered.

"Quite," said Holmes.

"What is your reply, sir?" asked the officer, in a cold, formal tone.

"My reply," said Holmes, "is that you may inform his lordship that we will not be passengers on the *Cormorant*."

"Very good, sir. His lordship requests that you call on him in one hour."

The sharpness with which the man pronounced those last two words made it clear that matters had at last come to a climax. Holmes and I returned to the breakfast table and informed the Widow of this distasteful turn of events.

"What will you do?" asked the Widow, in some agitation.

"We will call his lordship's bluff," said Holmes. "My commission comes from the cabinet, not his lordship. I still have the responsibility of investigating the deaths of Elizabeth Trent and Sir Roger. Until the cabinet acts, Lord Barington can threaten, but not coerce. I intend to confront him directly on this matter. In fact, I intend to press him for a ship."

In forty minutes' time Holmes and I stood before the imposing façade of Government House. It seemed appalling that the success or failure of our mission now lay entirely within the hands of our adversary. We had no independent lines of communication. The "news" from Singapore, as received in London, was whatever Lord Barington chose to make it. Despite the singular lustre of my friend's career, it seemed impossible that his mere stubborn refusal to admit defeat should in and of itself convince a wavering cabinet of the merit of his case, a cabinet that undoubtedly wished to concern itself with issues other than a scandalous charge against one of the highest-ranking peers in all of England. With these thoughts in mind, it is hardly surprising that I found the brief journey from the steps of Government House to Lord Barington's elegantly appointed offices profoundly disquieting.

Holmes, of course, was silent. The only hint to the profound inner turmoil he must have been enduring was the

masklike composure with which he concealed it. We arrived
at last at Lord Barington's suite. The broad mahogany doors
swung open, and we entered.

"Ah, Mr. Holmes," said his lordship genially, glancing up
from a pile of papers. "And the estimable Dr. Watson. I fear
the press of business has kept us from meeting as frequently
as I would like."

"It is kind of your lordship to say so," said Holmes.

"Please be seated, gentlemen. I see no reason to insist on
formality at this stage of our relationship. May I offer you a
cigar?"

"Thank you, no," said Holmes.

"Ah. Perhaps you will join me, Dr. Watson?"

I shook my head wordlessly and stared at my boots. I was
stunned by the change in Lord Barington's manner. Clearly, a
great weight had been lifted from his shoulders. The foreboding and suppressed rage that had almost mastered him in
our previous encounter had vanished entirely. We were in the
presence of a man possessed by an utter self-confidence, a
man who knew he had won and who had nothing to fear. In
contrast, Holmes and I sat as prisoners at the dock, men upon
whom sentence has already been pronounced, men who can
feel the rope already tightening about their necks.

Lord Barington was in no hurry. He lit his cigar with fastidious care, then leaned forward with both elbows on his
desk.

"Excellent," he said. "So often I find the temperature here
robs tobacco of its savour. However, the very air seems to
have changed. There is a remarkable freshness in Singapore
these days. Perhaps you have noticed, Mr. Holmes."

"No doubt," said Holmes. "It is fortunate indeed that your
lordship finds the weather pleasing."

My friend made an indifferent courtier. His remark, poorly
formed and indifferently delivered, brought a smile of insuf-
ferable blandness to the lips of our host.

"Yes, Mr. Holmes. The air has been singularly felicitous for
the past week. A most refreshing breeze, and a most welcome
one."

It appeared that his lordship was on the verge of saying more, but my friend interrupted him.

"My friend and I require," said Holmes, "a small ship, with a good crew, that can travel through the archipelago. We have indications that the adversary we seek is located on the island of Renggano."

If this information held any terrors for Lord Barington, he did not show it.

"Really, Mr. Holmes? How remarkable. This is most embarrassing."

"Why is that, your lordship?" asked Holmes.

"Because you have exposed a most egregious wrongdoing on my part."

"Of what kind?"

"I have important information for you, Mr. Holmes, and I have failed to impart it. You see, the missing rifles have been recovered. The case has been solved. Evidently, I failed to inform you of these matters. I am most distressed by my error. Please accept my apologies."

"Matters of the highest importance remain unsolved, your lordship," returned Holmes, obviously stung by the contemptuous manner with which he was being treated. "Matters that include the murder of Elizabeth Trent."

"Poor Mrs. Trent! A tragic case, Mr. Holmes. It is most regrettable that you were unable to assist the lady when she applied to you for help. But perhaps you should return to the scene of the crime. Singapore is hardly the place to be solving murders committed in London."

As Lord Barington uttered these shameless words, I could scarcely keep from throttling him then and there and let the consequences be what they may. To make malign sport of the murder of a most innocent and noble woman was almost more than I could bear.

"I must ask your lordship to return to the matter of the boat," said Holmes in a low voice. His face was dusky with anger, and his long, thin fingers gripped the arms of his chair convulsively. It was easy to see that he shared the same emotions as I.

"I fear that is impossible, Mr. Holmes. Her Majesty's Government has been most indulgent with you. You have ridden on great warships. You have enjoyed the hospitality of the great and mighty. Of course, you refused the fine villa that I placed at your disposal, but I take no offence. But now, Mr. Holmes, you have exhausted Her Majesty's hospitality. We will not supply you with a ship. Ships cost money, Mr. Holmes. Money should be spent on necessities, not on the pursuit of will-o'-the-wisps and old legends. I suggest you follow my example and begin planning your trip home to London."

"Your lordship is returning to London?"

"Indeed I am," said Lord Barington, with a genial laugh, that, under the circumstances, was less endurable than the most bloodcurdling scream. "I have been away a long time. I don't mind telling you, Mr. Holmes, that when I arrived here I was a broken man."

"I had heard something of the matter."

"Yes, perhaps you had, Mr. Holmes, perhaps you had. But fortune smiled on me here. Singapore has been good to me, but now it is time to return home. I suggest that you do the same."

With that, the interview ended. We rose, made our bows, and departed, the heartless laughter of the great lord still ringing in our ears.

"He is the fiend incarnate," I said as we strode down the steps.

"No, but he serves him," returned Holmes. "We must have a ship, Watson! We must have a ship!"

CHAPTER XXXIII

A Midnight Departure

 E MADE THE TRIP back to the Widow's in complete silence. For three days, Holmes seques-
tered himself in his study, not even appearing
for meals. Twice I made bold to enquire of
the Widow of his condition, but she only shook her head
wordlessly. On the fourth day, Holmes appeared around noon,
looking worn but excited.

"The Widow informs me that we have a craft, Watson," he
said. "We leave here shortly after midnight. Discuss this with
no one. You will excuse me if I attempt to recover some of
the sleep I have foregone over the past few days."

With that, he retired to his room. For my own part, the task
of keeping a check on both my hopes and fears almost led
me to wish that Holmes had kept me in the dark on the matter up until the moment of our departure, which indeed was
his common practice. More for diversion than anything else, I
disassembled, cleaned, and oiled my revolver. After that I
read through several issues of the *Straits Times* in a desultory
manner and smoked a cigar in the Widow's garden. After a
quiet dinner with the Widow, I attempted to obtain some
measure of rest in preparation for the rigours of our journey,

but the state of my nerves rendered that impossible. At last the hour arrived. A knock upon my door summoned me.

"Ready, Watson?" asked Holmes.

"Of course," I replied.

"You see, my dear, I am in the best of hands. There is no need for concern."

The Widow Han was beside him. I shall always remember her as she was that night, in a simple robe of white silk, with her gleaming, black hair, finer than the finest silk, spilling about her shoulders. She held Holmes' arm in hers and leaned forward to briefly embrace me.

"Good fortune, Doctor," she said. "The gods await you."

A few minutes later we were in the Widow's carriage once more, with Wu Shih at the reins, passing through the streets of Chinatown, still crowded with late-night revellers. As we approached the docks, the streets emptied, for in Singapore commerce confines itself to the daylight hours. The dark abandoned buildings and streets filled me with trepidation. Only the faintest crescent of a new moon shone in the sky, and even the brilliance of the Milky Way scarcely did more than dust the looming shadows with silver. I clutched my revolver in my pocket and looked nervously about me. At last we reached the harbour. Wu Shih drove the carriage directly out onto one of the docks, the clopping hooves of the horses echoing in the darkness. At the end of the dock a large junk waited. No other craft were visible except a much smaller junk that floated at anchor farther out in the harbour. Wu Shih brought the carriage to a halt beside the large junk. Holmes and I leapt out, while the boy gathered our baggage.

"Wu Shih, summon our captain," said Holmes.

Wu Shih spoke softly in Chinese, but received no response. He stepped on the deck of the vessel and raised his voice slightly, but again we heard, and saw, nothing.

"Deviltry, Watson," said Holmes, with a scowl on his face. "The man had specific orders. Hand me the bulls-eye and we'll have a look in the cabin."

Our search was as short as it was tragic. The first flame of the lantern displayed to us the body of the unfortunate captain, lying in a pool of blood, his throat cut from ear to ear.

"We move fast, but our adversary moves faster," said Holmes. "We had best leave before we share the captain's fate."

As we stepped from the cabin I noticed that the small junk, almost invisible against the black sea, had silently drifted in beside us and now lay close against the pier. A shadowy, powerful figure, his face concealed beneath the broad brim of a coolie hat, moved menacingly across the deck. Instinctively, my hand reached for my revolver in response to this new alarm.

"Careful, Watson," said Holmes, gripping my wrist. "You would not wish to injure an old friend."

The fellow lifted his head for an instant, and the faint rays of the shore lights glinted on his face. It was Captain MacDougall!

"You recognized me, Mr. Holmes," said the captain, with a chuckle. "What gave me away?"

"It is a curious junk that drifts toward shore while the tide is ebbing," said Holmes. "And one that bears verses of the Koran fluttering from its mast should be unique. The deduction was a simple one."

"Allah has brought me here, Mr. Holmes, but I cannot tarry. It is best that we leave immediately."

Holmes turned to Wu Shih. "We must go with the captain, Wu Shih," he said. "Do you think you can get yourself home safely?"

"You no worry about me, Boss Man Holmes," the boy returned. "You worry about yourself!"

"There's a good lad," said Holmes. "Keep this close about you."

The brief flash of a gold sovereign shone in the starlight. Wu Shih caught up the coin and tucked it in his pocketbook.

"You first-class boss man, Mr. Holmes," the boy said, wheeling the carriage about. "Gods await you."

Holmes and I watched him depart, and then stepped cautiously into the junk.

"Conceal yourselves beneath the canvas," said the captain. "It is imperative that we escape the harbour without being observed."

Holmes and I lay on the deck, together with our baggage, covered by a stout sheet of canvas. As the captain busied himself with adjustments to the sail, we felt the small craft turn about and head smoothly out to sea. Half an hour later the captain threw back the canvas and we felt the fresh sea air blow over us.

"We should be safe now," he said.

"How did you learn of our plight?" asked Holmes.

"We lost a mast a week ago in a typhoon off Borneo. We made port at Pontianak. A merchant from Singapore informed me how the odds had shifted in Barington's favour. When I learned that you were seeking passage to Renggano, I could not resist the temptation to lend a hand."

"Not Renggano precisely," said Holmes. "I gave that as our destination in the vain hope of concealing our hand. What we are seeking, Captain, is open water. I believe there is a ship, cruising off the Cocos Islands, Renggano, and Christmas Island, that bears our quarry."

"Excellent. We should be there in several days."

"Do you really expect to make such a journey in this craft?" asked Holmes. I shared his dismay, for the boat we were in was no more than ten feet long and, it seemed, hardly capable of prolonged sailing in the open sea.

"Of course not. I have obtained command of a small schooner. I chose this vessel as the most inconspicuous vehicle for my entry into Singapore Harbour. We will reach the schooner in a few hours."

"Excellent," said Holmes. "Would you possibly have a map at hand, and a lantern? I wish to orient myself as quickly as possible."

The captain passed an oilskin pouch to Holmes in reply.

"Here are the maps," he said. "Conceal yourself under the canvas if you use the lantern. My eyes are accustomed to the darkness, and I do not wish to lose that advantage. If we encounter another vessel, I want to see rather than be seen."

I must confess that the thought of sailing a small boat out into the open sea in the middle of the night with anyone except Captain MacDougall in command would have filled me with trepidation. Fortunately, the night, though dark, was otherwise ideal for sailing. The sea was calm and unruffled, with slow, even swells that hardly disturbed even our small boat, while a fresh, even breeze allowed the captain to guide us rapidly to our destination.

"The weather favours our venture," I remarked as we glided easily over the waves.

"For the present," the captain replied, "but I expect a higher wind shortly. She has been rising for hours. That is why I wish to reach the *Dulcinea* as soon as possible."

At length we spied a faint light shining through the darkness. As the captain had predicted, the wind was rising, and an occasional whitecap gleamed against the sea's darkness. As we drew nearer, the light separated itself in two, and as we drew nearer still, one of the lights split again.

"The *Dulcinea*," said the captain. "That is how I marked her."

Before long we were aboard the schooner, which was a two-master, close to seventy feet in length, with a crew of three. The men, from the look of them, had no relish for the voyage, but they went about their tasks with no complaint or delay. The weather continued fair, though with a strong wind, and we made our passage through the Sunda Strait ahead of schedule. As a precaution, Holmes and I remained below-decks throughout the daylight hours. The captain reported that when we passed the port of Bantam off Java, a small steamboat seemed to follow the *Dulcinea* for several hours, but then took a different course.

On the evening of our passage of the Sunda Strait, Holmes and I stood on the deck, the faint, misty outline of the coast of Sumatra just visible against the thickening sky.

"Somewhere on that island lies the most remarkable city in the world," said Holmes.

"You mean the home of the Bada?"

"Yes. When we finish with this business, it would be worth a month or two to track it down."

"You see no real difficulties in our current task?"

"I did not say that, Watson. But we are as prepared as we ever shall be. We have the captain's assistance, which is worth a great deal. As for the rest, it is sometimes best not to think too far ahead."

Later at dinner we conversed easily with the captain, who described for us the subterfuges he was obliged to employ in obtaining recognition of his rank with Archer & Company. Holmes responded with a long story of his first encounter as a consulting detective with Scotland Yard. As the two traded reminiscences, the foreboding I felt during my earlier conversation with Holmes faded from my mind, but several hours later, when I lay down in my narrow bunk, the fears suddenly sprang to life again. After an hour of restlessness, I finally slid into a troubled sleep, only to be shaken awake a few hours later.

"Watson, wake up!" I heard Holmes' fierce whisper in my ear and felt his powerful grip upon my shoulder. My confused eyes struggled to find their focus in the glare of the lantern he carried with him.

"What is it?" I asked.

"Murder," he said. "The crew have been murdered."

"The captain?"

"He is alive, or was when I left him. He roused me and went on deck. We must join him."

I dressed and armed myself in a matter of minutes. We hastened on deck and found the captain by the wheel, a revolver in one hand. At his feet lay the body of one of the crew, a broad dark stain spreading over the deck beneath his body.

"Knife wounds, all three," said the captain. "I have found no sign of a boarder. Doctor, I must ask you to go aloft. We cannot ignore the possibility that another ship is close by."

The captain's words were less than welcome. To climb a sixty-foot mast at any time is less than a welcome chore. To climb one at night, in a strong wind and a heavy sea, was a grim task indeed. But I had no choice other than to comply. Our position aboard that ship was precarious at best. At any moment we might be subject to assault by that mysterious foe whom we had sought to stalk, but who was now stalking us. I knotted a length of rope around my waist, that I might secure myself to the crow's nest when I reached the summit, and mounted the mast without demur, though the instinct to resist was so great that the release of each hand and foothold demanded from me the exercise of a conscious mental effort. Throughout the climb, I kept my gaze firmly fixed on the six inches of wood directly before my eyes, until at last my trembling fingers struck the iron rim of the tiny crow's nest that encircled the mast at its peak.

At that precise instant the ship struck a massive wave, and I felt that slow, horrible glide that pitched me first back, then forward, and then back again. Helpless as a leaf in a gale, I clung to the mast, which indeed seemed to tremble as much as I. The experience was so shattering that I knew I must pause awhile to recover my nerve before climbing at last into the nest and daring to look down at the sea from the terrifying heights of my perch. My stomach churning within me, I slid upward and at last completed the final short stretch of my ascent, fitting my feet to the absurdly slim iron spokes that provide the poor sailor with all the foothold he has. Steadying myself on the handrail, I knotted the free end of the rope around my waist to the rail, in a clumsy but serviceable version of the running bowline I had frequently completed under the cabin boy's tutelage aboard the *Prophet*. Then I looked out over the sea.

There are few sights more beautiful, and more terrible, than the night sea viewed from the crow's nest of a sailing vessel. Directly below your feet a great tower of canvas shimmers in the moonlight like a cloud. Above your head the true clouds rise like great, ghostly mountains. Their peaks shine and illuminate, while their valleys smoulder and blacken. The sea runs black as well, the great waves ever arriving and ever departing, splashed occasionally with crests of creamy foam, rolling off to the eternal horizon, where sea and sky become one.

Despite the rigour of my climb, I could hardly help responding to the mighty scene that played about me. But I knew that I could not absent myself from the deck an instant longer than necessary without incurring the captain's just wrath. I therefore strained my eyes in every direction in the hope of discovering some glimmer of light, some distant, shadowy shape, that might provide us with some assistance, either to extricate us from our peril or enable us to avoid greater danger. In the midst of my anxious reverie I was disturbed in the most dramatic manner, by the discharge of a revolver! I looked down, and as I did so I saw a powerful hand reaching for my boot! I drew my foot away in horror and, leaning forward precariously from my perch, beheld the foul visage of the perfidious Molo directly below me!

Struggling to maintain my balance, I drew my revolver and commenced firing. I cannot blame the reader for condemning me upon learning that even at this point-blank range my first three shots went wide of the mark. My shock at the suddenness of the vile creature's assault, combined with the violence of the ship's movement and the uncertainty of my footing, all conspired to undermine my aim. My fourth round, however, had some effect, for the villain gave out a howl of pain and slid down several feet, until the taut canvas of the topmost sail concealed him from my view. To my astonishment, however, he neither fell nor climbed down from the mainmast, but instead made a prodigious leap to the foremast, catching himself up safely at the base of the mainsail. Balancing easily on the crosstree despite the heavy rolling of the ship, he turned in my direction, made a bloodcurdling gesture of defiance, and then began climbing the foremast at a furious pace.

In the excitement of the moment, I foolishly fired off my remaining rounds, without doing the fellow the least harm. As the hammer of my revolver fell harmlessly on an empty chamber, I realized with a sinking feeling that the monster could now quite safely return to the mainmast and finish what he had begun. In my desperation, I looked down at the deck and beheld Holmes standing at some distance from the base of the foremast with his revolver drawn, but holding his fire.

Following Holmes' gaze with my own, I could see that he was watching not Molo but the captain, who was himself mounting the foremast with a speed and an alacrity that almost matched the pace of our apelike adversary.

As the captain made his way up the mast, I transferred my attention to his quarry, who now had reached the summit of the foremast and was evidently preparing to return to the mainmast. I aimed my revolver at him, and for a long moment he hesitated. I had gained a few seconds at most, but it proved to be enough, as the captain, now more than halfway up, began firing. A look of malignant rage, the image of which I shall carry forever in my memory, flashed over the creature's face. Then he disappeared from view behind the front of the sail. I could observe the captain fire his third or fourth round and then resume climbing.

As the captain reached the crosstree of the foremast, the loathsome creature somehow lunged upward from behind the sail, knocked the captain's pistol from his hand, and clutched him by the throat. My heart all but stopped within my breast when I saw the captain in such peril, for I could not imagine how he could escape, but somehow he broke the creature's grip. The two grappled furiously on the swaying mast, clinging to the ropes while they struggled. The captain broke free and scrambled upwards, then turned and gave Molo a powerful kick in the chest, sending the creature down and backward into the rigging. Yet he recovered with astounding agility, fairly flying back upwards hand over hand along the ropes. The captain continued his climb to the very top of the mast, then turned and pointed and shouted in my direction. His words were lost in the roar of wind and sea, but somehow his meaning flew instantly into my mind. I wrenched off my left boot and sent it hurtling toward him. As I did so the ship struck an enormous wave, which almost flung me from my perch. I could see nothing but the sweeping topsail and, far below, the shrunken deck of the *Dulcinea*.

When I recovered my balance, neither the captain nor Molo was visible. For a long minute I strained my eyes for some sign of either of them, glancing fearfully down at the deck and then back up along the foremast, but the billowing sails hid their secret well. At last I spied them, the captain balanced at the end of a crosstree and clinging to a guy rope, while Molo advanced toward him like a great spider. The hideous creature sprang forward, confident of his prey, but at the last second, the captain whipped out his hand and plunged the keen blade into the monster's belly. A piteous shriek rang out above the fierce rush of the wind, and the body of Molo, vanquished at last, hurtled to the deck below.

CHAPTER XXXIV

The End of the Quest

 REACHED THE DECK SOME minutes later, shaken indeed by the frightful encounter I had just endured aloft.

"Are you all right, Watson?" asked Holmes as I descended. "You have had quite a night of it."

"I have indeed," I said, trembling all over. "I would ask for a brandy and a cigar if this were a night for either."

"Here is your boot, at least," said Holmes. "The captain discarded it in his haste, but I was able to retrieve it for you."

"Here is your knife as well," said the captain, pulling the blade from the vile creature's belly and wiping the blood on his leg. "Your assistance was timely."

"As was yours," I returned. "Few men could have dispatched that brute."

"Indeed," said Holmes, "we both owe you our lives."

For a moment an almost boyish smile of pleasure seemed to break across the captain's face in mute salute to our praise. Then the sardonic reserve so characteristic of him emerged once more.

"Well enough," he said, "but our lives are still in danger. These sails must come down if we are to weather the night."

And come down they did, though hardly to the captain's satisfaction. The effort that lowering the seven sails of that ship cost us was astonishing. Our labours continued well past morning and left us with masts bare but intact. Though we were not faced with an actual storm, both wind and sea continued high. As the day lengthened, the constant rocking and wallowing of the ship, which we could not adequately control, wore heavily on me. I could not eat to relieve my hunger, nor sleep to relieve my fatigue. Though we were surely no more than two days' sail from the Sunda Strait, no ship had passed. I asked the captain if he were not concerned.

"I am concerned that my crew has been murdered by that foul monster," he said. "I am concerned that when we are towed back to Singapore we will be no further along to the solution of this conspiracy than we were before. I am concerned that Lord Barington will know our game and contrive to have you and Mr. Holmes returned to London whether you like it or no. But for the present, Doctor, I am not concerned for my life. If a sailor had no more in life to trouble him than this, he would be overpaid at any wage."

Such a speech left little room for reply. I returned to my post, staring out to sea while the long tropic evening light slowly waned to darkness. The sea quieted itself at last. I was able to eat a little and, with the pangs of my stomach eased, quickly fell into a deep slumber.

I must have slept for hours, though not nearly so long as I wished. I felt myself being violently roused.

"Wake up, Watson! There is a ship!"

It was Holmes' voice. I staggered to my feet like a half-wit, reaching for something to hold on to, and immediately fell flat on the deck, betrayed by the motion of the ship.

"Steady, Watson. You must wake up!"

I felt the cold splash of seawater on my face, a most unwelcome awakening.

"Here, drink this if you have a stomach for it," said Holmes, handing me a battered silver flask that smelled of brandy. I took a long drink and felt the spirits warm me.

"That's better, eh? Now, on your feet."

"Where is the ship?" I asked, still groggy with sleep.

"You shall see for yourself," said Holmes, with growing impatience. "There is no time to lose."

I staggered up the stairs, angry beyond measure at having been so roused, but aware from Holmes' manner that a moment of crisis had arrived. We found the captain on deck at the port bow, surveying the sea with his binoculars. Light clouds hid most of the moon's light, but I could clearly see a large black freighter no more than a thousand yards away.

"The *Duke of Buccleuch,* five thousand tons, a very fine ship," the captain said. "Reported lost at sea two years ago. Enderby & Cross paid off the investors in full."

No sooner had he spoken than a brilliant flash of light appeared on the ship, followed almost immediately by the eruption of an immense geyser of water within thirty yards of our vessel.

"They seem to have made some improvements on her," said Holmes dryly. "God help us if they intend to put us down."

There was another flash of light from the mystery ship. A shell whistled over our heads and crashed into the sea perhaps five hundred yards beyond us.

"Come now," said Holmes. "That was a poor shot. What do they mean to do?"

In answer a third shot crashed into the stern of the ship with an enormous explosion that sent planks splintering into the air. A fourth round followed with the same deadly accuracy, but then the gun fell silent. The *Dulcinea* settled slowly into the water.

"We have an hour at least, unless they give us another round," said the captain, glancing at the damage. "But I believe we had best abandon ship now."

"Yes," said Holmes, "for the moment they seem intent on making us their guests. It would be better not to give them a chance to alter their purpose."

I was struck by the look of calm, almost of satisfaction, that showed on the faces of the two men.

"What is their purpose?" I enquired.

"Oh, I am not sure that matters," said Holmes. "We have brought this affair far enough. I wrote out a full report of this entire investigation and made a copy as well. One copy is being sent to Monsieur Compte in Paris, along with the casket, aboard a French warship. He can reason out most of the pieces of the puzzle and can find those who can help him with the rest. The other copy remains with the Widow. While in London, I told my brother Mycroft the little that I then knew, and M. Compte will be in correspondence with him. These matters, which have been kept so dark, will come into the light at last, regardless of the outcome here."

Holmes' unconcern did not entirely inspire me, and my doubts must have shown on my face, for the captain clapped me on the shoulder in a gesture of reassurance.

"You should not worry yourself, Doctor," he said. "Allah would not bring us this far without a purpose. And if we can come this far, others can go further."

With that we set about lowering the whaleboat. I was glad for the opportunity to do something, however little, but once we were in the boat itself, the dark waves towering about us, my heart sank within me once more. Never, not even when I lay bleeding in Afghanistan, did I ever feel a greater sense of futility in my actions. My comrades' brave words failed to raise my spirits to the exalted pitch theirs had attained. To escape the burden of thought, I took to the oars and rowed us slowly away from the sinking *Dulcinea*.

"They mean for us to come on board," said Holmes, as the waves washed over the blasted schooner's deck. "I have handled this badly, Watson. And I owe you an apology as well, Captain. This was hardly what you bargained for back in Tangier."

"You need not fret yourself, Mr. Holmes," the captain said. "I am not surprised it has come to this. I put myself too far in to ever expect to get out."

He then sat and began to work the second pair of oars the whaleboat carried. We moved steadily toward the freighter, which remained motionless in the water. Since we had first sighted her, she had shown no sign of life other than the firing of her guns.

In a few minutes, our boat's wooden sides were scraping against the freighter's iron hull. Scarcely had we reached it, when a rope ladder was flung over the side by an unseen hand.

"Very well, then," said Holmes, grasping the ladder. "At last we get to the root of the matter."

With that he began climbing the ladder. As he disappeared over the side, I felt a sudden horror at the hideous fate that must await him. Determined to be at his side to witness the last, whatever it might be, I sprang forward and grasped the rungs. As the ship rose and fell, I clambered up the ladder and over the side.

CHAPTER XXXV

The Dance of Shiva

HEY WERE DRAWN IN A semicircle around us. They stood about three feet high and were covered with brown fur. They sat easily on their haunches like kangaroos, their long, naked tails curling behind them. Their forepaws were remarkably human in appearance, and many carried small daggers or firearms. Each wore a heavy leather belt that went both around the waist and over the left shoulder, as a kind of uniform. A soft murmur arose among them at the sight of us, a sort of clucking sound, whose individual words, if any, were indistinguishable to the human ear.

"More like rabbits than rats, wouldn't you say, Watson?" asked Holmes, as I joined him on deck. "The heads, I mean. Naturally, to be capable of rational thought the brainpan had to be remarkably enlarged."

Beholding these creatures, about whom we had speculated for so long, I scarcely felt capable of rational thought myself. I felt instead that I had fallen back into that strange, dreamlike world where I had earlier beheld one of their number. I was struggling to speak when the captain appeared by our side.

"Allah be praised," he said under his breath, "and Allah defend us."

"Do you think," I asked in as low a voice as possible, "that we could stand a chance against them?"

"I doubt that the moment for violence has arrived," said Holmes. "I don't fancy being pecked to death by derringer bullets, which would appear to be our most likely fate. Ah, they are clearing a way for us. Let us follow their lead."

Remarkably, a way did appear through the bizarre creatures, which closed behind us as we went. We arrived at a large door and entered.

We found ourselves in a large, high room of curious and unexpected luxury, brilliantly lit with electric lamps. The walls were lined with books, many of them elegantly bound. Above the bookcases were hung examples of exotic weaponry, cutlasses and pikes and antique rifles, some of which reminded me of the arms of the Afghan rebels I had fought as a youth. There were fine lacquer tables piled high with Oriental scrolls, reminiscent of the ones I had seen at the house of the Widow Han. The floor was covered by the most splendid carpets I have ever seen, offering up a profusion of colour and design that even in this extremity all but overwhelmed the eye. There were no chairs. The room was dominated by a massive desk, carved from what was undoubtedly English oak and surfaced with black leather. Curiously, the only object on it was a shotgun, which I instantly recognized as the elegant Purdy that Lord Barington had flourished before us only a week before. Behind the desk was a small table, with a silver salver that bore a fine crystal decanter and a pair of glasses. While I was attempting to take all this in, a broad door set in the far wall opened, and a figure appeared.

"Ah, Mr. Holmes," said the figure. "We meet at last."

I stared, unable to speak, unable even to believe my eyes. Our host was a giant rat, as tall as a man, even though bent over and hunched as though suffering from advanced age. He had an enormous, distorted head, with brilliant, inquisitive eyes, which burned with a malignant energy as he beheld us. His enlarged incisors, which were visible even when his mouth was closed, were like a pair of tremendous, blunt fangs. He had a heavy, black cape thrown over his shoulders, and he moved with a strange, hopping, shuffling gait, resting his weight on a heavy staff, his thick tail sliding behind him like an immense snake. With his eyes fixed upon us, he took up his place behind the desk and sat on his heels in the manner of the other creatures we had seen.

"No doubt you have some questions for me," said the creature, grinning in my friend's direction.

"Yes," said Holmes, cautiously. "I know nothing about you, other than a few rumours. I have had no evidence."

"But you do have evidence, Mr. Holmes. You simply do not know how to read it. But we shall discuss that in good time."

"Will Lord Barington be joining us?" Holmes asked.

"Lord Barington? Ah, you noticed his shotgun. Yes, his lordship is with us, in a manner of speaking. But first things first, Mr. Holmes. You have something of mine. I want it."

"You mean the scroll."

"I do."

"I hardly see how you can put forth any claim that the courts would recognize."

"I am the court, Mr. Holmes, and I find in my favour," said the rat, almost with a smile. "That scroll belongs to me, Mr. Holmes. It is the record of the greatest achievement this planet has witnessed, one that your puny race lacks the intellect even to comprehend."

"Really?" returned my friend, with a coolness of manner I could scarcely believe. "And what achievement is that?"

"The achievement of my birth. You are a fool, Mr. Holmes, to taunt me thus. I could be your saviour."

"I had no idea I was in need of salvation."

"You are in desperate need of salvation, as are your friends, unless you learn quickly to curb your tongue. I have hopes for you, Mr. Holmes. Great hopes."

The monstrous creature stared at us with his brilliant eyes, delighting in the confusion he provoked.

"Let me confess myself your admirer, Mr. Holmes," the creature continued. "Your discussions of the influence of the Mongolian steppe on human history showed remarkable perspicacity for one of your species."

"The thoughts of an idle moment," said Holmes.

"Surely you are too modest," said the creature, with a cunning smile. "When I first read your articles I thought I might have a rival. Though our premises differ, our conclusions, properly understood, are remarkably similar. Our union could have enormous consequences, and enormous benefits."

"I have heard such words before. Lord Barington's proposals did not interest me."

"Barington was a fool, but you were a greater fool to spurn him. I have much to offer you, Mr. Holmes. I can give you power, power undreamed of for centuries."

"I don't know that I should want to place myself in competition with his lordship."

"You need have no worries on that account, Mr. Holmes. His lordship is dead. I have a peculiar constitution, and peculiar needs. Lord Barington is now fulfilling those needs, to the best of his capabilities."

Having said this, the creature pulled open a drawer from the desk and took out a large bone, which I recognized with sickening clarity as a human radius, still "green," to use the brutal language of my profession. Regarding us with flaming eyes, the creature placed the bone between his great front teeth and shattered it with a single occlusion.

My soul sank within me after this monstrous display of wanton cruelty. The creature cackled with joy at my horror.

"My apologies, Doctor," it growled, "for assaulting your human sensibilities so directly. But I have waited a long time for this. Your race has much to answer for, and I will enforce the penalties due in full. But I must have the scroll, Mr. Holmes."

"Unfortunately, I neglected to bring it with me."

"I thought as much. But you will tell me where it is."

"I think not."

"Do not trifle with me, Mr. Holmes. Cross me and you will be destroyed. Join with me and I will grant you knowledge beyond your wildest dreams."

"Here? On this poor ship?"

"Yes, Mr. Holmes. Do you know what I am? You think me

one of the poor creatures you saw outside, blessed with the rudiments of reason, but condemned by lack of stature to fugitive existence by the heartless cruelty of your race. You call them less than human, Mr. Holmes, but you are all too human!"

As the rat spoke, his eyes flashed and his great forepaws clenched and unclenched. His harsh, grating voice shook with emotion, adding yet another touch of madness to the drama, which seemed to have risen bodily from the delirium of an opium eater's dream.

"I am an experiment, Mr. Holmes. I stand between two worlds, where no soul, no spirit has ever stood. Perhaps you know something of the voyages of Cheng-Ho."

"A trifle."

"A trifle indeed. Do you know that when the old emperor died and the admiral's new masters baulked at his expeditions, he made a last voyage without their assistance, from which he never returned?"

"That is well known."

"On that last, fateful voyage, Cheng-Ho took with him not only sailors, but craftsmen, scholars, soldiers, all who refused to stagnate under the feeble rule of a dying dynasty. He led a host of thousands, whose valour and enterprise would beggar the imagination of an Alexander, a Genghis Khan, or a Napoleon."

"No doubt."

"Do not provoke me, Mr. Holmes. I am telling you truths of immeasurable value. Cheng-Ho's fleet arrived at the island you call Singapore. His expedition, fleeing ignorance at home, had no wish to emulate it abroad. Instead of oppressing and murdering the Bada, the Chinese befriended them. But Cheng-Ho sailed on, to India, where he encountered the Muslim and the Hindu. The finest spirits, Mr. Holmes, have always rejected the petty orthodoxies to which your race is so addicted. Cheng-Ho gathered such men about him and created a new society, untrammelled by the superstitious fears that have condemned you humans to barbarism.

"He drew from many races—Chinese, Mongol, Turk,

Hindu, Persian, Arab, even African. Wisely, he excluded the Europeans, who destroy rather than create. He was succeeded by his nephew Meng-Wu. Their genius forged a society that this earth has never seen, a society of the intellect."

The great rat paused. He seemed to be in an ecstasy of excitement as he recounted this bizarre history. His dark, unfathomable eyes gleamed, and his massive head turned back and forth with quick, sharp jerks.

"Have you ever wondered, Mr. Holmes, what the free intellect could achieve if it were not weighed down with the vanity of princes and the envy of priests? Have you ever wondered what men could do if they dared, like Cheng-Ho, to step forward instead of falling back? I am the creation of those men, Mr. Holmes. I stand between two worlds, two races, two species. I offer to you the prospect of an intellect that commands flesh and blood rather than obeying it."

"What you say cannot be true."

"It is true. I am their creation."

"A descendant, you mean."

"No, their creation. I am over four hundred years old, Mr. Holmes, and for all that time I have been waiting for that scroll, which holds the secret of my birth. You will give it to me!"

"Again, I must decline. While I must confess that these facts are new to me, I grasped from the first the importance of the scroll, and thus have taken peculiar pains to guard it."

"You have not destroyed it."

"I have said enough."

"Very well. I have grown wise over the centuries, Mr. Holmes. I am old, but I am confident that soon I can reverse the process. Already you have seen evidence of my handiwork."

"Lord Barington's footman."

"Yes, Molo. You English pride yourself on your breeding. You cannot dream of what I can achieve. Your writings on the Mongolian steppe demonstrate an awareness of the plasticity of human cultures and their purely tentative and indifferent nature. What is true of culture is true of flesh as well. The scroll alone holds the complete secret, but even without it I have accomplished much. Consider, Mr. Holmes, what can happen if we substitute the will of the creator for the hand of chance."

To my amazement, Holmes seemed almost amused by the creature's remark.

"Pardon me. I had thought the point of my articles was the folly of assuming to master those tools that it is only given to Nature to employ. In any event, you are aware that we disposed of your creation."

"Molo was a beginning, nothing more. He served me. What I have done once, I can do again, and better. The entire animal world offers its resources. Allow me to show you."

So saying, the creature took a small, silver whistle from one of the pockets of his robe and blew upon it, though no sound was emitted. Almost instantly, there was a scratching outside the door through which he had entered. Then the door opened, and two dogs trotted in.

They were not such dogs as any man had ever seen. As tall as a Belgian shepherd, they were liver-coloured, with short hair, lean and lithe, and beautifully muscled. Their heads were overlarge, with fearsome jaws and gleaming teeth. They advanced silently, throwing a single glance at us, and then sitting before their master in a posture of alert obedience.

"These are Bel and Mar," said the creature, grinning evilly.

"Indeed," said Holmes. "Do they speak?"

"They do not speak, but they understand!" returned the rat, with a sudden flash of anger. "Bel! The bookcase on the far wall, to your right! The large red volume from the fifth shelf!"

Instantly the dog sprang to its feet and paced the length of the room. Rising to its hind legs, it inspected the books on the fifth shelf and carefully seized the proper volume with its jaws. So burdened, it trotted back to its master and laid the book upon the desk.

"There is so much to be done, Mr. Holmes. After the death of Meng-Wu, the brilliant society he had created fell to pieces under pressure from European traders. I learned the folly of even the greatest of your race. I was mocked and insulted, exhibited as a freak for the amusement of lords and ladies. They laughed at my very speech! But I escaped. I joined my brothers, the Bada, who took me in. I led their fight against your encroachments, your cruelties and wanton destructions. For centuries I have studied, hidden in the jungle with none but the Bada to care for me and to console me. But I have recovered much of what has been lost. My power grows. I must have the secrets of the scroll and of my birth. You cannot deny me."

"If you need the scroll so desperately, your achievements can hardly be as brilliant as you profess," said Holmes, in an icy voice. "Your meddling with the laws of evolution reflect a reason that has lost its way and the ramblings of your own disordered intellect, nothing more. As for power, you have none, other than this poor ship, which you could not create yourself."

"Do not goad me, Mr. Holmes," the creature roared. "I will not be goaded!"

"There is no need for that," said Holmes. "You are goaded by your own folly, which drives you to senseless crimes. There is an insanity in your blood, and it is claiming you."

"I had such hopes, Mr. Holmes. But you will not be taught," said the creature with a hideous snarl. "Very well."

With that, the monstrous rat lunged forward and grasped Holmes with its enormous paws. Holmes staggered backward under the brutal assault. As he did so, he whispered to me, "The Purdy, Watson."

In a flash I grasped Holmes' plan. While he grappled with the rat, he shielded me from the sight of the dogs. I snatched up the shotgun, pulled open the compartment in the butt, and took out three rounds. I chambered two of them and clicked the mechanism shut. As I did so, I saw the first of the dogs leaping towards me over the figures of Holmes and the rat. I drew the shotgun to my shoulder and fired. Almost immediately the second dog came flying around the side of the desk. My second round caught him in the side and sent him sprawling.

The rat, aroused by my actions, flung Holmes aside and seized me while I was breaking open the shotgun to load the final round. His immense paws held me in a death grip while he pulled me toward his hideous jaws. His foul breath was upon me, and I felt sure the next moment would be my last, when suddenly the creature released me, rearing upward with a high-pitched scream!

From the corner of my eye I saw what had happened. The captain had taken down one of the swords affixed to the walls and slashed off a portion of the monster's tail. The giant rat turned and, with a single, sweeping gesture, struck the sword from the captain's hand. A second blow sent him sprawling on the floor. Thanks to this reprieve I was able to chamber the final round and snap shut the breech. But the sound alerted the creature, who wheeled with amazing speed and seized me once more. I struggled desperately in his grip as he drew me again towards his reeking maw, almost fainting from the stench of his foetid breath. With the last, desperate effort of a doomed man, I managed to twist the shotgun until it pointed directly into the great rat's mouth. The shotgun roared, deafening me with its blast. I collapsed under the monstrous weight of the animal, and the room went dark.

When I awakened, Holmes and the captain were bending over me. I was covered with blood and still trembling with shock from the encounter. The captain was wiping blood from my features, wearing a large grin on his own face.

"That was most nicely done, Doctor," his powerful voice strained with emotion. "Allah chose well when he sent you to me. The battles are over, and the war is won."

"It is indeed, my dear fellow," said Holmes, clasping my hand in a grip of steel, "and the credit is entirely yours."

"But Holmes," I said, staggering to my feet, amazed that I was still alive, "how could you have known that the Purdy had three rounds in the stock?"

"I didn't know that it had any," he returned. "But what other chance was there? May I offer you a drink, Watson? Upon my word, no man ever deserved one more, and the creature appears to have kept a decent cellar, for a rat at least."

So saying, he poured me a glass from the decanter that sat on the table behind the creature's desk. I must have presented a remarkable picture, stupefied and smeared with blood from my late encounter, and clutching a glass of brandy. At length I ventured a sip, and then several mouthfuls of the warming spirits. I emptied the glass and set it down.

"I hope you are restored, Doctor," said the captain, amused by this display of European folly, "for we must be going. I hardly think the Bada will take kindly to the death of their king."

I could not help but be chilled by the captain's words. While Harat's monstrous plans had died with him, we ourselves were very far from freedom. Indeed, I could not see how we were to escape the ship. I was about to make some remark to this effect when, to my horror, I saw the face of one of the rats pressed against a porthole. When he saw the body of his slaughtered monarch, he let forth an uncanny wail that seemed to pierce my very soul. Almost instantly, other faces appeared at the remaining portholes. Soon, hundreds of throats were keening in ghostly unison, until the very ship seemed to vibrate with their sorrow. Grim-faced, Holmes barred the door to the exterior of the ship while the captain did the same for the door to the interior. We armed ourselves with swords, which seemed puny weapons indeed against the creatures, whom we knew to possess firearms.

But the feared battle was not to be. The keening rose and rose, ever fiercer in its intensity, for almost an hour, when suddenly the creatures fell silent. We could hear the soft rustlings of hundreds of feet. After a few minutes, which seemed endless, Holmes cautiously put his eye to one of the portholes.

"They're abandoning ship," he said, almost to himself.

The captain and I each flew to a porthole. Looking out over the deck, we could see waves of the strange creatures racing to the rail and over. Soon the deck was empty.

"I suggest you gentlemen consider the sailor's belief that rats decline passage on a sinking ship," said the captain, walking over to the door. "If the creatures are indeed all gone, it is best that we emulate their example."

So saying, he boldly opened the door, his cutlass at the ready. But there was nothing. We stepped outside, looking constantly around us, and made our way to the rail. The creatures were now a short distance from the ship, swimming furiously against the heavy swells.

"What can it mean?" I asked.

"Suicide," said the captain. He leaned on the rail, his hands far apart, staring down at the water. "They swim not to live, but to die. There is no land for miles. Even now they are going under. It is time we left this ship."

Even as he spoke the deck beneath our feet gave a sudden lurch and developed a pronounced list, which steadily worsened. We quickly located a lifeboat, equipped with a sail and two pairs of oars, as well as bottles of drinking water and other supplies. Under the captain's expert guidance, we lowered ourselves with surprising ease into the rolling sea, despite the darkness.

"Now, gentlemen," said the captain, once we were fairly well cast off. "We must row as men have never done before."

I could not understand why the captain did not avail himself of the sail, but his tone brooked no questions. He himself took one pair of oars and with a short series of brisk, powerful strokes, spun the long boat around and set our course directly into the wind. Holmes and I had no choice but to obey. Without so much as exchanging a glance, we each took up an oar and set to work.

Scarcely had we bent ourselves to the oars, when the abandoned ship was shaken by a huge explosion, which lit up the night sky with tongues of orange and yellow. Urged on by the captain's repeated commands of "row, gentlemen, row" and his own furious pace, Holmes and I bent our backs like galley slaves. We were no more than a hundred yards from the ship when a second explosion thundered across the waves, and then a third. The ship listed heavily to port, and then the stern began to sink.

"Pray she goes down fast, boys," said the captain, as the freighter's bow broke clear of the waves, "and be brisk with the oars."

We continued to row at a feverish pace, which took us but slowly away from the ship. With each stroke, I gasped for breath. Fatigue ran from my fingertips along my arms and up through my shoulders, down my back and through my legs, down to my feet and even my toes, straining for a grip on the whaleboat's rib. We rowed for an hour, and more. The captain's pace did not slacken. His oars hit the water with the regularity of a triphammer, and each stroke urged the boat forward with a light hiss of foam. His breath had the steady pant of a steam engine, and whenever I reached the point where it seemed I could not take another stroke, there would be his voice, muttering, "Row, gentlemen, row. Now, gentlemen, why don't you row?"

Every stroke became a torment, but there was no rest. The ceaseless physical exertion threw my brain, already all but overwhelmed by the incredible events of the last twenty-four hours, into a fit of delusive ramblings that, when viewed in retrospect, are hardly separable from lunacy. I silently cursed the captain for not setting the sail. Why had he set our course against the wind? We could be riding effortlessly with the wind, instead of labouring against it. What possible purpose could he have, I wondered, other than to deliberately inflict pointless agony on me—I, who had already suffered and done so much? Undoubtedly, he was joined with Holmes in some devilish conspiracy to insult and degrade me. They were only trailing their oars. It was my exertion, and mine alone, that was propelling the entire boat. It was impossible. It was criminal. I should strike them both dead, cast their lying, thieving bodies overboard, and make my way home to Singapore, where I would be hailed as the hero I was and granted the rewards I so richly deserved.

Such nonsense, and far worse, my tormented body teased from my tormented mind. Amid such agony I clung to my sanity as my exhausted fingers clung to the oar. I was as drenched

by my own sweat as if I had fallen into the sea. My breath
came in great, wrenching gasps. But still Holmes rowed silently beside me, and the captain behind, and still came the captain's low, urgent voice: "Row, gentlemen, row. I ask you, gentlemen, why won't you row?" Goaded by their examples, I
summoned the last ounces of my willpower to maintain the
pace.

The sinking ship blazed brightly, casting a hellish glow on
our proceedings. When the flames vanished at last beneath
the waves and the dark closed in around us, I gave a choked,
heartfelt cry of relief, for I thought that surely now the captain would slow his pace. But if anything he increased it. And
so we rowed in silent fury for at least another hour, with no
company but the sea beneath us and the stars overhead. My
body, and my brain, were dry. The wild thoughts that had
earlier whirled through my head vanished, replaced by the
numbed fatigue of an exhausted animal. In spite of all I could
do, I felt the oar slipping from my grasp. My fingers were no
longer a part of my body, and thus no longer subject to my
command. I stared wonderingly at them, amazed that they
could continue the long, slow pull of the oar when they were
no longer attached to my hands. How long I continued in this
insane reverie I do not know. At last I felt a hand on my
shoulder, shaking me.

"Doctor," said the captain, "Doctor, you must rest."

Unbelieving, I let the oar slip from my grasp, which the
captain caught and canted until the blade rested in the boat.
I was too exhausted to sleep, even to lie down. Instead, I sat
hunched on my bench, Holmes silent beside me, overwhelmed by the sheer fact that I no longer had to row. Dimly,
uncaring, I heard the continuing plash of the captain's oars.
The sweat dried in streaks upon my face. My weary brain
slowly recovered some grip on reality, to the point that I felt
I must ask the captain to surrender his position at the oars,
this despite the extremity of fatigue that wasted every nerve
and sinew of my frame. I was just at the verge of summoning
up the courage necessary to make this request, when, to my

utter and complete disbelief, the very sea behind and below us grew a brilliant white, as though a light of incredible intensity were burning far beneath the waters!

"The demon fire," said the captain. "Row, gentlemen, row!"

As he spoke, there was a great upwelling of the ocean from the point at which Harat's ship had gone down. The three of us stared as one while a great portion of the sea flung itself hundreds of feet into the sky, driven upward by an enormous blast of shrieking steam and glittering in the moonlight with a beauty and a horror beyond comprehension, an immense watery explosion that held the fury of ten thousand cataracts.

"Row, gentlemen!" demanded the captain. "We must escape the mist. It is death if we do not!"

The hideous grumbling thunder of the rising and falling water shattered our ears. I comprehended at last why the captain had set our course directly against the wind and had refused to use the sail. As a final gesture against his enemies, Harat had mined his ship with that fearsome explosive he had tested in the Maldives. As I held once more the cruel oar, I could see the sea mist, exploded a thousand feet into the air and more, form a dense fog over the spot in the ocean we had so lately quitted. With slow, painful strokes we bore ourselves away from the mist the captain feared so much. At last, when the dawn streaked the sky, we paused from our labours. The captain set his oars, took the water bottle I handed to him, and drank deeply.

"We have seen it, gentlemen," he said, "the dance of Shiva. Let it be Allah's will that no man see it again."

"Indeed," said Holmes. I glanced at my friend, whom I had almost forgotten in my long hours at the oar. Exhausted though he was, he managed a grim smile.

"A fearsome night, Watson," he said, with the same amused tone he might have used while sitting in his favourite chair at Baker Street. "I fear I must relieve myself of this."

To my surprise, he pulled off his boot and took out a small object wrapped in cloth. He discarded the cloth and revealed to us the mysterious scroll, for which the giant rat would have paid any price. He held the tiny device aloft in his fingers, and it gleamed in the morning sun, shining in light as golden as itself.

"Devilish tantalization of the gods, Watson," said Holmes, with a shake of his head. "Devilish tantalization of the gods."

He tossed the object overboard. It fell with a slight splash and slid downward, a golden trickle disappearing in the dark water, another possession of the silent and depthless sea, which holds its secrets forever.

Epilogue

CHAPTER XXXVI

The Return Home

E ROWED THROUGHOUT THE day, at a greatly slackened pace, of course, until late in the afternoon, the wind veered round and the captain deemed it permissible to raise the sail. Once freed of the burden of the oar, I fell almost instantly into a sound sleep. I awoke briefly during the night, staring into the brilliant stars above us, noticing with a start that the captain remained awake, guiding our small boat during the night. I awakened in the morning exhausted but with a most ravenous hunger, which I assuaged with a breakfast of hardtack and dried cod softened in fresh water, rude fare indeed, and made palatable only by the extraordinary exertions of the previous day.

Little did I know that in a short time I would consider such a meal a feast fit for the gods. The wind that had favoured us the night before failed utterly, and for the next four days we could do little more than drift beyond all sight of land, exhausting both our food and water, when we finally met with a large junk. Both captain and crew were Chinese, of course, but Captain MacDougall, known throughout these waters by reputation and possessing some command of their dialect, was able to convince them to take us on board their vessel, which was by great good fortune bound for Singapore by way of Tanjungpinang, a port on the island of Bintan, south of Singapore. Despite our appearance, which was by now nothing less than beggarly, we were treated with respect, although such necessities as clean clothes, soap and water, and a razor were denied us. However, Holmes did manage to obtain a supply of writing paper and began at once to put in writing an account of these momentous events, "in such form as will be believable in London," he told me. When I perused the document, I found that he had transformed Harat and all his monstrous band into a gang of human pirates. All that had been extraordinary in our adventures had been removed.

Three days after our rescue, we reached Tanjungpinang, where Captain MacDougall, in perhaps an excess of caution, made his departure. After idling several days, we returned at last to Singapore. It is difficult to describe the consternation with which our appearance was greeted, more than a week after our rescue by the junk. The entire port had been in a frenzy of speculation, thanks to the abrupt and unexplained disappearance of Lord Barington, Holmes, and myself. Holmes did little to dispel the mystery, refusing to discuss matters except in the most cursory fashion with Sir Warren Clayborne, Lord Barington's second in government. That unfortunate, uncomfortable, and contemptible man, who knew far more than he ever dared to admit, who had previously treated us with disdain, now welcomed us at the dock with fear and trembling. Holmes scarcely allotted the man five minutes before marching directly to the telegraph office, with Sir Warren at his heels. When we arrived, Holmes gave the clerk a document of ten pages, addressed to Lord Cromer. The transmission of that lengthy document, in an impenetrable code, under Sir Warren's very nose, was surely a trial of that man's temper, one that he had merited a thousand times over for his callous treatment of Elizabeth Trent.

Once the message was sent, Holmes and I immediately departed for the Widow Han's, where we remained in seclusion for several days, recovering from our ordeal. For the first two days of our confinement, I must confess that I did little more than eat and sleep. On the third day, I awakened no earlier than noon. Light-headed but relaxed, I descended the stairs to the Widow's delightful atrium to discover my friend and my hostess engaged in earnest conversation.

"Dr. Watson!" exclaimed the Widow. "You are most recovered."

"I begin to feel like myself again," I replied.

"But you must eat," she announced, clapping her hands to summon servants.

"By all means, Watson," said Holmes, "for your journeys begin again tomorrow."

"Tomorrow?" I asked.

"Yes. On a warship bound for Madras. I have received a message from Lord Cromer, and he is most anxious to hear of these matters directly from you."

"But you are coming with me?"

"No, I must remain here. Lord Cromer has appointed me his deputy and given me extraordinary powers to take matters here in hand, but that can only be confirmed by written orders from Calcutta. It will be weeks before I can act, and Lord Chromer can brook no delay if he is to defend me before the Cabinet."

I shook my head in confusion.

"But what am I to tell him?"

"Why, you are to tell him what I have written."

"And that will suffice?"

"Yes, Watson, that will suffice. You will, after all, have ample opportunity to refresh your memory aboard the *Heliotrope*."

"The *Heliotrope*? An unusual name of a warship."

"Yes, I confess that it strikes me as less than martial. However, H.M.S. *Heliotrope* is a destroyer of recent vintage, and the fastest ship in these waters. I have it from Lord Cromer that once you reach Madras you will transfer to the *Wrathful*, a fast cruiser. I understand that it too is an excellent ship. However, I fear you will lack for companionship, for his lordship informs me that while aboard the *Heliotrope* and the *Wrathful*, all officers and men will be under strict orders not to converse with you."

"You mean I will be under arrest?"

"Not entirely. A form of quarantine, perhaps. Lord Cromer is most anxious that nothing should appear in the papers."

"No doubt."

I was about to discuss the matter further when the Widow's servants appeared, bringing fresh fruit, warm breads, and green tea. The Widow, who had courteously disappeared when Holmes and I began our conversation, now returned, a suggestion, I thought, to turn the conversation to lighter matters.

"Your appetite is revived, Doctor?" she asked me.

"Yes, my head is much clearer," I told her. "I am only sorry that I will be leaving Singapore so soon."

"As am I."

"Our hostess has been accorded a rather fuller account of the proceedings than I supplied for Lord Cromer," said Holmes.

"Such remarkable and such tragic events," said the Widow, seating herself gracefully before us. "I am sorry that we will not be able to honour you properly for your services to Singapore."

"Why, to be here in your presence is sufficient honour for any man!" I exclaimed, perhaps too loudly. And, indeed, to behold once more those delicate features, that silken, raven hair, and elegant posture was infinite delight. I felt with a pang how I would miss our morning promenades and her gentle hand on my arm.

"Your are too kind, Doctor," she said with a modest smile.

The remainder of my time with the Widow passed all too swiftly. Although it was clear that Holmes had told her the true details of all of our adventures, I had no desire to relive those extraordinary events. Nor was I interested in learning the details of the public atmosphere in Singapore, which assuredly had not improved since the time that Holmes and I had arrived. We passed the time in quiet conversation, and in the evening, the Widow performed for us on her lute. Such was the last day that I was to spend in the company of that most remarkable woman.

My departure the next morning was early even by the standards of Singapore. I arose at three in the morning, dressing quickly and arming myself as I had for my first arrival in the port. I had made my farewells to Holmes and the Widow before retiring, and I was on the road to the Singapore docks before four o'clock, with no companion other than Wu Shih. At this hour, the silence of the dark streets was broken by little more than the clop of the horses' hooves. At the dock itself, however, the day's labour had already begun. I watched the busy figures around me with perhaps an excess of caution. Holmes had informed me that a launch from the *Heliotrope* would await me at the end of pier three. As we approached that pier, I observed a tall figure to step from the darkness. Instinctively, my hand gripped the butt of my revolver, but reason quickly corrected my alarm. I had no doubt as to the identity of the man who approached me.

"Captain MacDougall," I said, stepping from the carriage.

"You anticipated me, Doctor," he said.

"Not immediately. I am glad for this last opportunity to say farewell."

For a moment, the captain seemed embarrassed.

"I could not allow you to depart without presenting a gift," he said.

I could not conceal my surprise.

"A gift?"

"Yes. The one true gift. The holy book."

He handed me a small, leather-bound volume, which by his words I understood to be the Koran, the bible of the Mussulman.

"It is in English," he said. "I know there are many who say that it is sacrilege to translate the words of the Prophet, but a man such as yourself should be brought to Allah."

Such strange praise, so deeply felt, left me groping for speech.

"I shall read this," I told him at last.

"Yes, Doctor. Thank you. You have done much good."

And with these noble words, he strode from my presence, his great figure disappearing swiftly in the darkness. I slipped the book into my jacket pocket and climbed back into the carriage.

"Drive on, Wu Shih," I told the small, staring face that confronted me.

Hastily, he turned in his seat and directed the horse to take us to the end of the pier. When we arrived, I was greeted by a brawny young ensign by the name of Smithson, together with a small detachment of marines. I understood instantly from the ensign's demeanour that until I set foot in London I would be firmly in the hands of the British navy. I scarcely had time to bid farewell to Wu Shih and hand him all the silver I had in my pocket before I found myself seated in a swift motor launch and bound for the *Heliotrope*. That vessel in turn had already a full head of steam when we arrived, and I had not yet entered my cabin before we were under way. It was clear that my voyage home would be as rapid as the voyage out had been leisurely.

My cabin was remarkably commodious, considering that space is always at a premium aboard a military vessel, and featured the modern luxury of electric lighting. My bedroom was Spartan indeed, but the "parlour," if such term be appropriate, was quite comfortable, equipped with a fine leather reading chair and a small writing desk. I noted with amusement that pen, ink, pencils, and paper had all been removed.

I understood from Ensign Smithson that if I desired breakfast it should be brought to me at six A.M. I was not to venture outside my cabin prior to nine in the morning nor after six in the evening. These messages were delivered by the ensign with a sort of brusque courtesy, as though I might be a high-ranking officer from an unfriendly yet powerful state. Somewhat bemused by his manner, I set at once to unpacking my luggage, which consumed the better part of an hour, thanks to the plethora of fine clothing I had acquired at the Widow's urging while in Singapore. I had even purchased a bottle of Poindexter's Bay Rum to please her, a fragrance that I continue to use to this day.

My cabin aboard the *Heliotrope* had but a single porthole, which at this hour offered no more than an indifferent and unchanging view of the darkened horizon. However, my par-

lour was equipped with a small library, which I made haste
to inspect. To my dismay, it offered little more than tedious
accounts of naval history and tactics and the collected works
of Richardson. Presented with such a choice, I decided that as
a matter of duty I should consider the copy of the Koran that
the captain had given me. However, I confess that an hour's
study of that ecstatic, dogmatic treatise left me with little incli-
nation to read further. With some reluctance, I returned to the
bookcase and was reaching for the first volume of that
remarkably extended work known as *Pamela,* when a knock
at the door announced my breakfast. The *Heliotrope,* I discovered, did not stint on its meals for prisoners. It was a fine,
heavy English breakfast of eggs and kippers, which must have
come straight from the captain's table. When I had finished, I
settled in the reading chair with a pot of coffee and a cigar
and began my perusal of *Pamela.*

Of that work I can only say that it exceeded the Indian
Ocean in breadth if not depth. I arrived in Madras still uncertain of the ultimate fate of its eponymous heroine's chastity,
but heartily wishing that both she and her would-be seducer
were at the bottom of the sea I had so recently traversed.
Fortunately, the *Wrathful,* to whose broader decks I was
transferred, provided me with a more extended library,
including the works of both Smollett and Dickens. I gratefully quitted Pamela and embraced Pickwick and Clinker, jour-
neying through the Gulf of Mannar and across the full length
of both the Arabian and Mediterranean Seas in the company
of the creators of those two immortals.

Two better companions for a long and lonely sea voyage
could hardly be imagined, and I had great need of them. The
crews of both ships were as silent as Holmes had warned me
they would be. I believe I heard not ten words aboard the
Heliotrope and not twenty aboard the *Wrathful.* What the officers thought of me I have no idea, but the men had surely
concluded that I was the unfortunate victim of a rare and
deadly tropical disease. I took morning and afternoon consti-
tutionals on both ships and was invariably accompanied, at a
cautious distance, by a sullen young man with a long-handled

brush and bucket, who would scrub the decks wherever I had trod. Such unwelcome attention made it difficult to spend much time on deck, though I could not forebear taking advantage of the splendid weather by the simple expedient of sitting before my cabin in a camp chair.

In such a manner I completed a journey of over 11,000 miles, lasting shortly over six weeks. I arrived in London well-fed, well-read, and famished for human contact. When I arrived at the dock, I was taken immediately by the admiral for an interview with Lord Cromer. I had carefully rehearsed what I was to say and acquitted myself, if I may say, without error and to his lordship's satisfaction.

In the next several weeks, I was called upon several more times to deliver testimony to high government officials. During that time an assiduous reader of the London newspapers might have noticed a surprising number of abrupt resignations from our nation's diplomatic corps. Then the press positively exploded with announcements of arrests of high government officials in Singapore, as a result of an investigation led by the celebrated Mr. Sherlock Holmes.

At this point I began to attract the attention of the press as well. Lord Cromer's private secretary suggested that I might consider a winter vacation in Scotland. I fear I had the temerity, or even the vanity, to suggest the south of France as an alternative, but this was not well received. The following day I boarded a special train headed north, and my journey did not end until late in the evening, when I discovered myself to be in Aberdeen. I resided for almost two months at an unpretentious hotel, supposedly at government expense, but I suspect that the owners received scarce compensation for my presence, for I was obliged to tip the staff liberally to obtain even a modicum of polite service.

Aberdeen is endowed with many charms, but they are best enjoyed in the summer months. Only those who have endured a winter in that northern metropolis have an adequate knowledge of the confining nature of its near-arctic climate. I visited the university library with some hope of finding the essays on human evolution by my friend that had provoked such strange fascination in our monstrous adversary, but was unable to locate them. As a result, I whiled away the short days and long nights of the Scottish winter with the aid of Smollett's *History of England,* but once I had exhausted that excellent work, I had no other resource than the captain's copy of the Koran, which I confess I liked no better upon finishing than I had upon starting. I cannot say that I am a religious man, and when I considered all that I had experienced in the past year, I concluded that despite all there was to admire in the swordlike faith of the captain, and the ineffable Buddhist rituals of the Widow Han, and even the frenzied tropic growths of the Hindu temples, there was no reason to prefer them to the simple Christmas puddings of my youth.

During this entire time I had had not one communication from Holmes. No doubt he felt it unwise to place trust in the public mails or even the diplomatic pouch. Though it was obvious from the press that he had established himself as the dominant figure in Singapore, having the complete backing of the government at home, there must have been many in official position in Singapore and elsewhere who wished him nothing but ill.

I followed the case as well as possible through the London papers, but I confess that I learned little. Despite all that I knew, there were many mysteries yet to unravel and questions yet to be resolved. After much thought, I concluded that I should have to wait for the return of Holmes for their answers.

In late February, the government decided at last that it was safe for me to return to London, and I quitted Aberdeen's iron skies with some pleasure, travelling by overnight coach. I arrived at Baker Street after an entire day of travel on a bitterly cold morning. Fortunately, Mrs. Hudson, alerted of my arrival by my telegram, had prepared a brisk coal fire in the sitting room. In half an hour I was enjoying a fine breakfast of eggs poached with cream, roasted onions, grilled ham, and oatmeal, when Billy entered with a large, cream-coloured envelope bearing my name in elegant script. I opened it immediately and discovered to my amazement that it was an invitation to a "grand *soiree*" in honour of the "celebrated authoress" Miss Mary O'Hara and her remarkable novel, *Mary de Guize, or The Prince of the Iroquois*!

I noted with some disappointment that the evening's entertainment was organized by Lord Worthington, a well-heeled young aristocrat celebrated in the press as the keeper of one of the best studs in England. I had, indeed, no hope of retaining my former place in Miss O'Hara's affections, yet reality bears a sting that reason's anticipation can never disarm. Nonetheless, despite my weary frame and wounded spirit, I resolved that I should attend the evening's festivities and summoned Mrs. Hudson to prepare my evening dress.

I departed from Baker Street at eight P.M., feeling no little trepidation as I did so. On the carriage ride over, I bit my tongue repeatedly to reinforce my resolve not to provide Mary with a true account of my adventures in Singapore. Even if she believed them all, they could hardly counterbalance the youth, wealth, and social position of my rival. Better to quit the field gracefully than mount a clumsy counterassault that could only conclude in disaster. My distress rose to near fever pitch when I arrived at Lord Worthington's magnificent townhouse. Amid such elegant display I felt myself to be little more than an insect.

A liveried servant met me at the door and received my invitation with aplomb, conducting me down a large, well-lit hallway to an immense room that glowed with gilt, its walls hung with enormous paintings, the like of which I had never seen. Yet the ornately carved and painted ceiling, the gleaming chandeliers, the rich drapes, all faded in comparison to my hostess. Mary O'Hara had been a charming, passionate girl; she was now an elegant lady. Her thick, lustrous hair, arranged on top of her head, provided a perfect complement for her strong, yet graceful features. Her shimmering gown, her generous *décolletage*, and above all her dark, shining, joyous eyes bespoke the perfect confidence of a great beauty.

"Oh, Dr. Watson!" she cried, hastening to see me. "It is so good of you to come!"

"Why, nothing could keep me away," I replied. "You have done so well for yourself."

A slight smile, suggesting equally self-deprecation and self-knowledge, hovered at her lips.

"You are too good, Doctor. You will always be my first friend. Archie! Come meet Dr. Watson!"

A tall, young gentleman who could only be Lord Worthington appeared. If he minded being summoned in such an informal manner, he did not show it. Towering over me, he took my hand in a powerful grip.

"Dr. Watson, is it? Mary has told me quite a bit about you. Your friend Mr. Holmes is making a bit of a stir in Singapore, what?"

"Yes," I replied. "A sad business."

"Meeting Mr. Holmes and Dr. Watson was such an honour," Mary remarked. "Is Mr. Holmes still in Singapore?"

"According to the newspaper accounts he has departed," I said. "It is a very complex matter. Unfortunately, it is impossible to say more at this time."

"Dr. Watson is privy to a great many state secrets," said Mary, taking my arm.

"State secrets, is it?" said Lord Worthington, "I say, you're not a damned Liberal, are you?"

"My politics are my own concern," I said, with some dignity, unable to follow his lordship's reasoning, if such existed, but resenting his tone.

"Just so long as you're not a damned Liberal," he continued. "I hated that fellow Gladstone. Never would let a fellow alone. Do you keep horses?"

"No, but I have betted your stud religiously."

"Have you now? There's a good fellow. The Derby's good as won, you know."

We touched briefly on the merits of the various illustrious horses Lord Worthington had owned before he dashed off to greet someone else. I turned in the perhaps vain hope of continuing my conversation with Mary, but found her naturally surrounded by admirers. I helped myself to a glass or two of champagne, making some small talk among the unusual collection of guests that Mary and Lord Worthington had assembled, which included a fair number of actors and actresses, jockeys, racing track touts, cricket players, prizefighters, and wealthy young layabouts. After my third glass, I found myself engrossed in conversation with a flamboyantly dressed woman of approximately my own age with a strong Irish accent, whose boldness of attire, and even greater boldness of address, should have informed me at once of her identity, for she was, of course, none other than the mother of Mary O'Hara. However, I fear that this knowledge, if I ever did possess it, did not impress itself sufficiently on my mind. Seated on a large, comfortable couch, we shared a glass together, and then a second, and perhaps even a third, when Mary came unwittingly to my rescue.

"Oh, there you are, Johnnie!" she exclaimed. "You are a clever fellow to find Mother this way!"

There was in her tone a note of satisfaction so defined that it instantly dispelled the fog of alcohol that had hitherto obscured the operations of my intellect. I grasped at once that an involvement with Mary's mother, however innocently begun, could have no possible proper conclusion. My brain, once aroused, waxed perhaps too suspicious, and I wrung from Mary's brief words a distinctly matrimonial intention. The thought of being yoked with so extraordinary a creature reduced me to perfect sobriety, and at the very moment I confronted my hostess's sparkling eyes, I began to plot my rapid retreat.

I regret to say that I found such a manoeuvre easier to plan than execute. After the chill embrace of Aberdeen, the well-ripened charms of Mrs. O'Hara had an unrelenting appeal. And the mere sight of Mary, so delightful in her triumph, was a superb tonic, even when imbibed from afar. Yet there are times when duty must rule, and about half an hour later I departed from Lord Worthington's sumptuous lair.

The night, though cold, was crisp and invigorating. The stars shone above me like brilliant pinpricks in the black sky. Dispensing with the services of a hansom, I resolved to walk the five or six miles that lay between me and Baker Street. The excessive quantity of champagne I had consumed, and the frustrating unavailability of the female loveliness I had observed, combined to create in me an unhealthy restlessness that I felt could most harmlessly be dissipated by simple physical exercise. Several hours later I arrived at Baker Street, somewhat fatigued in body but quieted in mind. I undressed quickly and fell sound asleep, only to be awakened several hours later by the soft, almost human cry of a violin. Holmes had returned!

Despite my condition, I quickly rose from my bed and donned a robe. Stepping into the hallway, I walked towards the sitting room, where I beheld Holmes as I had so often seen him, slouched on the sofa with his violin on his chest, his dispatch boxes at his feet, and his keen, aquiline features barely illumined by the dying embers of the fire. I had meant, of course, to speak to him, but the tone of the air he played was so wild and melancholy, and the expression on his face so rapt and contemplative, that I dared not interrupt. Reversing my steps, I quietly returned to bed and fell once more into a profound slumber.

CHAPTER XXXVII

The Resolution of the Matter

OU ARE REVIVED, WATSON?" Holmes asked as I appeared at the breakfast table.

"My dear fellow!" I cried. "It is a pleasure to see you again after these several months. Is everything settled in Singapore? The *Times* implied that you would not be home for another fortnight."

"Yet another official ruse, I fear. For the past several weeks I have been the guest of Her Majesty's Government in Calais. From that location, it was easy to remain in touch with both the government and M. Compte in Paris."

"Monsieur Compte?"

"Yes. You may recall that prior to the culmination of our adventures I had arranged the conveyance to him of the unique materials that pertain to this case. To the extent that it is possible, given the extraordinary circumstances of the matter, the legal issues have been entirely resolved. How did you find Aberdeen? Less hospitable than Singapore, I should wager."

"I should not have chosen it myself," I said, taking a chair.

"The Home Office is frequently less than reasonable," Holmes said, passing me the teapot. "Even now the game is not over, for there will be appeals. But important as they are, these are secondary matters. The real match was played out long before."

He paused as Mrs. Hudson arrived with my breakfast, lamb kidneys on toast points.

"I hope you find them palatable," Holmes said. "I felt a celebration of sorts was in order. How was your evening with Miss Mary O'Hara?"

"It was hardly an evening. She appears to have chosen Lord Worthington as her champion, at least for the moment."

"How unfortunate."

"I had no other expectation."

"An intelligent judgment. I doubt that such a force as Miss O'Hara will ever be compassed by a single gentleman, however expansive his house and illustrious his lineage. At any rate, I look forward to reading her novel."

As we spoke, I helped myself to a pair of the delectable kidneys, which did little but stimulate my appetite, thanks to the prolonged exercise of the night before.

"Do you know, Holmes," I said as I took a second pair from the fine platter that Mrs. Hudson had laid before us, "I have lived through almost every moment of this case since the day that I received poor Elizabeth's letter, and yet when I reflect upon it, I find it to be nothing but a succession of mare's nests. To begin with, I never had the least understanding of who murdered Raleigh Trent or why, or if his death was not in fact suicide."

"It was scarcely suicide, Watson," Holmes said with sudden intensity. "Raleigh Trent was driven by his employers to take his own life. They had it in their power to destroy him, and destroy him they did. They chose him in the first place to take part in their schemes because they believed him to be more ambitious than honourable, and then destroyed him because he had become more fearful than ambitious. You recall Elizabeth telling us of his early enthusiasm that they would soon grow rich?"

"Yes."

"Surely there could be no other cause than that his superiors had introduced him to what we may call the 'private' side

of the business. There must have been any number of errands
that only an initiate could undertake. I have determined, for
example, that in 1891 Trent made a trip to the Egmont Islands,
south of the Maldives, a trip of several thousand miles, at his
employer's expense on a fast steamer that carried no ascer-
tainable cargo other than wood pulp, a product for which I
fancy there is little demand in that area of the world."

"For what purpose?"

"I can only guess that he travelled as a messenger of some
sort. You recall that the captain identified several of the
islands in the Maldives as way points for the slave trade engineered by Harat, as well as the location of what was assuredly the first test of that fearsome weapon that the captain
described as 'the dance of Shiva.'"

"But why was Trent involved in these matters at all? Surely
Harat could have made use of those gigantic rodents for his
errands."

"I think that unlikely. I doubt that many men would be willing, or even capable of conversing intelligently with the creatures, despite their undoubted ability to speak, read, and write
human languages such as English. Humans feel little enough
trust for their own kind. With all his mad genius, Harat's
power was severely circumscribed until he was able to form
an alliance with Lord Barington."

"So Barington was the key?"

"Yes, though it is hard to imagine how their partnership was
first established. I suspect that Harat must have had contact
with some humans, going back as far as fifty years, for there is
evidence of a smuggling operation based in Sumatra and operating in the Indonesian archipelago for that length of time. But
when he joined forces with Lord Barington and the principals
of Enderby & Cross, the two were able to construct a smuggling enterprise that reached easily around the entire world.
And Raleigh Trent found out more about it than was good for
him. Whether he actually threatened to expose his employers
is doubtful. Who could imagine bringing such a tale into court?"

Holmes paused to pour himself a cup of tea, while I
reached for the remaining two kidneys.

"In any event," Holmes continued, "Trent began to lose his nerve. Perhaps he caught sight of Harat himself in some inadvertent encounter. Whatever the cause, his employers could not but be aware that their man was falling apart, and Trent knew they knew. He made preparations for the worst, and did not resist when it came to him. He must have hoped that Elizabeth would accept his death and the mystery would end with him."

"But she did not."

"No. And because of my blindness, she paid for her courage with her life."

I had never in my life heard Holmes utter such a brutal self-reproach. I could think of nothing to say in reply and feared that our conversation was at an end. But after a pause, he recovered himself and began to speak again, almost as a sort of confession.

"You see, Watson, I had great curiosity for any news out of Singapore, thanks to the presence of Lord Barington in that port. When I heard Elizabeth's Trent's story, I felt that she was in great danger, for I had no doubt that Raleigh Trent's death, even if formally a suicide, was forced upon him. I concluded that for her own comfort and security, Mrs. Trent should give up her investigation and enjoy the benefits of the annuities that her unhappy husband had provided. I did not reckon on the inhuman ferocity of our foes."

"Then you think that it was Harat who decided that Elizabeth should die?"

"Yes. Barington was always a thorough scoundrel, but never likely to resort to physical violence unless backed into a corner. Harat was made of very different metal. Murder was his first choice, and I suspect he would have had Mrs. Trent killed in Singapore except for the intense scandal it would provoke."

"It might have cost Barington his position."

"Exactly. There is no doubt that Captain Manning was in league with Harat, whether directly or through Barington we shall never know, though I suspect the former. Such a cunning creature would always prefer to have several irons in the fire. Harat arranged to have one of the Bada travel on Manning's ship. Such a creature could hardly be expected to interpret the meaning of Elizabeth Trent's actions in London. It was Manning who concluded that she must die. I think it quite likely that he was aware of the lady's message to you that morning. Once he understood her purpose, he arranged for her murder."

"And so one of those grotesque creatures confronted Elizabeth and forced her to leave that note."

"Yes. Undoubtedly, the same great rat that bit me in the hold of Manning's ship. If you have finished with the kidneys, Watson, I suggest we retire to the sitting room. After so much travel, I find it reassuring to be in familiar surroundings once more. We will ask Mrs. Hudson to prepare another pot of tea. I think I should prefer the oolong at this point."

Though it was approaching noon, the sky outside wore the dull and menacing visage of a late winter evening. The weather had turned decidedly chill, and light hail spattered occasionally against the windows.

"You have brought your northern weather with you, Watson," Holmes said.

He picked up a large piece of coal and tossed it into the fire, striking the lump with a poker until it split in half. Then he settled back into his favourite armchair. Several dispatch boxes, which I had seen the night before, lay at his feet.

"All that is public of this case, and most that is private, are here in these boxes," he said. "The prosecutors, of course, have acres of documents, but I reserved the cream."

"What of the skeleton itself?" I said slowly, reluctant even to allude to such matters.

"Yes. With your approval, of course, I have consigned that and the accompanying artifacts to the care of my brother Mycroft, who now holds a modest position with the British Museum. Sometime in the future, after our deaths, no doubt, these facts must come to light. I hope you approve of the museum as the proper container for these secrets."

"I am sure it will do very well," I said, "but I hope you do not mind if I ask to continue our discussion. I find it most unfortunate, for example, that Captain Manning was never brought to justice for his involvement in this matter."

"Captain Manning escaped the law, but not justice," said Holmes, reaching into one of the dispatch boxes. "When I was in Calais, the government was so kind as to forward the accumulation of my mail. Among other things, I received this clipping. Yes, here it is."

He handed me several pages from a magazine, folded up into quarters. When I smoothed them out, I discovered a florid woodcut, depicting a buxom young woman in a low-cut dress in the act of shooting a man with a derringer. The article was entitled "Murder in San Francisco: Death of a Sea Captain."

"The article was taken from a remarkable American periodical known as *The Police Gazette*," said Holmes, "which is now available to London readers. It discusses, in most lurid fashion, the foul murder of one Captain Samuel Manning in a gambling den in San Francisco, a city on the west coast of the United States. The captain's demise occurred some seven or eight months ago."

"Witnesses say that Captain Manning was shot twice in the forehead with a small lady's derringer by a beautiful young woman with long, golden tresses," I said, adopting the language of the article.

"A young woman who, despite her striking appearance, has so far managed to elude capture," remarked Holmes.

"Has she been identified?" I asked, leafing through the article in search of that information.

"Ah, thank you, Mrs. Hudson," said Holmes, as that good woman appeared with a tray laden with a pot of tea and matching cups and saucers, all of fine Chinese porcelain, whose design I well remembered from our stay in Singapore.

"Just place it on the table," Holmes continued. "That will be all."

Holmes poured out two cups and passed one to me. Holmes drank gratefully from the cup.

"Most pleasant," he said. "Mrs. Hudson has such a sure hand in these matters. There was no lady in the case, Watson."

"Are you sure?"

"Did Captain Manning strike you as the sort of man who would allow himself to be murdered by a woman?"

"Perhaps not," I said, recalling that bluff, calculating individual.

"I am sure not. The captain was both cunning and heartless, and most unlikely to have fallen prey to a woman, with or without blond tresses. He was murdered, on Harat's orders, by one of Harat's rodents. Harat's plans for his war against humanity were maturing as we entered the case. Although Harat still had ample need for his human allies, he was beginning to eliminate those at the periphery of his operations. Manning had served his purposes. So, unfortunately, had Sir Roger Ainsby-Gore and, ultimately, Lord Barington himself."

"Where did you get this clipping?" I asked, returning it to him.

"From Miss O'Hara," he said. "The young lady has a most observant eye. Here is her note."

He handed me a folded sheet of stiff paper, tinted a rather startling shade of mauve. I read the following message, in Mary's bold yet feminine hand:

> Dear Mr. Holmes,
> I saw this article and thought you might be interested.
> Is this perhaps the same Captain Manning whom brave Johnnie gave such a thrashing? Please do catch the murderer of poor Mrs. Trent.

"I am very glad that she was able to be of assistance," I said.

"A most remarkable woman," said Holmes. "In coming years I am sure we shall read of her often in the popular press. But to return to the case, I confess that we may never know why Harat took such an extraordinary risk as to journey to Alexandria and confront Sir Roger in his residence. Sir Roger clearly feared the worst. What did Harat feel he might have gained by his journey?"

"Perhaps he was demanding that Sir Roger should have had us murdered," I conjectured.

"I think not, Watson. If Harat had wanted us dead, I am

confident that he could have accomplished the matter a hundred times over before we ever arrived in Singapore. That remarkable drawing of myself that we discovered during our passage to Alexandria was to alert the Bada to my presence, not to mark me for death. In our brief interview Harat was kind enough to compliment my intelligence. Up until the last he had hopes for some sort of alliance of the few against the many, a most unfortunate and misguided proposition—one, however, that served to preserve our lives. I think it more likely that it was Sir Roger who wanted us dead."

"And Harat travelled that great distance merely to dissuade him?"

"Not entirely. Remember that our involvement in the case was the first threat that Harat had experienced to his vast operations. He hoped somehow to enlist me as his ally, while those who already were his servants were demanding my death. While both Sir Roger and Lord Barington were creatures of his will, it appears that he had no base of power in India itself, which constituted a barrier to his control. When I was in Singapore, I made a close study of the official cable traffic between that city and other points of the Empire, Alexandria in particular. Sir Roger and Lord Barington were able to make some use of cables to exchange information, but only a minimum. Open and detailed discussion of their illicit strategies was clearly out of the question. They dared not attract the attention of Calcutta, through which all cable traffic must pass."

Holmes paused to refill his cup. He took fastidious care in the performance of this simple ritual, which suggested to my mind at least that he treasured even the slightest link to the life we enjoyed as guests of the Widow Han.

"Harat surely felt that he himself must come to Alexandria," Holmes continued. "Without his own immediate presence, he could have no guarantee that Sir Roger would carry out his orders. Clearly, Harat had no real human confidant, or we should have met such a person on board his ship. I can only conclude that Harat had visited Alexandria in the past, perhaps when first establishing his nefarious traffic in human souls, and had allies of a sort in that city. But he had no one whom he could trust to conduct negotiations on delicate matters. I strongly suspect that Sir Roger was insisting on our deaths, believing that his official position would allow him to ride out the ensuing storm. No doubt he was unable to appreciate the importance Harat attached to the possibility of my services. He pressed his case too strongly and suffered the consequences. After murdering Sir Roger, Harat must have concluded that it would be unsafe for him to remain in Alexandria and retreated to that solitude that had so long sustained him."

"And Lord Barington feared that he would suffer the same fate as Sir Roger."

"Yes. No doubt Barington felt he had trumped his master when he produced the stolen rifles and announced his return to London. Instead, he merely guaranteed his own death."

"Yet with Barington dead Harat had no allies other than those sad creatures aboard his ship."

"On the contrary, Watson. I fear you underestimate Harat's resources. His range extended as far east as west. I think it likely that he planned to establish himself on the island of Hainan, a large island off the coast of southern China. You may remember he expressed a certain sentimental attachment to the Chinese people. His connections among the Chinese population in Singapore were far larger than has been revealed. Shortly after our return to that city, more than a dozen of the leading Chinese merchants suddenly transferred their base of operations to Haikou, Hainan's largest port. Furthermore, they had all liquidated the larger portion of their holdings in Singapore some time previous to Barington's death. Had all gone to plan, I believe Hainan would quickly become famous in the European press as 'the workshop of Asia.' Fascinated readers would learn of the wonders emerging from that island, not realizing that these wonders would shortly be turned against them. Ultimately, Harat would have sought an alliance with the Emperor of China, the one figure who might assist him in his war against the Western nations, whom he most particularly despised among humans."

"What madness!"

"So it would seem. Would you care for more tea? I must instruct Mrs. Hudson to prepare a more intense liquor in the future. However, the lemon provides a pleasing astringency."

He passed me a cup, which was indeed astringent in the extreme.

"And what of the skeleton itself, and the scroll?" I said. "I could never understand why Harat had not obtained it, since he obviously knew of its existence."

"Yes. Although Harat never told us the home place of the remarkable culture that gave him birth, Captain MacDougall assured me that all evidence points to the island of Ceylon. Of all the cultures that have brushed against the Bada, it is the Hindu who know them best and could best defend against them. Much actual information about the Bada is available in Hindu writings, transformed by myth in a manner that makes it almost incomprehensible to outsiders. The keepers of the temple you visited were able to seal off all access to what was concealed beneath, revealing it to the proper man, Captain MacDougall, who in turn waited for our assistance to strike against the forces that had revived the exploitation of his people. It is clear, from your account, that he had been in contact with the temple priests. And more than once, you may recall, he spoke of our appearance as being providential."

"I always thought he spoke only in jest. But what of your writings on the Mongolian steppe? I sought to find them in Aberdeen, but could not."

"The articles so esteemed by Harat appeared in the *Delhi Antiquarian,* an obscure journal of Oriental studies based in that city. I confess I was taken aback by his enthusiasm."

"If your theory is correct, it was those articles alone that preserved our lives."

Holmes could not forebear from smiling.

"Rarely, I imagine, have the benefits of scholarship been so tangible. During the months of enforced leisure that followed the unfortunate demise of Professor Moriarty, I occupied myself with a close study of the collected works of the esteemed Dr. Darwin. My subsequent sojourn in the

Himalayas both hid me from the attentions of Captain Moran
and allowed me the opportunity to apply Dr. Darwin's methods and theories to a highly diverse set of phenomena. In my
guise as the Norwegian climber Sigerson, I spent a consider-
able amount of time with a party of German archaeologists,
who were concluding a most remarkable series of discoveries
along what is known among experts as the Silk Road, a trade
route that once stretched from China to ancient Rome. The
cultures of East and West mingle in a most extraordinary fashion in the lost cities that lie along this ancient route. From
their conversations, I began to think about the influences of
geography upon human civilizations, and to wonder if the
rise and fall of great empires might not be linked to such
mundane factors as the length of the grass on the Mongolian
steppe. Ultimately I embodied these thoughts in a series of
seven articles."

"And how could the length of grass affect an empire?"

"I was in the homeland of such conquerors as Attila the
Hun, Tamurlane, and Ghengis Khan. I wondered how it could
be an accident that three such men, so widely distributed
across a millennium, might spring from a common source and
have such a similar impact on such different civilizations. I
concluded that it was a confluence of fortuities, such as
remarkable advantages afforded by the physique and physi-
ology of the Mongolian pony, the development of the com-
pound Mongolian bow, the central geographical location of
the highlands, and indeed even the richness of the pastures,
that provided the fodder for the barbarian cavalries, that over
and over again brought proud civilizations to their knees. In
a series of six articles, I endeavoured to discuss simultane-
ously the physical and human environments that had given
birth to these unique events. In a seventh, I concluded with
some speculations as to how future civilizations might,
through a dispassionate consideration of Nature, seek to
shape the forces that once had shaped them, and move from
traditional patterns of alternating conquest and defeat to a
more harmonious cultivation of both the earth and the intellect. Apparently, Harat mistook the voluntary union I pro-

posed for the merciless experimentation he practiced. He misunderstood me greatly, but if he had not done so, his victory must have been certain."

Outside our windows, the sky had darkened further, and occasional gusts of wind caused the falling hail to rattle against the glass like bird shot. Inside, our thoughts remained fixed on the great events that had occurred in climes so far removed from our own.

"I cannot help wondering," I said, "whether any of those poor creatures survive. The Bada, I mean."

"Undoubtedly, though in what numbers it is impossible to ascertain. Perhaps they can reestablish themselves in the jungles of Sumatra. Perhaps someday our species will have the wisdom to erase the barriers that now hold us apart. It seems apparent that the Bada arose by a process of evolution separate from our own."

"You feel they have no relation to the African pigmy?"

"None. Clearly, they are descended from rodents. The dentition alone is conclusive, in my opinion, but you observed as well, perhaps, in the skeleton, both the similarities and differences in the structure of the hand."

"Yes. Still, the notion of a nonhuman intelligence, fairly equal to our own, is hard to grasp."

"True, Watson. But I feel that it was precisely this discontinuity that induced the precocious intellectual growth so characteristic of the brief period when human beings and the Bada joined together. The intellectual ferment must have been fantastic, to discover the deepest secrets of the vital forces of life itself, the forces needed to bring the creature Harat into being, and to have fashioned the device responsible for that great explosion we witnessed at sea. All the secrets of biological evolution, and many others, must have been laid out for all to see. I fear that civilization will spend a millennium to achieve the wisdom I discarded that day, yet I had no other choice. Such knowledge, cut off from common development of humanity, could only bring madness. Harat himself was a clear demonstration of that point."

Struck by the force of my friend's words, I lapsed into

wordless contemplation, but then took up the conversation once more, still unsatisfied.

"It seems almost inconceivable," I said at last, grappling with my thoughts, "how these ancient mysteries were finally brought to light in a manner that caused the death of so many, the death of Elizabeth in particular."

For a long moment Holmes remained so impassive at my statement, which I confess revealed my deepest feelings on the subject, that I could almost believe that he did not hear them. But at last he did speak, breaking the silence of the darkening room.

"There is no true wisdom without tragedy, Watson," he said, looking steadily into the fire.